THE GATEKEEPER'S STAFF
TJ YOUNG & THE ORISHAS

ANTOINE BANDELE

EDITED BY
FIONA MCLAREN

ILLUSTRATED BY
ARTHUR BOWLING

Publisher: Bandele Books
Interior Design: Vellum
Editors: Fiona McLaren, Callan Brown
Illustrator: Arthur Bowling
Cover Design: Mibl Art
Ornamental Break Design: Bolaji Olaloye

ISBN: 978-1-951905-02-6 (Ebook edition)

ISBN: 978-1-951905-16-3 (Paperback edition)

ISBN: 978-1-951905-13-2 (Hardback edition)

First Edition | May 16, 2021

CONTENTS

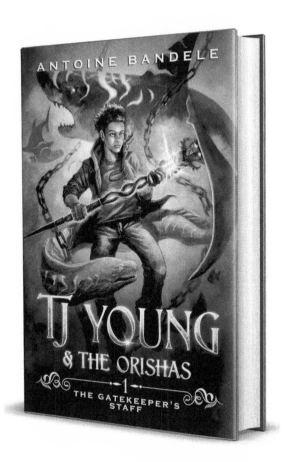

The Gatekeeper's Staff is the first book in the *TJ Young & The Orishas* series, a collection of stories based around lore and mythology from West Africa and the African diaspora.

If you enjoy this story and are interested in the rest of TJ's adventures you can join Antoine Bandele's e-mail alerts list. He'll send you notifications for new book releases, exclusive updates, and behind-the-page content.

Visit this link:
antoinebandele.com/stay-in-touch

Read the free prequel short story to
The Gatekeeper's Staff!

What happens when a deity needs a human body?
They go to the source, of course.

Eshu the Trickster needs a mortal form for his mischievous plans, but the only other Orisha who can help him swore off the practice ages ago.

It will take careful scheming to convince the Original Architect to come out of retirement. Any misstep and Eshu will be thrown from the Sky Realm.

What's worse, Eshu hasn't visited the heavens for several centuries. Would his former comrade even be the same? How can Eshu persuade someone he barely knows anymore?

Visit this link to read the prequel story:
antoinebandele.com/will-of-the-mischeif-maker

PRONUNCIATION GUIDE

Characters

A·de·ye·mi - a'dā'ye'mē
A·kan·de - a'kan'dā
A·yo·de·ji - ī'yo'de'gē
Bo·la·we - bō'la'wā
Du Bois - dü'bwa
Fran·cois - fran'swa
Ifedayo - ē'fā dī'yo
Man·uel·a - man'well'a
To·mo·ri Jo·mi·lo·ju - tō'mō'rē jō'mē'lo'jü
Gra·vés - gra'ves

Orishas

E·shu - e'shü
O·ba·ta·la - ō'ba'ta'la
O·du·du·wa - ō'dü'dü'wa
O·gi·yan - o'gē'yan
O·ko - ō'kō
O·lo·du·ma·re - ō'lō'dü'ma'rā
O·lo·kun - ō'lō'kün
O·lo·sa - ō'lō'sa
O·ri - ō'rē
O·run·mi·la - ō'rün'mē'la
O·sain - ō'sān
O·shun - ō'shün
O·ya - ōi'ya
Shan·go - shan'gō
Ye·mo·ja - ye'mō'ja
Ye·wa - ye'wa

Terms

A·she - a'shā
Ba·ba·la·wo - ba'ba'la'wō
Da·shi·ki - da'shē'kē
E·mi - e'mē
E·re I·da·ra·ya - e'rā ē'da'ra'ya
I·fa - ē'fa
Og·bon - ō'bōn
O·lo·shi - ō'lō'shē

Zo·bo - zō′bō

Locations
A·bu·ja - a′bü′ja
I·le-I·fe - ē′lā ē′fā
La·gos - lā′gōs
Man·da·wa·ca - man′də′wa′ca
O·yo - ȯi′yō

*This story is
a work of fantasy fiction
and not an accurate depiction of
the living practice of Ifa
and its many branches and followers
in the Motherland
and the diaspora.*

To my Yoruba family name,
I will follow you home.

NOT FIRST, NOT LAST

"HEADS UP, LUCKY CHARM!"

A basketball came hurling at TJ Young's head. Too slow to get his hands up, the ball smacked against his cheek and out of bounds. Lamar, one of his opponents, howled like a damned hyena—and considering his sharp jaw was contoured like a snout, that was a fair comparison.

TJ avoided Lamar's squinting eyes as the boy's laughter grew stronger with each passing moment, his teammates following suit with their own guffaws. One of them stomped their foot against the schoolyard asphalt for added effect.

"This dude really tried to catch it with his face, though!" he bawled.

"Some lucky charm he is," the stout Christian whispered to Jordan, the tallest girl in eighth grade.

TJ was sure they were regretting choosing him over Andy Wilkins. Andy was probably the worst fourteen-year-old dribbler in Los Angeles, but he could at least *catch* the ball. He must've looked much better than the flimsy "lucky charm" superstition bestowed upon TJ.

His nickname was sort of the worst.

The label never helped him charm the ladies or talk his way out of homework. It only helped him *not* get chosen last at pick-up basketball during lunch. But in recent weeks, it seemed like whichever team picked him won, despite his novice skill, so... the nickname stuck.

In short, his position on the team was more mascot than star player.

"Don't just stand there," Jordan snapped as her freckles scrunched up in a scowl. "Go get the ball, bro." She thumbed to the basketball, which then lay against the chain-link fence surrounding the school blacktop.

TJ gave her a nod and jogged off, embarrassed. He hadn't expected the ball to come to him in the fast break. Most of the time, Jordan and Christian passed the ball between the two of them while the rest of the team watched them in astonishment. The best any of them could hope to do was cheer them on with a slap on the back or an obligatory chant of "let's go!"

A group of pretty girls leaning back on the fence quieted their giggling as TJ approached. A red heat rose to his cheeks. He just hoped he didn't look like a clown—that's all he needed. Avoiding their judging side-eyes, he knelt to grab the ball, shielding his eyes with one hand from the hot, glistening blacktop.

When his fingers met the orange, pimpled rubber, a subtle sensation ran up his arm. It buzzed like a tiny static shock, as though touching a metal surface after rubbing your fingers together. It often happened while he played basketball.

The tingle meant that good things were to come.

His mother would've called it his *Ashe* at work: the force to make things happen and produce change. TJ just called it all a bunch of hocus pocus. He could never do anything with his own Ashe—if he had any at all. But his family were powerful diviners with the ability to produce magic on a whim.

Commune with your pet goldfish? Yup. Predicting the weather with cowries? Easy. Manifest fire out of nowhere? Without breaking a sweat—well, maybe a *little* sweat.

It all came easy to TJ's family, but in fourteen years, the only magic he could manifest was a belch after a good meal of chicken and jollof rice.

Despite all of that, TJ juggled the ball between his hands. He might not have believed he possessed magic, but luck? He could work with luck. He and luck were like peanut butter and jelly, after all. Heck, the kids *named* him after luck!

With a grin and a confident bounce in his step, he passed the ball to Lamar, whose face was still red from laughter.

Enjoy it now, TJ thought happily. *We got this in the bag.*

"Yeah, yeah, get your laughs in now." Christian guarded Lamar close, waving his stubby fingers in front of the boy's thin face. "We finna win it on the next possession."

Lamar spun around Christian with one fluid motion. "We're playing to eleven, fool."

"And we got nine, homie," Christian retorted, dashing after Lamar.

"I know you got held back, but damn, bro. Where you gonna pull out two points from? I know your silly butt ain't shootin' from distance."

They were playing with streetball rules. The first team to eleven would win, with each basket worth a single point and outside shots counting for double. But teams had to win by two in streetball. Christian must've thought they'd score a two-pointer on their next possession.

The kid never lacked in confidence, that was for sure. TJ smirked at that.

"Wipe that goofy-ass smile off your face," Jordan said to TJ as she defended another boy. "Get your head in the game!"

TJ shook the expression from his mouth as the boy he was *supposed* to be defending blew by him. Lamar passed the ball over TJ's head, and his teammate caught it with one hand... then took a jump shot way, way out. His shot was pretty, that same quick follow-through Steph Curry had but... without the range. The basketball *thunked* against the front of the double rim and flew high in the air.

"Shit! Box out, box out!" Christian shouted.

But the ball was too high, which left the perimeter open for an easy long rebound for the opposing team. And, of course, TJ totally forgot to block his opponent from the rebound.

"Damnit, TJ," Christian bellowed, his loose curls bouncing atop his head as he defended close against another player.

TJ's ears went hot as he got back on his man. He put one hand on the boy's sweaty school uniform, using his other to block any incoming pass. But it didn't matter.

Somehow Lamar got the ball again and was dancing around Jordan. He dribbled the ball between his lanky legs and behind his narrow back. It was like he was hypnotizing Jordan with his moves, lulling her into indecision until he was ready for his final ploy.

TJ had seen Lamar play enough to know he wouldn't take an outside shot; he had no jumper. All the dribbling he was doing was for show, and Jordan was falling for it.

Just as Lamar committed to his final crossover, he drove by

Jordan, nearly making the girl trip over her own feet. The boy had a clear path to the basket, so TJ curled away from his man and stood his ground before Lamar's bull rush.

That was a mistake.

The kid was at least twice TJ's size, but TJ had to make up for recent mistakes.

He closed his eyes and clenched his body for the impact. He watched the NBA enough to know that guys got pummeled like this all the time, but at least he could draw the foul.

TJ's thin forearms braced against Lamar's ripped body as he fell back into the hard asphalt. Lamar laid the ball in with a *thud* against the backboard and a *swish* through the net, tying the game nine to nine.

"Nah, nah, that's an offensive foul!" Christian called out as he waved his hands animatedly across his face.

TJ's brain kept spinning without end. Christian's meaty arms looked like they doubled through TJ's blurry vision as TJ rubbed at the knot welling between the naps of his small Afro. When he pulled his hand away, it was wet with blood between his middle and index fingers.

"Hell nah, bruh." Lamar sucked at his teeth. "There's no offensive fouls in pick-up; this ain't no NBA."

The boys argued as TJ waited for his head to get off its carousel. Lamar started pushing at Christian, and Jordan pushed back in retaliation.

"Guys…" TJ trailed off, lightheaded and unbalanced as he struggled to his feet.

The boys and girl didn't listen, clenching their fists and getting into each other's faces.

"Guys!" TJ shouted too loudly as the throbbing in his head rang violently against his skull.

They stopped their jawing and turned to TJ, who took a breath before he said, "Give 'em the point. We'll win it on the next one." He didn't want any easy calls coming his way. Lamar would just call him soft or something.

"See, even Lucky Charm knows that call was bull," Lamar said.

TJ, blood still dotting his fingers, snatched the ball from Lamar's hand. "It's our ball either way."

Lamar shrugged and strutted down the court with his team, ready to defend. Before TJ could take the ball out, Jordan slapped him across the chest. "Good lookin' out back there, Lucky Charm," she said. "He had me beat."

"Don't mention it." TJ craned his neck up to Jordan, whose braided head silhouetted against the high noon sun. "If I can't score, the least I can do is be a wall, right?"

TJ threw the ball to her.

"Nah, you take it up the court." She threw the ball back. "If you see a shot, take it."

TJ almost fumbled the ball in his shaking hands. Jordan didn't *actually* think he could win it for them, did she? The last time TJ scored a basket in a game was last year in the seventh grade — and it was his own team's hoop.

Sweat dripping down his hand and onto the ball, TJ did his best to dribble up the court. A group of other students who must've finished eating their lunch early huddled around, and the cute girls leaning on the fence drifted closer for a better look.

It seemed like everyone knew the game was coming to a close.

"*Great,*" TJ groaned to himself.

TJ drew in a long breath, looking for that same tingle he felt before. If one thing was true, whenever he *really* wanted his team to win, they did. The outcome shouldn't have been any different now that the ball was in his hands. Didn't his dad always say TJ had great court vision despite not having the best jumper?

He could do this.

Dribbling down the court, that faint sensation returned to him. He couldn't explain it even in his own head, but something about his focus changed. It was like his teammates had sharpened in focus, like some prism was filtering out all the noise. When he got like this, TJ felt like a puppet on a string. Something deep within him made the play call before he could even figure out what that call should be.

They weren't going to win this if he took the shot. The win would have to come through Jordan. It seemed like Lamar knew that too, who was already double-teaming the girl near the baseline.

TJ turned his attention to his other teammates. It was like a puzzle. He just needed to find a way to get Jordan open again. And unlike Lamar's team, she could actually hit her outside shots.

So TJ called for a screen at the top of the key, waving Christian over. The boy's eyes went wide with disbelief. It wasn't often that TJ called plays, let alone a pick and roll. Christian didn't even move until Jordan shouted, "Get over there and set 'im a screen!"

Christian did as he was told and rushed over to plant his body behind TJ's defender. The boy glimmered like a prism in TJ's vision, and a new crack in the path splintered for TJ to follow.

He lowered his dribble defensively and curled tight around Christian's screen—the boy's protruding belly coming in handy for that. Then TJ drove to the basket with an awkward burst of speed, putting his long legs to use. He had no intention of taking the layup —he knew he'd only miss it—but his commitment drew the attention of the other players who met him under the hoop to block his shot. TJ passed the ball back up top to Christian, who wasn't their best player but was at least a decent shooter.

Just as Christian caught the ball, a clarity seemed to drift across the boy's face. TJ's heart fluttered. He had set up the play perfectly; he just needed his teammate to finish it off. Scoring a long one-pointer, where Christian stood, would only continue the game— streetball rules required winning by two, after all. That meant getting the ball to Jordan on the outside corner.

With a pump fake, Christian forced Lamar to leave his double-team on Jordan. And the moment Lamar leaped into the air to block, Christian dished it out to Jordan at the corner. TJ clenched his fist, wanting nothing more than for Jordan to shoot and make the shot.

Please, please, please…

Jordan squared up, jumped, and followed through with a beautiful flick of her wrist. TJ bit his lip as the ball spun in a perfect revolution. It was over. He knew it would go in.

After all, he was the team's lucky charm.

Swish!

TJ's team went wild, throwing their fists in the air, jumping high in jubilation, and rushing Jordan with bear hug after bear hug.

"Splash!"

"Hand down, man down!"

"Was homie sleepin', or what?"

Everyone piled onto Jordan—the students who were watching, even the girls who were usually too cool to cheer. TJ couldn't help but smile. Were it not for his initial drive and his dish to Christian, Jordan might never have been open for such a good look.

"*We call those hockey assists,*" Dad would always say. "*One of the most undervalued plays in basketball.*"

"Good lookin' out, Christian," Jordan hollered through the crowd.

"Christian droppin' dimes like King James," another student said gleefully.

TJ frowned. No one turned to congratulate him, not even Jordan. He couldn't say that surprised him; he hardly ever got credit. Even so, no matter how used to it he was, it still stung. And there was no use making a case for himself. It would've just looked like he was stealing Christian and Jordan's thunder.

The other boys—Lamar chief among them—asked to run it back, but the bell rang, ending the lunch period. The sea of students broke up, each boy and girl grabbing their backpacks and lunch bags before heading off to their respective classes.

TJ joined none of them. Just the way he liked it.

He used to be friends with Christian, but they had grown apart. The boy decided who he wanted to be last year—an after-school juvie with the high schoolers: smoking, getting with girls, that sort of thing. TJ preferred after-school tabletop games, drinking slushies, and… well, he'd like to get with girls too if one would have him.

If it hadn't been for their shared interest in basketball, TJ would've never seen Christian anymore. It didn't matter, though. Friendships were overrated anyway, and not everyone was cut out for them—TJ included. Either TJ disappointed them, or they disappointed him. It was better just to be the lone wolf. Well, maybe not a lone wolf. No one would ever describe TJ as a wolf. Maybe a quiet puppy or modest fox, at best.

His parents just brushed off his reclusion at family reunions and birthday parties as being shy, but TJ figured he was just an introvert, which—according to the internet—meant he did better alone. He wasn't shy, exactly; he just didn't seek out attention.

There was only one person he may have considered a real friend, and as lame as it may have sounded, that person was his sister, Ifedayo Young—though TJ called her "Dayo."

She had been gone for three years now, though. She was too busy playing Wonder Woman in the streets of Abuja, or Old Oyo, or Lagos, or wherever in Nigeria she was at this point. No, not a cosplayer or one of those costumed people on Hollywood Boulevard, but an *actual* hero. At least that's what Mom and everyone else in the family always said.

TJ sighed and picked up his tattered backpack. It ripped at the bottom and barfed out a pile of folders and books. Grunting, TJ collected his supplies, hoping no one saw him.

"Uh… Tomori Jomiloju Young?" a gruff voice said from behind.

Great, of course *someone* saw him.

It was Principal Garcia. The stout man stood akimbo against the bright blue sky. His voice always sounded like something was caught in his throat, and he pronounced TJ's full name better than most — though it was still wrong.

"Just... TJ," he corrected him.

"TJ..." Garcia stopped, frowning. "What's that on your shirt?"

TJ looked down to find a few spots of blood. "Oh, nothing. Just wanted to see if red went well with the blue in my uniform. Answer: it doesn't."

Garcia sighed but didn't press the issue. "Listen, son." He cleared his throat, his eyes dropping briefly to the ground before glancing back to TJ. "I'm afraid I have some bad news."

TJ rolled his eyes. "Was it Tunde again?"

His brother Tunde always got himself in some sort of trouble. TJ told him he was too smart for his own good, always talking back to the teachers about their facts not being straight or riling up the wrong bullies, whose intelligence he often challenged. Granted, the kid was a little genius, already skipping two grades — one below TJ. He could almost hear his little brother's voice in his head saying, *"Don't worry, I'll skip another two so you won't embarrass me in the same classes."*

"I think it's best you come with me, son," Mr. Garcia said sadly.

An uncomfortable sensation trembled across TJ's body; Mr. Garcia wasn't one for the soft-handed approach.

"Sir, is Tunde all right?"

Garcia took in a deep inhale. "Tunde is fine, this..." Garcia's bushy brows were free of any humor. "This is about your sister."

TJ's stomach went empty. What did Dayo have to do with his principal? TJ gulped before asking, "W-what about her?"

Garcia drew a hand around TJ's shoulder. The gentleness in his touch only made TJ's unease worse. "Come with me, son. Your family is waiting for us in my office."

2

ALL THAT'S LEFT

TJ, YOUR SISTER PASSED AWAY...

Those words kept hammering into his head the entire car ride.

The short drive home, which that day felt more like an hour than its usual eight minutes, was often filled with chatter: "how was your day" and "do you have any homework"—that sort of thing.

That afternoon, however, the car seemed to move slower than a tortoise and was as silent as a library.

Dad didn't even play his typical chill tracks of Lauryn Hill or Mos Def, keeping his eyes locked to the road like it mattered, like he wasn't driving five-miles-an-hour.

Mom's glasses—which were two sizes too big for her small head but sat comfortably on her wide nose—magnified her red eyes, which had long been cried out.

TJ's little brother, Tunde, however, was a mess. Through the curtain of his sun-baked dreadlocks, he cried and cried. And with each sob, TJ bit on the inside of his lip to stop himself from joining him. That would only make it worse. He considered rubbing his brother's shoulder, but they hardly ever touched each other and it all felt very awkward.

As the slow rumble of the car went on, TJ turned away from his family, from Dad's bald, unmoving head, from Mom's running nose, and from Tunde's cheeks streaming with tears. So he looked down at the armrest at his side, where a multicolored stain was melted into the faux wood.

That had been his fault so many years ago. Mom told him not to leave his crayons in that little holder on a particularly warm summer's day, but TJ forgot. And when he ruined the car, it was his sister who took the blame.

Like she always did.

She wasn't like other sisters, the ones who were always annoyed with their little brother and too cool to be bothered to spend time with him. She was better. But now...

TJ, your sister is gone...

A sharp pain sliced through his chest. All the air he held in since he got in the car let out in quick staccato breaths. It couldn't be true. Dayo was untouchable. Everyone said so. How could she know all those spells and rituals and not be?

Mom threw him a sidelong glance, and TJ sucked in his heavy breathing. He hadn't cried in front of his parents for years.

Maybe whoever found Dayo was mistaken. Maybe they were just a normal person who didn't know about TJ's world and the extraordinary things that could be done within it. If they did, they wouldn't't've said Dayo had passed away from "cardiac arrest." Diviners didn't just... die. Not like that. If it was true, if she was really gone, something else must've happened.

Dayo's smile shone brightly in TJ's mind. He had just seen a video from her a week ago on her Instagram. Sure, her hair was a mess, and she looked like she could do for some sleep, but dead? Not a chance.

The worst thing of it all was that, while TJ gazed out the car window to the taco stands with hordes of people, and the delinquent teens skateboarding down the street, or the man flipping a real estate sign through the air... The world hadn't stopped. Everyone just went about their day like the kindest person TJ had ever known—ever would know—wasn't gone. It felt wrong, and TJ resented them for it.

TJ, your sister is dead...

☥

DURING THE WEEKEND, DAD CALLED INTO OBAMA CHARTER TO say TJ and Tunde wouldn't be coming back for the rest of the year. The school understood. There were only a little over two weeks left, so the boys wouldn't miss much. Principal Garcia had said they could be given the rest of the semester to grieve.

TJ didn't like that word... grief.

It meant he had to accept what he was still not ready to believe. The belief that he'd never hear Dayo's energetic laugh again, the kind that was contagious, the kind that made a standard joke feel like a stand-up comic's quip. He'd never see her in the mornings again, when she often drew her thumb through his eyes to get the sleep out.

But most of all, he'd never have someone to talk to like her.

TJ often got overlooked. It wasn't anyone's fault, necessarily. With Dayo being as talented as she was, and Tunde always testing in the top two percent in the country, it really was no wonder why TJ's mediocre efforts came as an afterthought in most circumstances. Why would anyone sit to listen to him when he couldn't conjure wind from his fingers or rebuild a computer motherboard from scratch?

But it was different with Dayo. She always made time to speak with him when she could. And she *actually* listened to him no matter what he was rambling about, from the trivial debates between nacho cheese or cool ranch Doritos to the more weighty topics of neighborhood displacement or police brutality that she'd made him read deeper into. Whatever was on TJ's mind, Dayo was there to nurture a dialogue with him, challenge him to think more broadly and with more compassion.

But all of that was gone now. Forever.

TJ had tried to take his mind off his sister, yet none of the things he usually liked doing seemed to work, not his mindless cellphone games, his favorite comics, or YouTube videos. The best thing he could do was sit and do nothing, just stare up at the stucco ceiling and let the late spring breeze drift across his face through his open window.

"Can you tell us what's going on?" a very fast-talking voice nagged from outside. "Do you know how Ifedayo Young died?"

TJ's toes curled at the sound of the word "died."

"Get out of here!" TJ heard his brother saying.

Flipping his legs over his bed, he rushed to his window and looked outside down to his front yard, where Tunde shooed away a squirrely-looking man in a beat-up old car.

"My mom said she didn't want to talk to you or any reporter. Go away, bro!"

"Just one question! Is it true Ifedayo Young was fighting against the—"

TJ didn't hear the rest of the man's question—Tunde waved the trash bag in his hand at the man like he was a pesky fly. Part of TJ wished Tunde hadn't done that. He wanted to know who Dayo was fighting against.

A constant scratching came at TJ's bedroom door, followed by light whimpering. He crossed his room and opened his door to find Simba, the family dog.

Before TJ could so much as pet him, the gold-and-white spotted Russell Terrier sped off downstairs. TJ followed the dog down to the foyer, which was littered with packages from people all over who gave their condolences. Simba bounded over hills of flowers and through tunnels of boxes like it was nothing. TJ followed as best he could, not wanting to crush the keepsake photo album his grandfather had sent from Nigeria, or the gourmet healing candles from Elder Akande in Louisiana, or the enchanted throw pillows that vaulted out of TJ's path from some *bruxa* in Brazil.

Simba didn't stop until he came to the sliding door at the back of the house, which led out into the backyard. This was his universal language for *"I gotta pee, fool."*

TJ tussled with the back door for a few moments—it often jammed up. Dad had said he'd fix it, but he simply didn't have the time between his work and basketball camps. And Mom didn't have the money to spare to call a repairman.

Everything in the house half-worked, not so broken that it needed immediate replacing, but enough of an inconvenience to earn complaints from everyone in the family.

After a few more tugs, TJ slid the door open, and Simba bounded for his special corner in the backyard—between the frog fountain and garden—to do his canine duties.

TJ had to admit it felt nice outside. The sky was cloudless, the wind delicate against his arms, and the birds sang a nice afternoon melody as smells of barbecue wafted over the backyard fence from one of the neighbors.

But like the rest of the weekend, TJ couldn't find any joy in the pleasantries. It didn't seem fair when Dayo lay on some cold slab of metal, getting poked and prodded by some mortician who didn't care or know her at all.

She would have loved the weather today. Spring was her favorite time of the year. She always took TJ to Kenneth Hahn Park to feed the ducks or watch the koi fish swim under large lily pads. Sometimes she did her best to teach TJ some magic, but he always failed her in that way. He tried to mumble one of the ritual phrases she shared with him, a simple incantation that was *supposed* to manifest water from his fingertips, but, like always, nothing had happened.

TJ grunted internally. Regardless of what he did or wherever he went, he could not take his mind off his sister.

"Psst, psst," a hissing voice came from the garden. But no one was there, save for Simba, who was just then covering his poop in the dirt. "Psst, psst."

"Um, hello?" TJ asked hesitantly to the open air.

"Over here!" A long strand of ivy that curled over the backyard's brick wall lifted up and down like someone waving. TJ sprang back, which made Simba yelp.

"Sorry, sorry, don't get all jumpy," the voice, or rather, the hanging, talking ivy said in a female Nigerian accent. "Name's Chika Ogunseye. I've just got a few questions from *The Eshu Messenger Press*. Hold on. I have them just here."

The talking ivy stretched out a second vine over the wall, this one holding a sheet of paper.

"My brother already told the other guy to get lost." TJ scowled. Simba bared his teeth at the intruder, growling all the while.

"Who? Akintemi from *Divination Today*? He's a bum. No, no, *The Eshu Press* is the real thing, very respectable."

"Says the talking vine who's intruding into my backyard."

The she-vine waved TJ's words away like a human would, then pulled out a third vine with glasses in its grip, which she used to read her sheet of paper—TJ couldn't see what for when she didn't even have any eyes.

"First question." She cleared her throat. "What was the true death of Ifedayo Young?"

"*True* death? What are you talking about?"

"The true death, young one. Everyone knows 'cardiac arrest' is code in the diviner community as—"

"*Afefe, wà si mi.*" A tiny gust of wind swirled at their side, and Tunde came running from the house. "We told you all to... get," he threw an uppercut, "out," a magical wind rushed up, "of," the ivy-woman swirled in a gust, "our house!"

With a final flourish of his hands, Tunde forced Chika the reporter off their wall and back out into the street, but not before she exclaimed, "You can't hide the truth!"

"Don't make me report you to the UCMP!" Tunde shouted back —the UCMP was the United Council of Magical Peoples. "This house is protected. We know our rights!"

As though reinforcing the point, Simba barked and growled at the wall at Tunde's heels. The lingering spellwind whipped at TJ's cheeks as his eyes went wide in astonishment. He'd seen his little brother use his Ashe before, but never with such force. Even if it was a tiny gust of wind, it still packed a punch. And the neighbors could've seen him — Mrs. Lindsey was always being nosey. They didn't live in one of the hidden magical hubs in the States, so they had to be careful.

Jumping up to peek over the fence, TJ could see a round woman toppled over on the sidewalk with little green vines sinking into her skin. She brushed dirt off her blouse, gave TJ a nasty look, then walked down the street as though nothing had happened.

"Don't tell Mom," Tunde spouted quickly to TJ, as though reading his older brother's thoughts. "One, I'm not supposed to use my Ashe during the day, and two, Mom told me to enchant the walls with a repelling spell last night, but then *Dad* asked me to do all these chores, you know how it go."

"Yeah, Mom asks me to do magic *all* the time."

Tunde punched TJ on the shoulder. "Ah, you'll get it, eventually."

"Fourteen years of my life disagrees with you."

"Yeah, well…" Tunde shrugged, gave TJ a blank stare for a moment, then took awkward steps backward. "So… um… I gotta do the rest of the walls. Clean this up for me, will you?"

TJ turned to see the garden left in a mess, including Simba's fresh droppings splattered on the brick wall. Cupping his hands over his mouth, TJ called out, "Dude, not cool! You know your ass can manifest some water or something and wash this up."

"Pfft, the hose is right there!" Tunde called back from around the corner, already out of sight.

TJ glanced at the disarray again, sighed, and got to work. After turning on the hose, he did three very lazy passes across the wall — he'd let his parents tell him he didn't do a good enough job later if they noticed. But just as he was wrapping the hose up again, he noticed a damp sheet of paper atop one of Mom's sunflowers. It looked like the same one that the reporter was holding. The ink was all blotchy from dews of water, but TJ could still read it.

Questions for Young Family

- *True Magical COD?*
- *Fight With Keepers?*

- *Vigilante?*
- *Quarreled with Elder Adeyemi?*
- *"I am the falling star. The falling star is me" — last words, perhaps?*

TJ stopped reading after that. It was a very, very long list. All the questions had their own intrigue, yet what halted him straight away was that fifth line about falling stars. He would've sworn he heard something like it before. Where though? And what had Dayo gotten herself into? TJ only vaguely recognized the name "Keepers" from when Mom watched *Divination Today*, but he wasn't sure who Elder Adeyemi was. And his sister, a vigilante? Was that a bad or good thing?

Then it occurred to him where he'd seen those words about falling stars before… Dayo's room!

3

WISHING ON A STAR

Wrapping the rest of the hose up, TJ fanned the reporter's notepaper dry, then tucked it into his pocket. As he made his way back to the backyard's sliding door into the house, Simba bounced at his heels. With three short heaves and a pair of jerks, TJ pried it open, but a mountain of fabric blocked his path. Simba jumped over a clump of red and blue clothes and raced into the cramped back room with the washer and dryer.

"I'm sorry, baby," Mom called from the end of the adjoining kitchen. "Let me get that out of your way."

She waved her fingers distractedly, and the fabric, which TJ could now see were cuts of aṣọ òkè, magically floated from the foot of the door to the top of the dryer where more clothing seemed to sew itself in intricate Yoruba designs.

What was Mom doing? Just an hour ago, she was weeping in her room like she had been all weekend, but now she hustled and bustled around the tiny kitchen as if stopping would bring back her sorrow.

TJ frowned as he realized she was doing the same thing he had tried to do—distract herself with anything, everything.

And now… she was busying herself with funeral preparations.

Yoruba funerals were not like normal American ones. For one, they weren't just a single day but a week-long affair. The day before, Mom had said Dayo's ceremony was going to start on Monday and end the following Sunday in a quasi-Yoruba-American funeral at Inglewood Cemetery. Mom was sewing the aṣọ òkè together for all the guests that would attend throughout the week. And judging by the fabrics that lay atop the cabinets, the drawers, the freezer, and the fridge, it seemed like half of Los Angeles was coming out.

Mom shuffled between the kitchen, dining, and washing room like a busy beaver as she recited the sewing ritual, which brought the rooms to life with self-sewing needles and floating scissors.

As Mom zigged and zagged, her towering dreadlocks seemed to sway like a palm tree in the wind, and just when it looked like her hair would topple over, it set itself straight again in perfect balance.

"Did you get in touch with Priest Glover, ìyà?" Mom asked what looked like a computer screen filled with cascading water, which dipped in and out of a large wooden bowl—a common communication device among diviners, not unlike a video call for non-magical people.

Despite not living in Nigeria for years, Mom always slipped back into that Naija cadence like she had never left.

Within the sheet of revolving water, an old wizened face with the same wide nose as Mom spoke with a thick Nigerian accent. "Why you always wanting Glover for, eh? Bàbáláwò Akande is always doing a better job if you want a proper celebration."

It wasn't uncommon for a Yoruba funeral to have professional dancers and the like among the procession. TJ had always thought of them as hype men or a studio audience, stirring up cheers and laughter. TJ never understood the tradition. Funerals were meant for quiet and introspection, not noise and jubilation.

"Glover doesn't get too loud," Mom said, orchestrating a set of needles through a new collection of fabrics. "Whenever Akande shows up, she whoops and hollers too much. People get uncomfortable."

Grandma sucked her teeth. "Too loud for you Americans. And what about the casket and flowers. How are you paying for it all?"

"Oh, I've got a favor to pull."

"Favor? You know we never take charity. An Abimbola always pays!"

"An Ambibola always pays," Mom repeated. "Don't worry, ìyá. They know I'm good for it. I just can't do it all at once."

Grandma looked unconvinced. "And don't go selling family heirlooms, you hear?" A scowl stretched across her face. Then her mouth shifted into a small "o" as her translucent eyes met TJ. "Is that Tomori Jomiloju? Tell him to stop hiding behind that wall and say hello to his ìyá àgbá."

"Hello, Grandma," TJ said sheepishly.

"No, no, no," she tsked tsked. "Ìyá àgbá, ẹ kásàn ṣe dãda ni?"

"Um…" TJ trailed off uncomfortably. He knew she said, "*you say to me, hello, Grandmother*" or something like that in Yoruba, and he knew how to respond, but he was always uneasy about verbalizing the words—he always got the intonation wrong. So he stood there with his eyebrows scrunched together.

"Oooh, you lookin' just like your *bàbà* every day, eh?" she beamed, water ripples flowing down her cheeks. "How are you feeling?"

TJ would've liked to pull out the note in his jeans and ask what they knew about it. He decided against it, of course. He'd rather figure it out on his own before getting Mom or Grandma involved. Mom was liable to take it from him and ask where he got it from. No, that wouldn't work. He *knew* he saw that line about falling stars somewhere in Dayo's room…

TJ must've put on a downer face in his turmoil because Mom cut in. "Ìyá, tell me if I'm doing this sewing spell right. I think the hems are too loose."

Grandma kissed her teeth again. "The hems are loose because you don't speak Yoruba enough anymore. When are you going to visit me?" She continued the rest of her tirade in her mother tongue, speaking too fast for TJ to keep up. Even if she spoke slowly and clearly, he still would've had an issue following what was essentially a foreign language to him.

Before she could turn her rapid-fire Yoruba back on him, TJ slipped out of the kitchen and into the family room. He was halfway back to the foyer with its obstacle course of gifts and keepsakes when a light sound of sniffling halted him.

He had entered from behind the sole couch in the room, unaware that his father had been lying there with his hand on his forehead. All TJ could see was his father's shiny bald head.

A lump welled up in TJ's throat.

Was his father… crying?

TJ had never as much as seen his father get teary-eyed, let alone this. Suddenly, an uncomfortable sensation washed over him, and he made sure not to press the heel of his foot into the loose floorboard under the rug as he stepped forward.

When TJ saw what his father was looking at, though, he couldn't blame his tears. Dad held his cellphone in his hand, scrolling through old videos of Dayo when she was a toddler. Even when she was young, her smiles and laughter were infectious. Each time she let out a giggle, the younger voice of his father snickered back, and the two found themselves in an endless ping pong of chuckles. However, it seemed like with each burst of laughter from past-Dad, it brought a new sob from present-day Dad—which the man tried to suppress with a hand.

TJ backpedaled from the room, holding his breath as not to disturb his father. As he climbed the stairs back up to the second floor, he found a whimpering Simba clawing at Dayo's bedroom door. TJ knelt to pet the little dog behind the ears and wondered if he knew what had happened to her. Dayo always said that animals were more in tune with their Ashe than humans in many ways.

TJ opened the door to the bright room of blues and lavenders, Dayo's favorite colors. Though the slanted ceiling made the room seem cramped, Dayo's room was still larger than TJ and Tunde's room, which the pair had to share as the only two boys in the family.

Dayo's room didn't have much. Only a small twin bed and a tiny desk sat in a nook near the room's only window. TJ could barely see the desk. Every inch of it was covered in all sorts of awards, from swim meets to writing achievements—most of the accolades, however, were humanitarian.

Mom had painted the walls with the images of the many Orishas, the ethereal forces that fueled diviners and their magic, from the sky deity Obatala to Oko of the earth, and Olokun of the deep blue sea. At night when the room grew dark, the paint glowed a majestic gold like fireflies in the night.

TJ had loved sneaking into Dayo's room when he was younger; they used to stay up late into the night talking about anything and everything until Mom and Dad banged on the walls.

"TJ. Dayo. Stop that noise and go to bed," they would say.

Despite himself, a curl of a smile crept across the edge of TJ's mouth at the memory.

Simba went straight for Dayo's bed, sinking his nose into her pillows. Even though she hadn't lived there for three years, it still smelled like her, that hint of honeydew fragrance she favored.

TJ went through her closet first, looking for anything that mentioned falling stars. Like everything in her room, it was immaculate and orderly. It felt wrong going through her things, but he kept everything as tidy as it was before he started looking. At the top of the closet was a shoebox that read: *Ifa Academy 2019*. TJ got to his tip-toes and clawed for it, but he couldn't quite reach. He stretched again, knocking his elbow into something hard.

A long shaft *thudded* against the shag carpet that rested under Dayo's bed. TJ stood with hunched shoulders, hoping no one heard the tumble.

It was Dayo's staff, the prized possession of a diviner. Mom must've put it there after her body came back Saturday morning. Tough mahogany wood made up its shaft, which twisted around a jagged crystal that shimmered a shade of lime against the afternoon light streaking through the room. Simba jumped from the bed to sniff the staff, then started licking the crystal as though it were a treat.

"No, stop that, Simba." TJ shooed the dog away as he picked the staff up.

Despite its twisting nature, it felt smoothed and polished yet firm to his grip, like something unseen locked his hand into place. When Dayo had first let him touch her staff, she told him it was his Ashe binding him to the wood.

Too bad he could do nothing with it.

But he could hear his sister's voice clear inside his head.

"Don't try so hard," she said kindly. *"You'll never get it to work if you try to force it out. You've got to breathe and be at peace. Feel how your Ashe flows through you and everything else in this room."*

Across the room rested a portrait of Dayo and her best friend, Adeola. They wrapped each other in a tight embrace with their graduation robes, smiles wide and bright. Around its frame in cursive writing read the words: *Wishing on a star, to follow where you are. May we find our shooting stars as they fall and rise with the guiding hands of Orunmila.*

That was it! But what did it even mean? It wasn't exactly a match to what was on the reporter's paper. TJ knew Orunmila was another Orisha, the one Dayo aligned with, but not much else.

The staff vibrated between TJ's fingers, and that familiar tingle rolled through their tips. Perhaps he could call the picture to his hand like Dayo sometimes did.

TJ lifted the staff above his head, recalling the lesson his sister tried to impart to him. Somehow it felt like she had never left, like she was there just at his shoulder giving him words of encouragement.

Don't try so hard, TJ told himself.

"*Àwòrán, wà sí mi,*" TJ recited the incantation, but nothing happened.

The picture didn't even move an inch.

TJ repeated himself, but still… the same result. Nothing.

After his third attempt, he closed his eyes, saying the words faster and faster, hoping to hear the rush of a picture frame soaring toward him.

He opened his eyes. Nothing changed.

Simba looked up to him with a lazy tongue and a wagging tail. It should've worked. He *knew* it was going to work, but for whatever reason, the staff didn't listen to him as it should've.

What did he have to do to get his Ashe to function properly? Everyone in his family—except Dad and his own family, who were very *un*magical—could do it. Maybe that was the problem. Perhaps he got Dad's non-magical genes, whereas his little brother and older sister lucked out with their mother's.

But TJ knew it wasn't true. Several times in his life he had felt the energy force his sister always talked about. He knew it was there, deep down, like it was behind some hidden veil he just couldn't see through.

Grunting, TJ twisted back to the closet and stuffed Dayo's staff back where he found it. When he closed the door, a gentle wind drifted past his neck. TJ looked to see if the window was open, but it was sealed shut. Simba started to sniff the air, whipping his head from left to right in search of something unseen. TJ turned to the picture again, but it still sat unmoving.

Where had that wind come from? He didn't just imagine it, did he?

TJ opened the closet and eyed the staff again. It could've been a trick of the light, yet it seemed like the crystal lodged in the wood glowed green. No, it couldn't have been the light—darkness shadowed the closet. Simba nuzzled TJ's leg, and the pair of them stared at each other.

They weren't alone in that room.

4

THE PROMISED CHILD

FOR THE NEXT WEEK, TJ MUST'VE VISITED DAYO'S ROOM A DOZEN times between all the days of her funeral arrangements. Yet never, not even once, did he feel or sense anything again. And he still couldn't for the life of him figure out what all the "falling star" business was about no matter how many times he listened to Rose Royce back and front.

During the first two days relegated to prayer and donations to fund the week's events—spiritually and monetarily alike—TJ had tried to replicate exactly what he did the first time he stepped into Dayo's room. But for the whole of those pair of days, all he could do was nearly give himself an aneurysm from all his wasted concentration and his obviously shoddy attempt at prayer.

He figured he should've appealed to Orunmila, Dayo's Orisha, but even that didn't seem to garner results.

On the next day of *Ìtàóku,* the day of feasting and celebration of life, when Simba kept asking TJ for table scraps, he remembered that his dog had been in the room with him when that weird sensation danced around his neck.

Yet despite putting his dog on the bed between Dayo's pillow like before, his pet's presence didn't change a thing.

On the next few days, which were filled with light-hearted games, TJ watched his cousins as they played Eshu's crossover, a magical game he could take no part in.

Unlike his typical pick-up games, crossover required more than mere tingling in the fingers or all-star teamwork. Many of his cousins used air-stepping to dodge and slip each other in a game more akin to ultimate frisbee or capture the flag than basketball—on magical steroids, of course.

That said, their movements inspired TJ to try the same wind magic in his sister's room; perhaps that would rekindle whatever sensation had been there before.

After hours of fiddling with Dayo's staff and reciting Yoruba phrases he was likely butchering, the best he could do was make himself go hoarse—though he thought he *was* getting somewhere when he smelled an odd odor.

It turned out to be Simba passing gas.

Despite his best efforts over the week, each time he stepped into her room, nothing happened, no ghostly gusts or odd sensations through his veins. Irked and defeated, TJ had finally resolved that whatever he felt that day was merely his imagination, a fixation his mind *wanted* desperately to be true.

So came the second to last day of the funeral festivities, *Ìrènòkú*, the most significant day. Though the week was filled with family and friends, almost like a mini-reunion brimming with tears and laughter, Mom said it was nothing compared to what they planned for the finale.

☦

THAT SATURDAY MORNING, THE FAMILY DROVE TO THE FINAL ceremonial day in silence, all dressed in traditional Yoruba clothing— TJ and Tunde in the back, Mom and Dad in the front.

Like everyone else in their immediate family, Mom wore a collection of blue and purple aṣọ òkè. Today she dressed in a big *gèlé* head tie with a *bùbá* blouse, *pèlè* shawl, and *ìró* wrap-around skirt. TJ and the rest of the males in the car wore *fìlà* caps, bùbá shirts, *àgbádà* tunics, and *ṣòkòtò* trousers. TJ thought he'd be hot in all the fabrics, but the wide cuffs and loose hangings crafted a nice breeze between his legs and arms.

As they rounded the corner of La Brea and Centinela, Tunde squinted and lifted his chin over his father's shoulder to ask, "Are all those people here for what I think they are?"

"Oh, my goodness," Mom gasped as she rolled down her window. The wind drifting through the car brought with it a scent of incense and spices, like the Pan-African festivals TJ's family often went to.

A horde of people garbed in African fabrics and headdresses filled the city streets like a rainbow sea of blues, greens, reds, and oranges. TJ tried to count them all as they drove by, but he stopped at one-hundred and twenty-three. At *least* a thousand clustered shoulder to shoulder as the crowd waited for the Youngs to arrive. When a few patrons in the crowd recognized their car, they waved merrily, some hopping up and down.

"Priest Glover said he lost count," Mom said, pride welling in her eyes. "Everyone from the diviner community must be here: from the West Coast, East Coast, down south, the islands, even all the way from Benin and Nigeria."

Tunde gasped from the seat beside TJ. "Dayo knew *all* these people?"

"Of course not, baby." Mom dabbed her eyes with a tissue. "But she meant a lot to very many."

"How long does this parade go on for?" TJ asked as Dad pulled their car into the grocery store lot where a banner reading "Funeral Parking" slung over a "Ralphs" sign.

Mom smiled brightly again. "We've shut down Centinela from La Brea all the way to the cemetery."

TJ gawked as his father turned off the car. He knew Dayo was some sort of hero in Nigeria, but he always thought it was local, not national, and definitely not… global. The sheet of paper in his pocket beneath all the garb brushed against his thigh like a pin-pricking reminder. It had said Dayo was being accused of being a vigilante, and he still hadn't worked out what that meant.

"I thought you diviners were supposed to be a secret," Dad grunted.

"It'll be all right." Mom waved a dismissive hand. "We've got officials from the UCMP watching over everything. No one's allowed to use their Ashe, and to any passerby, it'll look like a normal African-appreciation parade."

"*Normal* parade?" Dad questioned skeptically. "Y'all brought half the Motherland to South Central."

☨

WHEN THE YOUNG FAMILY FINALLY FOUND THEIR WAY TO THE center of the crowd where TJ's close cousins held up Dayo's casket, the parade began in merry fervor. Drums *thump-thumped*, trumpets belted loud tunes, and a woman TJ could not see through the masses sang out a traditional Yoruba song. The smell of fruits and berries wafted off everyone's clothes as they spun and tapped their feet to the music.

TJ walked alongside Dayo's casket bedecked in fresh lavenders and fragrant blue sea hollies, her favorite. It had been the closest he'd been to her body since she left. He thought if he strained his ears enough, he could hear her laughter, but it had to be his imagination.

Even as the men who held up the casket bounced up and down to the rhythmic music, the decorations remained in place. The casket was more secure than a military bunker. Mom must've wrangled enough money through donations to get Dayo the very best. But one side of the coffin hung low and lopsided as one man stomped instead of danced.

Though the others wore wide smiles and sang along with the hymns, Dad's eyes looked deadpan and vacant. Like TJ, he must've not found Dayo's death to be cause for celebration. Mom and Tunde, however, were swept up in the fervor, Mom clapping and Tunde pounding away on his àgbá drum.

Perhaps it was a cultural divide. Sometimes TJ only found common ground with his father when in the presence of the magical or, in this case, West Africans.

How could they be in such high spirits when Dayo lay dead only feet away? She'd never wake again, never sing or dance like the others, never pound on a drum, or cast another spell. All of that was taken from her without warning… because of some "cardiac arrest" that was apparently a code for something else TJ couldn't figure out.

TJ thought funerals were supposed to be quiet and somber, reflective and pensive, not loud and boisterous like the Lakers had just won a championship.

Noticing what must've been TJ's stony gaze, Mom put a hand around his shoulder and rubbed it gently. "It's great, isn't it?"

TJ wanted to say "he guessed so," but that would only make Mom sad. Who was he to bring her down? So instead he said, "It's… something."

She smiled, seemingly satisfied with TJ's response. "So many important people are here. This would mean so much to your sister." Mom pointed to the surrounding crowd. "Just there is Olufemi Bolawe." She pointed to a tall man with pores the size of craters in a black and orange tunic who, unlike the others, walked a steady pace with a neutral face. "He knew Ifedayo well. They were working together in Nigeria."

TJ gave the man a second examination. Maybe he knew what really happened to Dayo.

"And just there," Mom continued, shouting so she could be heard over the crowd, "a few feet from Bolawe is Elder Simisola Adeyemi. Some say she's the greatest diviner of her generation." She nodded to a woman equally as tall as the man with sparkling earrings. Though the woman was probably sixty, maybe even seventy, the shimmering makeup dabbed around her eyes looked like it belonged on someone half her age.

"And over there... that's Xavier Du Bois, one of the instructors at the summer camp down in—oh, is that?" Mom craned her head over a gleeful man plucking at a string instrument TJ didn't recognize. "Adeola, is that you?"

TJ's eyes widened at the sound of the name. Adeola was Dayo's best friend. He had met her a few times when he and Dayo visited her up in Oakland, or when she visited them in Los Angeles. He remembered having the biggest crush on her and getting instantly shut down. She made up for it by playing him in Mario Kart though, so that was cool.

"Mrs. Young?" Adeola called out as she pressed her way through the throng of people.

Like his mother, she wore an elaborate head tie and a vibrant dress, though her colors were emerald and canary. She and Dayo shared in their almond eyes and slender faces. Though, where Dayo's smile was straight, even, and wide, Adeola's grin always came at a thin slant, and TJ remembered that her nickname was Cheekbones because they were particularly distinct. Her nose, like always, was never free from some new nose piercing. And that day, she had a bull's nose ring.

"I thought that was you." Mom left TJ's side to embrace Adeola.

"I knew a lot of us would show up, but..." Adeola broke the hug to look around. Several Nigerian flags blocked out the sun and shadowed her face. "I never would have thought *this* many would pay their respects to Dayo."

The tears in Mom's eyes ran freely, renewed and ruining her makeup.

"Hey, Deola..." TJ said softly, eyes low. Maybe Adeola didn't remember him.

Adeola's expression brightened when she finally glanced to TJ. "No way... Tomori Jomiloju? That *can't* be you. You're taller than I am now."

"Dad says us Youngs hit our growth spurts right before high school."

"Go on. Go and say hello to the others," Adeola said to Mom. "Kiara and Titilayo are just over there. I'll look after Tomori. We got some catching up to do."

Mom gave Adeola two light kisses on her cheek and shuffled deeper in the crowd to say her hellos. TJ found himself transfixed by the *ìde* beads wrapped around Adeola's wrist. They were red, pink, and burgundy, and all seemed to shimmer in the daylight.

"Do you remember whose colors these are?" she asked TJ, who tried to act like he wasn't looking.

A familiar sting of embarrassment curled through his stomach whenever he was quizzed on the Orishas. How could anyone remember them all? The priests said there were at least four-hundred-and-one of them, possibly more.

"Um..." was all TJ could get out before Adeola jabbed him on the shoulder playfully.

"Don't trip," she chuckled. "Yewa isn't well known, even to the elders. These colors represent her. She's the Orisha of—"

"Graveyards," TJ finished sadly, remembering her role once Adeola named her. It made sense considering where they were.

"Yeah..." she trailed off. He could barely hear her over all the drums and commotion.

"I don't get it." TJ scowled, bumping shoulders with a teenage girl dancing with a sparkling sign of Dayo that winked magically on a loop—which was promptly taken away by a uniformed official wearing shades and all-white robes. "Everyone's cheering and singing like there's something to be happy about."

"Well," Adeola started, pursing her already thin lips as though considering her next words. "Your sister did a lot in life that's worth praise like this."

"I knew she was top of her class and all that... and yeah, she helped a lot of people, I know that, but... all of this." TJ gestured to the festivities. "There's something I gotta be missing." Then it hit him. How could he forget until just then? "Oh, dude! This reporter came to our house last week, and they dropped this." He fumbled in his robes as he pulled out the reporter's note. "Maybe you know something about it. It talks about the Keepers. And what does this stuff here mean about 'falling star.' It's on that frame of you guys in her room."

Adeola's eyes went sharp. "Your mother never told you about the promised child stuff?"

"Promised child? What's that?"

Adeola's narrowed eyes softened slightly. Her lips parted for a moment, but she bit down as though she were keeping herself from saying anything else. "If your mother didn't say anything, it's not my place to—"

"No, you can't just do that." TJ tugged at her arm. "What did she not tell me?"

Adeola's eyes shifted from left to right to the crowd as she removed TJ's hand from her arm. "I have to go, Tomori. We'll catch up later, yeah?" She walked off, stopped, turned back on her heel, then flitted her fingers toward TJ. "And *you* shouldn't have that."

The piece of paper started to wiggle out of TJ's fingers. TJ stared down at it as it did its little shimmy away from the pinch of his forefinger and thumb until it was finally free. It floated like a leaf in the wind until it landed in Adeola's hand.

"Wait, stop!" TJ outstretched a hand, but Adeola disappeared into the crowd.

After a few moments of shouldering through the sea of people—with one too many bump-ins with emerald-robed women he thought was Adeola, TJ gave up. A shaded part of the street covered by a maple tree became a resting point for him as he searched for Mom.

So, TJ thought, *Dayo was some sort of 'promised child.'*

What did that even mean? And why hadn't Mom told him about it? As he stared out to the crowd, the enormous, unending crowd, he wondered if they knew it too.

But they couldn't have.

He watched the same news everyone else did. *Divination Today* was on every morning in his house. Plus, he had a first-row seat to everything Dayo did—well, maybe not for the last three years. The last three years, it was more like he was in the nosebleeds. Not once though, did anyone mention her being a promised child.

A hero, sure. A humanitarian, all the time. Promised child? Never.

Maybe it was just a nickname, something interchangeable with all the other monikers Dayo picked up over the years.

TJ wondered where all the reporters were. This was all a pretty big event, after all. Surely they were doing their snooping. Then he remembered the big guy with the shades and the all-white robes. Now that he looked around a bit more astutely, he could see more men and women in similar robes on the edges of the parade, acting like they weren't over watching everyone else. There probably *were* some reporters snooping around but, like the little girl with her sign, they likely got shut down.

When TJ decided all his thinking was leading to a headache, he rejoined the crowd where he followed the hymns that surrounded his sister's casket. Eventually, he caught back up to Dad, Tunde, and Mom, who was still speaking with other people in the crowd. TJ wanted to butt in with questions of Dayo, even though it would've been rude. And once the sign reading *Inglewood Park Cemetery* crested over the congregation's caps and head ties, TJ finally mustered the courage to interrupt his mother.

"What's a 'promised child'?" he asked.

Mom's face went several shades lighter—a testament against her dark complexion. Despite the change of color in her skin, she acted as though she didn't hear TJ.

"Mom, did you hear me?" TJ asked again, but Mom waved to another guest and started a very loud conversation with him.

Fine, she could ignore him for now, but eventually she'd have to answer him. So TJ played along, waiting for the right moment to hit her with his questions.

But each time he thought he found a moment with Mom, something always came up: a new relative that wanted to catch up, a cemetery worker who needed something answered, or a friend or a stranger giving their condolences.

TJ would have gone looking for Adeola again on his own, but anytime he wandered off from his mother's side, she hissed and snapped her fingers, directing him to stand right back where he was. This was the only time she *didn't* ignore him, and anytime he opened his mouth in question, he was met with a "hush, not right now" from her.

☦

THE CROWD DWINDLED FROM A THOUSAND TO A FEW HUNDRED once TJ, his family, and select invited guests made their way through the private cemetery surrounded by high stone walls topped with spiked and black fences.

The wake ceremony was beautiful, set along the cemetery's lone lake with a simple fountain in its center. Green grass and tombstones flanked the water on all sides. And a great white tent covered the rows of chairs that faced Dayo's casket, shielding all from the high noon sun.

TJ barely noticed most of it. Throughout the ceremony and its speeches, despite sitting in the first row, TJ pondered on all that was said during the parade. He almost lost track of time when his brother poked him in the side.

"I-it's time to go look at her," Tunde said with a shaky voice.

He must've wanted TJ to go look first. TJ hesitated, a hefty weight magnetizing him to his seat.

Was he ready to see his sister?

Just last week he complained that he couldn't see her at the funeral home—now, he wasn't so sure he could take the four steps to see her at her own funeral.

Lifting himself from his seat with a stilted sigh, TJ followed behind his parents, who took the first turn to view Dayo's body. Along with the floral decorations atop the coffin, a collection of Dayo's personal possessions flanked the sides: a statuette of Orunmila, the Orisha of Wisdom, her staff, whose single emerald crystal gleamed under the afternoon light, a bowl of peaches, her favorite fruit, and many other items associated with Dayo in one way or another.

The mood had changed since the parade leading to the cemetery. Now it felt more like the tone TJ had anticipated, a respectful and almost eerie quiet punctured only by sniffles, blown noses, and the chirping of birds.

For the second time, Mom cried, though this time she sobbed into a handkerchief so her tears wouldn't fall on Dayo's body. Dad held a steady hand on her back, rubbing her only when her weeping grew to outright shakes. Unlike a week before, Dad held a strong face free of tears. He must've got all he needed out in the house. Perhaps that was a onetime occurrence TJ would never witness again.

After a few moments, it was TJ and Tunde's turn. TJ didn't know what he was expecting when he saw Dayo's body, but he didn't think he would feel so normal about it. It didn't look like she was dead at all. He'd even say she looked better than the time when she had been on Instagram a few weeks before.

Where her face once looked gaunt, now, thanks to the work done by whoever did her makeup, her skin looked healthy and full. It just looked like she was sleeping, as though she would wake up at any moment. But after staring at her for a full minute, the stillness in her chest made it all the more final.

TJ's eyes stung, stung like every onion in the world up and decided to relocate just under his lids.

He had cried several times over the past week, yet that was in the privacy of his own room when Tunde wasn't around.

This, however, was different.

A pang of guilt lanced through him, making him stiff and rigid. Why was he so embarrassed to cry in front of the guests? It was expected, encouraged. Why couldn't he let himself weep and mourn?

He knew why, deep down.

He just wasn't ready to admit it yet, knowing that the moment he did, it would be the final crack on top of the mounting grief he had suppressed that whole week.

That's what really fueled all his interest in the reporter's notes, what motivated all his questions to Mom as they entered the cemetery. To settle in one place and allow himself to think would only lead to the tears that dropped onto his folded hands at that moment. The reality of Dayo's inert body sank in in all its totality, and TJ's tears kept coming freely... and... he allowed them to.

He welcomed them.

Without thinking, TJ reached out to touch her arms folded across her chest. As his fingers brushed along her smooth hand, a shockwave spiked through his arms, making his skin prickle with goosebumps from an energy that he couldn't describe —yet, it felt familiar somehow. The vibrations were more like the way he felt when Dayo hugged him, like the way it felt when she laughed at his bad jokes. It was like she was... no, it couldn't be possible, he knew it couldn't. But it felt like her essence was inside him, coursing through his blood, racing down his spine.

Flashes of colors ran across his eyes and his body started to spasm.

Mom's scream came loud before his head hit the ground. Hard.

5

SHAPES & SOUNDS

"TJ, can you hear me?"

"Oh baby, please wake up."

"Is he breathing? What happened?"

The voices came in and out like a radio station being tuned in from too far a source. TJ could only make out a word or a phrase, but never full sentences.

His head swam in a space between reality and dreams. He couldn't see exactly, his sight replaced with a collage of colors like a kaleidoscope in his mind's eye.

He wanted to wake, wanted to tell the voices he was all right, but he couldn't find his sense of self. There was nothing of him any longer—no feet, no hands, no breathing even.

Just the shapes and sounds.

The hues swirling around him appeared almost as figures, colossal shapes that watched over him. One near the middle looked particularly familiar: almond-shaped eyes and a wide smile.

A deep tone pierced the abyss of sound, a rhythmic melody of a Yoruba prayer TJ didn't understand. As he listened to the words, he could feel his feet brush against the groove of his dress shoes, his toes rubbing against his cotton socks.

"Look there! Look there! Was that his feet?"

Yes, yes, it's my feet, TJ tried to say, but his own voice was still lost to the void.

The prayer continued, its words vibrating through his legs and up to his belly.

"He's breathing! Thank the Orishas, he's breathing."

TJ's fingers curled into a loose fist and he could feel a cool breeze trail across his knuckles, could feel blades of grass tickling his skin.

"Tomori Jomiloju, it's your mother. Listen to my voice."

Slowly, TJ opened his eyes to the white tent. Several shapes stood above him, not unlike the shapes in his dream, each of them silhouetted against the bright tent roof. Turning his head a bit, he could make out the green grass and the tombstones embedded in them next to the blue lake and the fountain within it.

Sweat soaked TJ's clothes. He felt like he had just played a game of full-court basketball.

"Give him some space, Yejide," came Dad's voice.

The shadowed figure that had to be Dad pulled at another with a large head tie... Mom.

TJ suddenly became aware of a large hand engulfing his forehead, two fingers at each side of his temples. The figure closest to him spoke with a strong baritone, reciting its prayer. Was that the voice he had heard in his reverie?

It had to be.

A tuft of grass brushed against the back of TJ's neck as his eyes focused in on the figure that loomed over him. The indistinct shadows materialized into features of people, of loved ones. Mom stood to his left, wrapped up in Dad's broad arms, blotched makeup spotted around her bloodshot eyes. Tunde stood just behind them, looking close to tears himself. But closest to TJ was the man Mom pointed out before, Olufemi Bolawe, if TJ remembered correctly. His eyes were serious and dark, sweat glistening atop his slightly protruded brow and into the valley of his deep crater-like pores.

"Thank you, Olufemi," Mom managed to choke out.

The man named Mr. Bolawe lifted his hand from TJ's forehead and wiped his own. "Thought we lost you there for a bit," he said deeply. "We can't stand to lose another Young so soon."

TJ gave him a weak smile, but it felt like he could only manage a grimace, at best.

"Olufemi." Mom put a light hand on the man's shoulder. "You look exhausted. Go get yourself some water from the bar."

"Yes, you're probably right..." he trailed off, his eyes shifting between TJ and something just out of view. The focus in his expression broke as fatigue truly set into the bags under his eyes. Whatever this Bolawe guy did to bring TJ back must've taken a lot out of him.

"Tomori, this is the man I was telling you about." Mom nodded to

Mr. Bolawe, seeming to read the confusion on TJ's face. "Olufemi Bolawe. He and your sister were close. He taught her in her first few years at Ifa Academy."

"Before I led a very unsuccessful political career," Bolawe grunted, lifting to his feet. He held a hand out for TJ, who took it and hefted himself up with the help of the man. "I'm truly sorry about your sister. Her death was a massive loss to our community. *Massive*."

The man's words sounded more genuine than the others TJ had heard all day. There was true sorrow in them, true gravity, and his words reached his eyes. TJ could see now that the man had many smile lines around his eyes, but in all the time he spoke he never as much as smirked.

How long had it been since he did, TJ wondered.

TJ surveyed the other people surrounding them. It sounded like half the guests were huddled around, judging by the number of murmuring voices.

TJ caught sight of the woman who had been speaking with Mr. Bolawe — Elder Adeyemi was her name, right? In the afternoon's light, she seemed to shimmer like the Orisha paintings in his sister's room, like specks atop the ocean. Even her dress flowed like the waters of the seas as she moved forward gracefully. It didn't even look like she took steps as she glided atop the grass as though she were on a pair of skates. The longer TJ stared at her outfit, the more at ease he felt, and he didn't come out of his trance until Elder Adeyemi finally spoke.

"My old friend is right," she phrased soothingly. "We cannot be without another Young. How are you feeling, um…"

"Tomori," TJ groaned, not sure why he gave her his full name. It just seemed like she commanded that kind of respect. "Tomori Jomiloju… or just, you know, TJ. And I'm feeling fine. I'm just a little dizzy."

"Did you faint when you touched her?"

"Y-yeah, I did." A few of the guests let out small gasps. TJ swallowed nervously, not meeting their eyes. "D-does that mean something?"

The elder drew down into a crouch like a queen of utter elegance. "It means you have connected."

"Connected… how?"

She smiled faintly. "That remains to be seen."

Looking at Mom askance, TJ was about to ask this Elder Adeyemi about what all this "promised child" business was about —

she seemed the type to know—when he heard shouting near Dayo's casket.

"The staff!" a man shouted. "It's glowing!"

Everyone turned their heads to the casket where Dayo's staff lay askew against it. Sure enough, the emerald at her staff's head pulsed brightly just as TJ had seen it a week before.

"Heavens!" a woman exclaimed from the crowd. "Praise Orunmila!"

Turning his head back to the others, TJ saw that everyone was staring at Dayo's staff in awe, all except Mr. Bolawe and Elder Adeyemi. Both of their gazes rested on TJ and TJ alone. For a moment, the two traded glances between one another as the glow within the staff's crystal finally dwindled.

"And so it is seen," Mr. Bolawe said in answer to Elder Adeyemi's previous statement.

Mom held her hand close to her mouth. "Oh my, she really is with us."

"This is… significant," Mr. Bolawe said to Mom. "She could be trying to speak to us now. Tomori, do you hear a voice? What did you see when you were out?"

"I-I…" TJ trailed off.

He couldn't concentrate with all the guests staring at him. It didn't help that everyone looked like they'd seen a ghost. Some of them were even looking over their shoulders and into the winds, not unlike TJ did the day he was in his sister's room.

"No, I didn't hear her. I mean, I didn't hear anything. Well, I *did*, but that was y'all's voices. I saw some figures in some smoke with all these colors, though. Does that mean anything?"

"Hmmm. It could be that Mr. Young here may have activated the latent Ashe in the staff in some way," Bolawe intoned mostly to Elder Adeyemi, then he turned to Mom. "May I ask why he's not at Ifa Academy this year?"

"W-well he—w-we've tried—i-it's just—" Mom stammered each of her answers. She always got like that when a diviner asked why TJ wasn't studying the Orisha or developing his Ashe. It was never easy for her to say he was distinctly magic-free, except for his intermittent tingling. "Y-you see—h-he hasn't really—"

Dad stood forward, ceasing his wife's stuttering. "Olufemi," he said as he pointed to the man's robes dampened with sweat. "Let me get you some water."

Mr. Bolawe broke his gaze with TJ, straightening his shirt before saying, "No, no, it's okay. I'll go myself. Please, excuse me for just a moment."

Mom wrapped her arms around TJ in a hug, pulling back to place his cheeks between her smooth palms. "Are you really okay, baby? Do you feel like you might pass out again?"

"Perhaps some water for Mr. Young as well, yes?" Elder Adeyemi suggested gently.

Mom slapped her forehead. "What am I thinking? Of course, you must be light-headed. I'll go get you some water, too."

She jogged away down the damp lawn, her *ìlẹkẹ* beads tapping together around her neck as she bounced.

"Mr. Young," Elder Adeyemi said. "How's your knuckle?"

"My knuckle?" TJ questioned with a raised eyebrow. He looked down at his hand. The space between his index and middle finger was bleeding, a piece of his skin hanging from his hand. "Oh, I slipped when I—"

"Let me get that for you." She grabbed his hand and spoke some words lightly under her breath. Her hand felt like satin despite its wrinkles and veins. "Excuse me for being so ill-mannered. My name is Simisola Adeyemi, headmistress of Ifa Academy."

"I know, my mom told me." This had been the first time he spoke to anyone from a magic school. It wasn't lost on TJ how much interest was laced in the old woman's voice either.

A cool sensation breezed across TJ's knuckle. He glanced down and watched as the small cut between his knuckle started to mend itself. Mom had done the charm work on him and his siblings plenty of times before. But now, he could almost see the energy surging between his fingers and Adeyemi's, could almost see how her words manifested the magical healing which weaved through his knuckle like a mist. It was almost like his basketball games at school, the same way he felt before making a pass to a teammate. Only now, it seemed more distinct, less of a feeling and something more tangible and concrete.

"Thank you, ma'am," TJ said as he examined his healed hand.

He met Adeyemi's gaze, almost regretting it the moment he did. It looked like she was searching deep into him, which made TJ a bit uncomfortable.

Mom returned, ambling along the lake's edge with a paper cup filled with water which splashed over her hands with each of her skips. By the time she reached TJ, the cup was only a quarter full.

"I'm so sorry, honey." She waved her hand over the cup, magically filling it with water once more. *"Ọṣun, mo gbãdurà ṣi ọ. Mu óunjẹ fun mi. Ṣé óngbẹ mi."* Again, TJ would have sworn he saw something like a fog between the cup and Mom's hand.

TJ grabbed the cup and drank. The cool water went down his throat, easy and smooth. He hadn't realized how thirsty he'd been, and, in two large gulps, he downed the whole cup.

"Want some more?" Mom asked eagerly.

TJ nodded. As his mother started to fill the cup again, TJ caught sight of a masked person with cream-colored robes at the back of the crowd holding a staff, a staff whose crystal was alighting crimson.

A woman nearby shrieked.

"Keepers!" shouted another man in the crowd, and a blast erupted next to the tent, throwing dirt and grass into the air.

6

THE KEEPERS

THE FUNERAL GUESTS RUSHED PAST TJ, JOSTLING AND BUMPING against his shoulders roughly as they screamed and ran into each other in a panic.

TJ tried to get up and follow everyone else but ended up falling back on his knees. Parents grabbed their children, and couples protected each other from the ground explosions that continued to blossom one after the other.

"Aaargh!" TJ cried as someone's shoe came crashing down on his fingers. The foot's owner didn't stop to apologize as they made a beeline for the nearby lake, diving in and disappearing in what looked like a whirlpool that manifested in the water. More diviners followed suit as they rotated their arms in large circles and opened more whirlpools that they dived in and vanished into.

A series of shouts brought TJ's attention back to the end of the tent, his pounding heart threatening to burst from his chest. Several figures dressed in white àgbádà tunics stomped forward like an avalanche from the cemetery entrance fifty yards away.

Each wore a different Yoruba-made mask, some wooden, some iron, but all of them depicting the facade of someone—or something—with narrow eyes. They held staffs in their hands, flipping and turning them overhead and sidelong as flares of fire, sheets of ice, and mounds of earth shot out from their tips and whistled into the ground where they exploded.

TJ covered his ears against the loud bangs.

Those guests brave enough to remain echoed the spell phrase, *"ọpá, wà ṣi mi."* As they said the words, staff after staff manifested in each diviner's hands.

From the tip of a Keeper's staff, an inferno stream roared for the tent. But before it could meet the white tarp, an invisible wall of wind halted its forward momentum, and it blossomed like a plume upon impact.

To his side, Mom lifted her own iron short-staff over her head as she bellowed, "Get behind me!" to TJ.

His chest, pulled by Mom's magical wind-grip, tugged him bodily behind her. As TJ was pulled, he snatched a horror-stricken Tunde roughly around the collar. Dragging his brother with him, TJ dove for an overturned table where Dad lay. Blood leaked down from his lip, into his goatee and onto his chin. He did his best to hold his expression firm and still, but his raised eyebrows—which disappeared into his headcap—betrayed the truth of his fear as blast after blast thumped against each of the defending diviners' wind shields.

The scale of the magic around was on a whole other level than what Tunde did to that reporter a week before. TJ's pounding heart knew no end among the chaos. Yet TJ braved a look over the table.

What are the Keepers doing here?

They'd always been in Nigeria, in news articles, some distant entity. Someone else's problem. Did they really chase Dayo's body all the way back to the States? And for what?

Mom and Elder Adeyemi stood shoulder to shoulder, blocking every rush of fire and lightning strike they could. But there were too many Keepers, and they had the advantage of surprise.

Where were they coming from, TJ thought. They couldn't have all snuck in.

None of the other diviners had time to regroup in a proper defense. They were spread out too wide and too thin. If they could just band together, maybe they'd have a fighting chance.

A thundering bass pounded in TJ's ears, and a familiar tingle came to his fingers. Again, his mind flashed back to last week's basketball game. But that was a different thing entirely. There, in a pick-up game, the worst that could happen was TJ taking a hard foul. Here, in the middle of a diviner duel, the cost was his life.

TJ glanced behind him. His sister's casket was still okay, untouched by the carnage all around, with the lake serving as a natural defense behind them.

TJ steeled some courage in the pit of his stomach as he tracked Mom's every movement. He'd never seen her fight before. The most impressive thing he'd ever witnessed her do before that day was water plants or fill their glasses at dinner. Now he understood why the elders always said she was the greatest water sorceress of her time, a true daughter of Yemoja.

The lake vibrated to the will of her iron staff, where she flung out ten-foot waves of water from it with deceptive ease as she warded the attackers off. It took a pair of Keepers teaming up with joint spells of fire plumes to halt her assault. It took a third to push her back. Even twenty yards away, the furious breath of heat licked at TJ's skin.

As Mom backstepped, Elder Adeyemi pushed forward, her staffwork even more impressive as she deflected the streaks of fire. But she didn't just fling the fire back the same way they came, instead splitting the flames and throwing them back like red-orange birds that countered against the attackers three and four at a time.

Despite both of their awesome skills, they could not defend the tent alone, as a streak of flame passed between them and straight toward TJ and his family.

Clenching his body tightly, TJ didn't have time to throw his hands in front of his face or twist out of the way as he watched the ball of flame rage forward. But at the last moment, it seemed to curve, careening harmlessly into a rock near the lake's edge. From behind Dayo's casket, Mr. Bolawe vaulted into the air with his own staff in hand, twirling it around like a baton.

"Diviners, on me!" he bellowed. "Form up around Adeyemi; make a barrier!"

The fighting diviners followed his commands. They hopped over chairs and tables and clustered closer together as the Keepers surrounded the tent in a semicircle.

Though Mr. Bolawe took a leading role, he was not the best diviner present. His water spouts were no bigger than a kiddy fountain, and the few lightning bolts he cast were as thin as linguini.

Mom doled out more protective wind charms, her staff's crystal lighting up and swallowing every attack in her reach, while Bolawe's waned like a dying light—it seemed the more powerful the magic, the more powerful the light.

Elder Adeyemi was working the impossible, manipulating blades of grass into sharp spears and daggers as she dodged and rolled with agility belonging to a college athlete, not an elderly woman.

The others were holding their own too, yet Mr. Bolawe was just a step slower, his reflexes just a touch less astute.

The man reminded TJ of himself.

Bolawe was like an orchestrator, always in the right place at the right time to support one diviner or another, ordering a pair to fill a gap or another trio to push forward. But the Keepers flanked wide at the sides. Bolawe couldn't lead all by himself.

Biting back his fear, TJ clutched at the edge of his table. He couldn't just stand there letting everyone else fight. He didn't know any spells or hexes, but maybe with Mr. Bolawe leading the charge, he could do *something…* anything.

Even if it was small, just like Bolawe's tiny spells.

But each thump that came against magical walls locked TJ's feet in place. For a moment, he toiled between fight and freeze. He fought against the voice telling him to stay put and the other one who told him not to be a wimp.

The second voice won out, beating heart and mounting fear be damned.

Turning, TJ looked for Dayo's staff. He spotted it on the ground. It had fallen over next to the peaches off the side of the casket. The crystal at its head glowed crimson instead of emerald. TJ reached out desperately for the staff, clamoring toward it. When he touched the shaft, the crystal's hue cooled to orange, then settled back into a dirty emerald, almost brown-looking.

"What are you doing?" his brother asked, ducking behind a folded chair.

"Fighting instead of hiding," TJ answered as he gripped the staff, rolled from under the table, and swung the mahogany wood around to the action.

Mr. Bolawe glanced over his shoulder toward TJ and the staff, then turned to the others to shout, "Forward! Hit them where it hurts!"

TJ's drive to help was for nothing, it seemed. Under Mr. Bolawe's command, the tides turned in the funeral guests' favor.

It didn't make sense, though. A moment ago, the Keepers were surrounding them, and now, for some reason, they backed off. One after the other, the Keepers covered each other's retreat as they too backpedaled toward the cemetery entrance, disappearing into holes in the ground, little whirlpools of dirt like the guest who escaped into the lake.

A glint of light against one of the Keeper's beads caught TJ's eyes, a blur of red, pink, and burgundy. Where had he seen that before? His gaze followed the Keeper, whose limp kept them farther back from the others, as they finally made it to the earth portal in the ground, disappearing into its muddy depths.

☨

IN THE END, THERE WERE NO BODIES OR INJURIES AS TJ would've expected, funeral guests and Keepers alike. The only impressions of a fight came by way of the overturned chairs and a corner of the tent kindling with embers.

"They already took my daughter from me. What more do those **òlòsí** want?" Mom roared, rifling into a tirade. Her red face looked wild—TJ had never seen her so angry before. When she finally ran out of curses to say in Yoruba, she started swearing in English. Dad had to lock her in a hug to stop her from lashing out.

So that's what a "cardiac arrest" meant. It wasn't code for a natural death.

It was code for murder.

TJ's stomach threatened to come up, and he couldn't blame Mom one bit. He wanted to blow up too, felt his breathing growing harsh in his chest. Whoever these Keepers were had defiled Dayo's funeral, and for what?

A wooden creak came at his side, and TJ saw that his hand was white-knuckled around his sister's staff. Then his gaze traveled along the disturbed earth in between the tombstones. He hoped one of the Keepers got hit in the leg or got left behind, too weak to conjure an earth portal. One of them would pay for what they did, one of them would explain why they did it at all.

But there was no one there. So, slowly, he released his grip, ignoring the pain.

"I don't understand. Their attack made no sense," Elder Adeyemi gritted as she slammed the bottom of her staff before her. It stood upright of its own accord. "The Keepers are brutal, but they don't provoke without reason."

"There were a lot of important people here today," Mr. Bolawe suggested, leaning on the edge of the tent's posts to catch his breath. "You least of all, Simi."

TJ couldn't help agreeing with Elder Adeyemi as adrenaline leaked from his fingertips, his sister's staff still creaking in his hand. He knew very little about the Keepers, but one thing he picked up from his little research over the week about Keeper attacks was that—

"They never leave survivors." Elder Adeyemi paced with a finger to her brow.

"They've never attacked while *you* were present, Elder," Mr. Bolawe reminded her. "And perhaps they changed their policy."

Adeyemi didn't have a response to that, still jabbing at her forehead. "Something doesn't feel right about it all. At the very least, they make a big show about why they're attacking. They always have their demands."

"TJ! What are you doing with that?" Mom's voice rang in his ear.

TJ gulped, looking down at his sister's staff. "I-I was just—"

"I told you to stay behind me!" She raced over to TJ with heated eyes.

"I know, but—"

Mr. Bolawe took a step between TJ and his mother. "It's okay, Mrs. Young. The kid just wanted to help. No one got hurt, thankfully."

Mom took a deep breath, her jaw grinding. Her face went through a bizarre metamorphosis, changing from a fierce expression of slanted eyebrows and pursed lips to wide eyes of sadness, then to tears as she turned to Dayo's casket. Fortunately, the casket and display had stayed intact, except for a few of Dayo's personal effects —like her staff—which had fallen over before TJ grabbed it. At least those damned Keepers didn't do anything to her body.

Mom slumped over to the coffin and dropped her head into Dayo's chest. "Senseless oloshi… they already won," she cried. "Why can't they just leave us be?"

TJ's throat went dry. For a moment, he thought he'd get a beating, but now he only felt shame for putting himself in danger. Mom had already lost one child; she didn't need to lose another. And everything was coming to light now, everything about his sister and the Keepers and what she was doing.

Dayo would've never stood down from them. She was too stubborn and too brave to.

He remembered what the reporter had said to Tunde. "*Is it true Ifedayo Young was fighting against the—*"

TJ didn't hear the rest, but now he knew what that statement was supposed to be: "*Is it true Ifedayo Young was fighting against the Keepers?*"

Why hadn't he known about any of this stuff? He couldn't bring himself to ask these things out loud, of course, not then. Not when Mom was like this. It was bad enough that her daughter—his own sister—was gone. It was all the worse that the Keepers came to ruin everything. As Elder Adeyemi had said, they accomplished nothing but pissing off a family.

Looking at Mr. Bolawe, who murmured to Elder Adeyemi, TJ couldn't help thinking they knew something he didn't. He'd never forget how they looked at him after coming back from his faint. TJ couldn't deny what he sensed afterward, how he felt at that moment.

Deep down, something within him had changed.

7

MANIFESTATION

THE UNITED COUNCIL OF MAGICAL PEOPLES HAD A TOUGH TIME covering up the attack at Dayo's funeral.

Luckily, many of the guests who attended the funeral were already familiar with the diviner community, and the attack was within the confines of the gated cemetery—which had enchanted protections.

Mom said there were only a handful of civilians driving by who noticed large flashes above the walls, but the UCMP was able to write it off as a fireworks show gone wrong.

When one of the local neighborhood watch women complained that fireworks should've never been set off within the cemetery and that she'd make an official complaint to the City of Inglewood, the council members assured everything would be taken care of. Mom told TJ later they had people in the city council who'd make sure the woman never got a proper response to her complaints.

Later that same day, TJ and Tunde watched the *Divination Today* story on the news site's live stream—which diviners and their households could only access. It seemed there was a mixed bag of reactions from the councilors on what happened and what they would do.

One of the American councilors, a woman from New Orleans with wild hair, skull-like face paint, and a boa around her neck, said the attack had been the first major one on American soil in over a decade and that their protocols were now a touch outdated.

Another, a man TJ thought could be related to the *real* Thor with his braided beard and blonde hair, said his nation would do all they could to help suppress the Keeper threat from returning.

And a Hindi councilor woman with more piercings than TJ could count said her government would watch their seas closely for any unauthorized transport and intervene if there was.

Over the next week, as the dust settled around the Keeper attack and Dayo's funeral, TJ was disappointed to find that he was just the same as before. The tingle he felt during the funeral never returned, and he remained positively magic*less*. Ordinary. Vanilla.

Several times during the week, he visited the family's ancestral altar to use Dayo's staff—which now hung alongside the other family staffs. Yet each time he gripped the wooden shaft, the only sensation that brushed against his palm was smooth mahogany, not the power of Ashe. Each night he went back and tried a new grip, or spoke a different prayer, only to find the same result.

Absolutely… *nothing.*

Since the funeral, the staff's crystal never glowed again, red or green. For hours at a time, he had stared at the face carved into the staff. He thought perhaps ogling at it long enough might unlock some sort of latent magic.

It didn't.

All it did was give him an eyesore.

It took another week for TJ to give up the notion that he was changed or special. Logic would have it that everything he felt was in his head, and he merely *wanted* to feel different.

Despite his less than encouraging results with magic, he still investigated the Keepers as much as he could. At first, he was glued to the *Divination Today* streams, but all their coverage of the Keepers was everything he already knew about them: they were a radical group in Southwest Nigeria who were in pursuit of bringing back the full power of the long-lost Orishas, no matter how many lives it would cost to do so.

When he got tired of hearing the same thing over and over, he went to Mom to ask her about them—and Dayo's relation to them. But each time he asked her a question, she responded with an "*it's very complicated,*" or, "*you wouldn't understand. I'll tell you when you're older.*"

So then he texted Adeola to see what she would tell him.

TJ: r u ok?
TJ: were u at the service??

Three dots popped up and bounced on his screen.

Adeola: I'm fine. I didn't stay but heard about what happened on DT.
Are you guys alright?
TJ: they killed Dayo.
TJ: the keepers killed her.
TJ: dyk about that??

Another three dots did their dance on screen.

Adeola: How's your mother doing?
TJ: did u see wat i just sent?

This time a long stream of three dots popped up, then went away for a while, popped up again, went away for a while, then showed up again.

Adeola: It's okay, I'll call her.

So, TJ shifted to Google, which quickly turned out to have nothing about any magical community—diviner or otherwise. The best he could find were articles and videos detailing the "mythology" of the Orishas, as though they weren't real, but there was nothing about a group of radical magic people in West Africa.

When he did a specific search for the story about the attack at Inglewood Cemetery, his results showed up with petty crime nearby, but nothing about an attack, not even the cover story of fireworks.

"You'll never find anything like that," his brother told him one morning.

TJ jumped with a start. His little brother always had a way of sneaking up on him—especially when he didn't want him to. TJ thought of closing his laptop, but it was too late. Tunde already knew what he was up to.

"And you know a better way?" TJ asked with a furrowed brow.

Tunde shrugged sheepishly. "The UCMP *stay* keepin' their stuff hidden online. Sometimes you'll find something that pops up for a few minutes, maybe an hour at most, but it'll be gone right after."

Though the boy was only ten, he was smarter than half the tech-heads working in Silicon Valley. During his very short childhood, he had already generated thousands of followers on social media, where he produced and taught others how to code in total anonymity. Not even their parents knew he went by the moniker "Nolaj" online. The only reason TJ knew was because Tunde wanted to gloat last summer.

"Let me guess..." TJ started. "You're not going to tell me how to look up what I need without something in return?"

"Yep," he said quickly. "Unless you tell me what you're looking for."

TJ considered it for a moment, but he wasn't sure what he'd find or where that information would lead him. Plus, he didn't want to put his brother in danger. And even beyond that, Tunde was terrible at keeping other people's secrets—especially TJ's.

"That's cold. Can't you just be a good brother for once?" TJ decided to ask.

Tunde ignored him. "What do you have to offer up?"

TJ bit down on his cheek. It was difficult to barter anything of value with Tunde. He had almost anything and everything he wanted. And whatever it was he didn't have, he always figured out a way to get it.

"What about... chores?" TJ asked hesitantly.

It was the only thing he could possibly offer his brother.

Tunde rubbed his hands together, his eyes looking to the ceiling in exaggerated thought. It was clear he knew this was where the conversation would lead. Dad was a stickler for a clean house—a carryover from his brief time in the military—and the mid-month deep clean was approaching rapidly.

"*We're training you to be good husbands when you grow up,*" Dad had always said.

The clean-up wasn't just making beds and putting towels away. It included clearing the cobwebs under the house, dusting every single surface in the kitchen, even mending the fences. And it didn't help that each month a new item in the house seemed to break down.

Worst of all, with Mom teaching weekends and nights, and their father always away at some sports camp, much of the work was dumped on the boys. TJ thought back on the jammed backdoor he'd likely have to fix himself. That alone would probably take a whole day to fix.

"I'd be open to you taking over mopping duties," Tunde finally decided. TJ relaxed a little. That was fair and easy enough. But Tunde wasn't finished. "And the dining room chandelier."

TJ sucked his teeth. "Nah! That's not fair. I did it last month."

The chandelier wasn't difficult to clean, strictly speaking, but it was certainly the most tedious. Their parents always told the boys to take the chandelier down and take it apart piece by piece to dust and clean each little hanging crystal. The entire task took, at best, three hours from disassembly, cleaning, and reassembly.

Tunde smiled. "That's the offer, bro. Take it or leave it."

Most times, TJ would have flat out denied his brother's request, spit out some foul language, and slammed the bedroom door in his face, yet the blinking cursor on his screen and the bold "0 results" flashing atop the search engine halted all his natural brotherly reactions.

So instead, he just grunted. "Ugh. Fine, I'll do the stupid chandelier."

"Bet." Tunde leered. "I figured you would."

TJ suppressed the irritation surfacing up his chest. "What are you doing here, anyway?"

"Oh, right." Tunde snapped his fingers. "Mom wants you downstairs."

"Dude, you took all that time to tell me?" TJ slammed his laptop shut, rushed past his brother—making sure to shove him in the shoulder—and hustled downstairs to where Mom tended to the ancestral altar in the living room with a bottle of polish in her hand.

Mom whipped her head up as TJ slid into a stop, his heel digging into the shag carpet for resistance. She chuckled. "What took you so long, honey?"

"Sorry, it was…" TJ was going to say it was Tunde's fault but thought better of it. He still needed information out of him; no need to ruffle feathers. "I… had to use the bathroom first."

"Well, you're here now." She pointed to the altar. "I just got done cleaning the table. Could you help me get all these things put back where they should go?"

"Why didn't you get Tunde to do it?" TJ whined.

"Because I asked *you*, Tomori Jomiloju." Mom didn't even need to look at TJ; her fierce voice was enough. TJ knew all too well that talk back was out of the equation on this one.

Holding back a sigh, he dipped to his knees and grabbed the first few items—pictures of TJ's great grandmother along with incense sticks. As he set the pictures where they belonged at the edge of the table, Mom spoke again.

"I know you've had a lot of questions over the past week or so." She stared at the frame in her hand: a picture of Dayo, one TJ knew well because of the fake smile she gave the camera. Mom had forced a photo out of her before her first day at Ifa Academy. "You know I love you, right, son?"

TJ nodded and gulped. Was Mom really about to tell him what he wanted to know? He wouldn't even need to do Tunde's chores if she did.

"I've been too short with you, and that's not fair. I haven't explained myself correctly." She finally set Dayo's picture next to the others. "The reason I haven't told you about your sister and everything else going on in Nigeria is that... I didn't want to worry you. You understand?"

TJ nodded again as he moved to the unscented candles next. He did his best to keep his expression flat as he set down two green crystals and a clear one on the table.

"I don't think it matters much now," she sighed. "If your Ashe was going to show itself, it would have happened already." She snapped her fingers thrice above each candle. After a short moment, each of them birthed tiny flames that appeared to dance. Again, TJ saw a wisp of a fog before each flame came to life. "When Ifedayo first attended Ifa, like all other students, the oracles put her through a test..."

Mom stopped herself for a moment, a finger at her lips.

"The promised child," TJ finished for her.

"Yes," she said. Her eyes looked distant, and the flames from the candles reflected majestically in her eyes. "That's when all that 'promised child' business started up."

"What does that mean?" TJ encased the lit candles in glass, lifting the cylinder from the floor and placing it on the center of the table.

"It's complicated..." she swallowed hard. Her eyebrows knitted together, a tension building in her forehead.

"It's okay, Mom. Take your time."

She sighed and stood before a wide and empty jug. Like she always did, she initiated her favorite water ritual, beginning with the first line: "Á kì í bọ́ ṣínú òmì tán ká mã ṣá fún òtútú."

Unlike the cup at the funeral, this jug took longer to fill. Fresh water materialized from the bottom of the jug and rose high at a snail's pace. Again, to TJ that odd fog blossomed before the water appeared in reality.

Mom turned to speak. "You see, your sister—" The kitchen telephone rang. "Give me a second, honey."

She shuffled to the kitchen, leaving TJ by himself with the altar. It only took a few minutes for him to finish organizing it as his mind raced. He couldn't imagine what had happened with his sister and those oracles, but he knew enough about legends to know she must have been special, powerful. That'd explain why she was so good at everything. Perhaps some Orisha had bestowed special magic for her to use. Whatever she had, it must've scared the Keepers enough to have her killed.

TJ stared at the water half filled in the jug. Before she was pulled away, Mom had only completed half the spell—which had ended the moment she went to answer the phone. TJ tried to recall the rest of the words. Mom used the phrase almost every day. He just wasn't sure if he'd get the annunciations right.

TJ took a moment to recite what he thought was correct in his head before he finally said out loud, in Yoruba, "*Ọ̀ṣun, mo gbàdúrà ṣi ọ. Mu óunjẹ fun mi. Ṣé óngbẹ mi.*"

As he spoke, a familiar tingle came to his fingertips. Slowly, the water rippled, then bubbled like a pot set to fire. A faint glow fluttered atop each bubble as they burst open, the same prism-fog TJ saw when he played basketball, the same radiance he saw just before a teammate scored.

A moment later and his gut went empty. To his utter surprise, the water within the jug rose again, not as quickly as it did with Mom, but sure enough, it lifted past the jug's midpoint and crawled to the brim.

A clinking sound echoed through the hallway, followed by the panting breaths of Simba. In an instant, the dog was at TJ's heels, jumping onto his knees and barking playfully. TJ had never seen the old dog vault so high before.

"I'm on the phone!" Mom hollered. "Can you get him to stop yapping, please?"

"Quiet, Simba, quiet." TJ tried to hold him down, but the dog was beside himself, turning around in circles and jumping without pause.

"Tomori, what did I tell you?"

"I'm tryin'. He won't stop."

Mom asked whoever she was on the phone with if they could excuse her, then she set the phone on the kitchen counter and stomped over to TJ.

"Simba." She snapped her fingers. "Relax."

Simba, who also knew the rage of Mom too well, stopped barking, though his tail wagged uncontrollably and his tongue hung from the side of his mouth.

Mom looked to the self-filling water, which had now nearly spilled over the top.

"*Itẹlọrun*," she uttered, and the water stopped rising, and with it, the glow. Was TJ the only one who could see it? "I would have sworn I didn't finish that spell..." She glanced at TJ, who stood still, his mouth agape. "Tomori Jomiloju, you didn't..."

TJ found all his words were caught at the back of his throat as his gaze flitted between Mom, Simba, and the jug. And again, just like before in his sister's room a few weeks back, something cool brushed against his neck. Goosebumps stuck out against TJ's arms.

Mom grabbed TJ's shoulders and stared at him straight on. "Tomori, tell me. Did you finish that spell?"

Slowly, very slowly, TJ nodded. He still didn't believe he did it himself. But now, with Mom saying the words out loud, he let himself believe it was actually him who did it, and not just a carryover from what Mom had done.

Mom clapped her hands to her mouth, and her eyes misted over. Turning on her heel, she shouted down the hallway. "Jalen, get me my water bowl from the closet!" She twisted again to TJ. Her expression had never appeared more proud before. "We need to call Priest Glover!"

8

A WILL AND A WAY

It took the better part of the afternoon, but Mom finally convinced Priest Glover to visit their home the next day. Despite that, Dad was less keen about TJ potentially going off to Ifa Academy as Dayo did.

"Seriously? The school responsible for our daughter's death? Now you want to send our boy?" he asked Mom as they all sat in the living room awaiting Priest Glover. Although TJ sat between them on their lumpy sofa, they spoke about him like he wasn't there.

"The Academy isn't responsible. She had already graduated before all that," Mom justified as she got up and adjusted one of Dayo's trophies hanging over the fireplace—which they never used. "And there's no safer place in Nigeria than Ifa Academy and New Ile-Ife."

Dad crossed his enormous arms, his frown making his goatee look like it was collapsing.

"The Orishas have chosen him for a reason..." Mom added.

"Didn't you say he only finished half a ritual—or spell—or whatnot?"

The lines on Mom's forehead scrunched together. She must've been thinking the same thing TJ had been in that moment. Ever since the ritual with the jug, TJ hadn't managed to manifest any other forms of magic. He was still crap with cowrie divinations, and all the rudimentary blood magic rituals his mother taught him manifested a whole lot of nothing. In the back of his mind, he had wondered if the magic had only worked because of some residual

Ashe left over from Mom. But he kept reminding himself that it was *him* who completed it.

He felt it; he *saw* it.

"That school was expensive enough when Dayo went," Dad continued in a grunt. "Magic schools ain't in the budget these days, you know."

"Oh, Jalen, I can take on extra hours at the school. We'd find a way."

Dad grumbled to himself and rubbed the back of his head vigorously—he did that when he had more to say but didn't feel like arguing. Instead of a rebuttal, he got up as well and paced the room in rhythm with his head rubs. A moment of gratification at seeing Dad sweat made TJ feel guilty, until he remembered his father's attitude yesterday.

A moment he was still trying to understand.

After Priest Glover had agreed to see TJ, Mom was about to tell TJ more about Dayo when his Dad came home. Overhearing them, Dad stepped in right away, shutting it down and saying that "the boy's too young to know about all that."

TJ didn't get it. In fact, he *hated* it. If his non-magical father could know, why couldn't he? What was the big deal? Frustration curled through his chest, but instead of pressing the issue, TJ turned his mind to the coming meeting. He had enough to worry about, especially when his examination would be under the observation of Priest Glover once again.

TJ knew his test would be under massive scrutiny. Had this been his first test, that might not have been the case. But this would be his third.

His first was well before he could remember, which occurred seven days after his birth. Obviously, he had failed that one, but he had no recollection, so it didn't wound his pride or anything like that.

When TJ was a toddler, the priests did a simple examination to determine which Orisha aligned with him the most. All the tests came back with a big zero. No mystical guardian for him, which apparently was an implausibility in and of itself. Even non-magical people had some association with Orishas like Shango or Yemoja.

As far as Priest Glover could tell, TJ was nothing more than an ordinary boy. Completely *un*magical. But that wasn't cause for concern, at least not then. Many young diviners didn't manifest their powers until later in childhood. So each week, Mom and Dayo did their best to teach TJ what they knew. And he disappointed them time and time again, year after year.

His second, third, and fourth birthdays—the ones when diviners were most likely to manifest—came and went without event. When it was time for TJ to attend kindergarten for the first time, the same year Dayo went off to Ifa Academy, Mom thought he'd predicted his acceptance to the Hughes Academy of Gifted Youths when TJ accidentally knocked over her set of cowries in the alignment of "educational success in the West." So she made him take a mail-in test for the less prestigious American school, but the following week they got the call that TJ's EAD—Early Ashe Detection—was too low.

Well, that was a lie.

They were actually nonexistent.

Though Mom did her best to nurture TJ's development, it wasn't a surprise six years later, the year before TJ could start at any of the diviner schools—including Ifa Academy—when he was officially rejected. The decision devastated Mom, though she never showed it in front of him. But he could always tell by the way she said "Ifa" in his presence, like it was a secret he wasn't allowed to hear.

TJ always figured it was her way of protecting his feelings.

But ever since he completed that water spell, his mother said "Ifa" with the same warm energy she did before his eleventh birthday.

Though his demonstration of magic was less than impressive, it was also the *only* demonstration to prove he might have some Ashe in him after all. Still, his little trick with the water didn't entertain confidence within his gut, which at the moment had felt empty despite Dad feeding him a "breakfast of champions" that included a mountain of potatoes, a filet of salmon, a whole avocado, and a super green mystery shake to wash it all down.

"*Well, if ya gonna take the tests, you better do 'em right,*" Dad had said as TJ did his best to keep down what he figured was a ginger afterkick from the shake.

TJ gazed up and around the living room filled with the awards and certificates Dayo couldn't fit in her own room. The living room was a bit drab, filled with faded grays and browns, but the glistening trophies brightened it with shimmers of silver and gold—Dayo hardly ever earned bronze. TJ always figured Mom put them up to inspire him and Tunde, but they only ever served to intimidate him. How could he ever match someone like her?

A knock at the front door made TJ jump. Dad didn't move at all.

Mom sprung up and nearly skipped to the front door to greet Priest Glover and, to TJ's surprise, a second visitor.

"Oh, Elder Adeyemi!" Mom exclaimed. "I'm sorry, we weren't expecting you."

TJ could only see Mom's back dipping low in a formal Yoruba curtsy. TJ tried to hide his shock as he stole a glance at his father. Dad's squared jaw and sharp brow didn't change at all. TJ couldn't blame him. He didn't understand who Simisola Adeyemi was. And up to a little while ago, TJ hadn't known she was one of the most celebrated diviners in the world. She came up a bunch of times in his searches for Dayo and the Keepers after his brother helped him out, though.

What is she doing here? TJ thought as his heart decided to start a drumline in his chest.

It was bad enough that Priest Glover was there to deny him for probably the third time… but in the Headmistress' presence on top of it all? It seemed excessive.

"Please, come inside. You must be hot." Mom waved a hand into her home, revealing Priest Glover's chunky, broad face and Elder Adeyemi's long, slender one.

Like before, Adeyemi wore an outfit of deep blue sprinkled with dots of white. It looked almost like a galaxy shifted within her clothes. With her usual glide, she slid into the house and brightened the living room, the gilded trophies and awards seeming to reach out to her with small bright eyes.

She bowed her head slightly, directing her words to Dad. "Good afternoon, Mr. Young." She turned a smile to TJ. "And to you, Mr. Young."

Priest Glover stomped in after her. He cleared his nose loudly and grunted as a form of salutation. Dad snorted his own greeting, and TJ let out a meek "hello" as Mom served their guests glasses of *zobo*, a refreshing red Nigerian hibiscus juice, perfect for a hot day.

"Summer's starting with some real heat this year, isn't it?" Mom asked as she directed Glover and Adeyemi to a pair of lumpy sofa chairs that had been in the family, TJ thought, since the civil war.

Elder Adeyemi responded with a comment about similar weather in Lagos, and the adults continued with their small talk for a few moments. Priest Glover seemed less than enthused, his arms crossed around his chest like he was restraining himself in his own invisible straightjacket.

After a few minutes, he cleared his throat gruffly. "Headmistress

Adeyemi has very limited time with us today. Shall we begin with the..." Priest Glover's tone turned nasty, "Erm... prospect?"

"Right." Elder Adeyemi set down the glass of her half-drunk zobo. "I am most intrigued to start today's session."

"Not that there's anything wrong with it, Headmistress..." Mom started, her voice deferential. "But may I ask why you've come with Priest Glover today?"

TJ steadied his gaze on the elder, anticipating her response.

"It's very uncommon for the academy to accept a new student so late," she began. "If TJ is accepted today, there will be a lot to consider. He would have already missed two years of instruction, and, as you may know, the third year at Ifa is an evaluation year. Were he accepted, he'd have to be held back."

"Unless the boy can pass all the preliminary tests." Priest Glover huffed as though he were suppressing a laugh.

TJ remembered Dayo saying something about the third-year tests. She had been so stressed then, staying up late even when she was on winter vacation. It was bad enough that Priest Glover seemed keen to fail TJ before their examination began. Now, it was near impossible to impress them enough to believe that, one, TJ had enough Ashe to attend the school, and two, that he was astute enough to catch up on two years of missed training.

"I'm only here to observe," Adeyemi continued. "When all the preliminaries are complete, both Bàbálàwò Glover and I will decide if TJ is ready under these special circumstances."

"Great," Mom said. "Do we start now?"

Priest Glover sat forward, his backside conducting a chorus of creaks. "Yes. But we will have to ask both parents to leave."

"Is that really necessary?" Mom questioned Elder Adeyemi. "Both times before, they allowed me to stay."

"True." Adeyemi's voice came as gentle as a breeze. "But considering the unique circumstances we've found ourselves in, we think it's best to test the boy alone without any... distractions."

TJ shifted uncomfortably between his parents. When Mom sat forward, TJ didn't like how he could no longer feel her arm pressed against his.

Mom must've been thinking the same thing because she said, "I don't see how my being here for my son would change anything."

"He won't have his mother with him at Ifa, after all," Priest Glover added coldly. "Best he gets used to such a thing if he," Glover waved his hand, clearly finding even the possibility of TJ succeeding being ridiculous enough to even speak aloud, "*if* he does find a place at the academy."

TJ didn't like the way the man's lips curled at their edges or how his wide nostrils flared like a giant pig's.

"I'm sure there's something we could do while we wait." Dad sat and clapped his hands together. He seemed pleased he didn't have to sit through what would likely be a grueling session.

TJ's shoulders slumped with the thought he'd fail again, another pin of disappointment, and in a room full of Dayo's achievements to top it off.

"I can assure you everything will be fine, Mrs. Young." Elder Adeyemi placated Mom with a sensitive and warm expression. TJ couldn't help noticing there always seemed to be a deep sympathy in her words, like she had seen a lot of stuff in life, like she could feel what others did at every moment.

"To be honest, Mrs. Young," Priest Glover said. "We need to be sure your son's expression of Ashe is his own."

Mom leaned back on the sofa, utterly sinking into it. TJ didn't look at her face, but he was sure she was fixing the priest with a brutal stare. "I *know* you're not thinking I'm trying to pull something over on you? On Elder Simisola Adeyemi, of all diviners?"

Priest Glover shook his head. "Of course not, Mrs. Yo —"

"Then what are you insinuating?" Mom's voice was dark.

Elder Adeyemi lifted her hands gracefully. As her arms rose, the stars on her dress shifted like a meteor shower in the night. "We do not mean ill by our request. We merely need to replicate the scenarios Mr. Young will experience in the academy. Scenarios that do not involve a parent present."

Dad, who had already stood up, looked between the room of diviners nervously. He blew large shoots of air through his cheeks, making them look like skin-colored balloons. Rubbing the back of his head again, he turned to Mom. "Let 'em do their tests like they want to, honey."

Mom didn't look at him at all, instead glaring at Priest Glover. Like TJ, she seemed to know it was he who suggested a solo examination. It didn't help that now he looked to be accusing her of some sort of fraudulent behavior.

"Okay, then," she finally said, breaking the mounting tension in the room. "As the *Headmistress* wants it."

She shot up from her seat and marched out of the room. Each step she took upstairs sounded like an earthquake rumbling through the whole of the old house. Dad followed after her sheepishly as he gave the guests brief apologies.

✝

A FEW MOMENTS AFTER THAT, TJ, PRIEST GLOVER, AND ELDER Adeyemi sat in silence. Well, not exact silence. TJ thought it was more like him sitting quietly while the two diviners fixed him with discomforting stares, looking him up and down like some show-dog before a contest as they mumbled to each other in Yoruba he didn't *quite* understand.

"So..." TJ started. "Do I start or do you—"

"I do not sense any Orisha within him," Priest Glover finally said, ignoring him. He never looked at Elder Adeyemi as he spoke but straight at TJ without breaking eye contact.

Adeyemi stroked the bottom of her chin. Though she definitely would have classified as a senior citizen, her skin did not betray her age. The only way TJ knew she was an elder was by the way she moved, the way she spoke with that assured sense of wisdom.

"I wouldn't be so sure of that assessment," she said. "True, there is no direct correlation to pick up on, but there is something hidden just under the veil. Don't you sense it?"

Glover inhaled deeply and exhaled emphatically. "I'll admit. He's reading differently from the other times I've judged him. But it means little."

"This isn't unheard of," Adeyemi added. "After all, we do not finalize Orisha alignment until the end of the third year."

TJ would've thought they had forgotten he was there with how they were talking *at* him, not *with* him.

"Do I get any say in this?" he asked with a little irritation. When he spoke, both of the diviners' trance-like gazes seemed to break.

"Yes, I suppose you do." Elder Adeyemi interlaced her fingers into her lap. "You are familiar with the Orishas, yes?"

TJ wasn't sure what Adeyemi meant by the question. He knew this was a test, though. And with such tests, there was often a double meaning to the words. Was the headmistress asking if TJ knew all the names? Did she mean if he knew all their spirits? Did she mean if TJ communed with them during his daily rituals?

A simple "yes" was the safest answer TJ could think to give. But then he thought back on the funeral and his sister. He *definitely* felt something with her. Was that the answer the headmistress was looking for? Probably not. Dayo wasn't an Orisha, just a diviner.

Elder Adeyemi continued to stare with those deep, brilliant eyes of her. What answer would she want to hear, TJ wondered?

Before TJ could muster a response to their first question, Adeyemi *hmmmed* and nodded. "I don't think we'll determine anything with his alignment. Let's move onto our follow-up evaluations."

"Wait," TJ said. "So this whole sitting thing was a test? I wasn't doing anything. Don't I have to concentrate or something like that? That's how I did it yesterday."

But again, the elders ignored his words and continued to watch him. TJ wondered if this was normal. What was the point of not answering him?

A few moments later, Elder Adeyemi downed the rest of her zobo drink and rested the empty cup on the table. "Please," she gestured to the glass, "fill this cup with water."

This was the moment TJ had been dreading. He couldn't get the damned spell to work without Mom being around. And seeing as they forced her to retreat to her room, there was nothing for him to latch onto.

"Your mother tells us you can summon drinking water," Priest Glover said. "Is this true?"

TJ nodded silently. He knew what was *supposed* to come next, but he couldn't do it. If life were fair—if life were simple—he'd start reciting the spell word for word with no mistakes and fill the cup with water. Adeyemi would drink it and say, "this tastes wonderful," shake his hand and officially invite him to Ifa Academy, where he would go on to train like his sister had, maybe even take on her role as the Hero of Nigeria.

But life was never so easy.

For the next painstaking minutes, TJ sat mumbling the watering spell without as much as producing a droplet.

"You see!" Priest Glover sucked his teeth. "The boy cannot be accepted."

Elder Adeyemi sighed. "Manifesting drinking water is complicated magic. We couldn't expect Mr. Young to replicate what must have been a fluke."

TJ gritted his teeth. It wasn't a fluke. He had done it before. He just didn't know *how*... but he *did*.

"Hold on, give me a second." TJ lifted his hands to halt them from making any hasty decisions. "Sometimes I get this feeling in my fingers. A little tingle."

TJ clapped his hands together and rubbed them, aiming for that familiar sensation. But all he managed to do was heat his hands like it was a cold day. Priest Glover rolled his bored eyes to Adeyemi.

For whatever reason, though, Elder Adeyemi kept testing TJ no matter how many times he failed. First, with his skills in alchemy, where he was directed to brew a simple healing balm for chapped lips. Then on his skill to predict the next day's weather, yet all he could see in the spread of cowries along a divination board was just that: a cluster of sea snail armor atop a wooden circle.

"Why don't I just use my cellphone to predict the weather?" TJ asked the diviners, his frustration getting the better of him.

Priest Glover responded by saying that the "clouded scientists" couldn't predict the weather if their lives depended on it. He said their "educated guesses" were more fickle than their stock market. TJ noticed Glover enjoyed saying "clouded" a lot in a very rude way when referring to non-magical people.

"It's a simple prediction, Mr. Young." Glover spat over TJ's shoulder. His breath smelled like hot garbage. "First-year students in Junior Secondary School can do this in their sleep."

Despite another failure to produce magic, Elder Adeyemi continued her tests. Frustration settled in TJ's tight grip as he punched the cowries when the diviners weren't looking. Why did they keep testing him over and over? It was obvious they were right. TJ was just a fluke, like they said.

"Ok, you've proven your point," TJ said as he followed the diviners to the backyard. "I suck. I can't do any of this magic stuff. Why don't you just call my mom back down and tell her I wasted your time?"

Priest Glover looked half ready to turn on his heel and oblige, yet it was Elder Adeyemi who stood in front of him. Then she knelt down to TJ.

With a gentle smile, she placed a hand on TJ's cheek. "Young man, all day, I have put you through many trials. Why do you think that is?"

"So that Priest Glover can make fun of me with his domino buddies on Friday nights?" TJ sniped.

It surprised him to hear a legit chuckle from the Priest. TJ was about to give him a scowl when Elder Adeyemi cuffed his chin and locked it in place, forcing him to look at her straight on.

"You do that a lot, don't you?" Adeyemi asked.

"What?"

"Cover your insecurities with humor. Ifedayo did it too in her first year."

A shiver careened through TJ's spine at the sound of his sister's name. Maybe it was the way the elder said it. Her Nigeria accent suited Dayo's name perfectly—go figure. But it was more than just the intonation. It was like something inside him had jumpstarted.

"Did you ever talk to her?" TJ asked. "At the school, I mean."

Adeyemi's eyes shifted slightly. For once, they looked human, brown instead of that endless deep. "As well as I did any other student," she said, looking down and back up to TJ. "And more."

Priest Glover tapped his foot impatiently. "Headmistress, I think we should continue."

"I believe in you, Tomori Jomiloju." She disregarded Glover's edginess. "Open your mind and heart to the Orishas. They will guide you in all things, Ashe or no."

Lifting herself to her feet, Elder Adeyemi led them to the small garden where weeds encroached on a set of dying poppies. TJ suppressed an internal groan. Those weeds would be waiting for him soon once Dad's deep cleaning session kicked off.

"You may not know this, Mr. Young," Adeyemi chimed, "but Bàbáláwò Glover here has an affinity for Oko's magic." TJ tried his best to rack his brain for which Orisha that was. The deity had something to do with plants, he thought. "The Bàbáláwò will demonstrate a simple healing ritual to uproot the weeds and cure these flowers. Watch closely."

"I'll only do it once," Glover droned.

The man knelt down on a knee and spoke words TJ was actually familiar with for once. It was another phrase Mom used often when she tended to the garden.

"Watch," Elder Adeyemi whispered in his ear. Her breath, unlike Glover's, was as cool as an ocean breeze. "See how he moves his hands. Listen to how he says his words. *Feel* the Ashe he draws on."

For a moment, TJ saw the fog he had become familiar with. It sprang between Glover's hands and the plants, as the weeds receded back into the earth, almost like they knew their time was up, and the dying flowers rose up to the afternoon sun, their petals sprouting anew, the purple as vibrant as the first day they bloomed.

"Yeah, I can see it," he murmured to Adeyemi.

"You mean you *feel* it," she corrected him.

TJ didn't have the heart to correct her. After all, who knew more... a teenager who had never done magic before, or an elder who had been steeped in it for her whole, very long life?

"Yeah, I meant feel it."

"Now, you do it," Priest Glover ordered, but his deadpan said he expected another failure.

TJ walked to the tiny garden, then knelt once he reached one of the flowers Glover left dead. He recited the words perfectly, confidently. He did as Elder Adeyemi said. He moved his hands like Glover, but most of all, he *felt* as he thought Glover had. And for an instant, as Glover glared over his shoulder, he could sense Ashe pouring off of the old man, the residual magic he had used before. It was almost like the way he felt after Mom left the water ritual unfinished. Only now, TJ was doing it all on his own.

Slowly—very slowly—but surely, the wilted flower started to spread wide to the sun. It did not fan out as broadly as Glover's, the lavender colors of the lily lighter than they should be, but it was something.

It was magic!

TJ smiled, Adeyemi beamed, and Glover, for once, was free of his usual scowl.

9

THE DECISION

WHEN TJ, PRIEST GLOVER, AND ELDER ADEYEMI RETURNED indoors, TJ had his guests wait in the family room. Then he walked into the foyer and called up to his parents that he was done with his tests. Almost before TJ finished his sentence, Mom appeared at the top of the stairs, her eyes wide and hopeful, magnified by her large glasses. Pressing a finger to her lips, she gestured a thumbs up or thumbs down to TJ before pointing at him. TJ smiled awkwardly and returned her voiceless questions with a shrug coupled with a "so-so" shake of his hand. Mom's shoulders fell, but her eyes still bulged, like she was in shock that he hadn't outright failed.

"The hell y'all doin'?" Dad whispered.

TJ and Mom jumped at the same time, TJ gripping the stair railing and Mom flinging her hand to her chest in surprise. But in the next moment, Mom hit Dad around his shoulder playfully as TJ tried not to laugh.

If he were honest, he wasn't exactly sure how his session went. For a majority of it, it seemed like he was doomed to fail. Yet in the end, it seemed like he finally made *some* progress. Is that all the Priest and the Headmistress needed to see? Perhaps all he had to demonstrate was *any* form of magic, no matter how small. After all, that's what schools were for, right? To make him and the other students better.

"Is everything all right in there?" came Elder Adeyemi's voice echoing down the hall.

"Yes. We're coming right now!" Mom called back as she hustled down the stairs. Dad lumbered behind her.

A few moments later, they were all back in the living room where the meeting had started. TJ sat between his parents on the couch once more, their guests sat across from them on the old sofas, and Dayo's awards watched over them all.

For a few silent moments, Priest Glover held a notebook in hand, the staccato beat of his pen scratching atop the paper interrupted only by the flipping of pages. TJ fiddled with his thumbs, and he swore he could feel his mother's rapid heartbeat through the pressure of her arm against his. If the Priest was taking this long, that had to mean a good thing. He remembered Mom telling him that in court cases decided by a jury, a long deliberation usually meant an innocent verdict. Perhaps in this situation, it meant a positive outcome.

After some more rustling of papers and etching of pens, Priest Glover said, "We conducted several tests for Mr. Young today. In our first test, he failed to show any alignment with any Orisha—"

"Something that's not relevant officially until the first year of Senior Secondary School, at best," Mom reminded him.

"And in the following examinations," Glover continued without missing a beat. "The prospect showed little to no signs of Ashe."

"But what about that flower I cured?" TJ interrupted.

He hadn't noticed that his butt was now on the edge of the couch or that his nails were digging into his hands.

"That counts for something, doesn't it?" Mom joined in, but TJ couldn't help noticing a shift in her tone. She must've known that curing flowers wasn't impressive enough to be accepted into the Harvard University of magical schools. But that still left room for another school for gifted children in the States, TJ hoped.

"It counts..." Glover conceded. TJ knew there was a but coming though. "*But,* I cannot, in good confidence, say Mr. Young would succeed at Ifa Academy."

That wasn't a no.

TJ's breath quickened as he glanced at Elder Adeyemi, who sat still as a placid lake. Was she really about to accept him? Is that why the Priest looked so disgruntled? Because he disagreed with her decision?

"He is not ready," Glover continued. "However..."

TJ's heartbeat hammered in his throat. He couldn't believe it. He was going to finally go off and learn all the things his sister did. With enough time, maybe even his cousins would let him play their games with him. And then he'd finally have a leg up on Tunde, for once.

"He's going to Ifa Academy!" Mom couldn't contain herself. She clapped her hands together and pressed them into her nose like a prayer.

Priest Glover's eyes looked like they'd pop out of their sockets, and TJ never thought he'd see a man's eyebrows raise so high. "Heavens, no!"

TJ and Mom sat back at the same time, wearing twin frowns. Were it not for the couch's support, they'd've sunk straight to the floor. TJ felt terrible, like something rancid could come up his throat.

"W-what do you mean?" Mom asked.

"If the man says he ain't ready, he ain't ready," Dad said, then leaned in close to TJ. "You did your best, son. Can't ask for more than that." He looked almost relieved. Mom gave him a look that clearly read he needed to shut *all the way* up.

TJ dropped his head and pretended he was very interested in the chipped wood paneling under his feet. He couldn't bear to see Mom's face. He'd seen her disappointed too many times before. And he had *really* thought for a moment he'd been able to go, even if they put him into some extra classes or something like that.

"Mr. Young will not be accepted to Ifa Academy," Elder Adeyemi reiterated. Her cool voice had a finality to it like ice. "But if he accepts..." TJ peeked up slowly. "We will admit him to attend Camp Olosa."

TJ's head flew up in surprise. Sure, camp was no Ifa, but at least TJ could get some sort of training with his Ashe.

"You people got camps for this now?" Dad asked, half impressed. TJ tried to ignore that he said, "you people."

"Not many," Priest Glover said. "Only the one, Camp Olosa, in the States, for those who practice under the Orishas, and of course for the others, like the natives down south in Mexico, the Shaman Enclaves in some of the American reservations, even the Norse got a camp in British Columbia."

"It's a developmental camp," Elder Adeyemi explained. "Many of the campers there are like Mr. Young. Late bloomers. Or those who need additional training between schooling years."

Mom didn't move from her slumped position. "So he can still get into Ifa Academy?"

"Or into any of the others." Adeyemi lifted an elegant finger as Mom shot up again. "I don't want to get your hopes up. Most campers there attend just to hone the little they have. Not many go on to the proper schools. But that doesn't necessarily matter. Quite a few go on to have wonderful careers just by attending the camp. Enchanting farmers. Magical service workers. Sanitation and the like."

It sounded like Adeyemi was trying to sell them a used car. To TJ, it sounded like the second chance he was looking for. Now that he thought on it, he would've sworn Dayo went to the camp a few times.

"It lacks a certain prestige," Priest Glover said. "It's a remedial institution, to put it more bluntly than the Headmistress has."

"Remedial?" Mom stirred in her seat once more. "Ifedayo went there three summers straight."

"You said it was just a regular summer camp!" Dad said incredulously.

"It was... expensive," Mom murmured to him. "I'll explain later."

Priest Glover cleared his throat. "That's right. Miss Young went when she was *supposed* to. For Mr. Young here, while he *should* already be entering his third year at the diviner schools, his position in the camp will be on a probationary status. But judging by your expression, you don't seem to find this acceptable. Believe you me, I think the boy shouldn't be accepted at all, even to the camp. It'd be no issue. We could—"

"No, no, he'll go." Mom sat up straight. "When does it start again?"

"A week from today, actually," Elder Adeyemi answered. "Marvelous timing."

Super dope *timing, more like it*, TJ thought as the fluttering in his stomach ramped up.

Camp Olosa was sounding like summer school, but for a subject he *actually* cared about. He'd always asked his parents if he could go to a sleep-away camp, but they never could afford it. Plus, it was the first time someone accepted him to anything magical. Even his own cousins didn't allow their "clouded" relative to play their mystical games with them. Maybe he wouldn't get to Ifa Academy, but he could at least learn a few more things while having some fun for a couple of months.

"Is it far?" TJ asked, excited at the idea he might get to travel.

Elder Adeyemi blinked and smiled at TJ's rising enthusiasm. "It's in New Orleans."

10

NOT ANY OTHER BIRD

ON THE MORNING THAT TJ WAS TO BOARD THE PLANE TO CAMP Olosa, he felt like the only one who cared about being on time. TJ had come to realize that "colored-people time"—the stereotype of Black Americans and Nigerians being late to everything—was astronomically true for his parents.

Mom and Dad met each other in their sophomore year at UCLA. They both shared a general education class for Biology, where more times than not, they showed up late. They both said it was because of a lack of interest in the subject, but TJ knew different... especially that day.

Unlike his parents, he had read all about the TSA and how long it took on average for someone to get through the airport checkpoints. The recommended time was two hours before any domestic flight, which meant TJ and his family should have been out of the house thirty minutes prior.

TJ didn't understand why it took so long for them to get everything and everyone together and out of the house. It wasn't like they were all going on vacation together. TJ was the only one who needed to pack, which he got done an hour after Elder Adeyemi and Glover had left their house.

Mom rushed up and down the stairs to make sure they forgot nothing, a wet toothbrush lodged between her high-top dreadlocks. Meanwhile, Dad fixed up another large breakfast. TJ wasn't allowed to leave the table until he finished the bright red beet smoothie in front of him. And Tunde did his best to keep out of the way of the bustling morning maelstrom.

While Mom made her fourth lap up the stairs, TJ's eyes flipped between his disgusting smoothie and his phone on the table. As promised, he cleaned the chandelier for Tunde, and in return, his brother showed him how to access "Evo"—short for Evocation—a special browser for news and information about the magical community you wouldn't find on the major networks like *Divination Today* or the *Eshu Messenger Press*.

TJ almost felt like he was on the dark web.

For the past week, he had done as much research as he could, further rushed once he found out one of the primary rules at Camp Olosa was that campers could not bring any personal cellphones.

For his first day of research, TJ tried to find anything relating to a "promised child," but even *with* Evo, nothing popped up.

Then he looked up topics about the Keepers, and the results returned in the thousands. Unfortunately, most of it he already knew. They were a radical group who intended to bring back the Orishas to live among mortals. What he did learn, however, was that their methods were complicated... and never ended well for anyone. They often revealed themselves to the non-magical community, either by putting them at risk or worse. As a whole, atrocities aside, revealing yourself as magical had been a huge no-no for many, many years, making the Keepers enemy number one among magical Nigerian authorities—and even international ones.

However, when he tried to learn more, it turned out most of the articles TJ found were more speculation than fact where the Keepers were concerned. They were something like a secret society—even within the secret society of divinerkind. No one even knew if their leader, named Olugbala, was a man or woman, young or old, one person or a collective. And every time this Olugbala made demands against divinerkind, he, she, or they wore a mask, just like the other Keepers did.

"What's got you looking sick, honey?" his mother asked just as he scrolled past a particularly nasty photo of a diviner whose face looked like it had been stuck in a beehive. Apparently, they had tried to fight against Olugbala. "Honey, what's that you have in your hand?"

Without looking, TJ fumbled his phone to scroll to a safety tab on his browser that he had prepped in anticipation for situations just like that one. He nearly dropped his phone before he flipped the screen to Mom. If his no-look switch-up was right, his phone should have depicted a page detailing standard shield charms and the theory of their applications against opponents with more powerful Ashe.

Mom's inquisitive eyes turned sharp, however, and TJ's heart dropped into his butt.

"Where did you find that website?" she asked with a frown, snatching the phone from his hand to examine it more closely.

TJ flitted a quick look to Tunde, who crunched down loudly on his cereal like he couldn't hear a thing.

"U-u-um..." TJ stuttered, sweat building on his palms. "I can explain..."

"'Though the și lọna charm may be considered controversial,'" Mom began to read. "It has come in handy for many diviners finding difficulty generating their own Ashe. The technique is simple, and I liken it to the Japanese martial art, jiujitsu, where the practitioner uses their opponent's strength against them.'"

As Mom continued farther into the article, TJ felt the heartbeat thundering in his ears finally subside. She hadn't seen the grotesque picture after all. Still, the ridicule across her brow was unmistakable.

"Who wrote this?" Mom asked as she scrolled her thumb through the phone. "Ah, just as I thought. Olu Olowokandi. I went to Ifa with him, you know. He always looked for shortcuts and fake initiations." She turned the phone to TJ. "Why didn't you ask me to help you? This sort of rubbish is what will get you hurt."

TJ bit at his lip, then rubbed the back of his head like his father always did. TJ had read that part of Camp Olosa's extracurricular activities included dueling, and he didn't want to look like a complete novice.

Mom's steadied gaze was disconcerting, her glasses framing her slitted eyes like an intimidating mask. She waited for his response, holding out his phone with a lazy grip. "Well, why didn't you ask?"

TJ cleared his throat, surprised at its tightness. "I don't know. I didn't want to bother you."

"Bother me? The day before you go off to Olosa?"

TJ picked at his spoon, and his voice came out low. "It's like Priest Glover said... I won't have you around, so I gotta figure it out some way."

Mom set TJ's phone in front of him. "That's fine, I understand." She pointed a sharp finger at the screen. "But don't listen to this man, you hear me? He'll have you burning off your eyebrows instead of whatever it is he's scheming up these days."

"Yes, ma'am." TJ took his phone back and slipped it under the table again.

The conversation with his mom had culminated in his palms becoming very sweaty. His hands were so damp he couldn't keep a grip around his phone. Slipping out of his hand, his phone banged against the ground, drawing the attention of Dad, who had just walked by the kitchen door.

"Boy, stop playin' around with your phone and finish your drink," he said through a mouthful of grapefruit.

A dozen tiny gulps and a few dry heaves later, TJ finished the maroon concoction, and Dad finally dismissed him from the table.

Despite all his research, he still didn't feel confident he'd succeed at Camp Olosa. A lot of the campers were teenagers with a few years head start on him. Though the tingle at his fingers came more frequently, he still couldn't muster his own forms of magic consistently, and his Ashe was strongest with Mom around or in the presence of his sister's staff.

Dayo's staff! TJ thought just as he walked past the altar in the family room.

Obviously, he couldn't have Mom with him during the summer; Priest Glover was right about that. But in a way, he could take his sister with him if he took her staff. That way, he could have a fallback if the camp was too tough. The only issue was that he wasn't allowed a staff until he was fifteen-and-a-half—or in his first year of Senior Secondary School.

Plus, Mom would've had an outright fit.

"How you feelin'?" Dad's voice came from behind, making TJ jump. "Nervous?"

"Me? Nervous?" TJ snorted through his nose. "What do I have to be nervous about?"

TJ did his best to keep the shakiness in his voice steady. Dad preferred it when he was confident, especially before "the big game." He might not have cared about Camp Olosa or Ifa Academy, but he understood the concept of rising to the occasion.

"It's a big step," Dad said. "I remember how twitchy Dayo got when she was going off to that academy. She had the same look you got now."

TJ flattened his expression. "I'm fine, Dad. Worst-case scenario,

I'll blow my hand off or something. Shoot, I might not even be able to do that."

Dad frowned. "I've been watching you this week. You're doing better with this stuff. Just the other day, you did that thing with the plants... What do you call it? Curing?"

TJ nodded but pouted. In his early research, he discovered that that was one of the most simple forms of magic. Not very impressive next to fireballs and fortune-telling.

Dad drew a line around his goatee with thumb and forefinger, then gestured to the trinkets and staffs near the altar. "Does it help you practice when you're at this table?"

TJ nodded again, solemnly. He couldn't deny that it brought him strength.

"Hmmm... they got baseball at this camp of yours?" Dad asked with a grunt.

TJ turned a questioning look on Dad, who smiled and grabbed Dayo's staff from its pedestal. He hefted it in his large hands. "Yeah... this looks like the right length. Maybe a little lighter than a metal bat, but..."

"What are you talking about?" TJ asked as Dad disappeared into a side closet. A moment later, he pulled out a baseball bag, took the staff, and stuffed it into the compartment specifically designed for a baseball bat.

"It's a perfect fit." He handed the bag off to TJ.

TJ held it close to his chest. It *was* a perfect fit, but it had one gaping flaw. "I'm not allowed to have a staff with me at camp. And Mom will be mad if Dayo's staff is gone."

Dad shrugged. "If they see it in your bag, just tell 'em your *clouded* father put it in there. We'll just say I'm ignorant." He winked. "Plus, I heard that Mr. Bolawe was talking to your mother on that water phone. He said staff magic is strong, and you should use every advantage you can get. And if your mom asks, well... I'm sure I'll come up with something."

TJ grabbed Dad around the middle without thinking. "Thanks, Dad."

A few minutes later, Mom dashed down the stairs screaming for everyone to get in the car. TJ pulled out his phone. They only had an hour until his flight left. Lucky for them, Dad was the kind of driver who split lanes and ran through yellow lights.

In fifteen minutes flat, they screeched into the Delta Airlines departure terminal.

Dad and Tunde said their goodbyes. Tunde jeered, reminding TJ the family would still love him even if he failed a remedial summer camp. TJ couldn't help smiling at that. He knew that was the closest thing to encouragement he'd get from his brother.

"Let's go, Tomori," Mom said, rolling a bag behind her. "Your flight boards in thirty minutes."

TJ bit back his retort. If he told Mom he had been ready for hours and it was *her* fault they were late, he was sure to get popped in the mouth. So he waved to Tunde and Dad and shuffled behind Mom into the airport.

He and Mom speed-walked to check their bags, their feet moving so fast that the *click-clack* of Mom's flats and the *squeak-squeak* of TJ's Jordans turned heads. Thankfully, the man at the desk didn't question the oddly shaped "bat" in TJ's baseball bag. Then they were through their gate, through TSA, and straight to the announcement of: "Flight Zero-Zero-One-Ten, now boarding."

"Got here just in time," Mom sighed through labored breaths.

TJ would never understand why she always insisted on stressing herself out. He would've preferred being early and bored than sweating buckets and nearly late.

✝

THE FLIGHT WASN'T BAD, ONLY FOUR HOURS TO NEW ORLEANS, much better than TJ's first flight, which had been to Lagos, Nigeria. That had been a full day of travel, including two layovers. On this flight, TJ had only been subjected to two foul odors during the entire trip, and there were no crying babies in sight—he hoped that was a good omen for what was to come.

The view outside his window seat was spotless, except for a few gray clouds covering the distant desert below, which he assumed was Arizona or New Mexico. For a few moments, he wondered if there were other young diviners down there like him getting ready to go to camp or discovering their own Ashe.

Then he thought about the other campers he'd meet. If Camp Olosa really was for remedial diviners, maybe they'd be just as nervous as he was now.

That would make things a whole lot easier.

TJ pulled out his camp brochure to read up more on what to expect. He'd gone over it two or three hundred times, and the only thing of value he could really pull from it was that Olosa, the Orisha of Lagoons, traditionally took sheep as offerings which she fed to her alligator messengers.

After reading the brochure another hundred times, he gazed back out of the window. When the landscape turned from the reds and browns of the deserts into the marsh and clouded skies of swamps, TJ felt a hand brush against the back of his own.

"How are you feeling, honey bunny?" Mom asked with a serious yet gentle tone.

TJ could barely hear her, though; his ears always clogged up on airplanes.

"I'm a little... gassy," TJ joked, though it had been true. The airplane cheese wasn't sitting well with his stomach, and he wasn't trying to be the third stinker on the trip.

Mom slapped him playfully across the arm. "You know what I mean, silly."

TJ shrugged. Now that they were so close to their destination, he was surprisingly even-tempered. But he knew that only meant he was liable to burst at any moment.

"Did you tell any of your friends where you are going?" she asked.

TJ rolled his eyes. "Oh yes, all zero of them."

TJ knew Mom was making sure he didn't tell anyone about the magic camp he was attending, but he couldn't help being blunt despite her giving him bug eyes. "Don't worry, Mom. I'm only joking. Siri knows I'll only be away for the summer." TJ did his best not to burst out laughing as he tapped at his iPhone's screen. "She was sad at first, but I think she'll come around."

"Don't play like that. You have friends." Mom's shoulders turned squarely on TJ. "What about that one boy, Gabriel?"

"You mean my study partner in fifth grade?"

"You weren't friends?"

"If a guy who spoke to me just to ace our project on California missions counts as a friend, then yeah, I guess."

Mom's brow furrowed. "What about that Christian Flores boy? I take him home all the time."

"That's because he likes *you*, Mom. Not me. And don't look at me like that. It's a personal choice. I read somewhere that introverts like me thrive better by ourselves."

That was a half-truth. Sure, TJ didn't feel the need to make friends to be happy, but he also didn't have the best luck with graduating from being a mere acquaintance with most of his classmates. He just never fit in nicely with anyone, was all. They all grew up to do teenager stuff, and he was still stuck on cartoons—the not-so-cool kind. But like Dayo always said, sometimes it took time to "find your tribe." It was just taking him a little longer to find his.

But he could wait.

"Nu-uh." Mom sucked her teeth, her old Nigerian accent slipping through. "This summer, you're going to make some friends."

"I thought I was supposed to focus on my studies."

"You can do both, Tomori!" she said a bit too loudly—the snoring man next to her stirred—so she lowered her voice. "You know I'm proud of you no matter what you do. I just want what's best for you."

TJ didn't know what came over him, but something about what Mom said didn't sit well with him. Her words felt generic, hollow. So he had to ask, "Then why didn't you or anyone else ever notice me?"

Mom closed her mouth and looked down in thought. TJ hadn't meant to make her uncomfortable. It just came out. And for whatever reason, he wasn't done. "Everyone at the funeral loved Dayo. They really *loved* her. It was like they lost a sister, like they were closer to her than I was. And you won't even tell me why."

Mom stayed quiet for a long while. TJ thought she was going to ignore him for the whole rest of the flight until they landed. But even when she opened her mouth on occasion, she fiddled with the menu in the seat in front of her or the headphones she had plugged in.

"I can't shield you from the truth once you step foot onto the campgrounds," she finally said, sighing. Looking around briefly before lowering her voice, she continued. "Most of the elders there are bound to know about Ifedayo. You see, all that promised child stuff happened three years ago."

The same time we started growing apart, TJ thought.

"It wasn't until she graduated from Ifa Academy that the oracle's reading started making sense. They said that Ifedayo would…" she trailed off, her eyes glistening.

TJ rubbed the inside of her palm to encourage her to go on.

"I don't know the whole thing," she said. "No one does. But the oracles said that she would have special powers. Powers beyond a typical diviner. A power that would rival the Orishas themselves. It was said she would awaken an Orisha long lost. It all seemed to add up. You don't know this, but many of the priests believe the Orishas have gone, though their power remains. For centuries, no one has communed with them directly. Well, there was a brief time back in the sixties when people thought they would come back. The war then was so similar to some of the old stories..."

"What war?" TJ asked, sitting up straight.

"The Biafra War... The civil war that nearly tore Nigeria apart..." Mom's words came slowly. "We don't talk about it. I wasn't even alive when it happened. But my mother immigrated to the States after my father died because of it."

TJ scrunched his eyebrows curiously. "So Dayo was supposed to do.... what exactly?"

"Outside of uncovering a lost Orisha... that I don't know. Many suspected she was destined to open the gate back to the Orishas — if the connection was really lost at all. Then she..."

Then she died, TJ thought.

"So the oracles were wrong, then," TJ said almost to himself.

"It happens from time to time."

"And I'm following all of *that.*" A heat rose through TJ's spine.

That's why Mom didn't want him to know. It was a lot of pressure to live up to. And that pressure was making him sweat again. He took off his zip-up hoodie and loosened the button at the top of his shirt, drawing a worrying look from Mom. How could anyone expect him to amount to much? No wonder everyone was so devastated. Dayo was marked to do phenomenal things. And him... not so much.

"I know you would never say this," he turned to Mom after stuffing his jacket under his seat, "but I know Dayo was the favorite. You and Dad love Tunde, too. And I'm number three on the list."

"Don't say that." Mom jabbed a finger at him, accidentally elbowing the sleeping man next to her. "Don't you ever. You know we love you all the same."

"Sure, you love us the same. But don't give me that stuff about no favorites. Everyone has 'em. I'll admit it. Dayo was my favorite, too."

Mom hung her head low again, searching for words within her hands, which were now twiddling with the stitching on her airplane blanket. "My bond with Ifedayo was different, that's true. But that shouldn't matter. Sometimes people put too much faith in 'promised children' or those who are more *apparently* talented."

"And then there's teenagers like me. The ones who do best cheering from the bench. Which works fine for me, honestly." He tried for a smile, though it probably came off as an awkward grimace. "Besides, like Priest Glover says, I could just be a fluke."

Mom sighed before saying, "*Adé orí òkín kò lè ṣe déédé orí eyekéye.*"

TJ's eyes glazed over.

Mom laughed a little. "Don't worry. This summer you'll learn the language well enough. What I said means, 'the crest on the head of the peacock simply won't fit any other bird.'"

If that was supposed to be clearer, it didn't help TJ's comprehension one bit. He never liked the proverbs his mother told him. Why couldn't she just say what she meant to say? It would be a whole hell of a lot easier in the communication department.

Mom leaned in close to TJ, whispering so that he knew her words were only for him. "We are all differently endowed, Tomori. Be secure in who you are; envy no one."

11

NOLA

THERE'S A QUOTE THAT GOES: "IF THERE WAS NO NEW ORLEANS, America would just be a bunch of free people dying of boredom." TJ wouldn't call himself the best judge of cities, but thinking back on those words as he and Mom walked through the Delta Airlines terminal, he couldn't help but admit there was a liveliness to the city he'd never experienced before.

Granted, he had only seen the airport so far.

The scent of cajun spices spilling out of creole kitchens filled each corner they turned down. Gift shops flanking the long, open concourses sold jerseys for the Saints and Pelicans. A few of the restaurants even had live jazz in front of their establishments, with men blowing into saxophones and women singing sultry melodies.

TJ could easily pick out the tourists from the locals. Sure, the visitors couldn't help bobbing their heads or shifting their shoulders —TJ caught himself tapping his foot at one point—but the locals went into full shimmies whenever the music caught them in its web.

"Ooo, ain't you so handsome! Come over here and shimmy with me, young man." One elderly woman tried to pull TJ into a dance, which he denied, though he couldn't hold on to a nervous giggle that slipped out.

Finding a cab wasn't as easy as getting a dance, however. It had been thirty minutes, and Mom still hadn't found the "right" one— whatever that meant. TJ had counted at least three dozen yellow cabs since they arrived. He'd even suggested they call an Uber or Lyft, but Mom kept hushing him and saying, "maybe I missed it," as she placed her hand over her forehead and peered into the mass of cars.

TJ pulled out his phone for the hundredth time. Since it would be taken from him at camp, TJ spent his last precious hours with his iPhone scrolling through memes. TJ didn't admit this to anyone, but most of his comical inventory came from trivial internet jokes sourced from online message boards or social media apps. As he stood there laughing to himself, a large man bumped into him.

"Sorry about that, li'l man," he said with what sounded like a Spanish accent. His skin was darker than midnight, stark against his short snow-white hair and beard.

"S'ok," TJ replied lightly, disregarding the slight throbbing in his elbow. He went back to his phone when the man spoke again.

"'Ey, Manuela." He tapped at someone's back. "What do you call a disease you catch at an airport?"

"Hmmm," came another voice. It sounded like a girl's. TJ lifted his head out of curiosity—as any teenage boy would. The man's broad middle covered her, though, whoever she was. But TJ could see a large mass of hair at the edges of the man's elbow.

"I don't know, tell me," she said. Her accent sounded something between what TJ assumed was her father's and a New Yorker's inflection.

The man laughed before saying, "Terminal illness."

The girl canted her head, revealing her face and her bushy curls, which fell to her shoulders. Her nose wrinkled up in a cute way, as though she were stifling a sneeze. TJ noticed a small birthmark just above her nostril.

He had expected her to roll her eyes or shake her head at the dad joke, but, at the edge of her cheek, the impressions of a dimple sunk into her brown skin. Then she couldn't hold it in any longer. She gave her father a huge beam and chuckled.

"Better be safe and take an *air*borne," she shot back, her cheeks pushing up on her face in a grin.

Her laugh came with mirth, more genuine than most of the ones TJ heard—the kind that was contagious. Then, her eyes traveled to TJ's, and their gazes locked.

TJ's breath hitched as he realized he had been smiling at her. Quickly he dropped his grin into a flat line, but he couldn't pull his stare from her. Every little voice within him told him to look away, to stop. But he couldn't.

The girl stopped laughing and considered TJ with a subtle half-grin. None of it made sense. She was *supposed* to give him the stink eye, to tell him to "take a picture, it'll last longer."

Neither of which happened.

She just held his gaze with curiosity, her thick eyebrows riding up her forehead.

They probably would have continued staring at each other had it not been for Mom tugging at TJ's shoulder. "TJ, what are you doing? Our cab is here."

TJ turned to Mom, who was already rolling his bags into a clunker of a van painted a faded blue and white with a cartoon alligator plastered on its side. Black smoke billowed from its exhaust, and every few seconds, it popped, drawing the attention of the other hailers waiting to be picked up.

"Sorry, I'm late." An old man wearing a blue dashiki and a white aṣọ òkè cap came shuffling out of the van to help Mom with the bags. "The traffic gettin' back was terrible. And the bosses said I ain't allowed to use no Ashe—" Mom shot him a look to silence him, her head turning over each shoulder for any onlookers. "Ah, you know what I mean. Gettin' 'round like the clouded do is slow business."

"Well, you're here now," Mom said as she waved TJ over. "Come on, get in, honey."

TJ walked forward and lowered his head into the van. It seated two in front, two in the middle, and three in the back. Most of the seats look like a dog had used them all as a chew toy, and it smelled like must and mildew. The back looked the worst of the two, so TJ made for the middle. But as he sat down, Mom tapped him on the shoulder.

"Take the back seat," she whispered. "We have another family behind us."

TJ turned to see who she was talking about, but Mom's tall honeycomb dreadlocks blocked his view. Was she talking about that girl and her dad from before?

After another snap from his Mom's fingers, TJ shifted to the back and searched for a portion of seat that didn't have springs coming out of it. When he sat, he saw a familiar bush of dark hair duck its way into the van. It *was* the girl from before. Her eyes met TJ's again for the briefest of moments, and she gave him a small wave.

TJ lifted his head and said "sup" in the most cavalier tone he could muster, trying to look cool. Then he proceeded to gape at the back of her head, waiting for each moment she turned to her father so he could get another glance at her face.

She looked just as fine from the side.

"Why's the van all beat up?" TJ muttered to his mother. The girl up front seemed to listen in. "I mean, this is the van taking us to camp, right? How do we know we aren't gonna break down on the highway?"

Almost on cue, the exhaust popped for the dozenth time.

"Enchanted items can't be messed with too much," Mom said as she shifted her weight in her seat in search of a comfortable spot—an impossible task. "If anyone cleans it the wrong way or replaces the wrong part, all the magic could fall apart."

TJ turned back to the girl, wondering if she, too, was a diviner. She must've been—why else was she sitting with them in the dingy cab?

"All right," the cab driver announced. "Everybody buckled in?"

TJ inspected his seat but saw nothing but stains and plush. "Um, we seem to be lacking in the seatbelt department here..."

"Seatbelts?" the cab driver cackled.

"Oh, sorry, honey." Mom turned to him and waved a hand over his chest.

TJ felt an invisible force plant him to his seat like a roller coaster harness. The girl in front did the same for her father, and TJ's chest caved. She *was* a diviner after all—her father must've been normal. Did she see he couldn't do the magic himself, that his mother had to tuck him in like a baby?

TJ groaned inwardly.

"It's a simple wind charm," Mom whispered to him. "It's what's binding you to the seat. If you listen hard enough, you can even hear it rolling around your body. Sorry, I should have taught you that one back home. It comes in handy."

Thanks, mom. TJ thought as he swallowed deeply. But she was right. Glancing down, TJ could see that faint mist curling around his chest.

The girl's father glanced over his shoulder, his wide and open mouth sparkling with pearly whites. "Is it your first time to the camp?"

"Yes, but it's only temporary," Mom spoke for TJ, her voice cutting sharp and quick. "Until he can get to Ifa Academy."

"Oh, Ifa," the girl's father said with raised eyebrows. "Manuela was there last year, but—"

"Dad..." the girl named Manuela mumbled.

"Oh, right, right," he said as though reminded of something.

"Well, name's Zé." He stretched a long hand out to Mom. "Zé Martinez. And this is my daughter Manuela."

Mom took his hand and shook it. "I'm Yejide Young. And this is my son, Tomori Jomiloju."

Manuela's eyes seemed to brighten knowingly at Mom's name. TJ had to remind himself that their family name would have been well known among diviners. Not only was his sister famous, but his mother was held in high esteem whenever they traveled to Nigeria. But... Manuela and her father were Americans. Maybe TJ had only imagined it.

"You okay there, li'l man?" Manuela's father asked. "Your face looks a bit red."

TJ tilted his head down to cover his face. At the edge of his vision, he could see Manuela looking at him through her thick hair.

"Don't sweat it. There's nothing to worry about," Mr. Martinez said. "This is my daughter's fourth year back to Camp Olosa. She'll show you around."

Well, that doesn't sound so bad.

TJ lifted his eyes from the hole beneath his feet—which had given him a perfect view of the street below—and met Manuela's. There was no way her dimples could be any more perfect.

12

OL' SALLY

As they drove along the highway, TJ knew that if the cab wasn't functioning because of magic, it would've fallen apart. Everything rattled as the driver dodged potholes and uneven roads. At one point, TJ would've sworn the undercarriage would split beneath his feet, but as it seemed to pull away, an unseen force snapped it back together like a magnet.

TJ spent most of his time watching how Manuela's fluffy curls bounced with the car's jerks. Some of her hair coils were dyed a golden brown. He wondered how she chose which strands to dye and which to leave alone. TJ ran his fingers through his own naps. Would that be a good conversation starter when they got to camp? Ask if he should dye his hair with streaks, too?

Between his stolen glances, TJ considered the many ways he could make a fool of himself in front of Manuela. What if every guy she spoke to made comments about her hair? What if his voice cracked? Or what if she was just being nice to him before because her father was there?

He tried to distract himself from his imagined worst-case scenarios by staring out the window where they passed dark bayous of black lakes and green marshes of twinkling swamps. At one point, he rolled down the window to free his nose from the car's mildew smell, but the thick, rotten egg stink of the wetlands wasn't much better.

Taking his mind off Manuela proved difficult when she spoke so animatedly with her father. So TJ decided to give it up and listen in to everything they said. Without shame.

From their conversation, TJ picked up that they were definitely from somewhere in New York. And the only thing he could think about was asking how good New York pizza *actually* was. But that was too lame. He needed to think of something else, something better, something more interesting.

Mr. Martinez seemed to like soccer quite a bit. He kept debating who was the best dribbler in the sport with the cab driver and Manuela. The cab driver—who liked to talk with his hands a lot, sending the van careening intermittently—seemed to back someone named Messi, a player Manuela agreed was great. Mr. Martinez, however, kept making a case for another player named Pelé.

"Bah, I expected Messi from the *jovem*." He threw up his hands theatrically. "But you, amigo? I thought a *velho* like yourself would know better about *futebol*."

TJ couldn't quite pin down what Mr. Martinez said half the time. Frequently, he switched between English and what TJ assumed was Spanish. TJ knew a little Spanish from school, so he could pull a few phrases out of the chitchat between Mr. Martinez and Manuela, but the few he caught didn't exactly make sense without the rest. Beyond that, their accents sounded a bit off from what he was used to in Southern California. Maybe West Coast and East Coast Spanish had different dialects, like with English.

The one thing TJ was confident he could relate to was Manuela's humor. She and her father were like a ping pong match of joke after joke. It seemed like anything made her laugh, especially Mr. Martinez's dad jokes. And like that, TJ knew his perfect opening. All he had to do was think up the perfect one-liner, and he'd be golden.

Before he had the chance, though, the cab jerked to a sudden stop.

"*Bonjour, Monsieur Francois*," the cab driver said to what looked like nothing.

They had approached a chain-link fence surrounding a thick marsh. Nearby a sign that looked like it had once been white hung from its side, red lettering reading:

NO TRESPASSING, TOXIC WASTE AHEAD.

"*Bonjour, Monsieur Deji*," came a French-accented voice from nowhere.

There was nothing but bundles of overgrown weeds crawling up the fence and a barren tree at its side. TJ had expected something off-trail, but this seemed a bit sketchy. Plus, just on the other side of the fence was a green lake unfit for a shabby old van that probably lacked four-wheel drive. TJ stole a glance toward his Mom, but she appeared perfectly at ease.

Still, the cab driver kept speaking to the air. "I think I got the last of the children. Elder Akande went back with another van to see if there's any lost ducklings left."

"Is he a ventriloquist or something?" TJ whispered to Mom. She only smiled and pointed to the front.

TJ took a second look and saw that the barren tree moved its gray arms. It must've been a transformed man, just like that reporter in his backyard with the ivy.

"Be careful on the first bend," the voice said. "Ol' Sally came back. Probably just curious to see the campers coming in."

Now TJ could see that there was a face carved into the tree. Two pieces of bark near its top lifted in the motion of lips. Mouth agape, TJ lifted his phone to take a video, but his screen only showed a regular tree with no moving lips or shifting arms.

"I thought Akande woulda had Ol' Sally moved off by now," the cab driver said, sighing. "You ain't have no more offerings, do ya?"

"Nothing here," the tree said. "But give it some time. She'll move off if she's still hanging about."

"Offerings? Ol' Sally?" TJ asked Mom, but she answered with a finger pressed to her lips.

"Good to see you again, Francois," she said through a cupped hand.

The tree man bent low and angled one of his branches in a creaking wave. "Is that Yejide? My oh my, it's good to see you! Who's that you've got with you?"

"My son, Tomori Jomiloju."

The tree man bent the other way, his oak brow rising in his unique expression of surprise. "Oh yes, of course. He's got his sister's hair and everything. Well, when she was younger. I never saw much of her once she went off to that big fancy school. I heard the news, of course. Very sorry to hear it, Yejide, very sorry to hear it. She was a wonderful young woman when I knew her."

Mom inclined her head.

"Well, let me not keep you. I'm sure I'll get to know your son well enough this summer."

The tree shoveled its branches into the base of the fence and lifted it, roots and all, as though it were just a swing up garage door. The cab rumbled again, and the pieces under TJ's feet shifted in and out until they formed a curved floor like a rowboat. The roof crunched and fell inward. Grabbing hold of Mom's arm, TJ held on, eyes shut tightly, believing he was either about to be crushed by the roof or fall straight through and onto his butt, which was the last thing he needed with Manuela in front.

When nothing happened to him, he cracked open an eye and watched, almost in awe, as the top of the car shifted away in fragments. It reminded him of the Transformers movies Dayo had shown him as one of her "guilty pleasures." The pieces around them shifted like a convertible, creaking at the sides with each movement until it opened up at the top, revealing the afternoon sky. It wasn't long until TJ realized the cab had transformed and put itself back together into a bonafide bayou boat.

Now he understood where the mildew smell came from.

Tipping his folded cap to the tree man, the cab driver pushed forward on what had been his gear shift a moment ago. Now, it was a throttle control for the airboat. TJ's back sunk into his seat as they propelled forward, straight over the marsh.

☦

THEY CONTINUED AROUND CAREENING BENDS OF THE SWAMP rivers for several minutes—TJ gripping tightly around his seat—as the wetlands grew thicker and thicker with mossy trees which sprouted from the green waters. TJ half wondered which of the putrid plants was casting off the musty smell that seemed to stew in the humidity, though after a four-hour plane ride, it could've just been him.

TJ soon found that marshes like this meant he needed to keep a swatting hand at the ready at all times. Already, several mosquitos made attempts at making his exposed forearm their midday meal.

"It's pretty loud," TJ shouted to Mom. "Won't someone hear us?"

"Not with Monsieur Francois mannin' the gate," the cab driver called back. TJ had no idea how the man's folded cap stayed secured on his head through the gust. "He does a little ritual every day or so to make it look like ain't nothin' interestin' is out here at all. And he cuts off the sound usin' Oya's wind... Don't worry yourself none. You gonna learn all 'bout it soon."

TJ shouted up front again. "Do any normal people ever get in?"

"You mean like Mr. Martinez here?" the cab driver asked. TJ traded a look with the bearded man who gave him another short wave.

"No, not like him. I mean, people who aren't... allowed."

The cab driver beamed a jagged row of teeth as he cut between two narrow trees. "One or two of them little hoodlums get past every now and then. Well, that's until they get a good look at Ol' Sally."

"Ol' Sally?" TJ questioned.

There was that name again. Who was she? Some swamp witch or something? TJ could imagine some ragged old lady with wires for hair and a boil threatening to burst on a long hooked nose.

"Ol' Sally," the cab driver repeated, pointing ahead to the first bend in the path which led into a dark, low-hanging canopy. The leaves huddled around a dark pool of water, and from within the depths rose the largest alligator TJ had ever seen.

"Meet Camp Olosa's mascot." The cab driver nodded to the giant thing blocking their path.

The alligator stretched out longer than the fallen, decaying tree it skulked by and was at least two times as wide. TJ couldn't slow the pounding in his chest even if he wanted to as the gator flipped its tail up from the murky waters. If it felt like it, it could crush their whole boat in two bites.

Ol' Sally seemed to put Manuela on edge as well. She shifted in her seat uncomfortably, her hand pressed into a fist against her seat.

"She's never been so close before," she said with a hint of a crack in her voice. Around her fist, TJ could have sworn he saw a few loose leaf shavings floating around her knuckles.

"Just keep calm." The cab driver appeared entirely unphased. "She'll leave... eventually."

"Define 'eventually,'" Manuela asked as the giant alligator tore strips casually from a tree base.

The cab driver shrugged. "If she hasn't had her nap yet, it cain't be more than two or three hours."

"Three hours!?" Mr. Martinez blurted, slamming his palm against his knee.

Mom lifted from her seat for a better view. "Is there no other way into the camp?"

"This here's the one and only," the cab driver said. He already had his legs up and crossed over the hood of the boat, his hands interlaced behind his hat.

TJ kept his focus on Ol' Sally. A mosquito buzzed by his neck, but its bite was nothing compared to what Ol' Sally could inflict. Her breathing against the water came out so harsh that it brought up waves that ebbed against the cab's "hull." Then she took in a sharp, rapid breath. She had caught the scent of something—her eyes turned to the boat—or some*one*.

The cab driver stood up and squinted. "I ain't never seen her like this."

The fact that the man traded his offhanded tone for an earnest one made TJ uneasy.

"Is she sick?" Manuela edged back against her seat.

And of course, because TJ's luck always ran that way, Ol' Sally's bulbous eyes shifted from the boat itself and straight to him. TJ tried to convince himself that it was his overactive imagination again. Yet when he shifted his glance to the others, he knew they knew it too.

The creature had him marked.

TJ's knees locked as Ol' Sally grunted and bellowed, her jaw snapping as she watched him. Then, suddenly and without warning, she slid her head underwater and disappeared. TJ held his breath, bracing himself, his gaze darting throughout the cloudy green waters covered in weeds.

"That's new…" the cab driver trailed off as he stepped closer to the boat's center. He spoke some words under his breath, and a jagged oak staff materialized in his hands. "Everyone, keep from them edges, please."

Mom manifested her own staff as everyone huddled to the center of the boat. Silence hung in the air as TJ strained his ears for any kind of sound. But all he could hear were the croaking of distant frogs and the chirping of crickets.

"Boy," the cab driver said through thin lips, deadly serious. "Don't. Move. None. She right behind you."

TJ's back stiffened. Despite the cab driver's advice, he moved. With a slow turn, he peered over his shoulder to find one large oval eye staring directly at him.

"Don't make no sudden movements," the cab driver said. "She just gettin' the measure of you, is all."

"Easy for you to say," TJ mumbled out the side of his mouth as he did his best to keep from pooping himself.

Ol' Sally lifted the whole of her head from the water, her snout only inches from TJ. If he stuck out his fist, it could rest comfortably within one of the alligator's nostrils.

What if she snaps at me?

Would he be fast enough to duck so the adults could blast her with a spell? No, if he did that, the alligator might miss him and get Mom. He'd have to stand his ground, he decided.

But he didn't have to. The giant alligator just stared at TJ with an almost human expression, as though assessing him. With a single blink, the stare-off broke. And then, with a snort that blew back his tiny Afro, Ol' Sally sunk back into the water and turned away, leaving their new path open.

"Well, I'll be damned," the cab driver gasped. "I ain't never seen the ol' girl take to someone like that, 'cept Elder Akande, maybe."

TJ shrugged, trying his best not to let his voice crack. "What can I say? I have a way with giant man-eating alligators."

Manuela giggled, and TJ couldn't help smiling.

Those dimples of hers were too much.

"Well, ain't much farther now." The cab driver took his position back at the helm, and the boat lurched forward again. "Just a little ways mo', and we can get y'all two set up in ya cabins."

13

WELCOME TO CAMP OLOSA

A FEW TWISTS AND TURNS THROUGH THE BAYOU LATER, AND TJ remembered how much he hated "first days." In all his excitement, after staring down a giant alligator, he had forgotten how many other campers there could be. In the five minutes it took for Mom to argue the taxi fare with their driver—"What do you mean it's extra because of the giant alligator?"—TJ counted at least three dozen other campers on the rickety dock they had arrived on. There were even more farther along the muddy path where stacks of cabins could be seen through pockets of trees.

Some of the campers held their heads low, and, like him, their hands fidgeted as they watched the others skip and smile, ready for another summer. A pair of tall boys even greeted each other with a personalized handshake and dap that involved a floating set of leaves swirling around their arms, capitalized with fire manifested from their mouths like dragons.

"LaVont! Jimoh! No magic until you're on the grounds!" shouted a thin woman in an all-white dashiki, who TJ assumed was a counselor.

The boys turned to her in protest, gesturing their hands down at the dock. "Ah, come on," one of them said with a Nigerian accent. "How is this not technically on camp grounds?"

Manuela was among the excited group of campers. The moment she and TJ anchored near the camp's lop-sided deck, she had bolted for her friends, two albino girls who looked like they could be twins. Their blue and white-trimmed dashiki, which had been the standard for all campers, contrasted nicely with their braided auburn hair.

TJ blew out a long breath. It would've been difficult to talk to Manuela alone at that moment. The rate of her speech exploded as she and her friends caught up with one another. Heck, she didn't look like she'd stop talking until tomorrow.

"And then this boy on the boat made Ol' Sally go away," TJ caught her saying just before all three girls turned to him.

He shifted his gaze quickly, forcing his hand to stop zipping and unzipping his jacket nervously. They'd be looking at him, and he needed to appear as cool as possible.

Problem was, he wasn't exactly sure how to do that.

Did he cross his arms? Put his hands in his pockets? And which pockets? His jacket pocket, his front pockets, his back pocket?

He finally decided on interlacing his fingers and setting his hands at his stomach. He regretted the moment he did it. He probably looked like some pretentious dork. The twins giggled that familiar giggle he knew oh too well from the blacktop at school.

Taking his mind off the girls and forcing himself not to give them sidelong glances, his new gaze settled on the camp's entrance. Two long poles stuck in the ground at a slant that held up a splintered sign that read: CAMP OLOSA. Vines and moss covered the "Os" making them look like eyebrows, with the "L" looking like a nose. TJ wondered if that was intentional. Then he wondered if the "Os" really *were* eyes and if the sign would start talking to him like the tree man off the highway or the reporter from his backyard.

"Girls will check in to the left. Boys to the right," roared another woman at the end of the dock.

It looked like there were rocks stuck under her large arms. She must've been strong. She was also the tallest woman TJ had ever seen. She wasn't just fit in the typical mid-30s athletic way—she looked more like some Dora Milaje warrior towering over a wooden table next to several other counselors. Like the others, she too wore an all-white dashiki with black trim. Through the sea of campers who already wore their blue-and-white dashikis, interspersed with others, like TJ and Manuela, who still wore their street clothes, it looked like the counselors were tiny moons directing a sea of blue down the camp's swamp paths of brown and green.

Manuela and her friends peeled off to the left side of the dock, where it spread into a thick and solid mud path where they could find their land legs. TJ watched them as they went. He half hoped they were still talking about him. He thought he did a decent enough job impressing Manuela, but she seemed to forget about him completely.

"Look, Mr. Martinez here went and paid the little extra. It's only fair," TJ overheard the cab driver say to Mom.

Mom had a single hand at her hip, her head canted, and her lips pursed. That meant bad news for the driver. "Oh, no," she raised her voice. "You got me twisted if you think you're finna—"

TJ didn't stick around to hear the rest of what she said as he shouldered between a family to avoid being associated with one of Mom's infamous eruptions. He didn't stop until at least a dozen other boy campers were between him and the dock, where he found himself between a father who wore a faded camp dashiki and his young son who refused to put on his own.

The little boy held back watery eyes, each of his sniffles fighting against an outburst. TJ knew that face all too well. He could almost hear one of his own parents saying, *"You better fix that face before I really give you something to cry about."*

Another camper TJ's age shook his head, tilting down his designer sunglasses to the bridge of his nose like he couldn't believe what he was seeing. Then he rolled his eyes and took his space in line again.

What's he need shades for in a swamp? TJ thought as he looked up through the canopy of trees backdropped by an overcast sky.

Everything about the boy spoke of money. His fade was clean, TJ had to admit. He had braids rolled into a topknot, and TJ assumed his name was "Ayo" since it was cut into the side of his taper. The boy wore silver bracelets, two gold chains, and a designer t-shirt he could've easily bought from a department store, but since it had a little designer logo near the chest, it probably cost four times as much. His fresh sneakers were nice too, but the high-end skinny jeans were not doing his lumpy calves any favors. In fact, he didn't seem to care at all about the muffin top protruding from under his t-shirt line.

In short, the kid was TJ's least favorite kind of person.

Leaning down on a knee, TJ whispered to the little sniffling boy. "Hey, little dude, don't worry about it."

The boy turned, his loose Afro curls heaving as he did his best to stop himself from weeping.

"What's your name?"

"G-Gary," he mumbled.

"I'm TJ. This your first time?"

Gary nodded.

"Me too. But I bet you're way better than me. I couldn't even fill a cup with water until a week ago."

It was the truth, but the boy didn't need to know that.

"Really? That's so easy," Gary said with a bit more volume, side-eyeing his father.

TJ gave him a slight smirk and crossed his arms. "Is it? Could you teach me how to do it better?"

Again, the boy stared up at his father. The thick-eyebrowed man gave his son an approving wink.

Wiping his nose, Gary muttered the ritual phrase just as Mom had always done. Instead of waving his fingers, though, he swayed his arms like he was wading through a shallow river.

"Dad says this is the wrong way to do it." The boy stuck his tongue out in concentration. "But it works for me."

After only a few moments, water sprinkled from the tips of Gary's fingers like a tiny fountain. TJ gave him a short applause and a smile. The boy giggled and started spraying his father. A few droplets fell on the man's old camp shirt before he waved his hands in the air, producing a wind wall that protected him from his son's Super Soaker fingers.

"How about you?" Gary asked. "You try."

TJ shook a hand in front of his face. "No, no, I'll just embarrass myself."

"C'mon. Show me!"

TJ took in a big sigh and said, "Well... you asked for it."

After a few grunts and shakes that made it look like TJ was having a fit of shivers, only a single spout of water shot from his thumb.

Gary tittered through his knuckles. "You're right. I *am* way better."

"Right..." TJ said, doing his best to play along.

That was, after all, really his best effort.

Gary's father tapped TJ at the shoulder and murmured a thank you in his ear. At least the pair of them thought he was being nice. That was a lot better than looks of disappointment and raised eyebrows.

"Don't worry, you'll do better," came Mom's voice from behind.

TJ jumped, then hung his head low. "You weren't supposed to see any of that..."

"This is what the camp is for, eh?" Mom reminded him as she handed him his baseball bag.

His eyes went wide as he clutched at its straps. How could he almost forget to bring it with him? No wonder his water manifestation sucked so hard. He needed his sister's staff closeby.

"Listen," Mom continued. "I've got to check in with the Director about a few things. Will you be okay checking in by yourself? I'll meet you at your cabin."

"Yeah, I-I'm good," TJ said.

Mom brought her hand to TJ's cheek. "Oh, my little man. Growing up."

"Mom…"

"I'm so proud of you. You know that?"

"Mom…"

She cupped his chin and started kissing him on the cheeks. TJ stiffened, hoping none of the others saw his mother giving her teenage son a kiss like she was seeing him off to preschool. Manuela was just down the path. If she took just a second to look over, she would—

"Mom!" TJ gritted without shouting.

"Oh hush, I never get to kiss you anymore."

"And you chose *now* as the best time to start?"

Despite her previous need to see the Director, Mom wouldn't let him go. "Do you have your toothbrush? Dashiki? Towel? Remember, the basic healing incantation is said with an intonation. You need to change tone like with the other—"

"Mom, I'm fine," TJ cut in. "For real."

"Okay, okay, I'm going," she said quickly, then shuffled between the girls' and boys' line to the front. When she passed by Manuela, she waved over to TJ, then threw up an "a-ok" hand gesture. How did she know so fast?

TJ rolled his eyes but couldn't help chuckling at Mom's giddiness. He knew he should cherish the moment. If the best magic he could do was a single water jet from his thumb, these semi-prideful moments with her would become far fewer.

14

FRESH MEAT

THE COUNSELOR'S CHECK-IN DESK TOOK LONGER TO GET TO THAN TJ expected. Not because they had to stop due to one of the elder counselors having to fix his "contraband mask," as he called it — which apparently was supposed to see through bags. Not because one of the tall living wooden statues had trouble spelling the names of "Madhavaditya" and "Abhimanyu" — two foreign campers who were new to the camp whose name tags ended up saying "M" and "A." No. It took so long because every time TJ introduced himself, each counselor spent the next several minutes giving him their condolences. It seemed like each of them had their own favorite story about his sister.

"Best crossover player I've ever seen," one counselor said.

"I would have never made it off that cliff if it wasn't for her," said another.

"She was one in a million."

Then, finally, TJ met someone who didn't shower him with words of sorrow or remembrance. There was no way TJ could forget the face of the man with the deep pores and serious eyes, the one who led the charge at the funeral even though his Ashe wasn't as powerful as the others.

At the end of the table sat Mr. Bolawe, who beckoned another camper forward. When TJ caught the man's attention, he waved brightly, and Bolawe returned his greeting with an expression of recognition and a cheerful grin. At least there was one person TJ knew, though they had barely spoken back at the funeral.

Mr. Bolawe and another man with a very severe-looking face, slicked-back hair, and an old-school pencil mustache were checking the campers' belongings, taking over for the elder who was now smacking his "contraband mask" against a rock and calling it "a sorry piece of junk."

TJ clutched tightly at his baseball bag, feeling the groove of the staff inside.

The little boy Gary and his father went ahead to Mr. Bolawe, but the kid with a topknot named Ayo was with the mean-looking guy. It seemed like Ayo had tried to smuggle in just about everything on the "leave at home" list, including an iPhone, an enchanted water bowl, an old iPod—apparently as a backup in case they took his iPhone—cash, food, t-shirts with derogatory terms, and all his expensive jewelry.

Some form of magic hid all the items. Though many of Ayo's bags looked empty on initial inspection, the counselor with the pencil-thin mustache tapped his staff along their edges and rubbed his hands on the inner-lining until he pulled out item after item like a magician pulling rabbits from hats.

Again, TJ gripped his baseball bag. Even if he knew how to make his staff disappear like the adults, which he didn't, he'd be no match for whoever that counselor was. Cellphones and food were one thing. But TJ was bringing in a staff, something even this Ayo kid didn't dare to bring. If the counselor found his, TJ wouldn't just get a foul look. He might get kicked out before the first day.

Ayo sucked at his teeth. "C'mon, Mr. Du Bois. You really gotta take my chains, though?" His accent was odd. It sounded like a Nigerian accent being covered up by a stereotypical Black American dialect.

"You know the rules, Ayodeji," said the stern counselor called Mr. Du Bois in a creole accent. He had the kind of voice that demanded no nonsense.

"Whatever, man." The boy named Ayo—or Ayodeji—grunted and pulled off his golden chains. After he packed all his "camp approved" items back into his bag, he stomped off.

"Next," Mr. Du Bois droned.

TJ shivered, and goosebumps sprouted against his hoodie. Maybe he could explain that he had misread the rules. Or perhaps he could fake a stomachache after all that careening through the swamp. The cab driver would vouch for him—he might even say something about Ol' Sally. Maybe then the man would be too distracted and let him through.

But before TJ could decide on a plan of action, Mr. Du Bois tapped his iron staff against the desk with a tiny bird figurehead atop it, indicating that TJ needed to place his bag down—and that his patience was running thin.

TJ gulped, an uncomfortable burn roiling through his chest. There wasn't much else to do but dump his bag in front of Mr. Du Bois and hope he'd be allowed to stay without punishment.

Before the counselor could start his inspection, however, the crystal in his bird staff already alight, Mr. Bolawe lifted a finger to intercede. "I'll take him, Xavier. This is Ifedayo's little brother."

"Oh, is that so?" Mr. Du Bois examined TJ up and down. "Oh yes, I do see the resemblance. I was at the funeral." TJ vaguely remembered his mother pointing out someone named Du Bois. "My deepest condolences. And that nasty business with the Keepers…"

"Was messed up," TJ finished for him, his voice stronger than he intended.

"Yes…" TJ didn't like the way Du Bois was looking at him. "'Messed up', as you put it." The man held his gaze a little longer before saying, "Yes, Olufemi. Go ahead and take him. I'll get the next boy. You," he called to the kid behind TJ, "Yes, you with the baseball cap. Take it off, and let me see what you got under there."

TJ let out half a sigh. That was a close one, but he wasn't out of the swamp yet. Mr. Bolawe might've been friendly to him, sure, but that didn't mean he wasn't a stickler for rules too. That said, TJ had one play he could use against Bolawe that he didn't with Du Bois: they *actually* had something to talk about. So long as he could keep up an interesting enough conversation, then perhaps Bolawe would just give his bags a once over without doing a full check.

"I didn't know you were a counselor here," TJ began casually as he slid his bag down the table.

Mr. Bolawe unzipped the bag and felt around with his hand. "No, just volunteering for registration day. Though Director Simmons knows she can call on me at any time."

"I never asked at the funeral what you did." TJ watched Mr. Bolawe's hands closely, perhaps a bit too fiercely. He couldn't look into the bag; that'd be a dead giveaway. Just a little longer, and Bolawe would just pass right over the staff. Maybe he didn't even notice the additional compartment that housed what should have been a baseball bat.

Loosen up, TJ. Don't stare at him. That'll give it away. "You said something about politics?"

"A little while ago, yeah." His hand stopped like it found something. Instead of sliding back and forth, it circled one particular area. "I'm not sure what to call myself these days," he continued offhandedly.

Yeah, his hand was definitely hovering over where the crystal was lodged into the face of the staff. TJ could only hope Mr. Bolawe thought it was a softball or something.

"You know something?" Mr. Bolawe chuckled. "They don't play baseball in this camp, I think. What kind of bat is this?"

TJ went dead quiet as all the blood rushed from his face. Mr. Bolawe's wry grin fell into a questioning, thin line. Without looking away, the man unzipped the compartment. Then he looked down and examined what was inside, his eyes traveling over the taboo item. The friendly twinkle in his eyes grew serious. This was it. TJ would hear it now. But he had one more thing he could still pull.

"My ignorant dad's a cloud," he muttered all at once, jumbling the order of his words around. He had meant to say his *"dad's clouded, and he's ignorant."* Shoot, even hearing that in his head didn't sound so great.

Mr. Bolawe didn't frown, though. He didn't seem angry or anything like that. In fact, the corner of his lips seemed to curl up, not down.

He laughed low through his nose, then peered up to TJ knowingly. He put a single finger to his lips then murmured, "These kinds of bats aren't allowed in any of the leagues here."

"I know, I know," TJ said as he gave a sidelong glance to Mr. Du Bois, who was now busy tracing his staff between the other boy's thick cornrows. "But I had to bring it. It's the only way I can do mag—"

"I'll keep your secret." Mr. Bolawe zipped up the bag and handed it back to TJ. "But you best do a better job at hiding it."

"I will," TJ said earnestly, amazed that he could keep his sister's staff, astonished that he wasn't getting kicked out.

"The cabins are known to have a few loose floorboards." Bolawe winked.

A bout of laughter rang out a few feet away. Down the path, Ayodeji and those tall boys spoke loudly about what they called "Gary's jacked up hairline." TJ didn't see anything wrong with the boy's hair. Sure, his haircut wasn't crisp like Ayodeji's, but it was a natural hairline, one not manufactured by a barber.

"Ayodeji!" the female counselor with tree trunks for arms shouted.

Ayodeji covered his mouth, pretending like he hadn't said anything at all. But the counselor wasn't fooled. "Since you've got jokes, you can give some of our new arrivals a tour of the campgrounds. Considering it's your second year back because you couldn't act right, you should know the lay of the land well enough. And I know damn well you didn't just roll your eyes at *me*, little boy. Do you hear me?"

Ayodeji looked like he wanted to groan again, but he stopped himself with a forced smile. "Yes, I hear you."

"'I hear you, *ma'am*,'" she corrected him.

"Yes, I hear you, ma'am," Ayodeji returned flatly.

"Good." The woman turned her broad shoulders to TJ. "It's Tomori's first time. Show him where the boys at preparatory level sleep."

TJ tilted his head to Ayodeji, who scrunched up his face like he was battling a stomach ache.

"Well, don't just stand there staring," he told TJ. "C'mon, I gotta show you what's what 'round these parts."

Ayodeji gave each of his friends a shake and a dap that included that same trick with the wind and fire—this time, the counselors couldn't say they weren't allowed. Then, without waiting or even looking back, Ayodeji walked off farther into the camp.

TJ quickly thanked Mr. Bolawe again and slung his bags over his shoulders. He jogged behind Ayodeji, catching up to the boy just before an area that looked like it was set up for a military boot camp. Ayodeji explained the setup was for *Ere Idaraya* training, which he described to basically be physical education on steroids.

"Miss Graves is our drill sergeant," Ayodeji droned as he lazily hopped between a set of old tires laid out on the ground. "That broad who was chewing me out."

"Miss Graves. Got it." TJ followed alongside him, avoiding the tires.

"The breakdown here is pretty simple," Ayodeji went on. "The scrubs are at elementary level, mostly for the five to seven-year-olds." After his last hop and skip, he lifted two fingers. "Then there's the intermediates for the eight to eleven-year-olds, though sometimes people get held back, like that Jamaican girl Marie did last year." He stuck out a third finger. "Then there's the preparatory levels for those trying to get into one of the magic schools."

Next, they passed a large clearing of manicured grass with white lines around it. The field was sandwiched between a thicket of trees and mossy rocks. TJ recognized the markings on the ground for the favored magical sport in West Africa, Eshu's crossover. Ayodeji called the playing field a pitch, the first slip up in his fake American accent.

Farther down the path, they passed by a massive lagoon that Ayodeji called Olosa's Domain. It twinkled in the afternoon light, and TJ thought he might have seen something glow just under the placid waters for a short moment. He found himself gawking at it a step too long as a faint buzzing swirled in his ears, and he nearly bumped into Ayodeji in the process. But he stopped himself with a locked knee just before he collided with the boy's lumpy back.

"None of the campers are allowed there unless under adult supervision," Ayodeji said as he continued on.

All the while, as he pointed out each landmark, he drawled with a tone of utter disinterest. And anytime he mentioned the curriculum, he acted as though it was beneath him, like he was supposed to be somewhere else. Priest Glover's proclamations about the camp being remedial started to sink in the more Ayodeji talked down on the various classes and activities.

"Baby stuff," he kept saying over and over. "Ifa Academy is way more challenging."

TJ didn't care. If anything, it was better that way. It meant the elders and counselors expected less from the campers, not like what he'd be put through if he was actually going to Ifa, where they studied all sorts of advanced magic. Here, he could probably just clean up a puddle of dirty swamp water and get good grades.

"So, who's your Orisha?" Ayodeji asked as they finally approached the boys' cabins.

The wooden shacks, like the dock, canted at odd angles, their foundations sunk deep into the murky swamp. A long row of wooden slats led from the half-mud, half-grass earth to mid-lake where the cabins seemed to float, reflected against the waters.

As TJ took his first step, the wood squeaked underfoot. He highly doubted the path to their lodgings was very secure, but like everything else in this place, it held together despite all logic saying it should break apart.

"What did you say?" TJ asked, distracted by his precarious

balancing act.

Ayodeji walked the path like it was as flat and even as a city block sidewalk. "I asked who's your Orisha."

"Oh, that… the priest who saw me says he doesn't know yet."

"But you've got Ashe, right?" Ayodeji asked suspiciously.

"Oh, yeah… a bunch."

Ayodeji considered TJ's response with pursed lips. He probably didn't believe him, but he continued anyway. "My family has strong ties to Shango."

TJ had no trouble recognizing *that* Orisha. Shango was perhaps the most famous and well-known Orisha with his power of lightning and his key traits of confidence and strength. Mom always said he was overrated despite his great power.

It was no wonder Ayodeji thought himself aligned with him.

With a slight scowl on his face, TJ followed behind Ayodeji as they passed by another weathered sign that read: BOYS' CABIN. A row of four cabins stretched along the wooden porch.

"That first one's for the male instructors and guests." Ayodeji pointed casually. "This next one is for the scrubs, and that one after that is for the intermediate campers."

Each of the cabins was narrow and long, every door topped with a wooden carving TJ assumed was a depiction of Olosa, the Orisha of the Lagoon. She was long-haired and young. Jumping fish and alligators flanked her to the left and right. TJ had to walk back and forth twice to realize that each carving—Orishas, fish, and alligators alike—followed his every move. One Olosa carving even waved to him.

Already this camp was giving him the creeps, and the first day hadn't even started yet.

"How about your family?" Ayodeji asked as he knocked on the last cabin door at the end of the row, which TJ assumed was for the teenagers at preparatory levels, like them. "What's their Orisha?"

TJ dropped his bags at his feet. "My mother speaks to Yemoja, and my sister was closest with Orunmila, I think."

"That's what's up, that's what's up." Ayodeji bobbed his head with approval.

For the first time, he really took TJ in. TJ didn't realize that those two Orishas commanded so much respect. He always figured they weren't flashy enough to garner much interest.

"Yo!" Ayodeji knocked on the cabin door again. "Elder Wale, where you at?" He cupped his hand around his mouth and muttered to TJ. "The old dude stay sleepin'. He says he needs his beauty rest or whatever. But when you see him, you'll know that shit clearly ain't working for him. Just remember to always look at his left eye."

"What's wrong with his right eye?"

"It's a little… slow to catch up, you feel me?" Ayodeji let out a small chuckle and hit TJ across the shoulder. TJ knew he was supposed to laugh, but he just didn't find the boy all that funny. "Hey, I never asked. What's your family name?"

"Young," TJ answered. "Tomori Jomiloju Young is my full name, but I just go by TJ most of the time."

Ayodeji's expression changed completely, all humor erased from his round face. He lifted his sunglasses from his eyes, revealing them to be brown and fierce. "You're shittin' me, aren't you?"

"Um…" TJ looked between the cabin and the trees as though they could give him a better answer. "Um… No? No, I'm—I'm not messin' with you."

"You're related to *the* Ifedayo?"

"Mmhm."

An uneasy silence passed between the two as Ayodeji ogled, and TJ did his best not to appear too uncomfortable.

"Don't think just 'cause your sister was some prodigy that'll give you special treatment here," Ayodeji finally said, his previous drone all but evaporated under a new heat.

TJ raised an eyebrow. "What are you talking about?"

"Only one or two campers get picked to go to Ifa Academy at the end of the summer." In the boy's anger, he forgot to cover up his Nigerian accent for once. "Last year, they didn't even take no one. A few got taken to that Hughes school, but who'd want to go there? But this year's gonna be different. And one of their selections is gonna be me."

For a moment, TJ thought about just standing there and saying nothing to see how Ayodeji reacted. He was about to tell the boy he didn't know anything about special treatment or selection processes when the cabin door swung open, and a wily-looking old man stuck his head out, speaking gibberish.

"*Wha-goin-on-ada-hurr?*" he bellowed. "Ol' Sally come through here again?"

Ayodeji was right about the lazy eye. This must've been Elder Wale.

"Nah," Ayodeji responded. He stared TJ dead in the eye. "It's just fresh meat ready to get chomped up and spit out again."

15

MORNIN' ON THE BAYOU

THAT NIGHT AFTER EVERYONE GOT SETTLED, TJ SAID GOODBYE TO Mom, who attacked him with a dozen more kisses right in the middle of the boys' cabin. After an hour of "mama's boy" from the broken records that were Ayodeji and his tall friends, LaVont and Jimoh, Elder Wale called "lights out."

TJ slumped his head against his pillow, turned, then slumped again. It was the dozenth time in the span of a minute. He just couldn't sleep with Ayodeji's words of "fresh meat" stuck in his mind, playing back on repeat.

All the other boys were knocked out. There were fourteen others, not including TJ; he was one of two new boys to the preparatory level group. The other was a big fluff of a boy named Joshua Reed, who snored for two hours straight. It didn't help that, as the other new kid, they bunked him with TJ.

TJ pressed his pillow to his ears and rolled to the rest of the cabin where the other campers slept. Some boys, like Ayodeji, were there on "academic probation"—basically rejects from Ifa Academy or elsewhere. But most, like the mousey boy named Stephen Christopher, had been going to Camp Olosa since they were kids, never getting accepted anywhere. TJ thought of them as the OG rejects. Had he manifested his magic a little sooner, he might've been just like Stephen, attending Camp Olosa without moving on up. The boy seemed happy about it, though. Before they slept, he talked about all the things they'd do that summer, from lake time to dodgeball to storytelling at the end of each day around a bonfire.

TJ couldn't help noticing that none of the things he was excited for pertained to magic.

Ayodeji hadn't been any nicer in the second half of the day. The boy didn't seem like the most friendly person TJ ever knew to start, but he couldn't forget how Ayodeji's tone completely changed when TJ mentioned his sister's name.

TJ was lucky to be accepted to Camp Olosa to begin with, but getting to the big school? That was something else. But... what if he could pull it off?

He just needed to be the best of the worst.

Mom would've been so proud. His brother would stop making fun of him. And he might just have a sliver of what Dayo had. Maybe he could continue whatever she was doing before. And if the Keepers showed up again, he'd know some *real* magic. The kind of magic where he didn't have to hide behind overturned chairs at a funeral. The kind of magic where he could stand shoulder to shoulder with Mom, or Elder Adeyemi, or Mr. Bolawe, who'd direct them all.

But a nagging voice in his mind told him he was wrong, that he would fail. Ayodeji probably thought TJ was some prodigy like his sister. The moment TJ attempted his first camp activity that would be it. He'd be exposed. Then everyone would know he was nothing like his sister. Everyone would know he was a loser who was only good enough to be some silly lucky charm.

But he still had a few hours before any of that would happen.

After realizing he'd get no sleep, he pulled out the only book required for the camp: *Ashe - A Guide for Everyday Diviners by Amos Isola*. TJ had read the first chapter before coming to camp, but even the exercises on the first few pages were too much for him. Reading it a second time didn't help, and the light was so low he had to squint.

"What does that say..." he murmured to himself.

"*Before we begin, we must first observe before all things, our ancestors and our Orisha,*" a voice from nowhere rang out. It took TJ a moment to realize that his book had emitted the scholarly disembodied voice of Amos Isola herself. "*And before we create a relationship with our Orisha, we must give an offering to Eshu first and—*"

TJ slammed the book shut before any of the other boys woke.

"That was incredibly rude," the book said, voice muffled.

TJ had heard Mom's books speaking out loud to her, mainly in the kitchen when she made breakfast on the weekends, but he'd never had a book of his own talk back to him.

TJ dipped his head to the cover and whispered, "You're going to wake everyone up."

"Well, how am I expected to be heard if I whisper?" it muffled again.

But TJ didn't answer, deciding to try again in the morning when his mind was clearer.

But between TJ's nerves and the snoring of Joshua, there was no way he was going to cop any z's. He tried staring at the wooden slats above his head to find rest in their boring design, but it didn't help when Joshua's heavy breathing creaked against the wood.

The snoring and creaking wouldn't have been so bad if there wasn't also the annoying chirping of crickets just outside the *closed* windows, though from the sound of them, you'd think they were under his bed. The crickets in Los Angeles weren't nearly as loud. But here in the swamp, it sounded like an insect horde was meeting to take over the world.

If this is how the night was going, his first day was going to suck. He had initially thought everyone at camp would be late bloomers like him. But thinking back on that little kid, Gary, he knew that wasn't the case. Maybe no one here was advanced, but they were, at worst, ordinary—by magical standards.

In the few hours TJ had spent on the campgrounds, he'd seen several campers use magic casually with each other. Things that seemed impossible to TJ—like lighting lanterns with a snap of a finger or communicating with birds to see what kind of bread was their favorite—were mere child's play to everyone else.

The other boys seemed nice, but TJ thought that was just because of his sister. Everyone already seemed to know he was Ifedayo's little brother, and there was already talk among the other campers of what TJ was capable of doing. He'd even heard Stephen Christopher whisper something about Ol' Sally backing down from him because his irises glowed red like lava.

All attention was on him.

It was the last thing he wanted.

After a few more hours in his bunk, the crickets seemed to quiet, and Joshua's snoring downgraded from sustained moans to stuttered grunts. TJ's eyes, finally, grew heavy as he drifted to a much needed—

"Wake up! Wake up!" bellowed Elder Wale in chorus with a cowbell.

TJ groaned. Had he slept at all? His heart fluttered with exhaustion and utter fatigue. He would've thought the old man's booming voice was almost sing-songy if he, TJ, wasn't so cranky.

Just to Elder Wale's left, another young man who must've barely been out of high school waved a mossy staff in the air and shouted, "Let's go, Cabin Four!"

His name was Franklin—TJ had learned yesterday—the assistant counselor of Cabin Four and Stephen Christopher's older brother. Ayodeji called the brothers professional losers. His mossy, dingy-looking staff didn't help to dispel that argument.

"Let's go! Another summer! Mo' learnin', mo' knowledge," shouted the junior counselor. His voice was thin and oddly reedy, a perfect match for his lanky body. TJ had only said a brief hello to him the day before. The only thing he knew about him was that he went by the name of Juice—only the Orishas knew why.

The cowbells continued their heavy ringing, but TJ couldn't see where they came from. Then his eyes traveled up, just above each of the counselor's staffs, which swayed back and forth. A trio of bells floated above them of their own accord, swaying in unison with the counselor's staffs as they moved back and forth.

TJ's shoulders weighed down like bricks as he pulled his blanket over his head. Maybe if he hid well enough while the other boys woke up, he could catch a few more minutes of sleep. Just a few more minutes would be enough...

But as soon as he relaxed, his blanket flew into the air and folded itself under his bed. Cold, morning air nipped at TJ's feet. He turned his head to see how his very warm blanket was stolen from him, only to find Elder Wale's mismatched eyes inches from his face.

Despite his best courtesies, TJ screamed and fell out of bed.

"Gets the fresh meat every time," the elder cackled, holding his side.

He turned to the other beds and waved his staff at each of them. Blanket after blanket flung off each boy, all of which woke up with quick and sudden stirs, though none of them were nearly as surprised as TJ. Joshua, as far as TJ could tell, hadn't moved at all, still snoring louder than even the bells tolled.

"All right, boys," Elder Wale said. "Let's get this place cleaned up."

A few minutes later, when TJ finally got his first foot out of bed, Joshua peered down from the top bunk. Everything about his face was wide, his nose, ears, eyes, forehead, you name it. Yet, there was an innocent quality to his pudgy cheeks that made him seem easygoing.

"You sleep okay, TJ?" he asked with a yawn.

TJ rubbed his eyes languidly. "I've slept better…"

"Sorry," Joshua hefted himself from his bed and landed with a thud next to TJ. "My uh… mom forgot to pack my nose clips. I gotta ask one of the counselors if I can call her to send me some."

"It's okay, really," TJ reassured him, but his drooping head said otherwise.

Joshua dipped his thick fingers under TJ's armpits and lifted him in one tug, setting TJ upright. "Wale got you good, didn't he?" Joshua asked under the start of a giggle. TJ didn't answer, doing his best to hide the shock still wearing off from the elder's surprise. "Don't worry about it. He does that to all the new campers. You get used to it."

"Aren't you new here too?"

"Yeah, yeah. I just heard the other campers saying Wale's crazy," he said nervously, then awkwardly patted TJ on the back, grabbed his toothbrush, and ambled to the bathroom. TJ followed suit, grabbing his travel bag.

He trudged to the back of the cabin, where two lines formed for the bathroom, one for the showers and the other for the sinks. Through the other boys' shoulders, he could see the others washing their faces with floating towels. Their toothbrushes ran up and down their teeth, hovering on their own.

"That's pretty cool," TJ said to Joshua. "The towels are self-washing?"

Joshua turned his head with a raised eyebrow. "Self-washing? For *this* camp? Hah! Enchanted towels are expensive. Nah, we gotta enchant everything ourselves. It's easy, though—just don't last all that long."

Just then, one boy's towel fell into the sink. He picked it back up, said some words TJ couldn't hear, and the towel started digging the sleep from the boy's eyes again. Not wanting to be seen doing his morning routine without magic, TJ took a sidestep to the shower line instead.

"Hey, where are you going?" Joshua asked.

TJ smacked his head theatrically. "I-I thought I was in line for the showers. I'm a morning shower kind of dude."

That was a lie, of course. TJ just figured he could do all his bathing, teeth brushing, face washing, and all that in the privacy of a shower. He still had a few hours before he'd have to embarrass himself—no need to do it first thing in the morning.

16

MISS GRAVÉS

AT BREAKFAST, JOSHUA WOLFED DOWN A LARGE POTATO OMELET, a lop of grits, a bunch of sweet potato waffles, a tower of biscuits covered in gravy, all with a tiny cup of orange juice.

"Only thing this meal is missing is some yams," he said as he downed his first cup.

TJ sat staring at him with his mouth agape. Then he pushed over his own cup of apple juice. "Here, take it."

"Thanks, man," Joshua said through a mouthful of egg. "But I'm telling you, you didn't need to give me your juice. And the first session for preparatory levels is with Miss Gravés. You'll need all the energy you can get. I heard she has us—"

"It's okay, Joshua." TJ lifted a hand to shield his face from the flecks of potato coming from Joshua's mouth. "I wasn't hungry, anyway."

TJ's stomach was empty, and he had no appetite. He wasn't even sure how he was supposed to prepare for the first session. His schedule simply read Ere Idaraya Training, something he could not understand. He remembered Ayodeji mentioning something about it but couldn't recall what it translated to. It could have said they were training to fight killer trees, or something about cleaning out Ol' Sally's mouth, for all he knew.

A half-hour later, TJ quickly realized there were no tree men nor any giant alligators.

It was worse.

It was physical education.

Miss Gravés must've lied on her application to Camp Olosa. She wasn't a diviner; she really *was* a drill sergeant. Just like Ayodeji said.

In the space of twenty minutes, she had the campers doing butt kicks, flutter kicks, burpees, crab walks, and lunges one after the other with no breaks—well, except for the stationary forearm planks, TJ's favorite. But each time he caught his breath, it was onto the next workout. Worse, she didn't count their reps like a normal P.E. teacher. Instead, using a military count of one, two, and three before counting a single rep.

"One, two, three," she would shout.

"One," the campers would call out.

"One, two, three," she'd bellow again.

"Two," the campers echoed.

And on and on it went. TJ's entire body felt like it was on fire from within. His sweat did a poor job cooling him down, and his stomach grumbled loudly. TJ placed a hand to his belly, apologizing to his body for not giving it any food.

He should've listened to Joshua's advice. But the large boy didn't look like he was doing any better. He clutched at his own stomach like he was suffering from a cramp. Then, suddenly, all of his breakfast came up on the grass in a sludge.

For a moment, TJ thought the boy had second servings at breakfast just so he could throw up and get dismissed. Even if that was his intention, Miss Gravés didn't care.

She sat him up straight, used her staff to clean up his mess, and turned to the class. "All right, everyone," she said with hands at her hips. Sweat beaded her forehead, but she didn't breathe heavily or hunch over like the rest of the campers. "Let's take thirty."

"Oh, thank God," TJ gasped, falling back on the grass in a heap. He didn't even get this much exercise in his own school. Did Mom leave him at the right camp? All of this was feeling like some military academy.

"Don't get too comfortable. She means thirty seconds, not thirty minutes," a voice labored to his side.

TJ turned his head to a girl who was red in the face, her curly hair pulled back in a tight bun. It wasn't until she smiled at him with two deep dimples that he recognized her as Manuela.

She looked different from the day before. For one, her golden tips had been re-dyed to match the rest of her dark hair. And yesterday, she wore lip gloss, and her bushy hair had covered the frame of her heart-shaped face. And now her dashiki-designed tank top exposed her toned arms, and her perfect legs stretched long against the grass.

"Hey, Manuela... right?" TJ asked. He strained his voice, fighting against the fatigue that threatened to make him sound wheezy. Not smooth at all.

Manuela winced like she heard something offensive. "No, only my parents call me Manuela—mostly when I'm in trouble, or when they try being formal. Just... Manny is fine."

"I'm sorry, uh... Manny." TJ lost the battle with his cracking voice. He almost stopped talking altogether after that, but he wanted to make himself clear. "I didn't mean to—"

"All right, break's over," Miss Gravés announced with a clap of her hands. Manny wasn't joking about the thirty seconds. "Everyone, line up behind me. We're going to start today's assessment: Your mile run."

The campers groaned and shuffled behind her. TJ searched for Manny, but she was already high stepping toward Miss Gravés, stopping only to stretch out her muscles every other step.

So much for making good impressions. Maybe he could run alongside Manny and make up for the misuse of her name. He knew all too well about preferences for nicknames.

"Damn, she bad," TJ heard Ayodeji say from the side with his friends.

"Bet you can't get her number, though," LaVont told him.

Ayodeji sucked his teeth. "Shooooot, I stay gettin' numbers, bro. Trust."

Nerves rippled through TJ. Of course the other boys at camp would've noticed Manny too. And TJ never did well with competition.

"I don't expect most of you kept up with your exercises at school," Miss Gravés announced as she twisted her hips and arms. "The grading scale is the same as always. Complete your run within a minute of mine for top marks. For every thirty seconds thereafter, your grade will fall a full letter. Got it?"

"Got it..." a few campers droned in unison.

TJ leaned into Joshua, who lumbered to his side. There was still a bit of vomit on the edge of his lip. "How fast does Miss Gravés usually run her miles?"

Joshua raised his eyes into the morning sun, looking for an answer. "I think I heard she averages a little over seven minutes. Under, on a good day."

"What!?" TJ blurted as Gravés started her run.

The rest of the campers shoved him as they rushed after her, leaving TJ with his mouth hanging open. The best he ever did at school was ten and a half minutes flat. And apparently, even running a *nine*-minute mile was only considered barely passing.

TJ had to remind himself that he needed to catch up to Manny. So he dug in his heels and pelted off with the fastest sprint he could muster.

That was a mistake.

Mile runs were a test of endurance, not pure speed. Within half a lap, he was already gassed, and he barely got twenty yards from the leading group, which included Gravés, Manny, and a few others.

TJ had to give Miss Gravés credit. All the P.E. teachers he ever had sat on their asses and yelled at their students to work harder. From the start of their session, she did everything with her campers, no matter what she asked of them.

Within two laps, Miss Gravés passed TJ, kicking up dirt as she blazed by. "Come on, Mr. Young, use them Daddy Long Legs of yours."

He didn't know how she did it. It wasn't like she was running exactly, just jogging very fast. Even her casual run was faster than TJ's sprint.

Second to pass him was Manny, who trailed behind Gravés by several yards. TJ tried to kick up his speed to match her and speak to her again, but his gangly chicken legs screamed in protest. It didn't help that the surrounding swamp was humid and sticky, making his dashiki tank top stick to his skin like glue.

At least he could find solace that he wasn't the slowest camper. Behind him, Joshua and Ayodeji dragged their feet, complaining all the while.

"Why. Is. This. So. Hard!" Joshua shouted at his feet.

"This is stupid," Ayodeji heaved from behind when TJ rounded his third lap. "This ain't got nothin' to do with my Ashe."

After another lap and a few dry heaves, TJ finally approached the last leg. He glanced behind him to see if Manny would lap him again, but he couldn't see her anywhere. He looked ahead instead, searching for her hair bun. He dropped his jaw when he saw her only twenty yards ahead of him.

How did that happen?

She was nearly keeping pace with Gravés, who was already doing a post-stretch that looked like some sort of complicated yoga. So how was it that TJ was about to catch up? Maybe Manny burned herself out as he had. Yet that didn't make sense either. Her pace definitely looked more lumbered, but she didn't look exhausted like the other campers, free of any haggard breaths.

"Hey, Miss Martinez!" Miss Gravés called out. "I see you doggin' it. Pick it up. We both know you're better than that."

When TJ finished with the best time in his life—ten minutes and twenty-six seconds—he was shocked to hear Manny finished with a ten flat. As Ayodeji came in with his eleven-fifty-two and Joshua with his twelve-twelve, Miss Gravés declared her final run time was six minutes and fifty-five seconds. TJ didn't need to do the math to know he failed—even though he totally did do the math. But for Manny, he guessed she got a "D" or close to it.

Everyone caught their breath, gasping for air and hunching over like the grass below them would somehow give them extra air. Joshua sounded like he had a frog in his throat, and TJ did his best to inhale long and deep as his father had shown him.

Thinking on it, Dad would've loved Miss Gravés.

"Ere Idaraya probably won't be your favorite subject this year," Gravés said, continuing her pretzel-shaped stretches. "But it will be the most important to establish a solid foundation for your connection to the Orishas and our Ashe."

"I'm sorry, but I don't see how jogging helps me do magic," Ayodeji complained, his designer glasses slipping off his nose. He slumped over on his side, and it looked like Victoria Falls was crashing down from his braided topknot.

Miss Gravés gave him a smirk, looking as though she was waiting for that very response. "Oh sure, you'll be able to get off a few spells, maybe a nice long ritual. But keep it up, and you'll get tired real quick. Drawing from Ashe takes a toll on the human body. What we do as diviners is more than just saying words or waving staffs. Our magic is spirit-based, and it can drain one quickly if ill-prepared."

"But my bàbà tells me none of this matters once we get our staffs," Ayodeji retorted.

"That's true... to an extent. Staffs do funnel much of the Ashe that drains us, but we should never depend on them. They are a tool, an extension, but I've seen too many diviners rely on their staffs only to find their talent without them diminished." TJ's shameful thoughts trailed back to his cabin, where he hid his sister's staff. "What if, for instance, you're disarmed of your staff? Elders like Akande and Adeyemi can still function almost as well without one."

"Shooooot," Ayo smacked his lips, "I *wish* someone tried to disarm me."

TJ couldn't help thinking back to the Keepers at the funeral. He'd bet they all were more than capable of disarming a fourteen-year-old. They must've been just as fit as Miss Gravés, too, with all the dueling they must've done. If TJ wanted to be good enough to face them one day, he knew he'd need to take Miss Gravés's words to heart. Tomorrow, he'd get his mile within a passing grade no matter how much his legs throbbed.

17

MR. DU BOIS

WHEN MISS GRAVÉS DISMISSED THE STUDENTS, TJ ONLY HAD A few minutes to rush back to his cabin to shower, switch out of his dashiki tank top to a traditional dashiki, and hustle to his next class: *Ogbon* Studies.

As TJ stepped into the Ogbon cabin, aromas of sweet basil mixed with cinnamon-scented incense met him. The space was a large one, able to seat thirty campers at a time, just enough for the boys and girls who filed in one after the other. Each seat was designed with blue and white beaded diamond shapes, and a tiny desk rested just before each. Several odd crowns with U-shaped beads hanging from underneath lined the wall over a blackboard. TJ recognized them as Olosa masks.

TJ took a deep breath. If there was any time for him to do some cramming from his book, this would be it.

"Yes, take it all in," said their instructor, Mr. Du Bois, the mean-looking counselor with the slicked-back hair and glasses. He wore a slouched fìlà cap of white with a matching dashiki. The man's tone seemed kinder today, less stern than the day before when he was confiscating Ayodeji's personal items. "Let the fragrances clear your mind. I trust you can all find your seats."

TJ looked for a seat close to Manny, but by the time he saw her, she was already sandwiched between the Santos Sisters—the albino twins from the day before. He didn't know how she did it, but in the ten minutes between their first and second class, she had reapplied a full—yet subtle—face of makeup, and her hair hung loose around her shoulders with orange dye tips as though she never had it in a bun before.

Turning to look for another seat, TJ saw Ayodeji at the front of the class, a position he'd never thought to see the boy in. There was a seat open next to him, but TJ sure as hell wasn't going to take it.

He twisted his head to the right of the class where Joshua, who coughed loudly into a tissue, sat. He must've still been getting over all that running. A quartet of unoccupied chairs surrounded the large boy. None of the other students sat within seven feet of him.

TJ didn't see many other choices, and Joshua was friendly enough to him, so he slid into one of the seats next to him. The moment TJ rested his behind in what he discovered was a very comfortable chair, he instantly regretted it.

If he thought *he* had smelled bad, it was nowhere near to the stench coming from Joshua's pit stains. And each time he coughed, it seemed to spread the funk in a seven-foot radius. As rude as the boy's stink was, TJ didn't have the heart to move away when he had just sat down. It also didn't help that Joshua immediately started chatting up a storm the moment TJ took his seat.

"I hear this class is way easier," he said in a blurt. "So long as you can keep up with everything Mr. D says, you'll be all right. He's very clear, but he has one rule—"

"I do not repeat myself twice. So, listen closely," Mr. Du Bois announced.

"Yup, that's the one," Joshua said as he jabbed his pencil toward the instructor.

TJ took out his book and hoisted it onto his desk. "So, did I need to read the first chapter before coming in today?"

"Oh no, we don't do anything with Ashe in this class. It's mostly brain teasers, some philosophy, debate, a bit of math, language—"

"Are you sure this is a camp for diviners?" TJ questioned. "This is feeling a lot like regular—"

"Did you have a question, Mr. Young?" That stern voice returned to Mr. Du Bois's lips.

TJ shifted in his seat toward the instructor, who had already started writing on the blackboard.

"Sorry, sir. I was asking Joshua if—"

"Funny," Mr. Du Bois cut in. "I didn't know Mr. Reed was instructing the class." TJ swallowed hard. "If you have a question, young man, you direct it to me, and only me. And Mr. Reed," His pencil-thin mustache disappeared into his pursed lips, "Refrain from distracting the other students."

"Sorry, Mr. D, just catching him up," Joshua said, smiling.

"What did you just call me?" Mr. Du Bois said, appalled.

"Du Bois, Du Bois," Joshua spluttered, completely butchering the name. "My bad. I'm bad with the French. It don't come out right with this mouth."

"Ooooo!" cooed one of the students. Their exclamation was met with a few stints of laughter. TJ didn't lift his head to look to see who was making fun of them, but he couldn't help catching a slitted expression coming from Ayodeji and his friends LaVont and Jimoh.

Oh, what TJ would have paid to smack that wry smirk off the boy's face.

For the rest of class, TJ waited until Ayodeji talked out of turn or got an answer incorrect just so he could do some gloating of his own. Yet the boy was an ace with each subject, each activity, from Mr. Du Bois's riddles to his advanced algebra instruction. The kid was in his element, always first to raise his hand. TJ thought he must've been trying to make up for his astronomical fail during the mile run with Miss Graves. After all, *"one of Ifa's selections was gonna be him,"* right?

TJ still couldn't fathom how any of this related to Ashe or Orishas. Worse yet, as "normal" as it was, the curriculum was well above the material he was learning in his regular school district, even if he was in a charter school.

Just as TJ was about to raise his hand to ask when they'd learn something, well, magical, Mr. Du Bois wrote the word "Ori" on the board with three underlines beneath it.

"Who can tell me what this is?" Mr. Du Bois asked the class.

Again, Ayodeji's hand shot straight into the air, but this time Du Bois was looking for other participants. For the first time, TJ felt he knew the answer. Slowly, he raised his hand in the air, and Mr. Du Bois pointed his piece of chalk at him.

"It means…" TJ swallowed deeply. At the corner of his vision, he could see more than enough eyes on him to make him sweat; Manny's among them. "It means the Wise and Sacred head."

"That's a base definition, surface level. You can do better. Tell me more of what it *really* means."

"I—I…" TJ stuttered.

Wise and sacred was the best he could come up with.

"That won't cut it, Mr. Young. You're in preparatory levels, not with the children. Though, if you wish to join them, that could be arranged. There's no shame in starting from the basics."

That one stung TJ.

Ayodeji stifled a laugh before he raised his hand again. When no one else dared to say their piece, Mr. Du Bois finally settled on the boy.

Once called on, Ayodeji sat straight up in his chair. TJ noticed that his Nigerian accent came through clearly when he answered questions. "While yes, ori in Yoruba simply means head, the term is multi-faceted, especially how it's applied to our connection to our Ashe and, more importantly, the Orisha. Ori resides in two parts, the inner and outer head. Ori also relates to the destiny bestowed on us from birth—"

"All right, all right, slow down," Mr. Du Bois chuckled, writing down Ayodeji's answer on the board as fast as his chicken scratch could go. "Yes, Mr. Oyelowo. That is correct. And do you know why it's so important that we train with ori daily?"

Ayodeji shook his head. Finally, something he didn't know.

"*Ori la ba bo, a ba f'orisa sile*," Mr. Du Bois said in Yoruba. "For those of you not yet fluent in the tongue, it means, 'it is the inner self we ought to venerate and let divinity be.'"

Du Bois set a knuckled grip on his hip. "This summer, you will be challenged, perhaps beyond your comfort level. But remember, it is not the Orishas who empower us; it's *this*." He pointed to his head with his chalk, and a bit of dust came away at his cap. "Put your mind first, and the Orisha will come, do you understand?" His large eyes reflected through his glasses, waiting for the campers to nod affirmation. "We may sound like broken records to you—I'm sure Miss Graves already explained it from her perspective—but we are more than our mystical abilities. If you truly want to succeed in this camp and, for some of you beyond that, you'll do well to remember this. You need to clear your ori. Just as you've learned to feed your body, you will learn to feed your minds here. All these things are connected."

Mr. Du Bois let a silence settle in the room, giving the students time to process what they heard. TJ thought he had a better understanding of it all now, yet that still didn't make it easier to swallow. Camp Olosa wasn't going to be as easy as saying "hocus pocus." It was going to take hard work and a discipline he wasn't sure he had.

"And with that," Mr. Du Bois said as he took a glance at his watch. "You are dismissed."

Desks scrapped, chatter swelled, and the campers started out.

Mr. Du Bois cupped his hand over his mouth. "And remember, if any of you need additional help, the camp offers tutoring after lunch period."

Those last words sounded like they were meant specifically for TJ, and he blushed for it.

⁜

A FEW MINUTES LATER, TJ AND JOSHUA WALKED TOGETHER TO their next activity: *Emi* Guidance. The session took place through the whispering willows wood and just off the camp's largest lagoon, which Ayodeji had called "Olosa's Domain" the day before.

"Sorry about getting you in trouble back there," Joshua said as they entered under the willows.

They passed a group of child campers who trotted from the woods toward what TJ assumed was their own Ogbon instruction. Some of them were using their dashiki as headscarves to cover themselves from the near-noon sun, to which their junior counselor scolded them to put them back on.

Oh, to be young again, TJ thought. *No worries, no cares.*

"Don't mention it." TJ waved a dismissive hand toward Josh. "I don't think Mr. Du Bois ever liked me to begin with."

"Nah, he seems all right with you." Joshua patted him on the back. "But did you see the way he came at *me*?"

TJ sighed. "He seemed fine with Ayodeji."

"Well," Joshua shrugged, "he got everything right, didn't he?"

TJ thought again of what they would have to do in the next session, *A Guide for Everyday Diviners* prominent on his mind. The first exercise in the book detailed the ability to stave off hiccups, but as soon as TJ realized their next session was at the lagoon, he figured they'd be doing something water-based or some sort of protection against parasites or leeches within the swamp.

The book's concepts seemed easy enough, but TJ always found concepts easier to grasp than active practice. Now that he thought of the lagoon yesterday, which had looked like a cesspool ready to swallow him whole, he wasn't so sure.

As TJ and Joshua continued across the main lawn, through Miss Gravés's rope-slung obstacle course, and through a second thicket of trees, TJ overheard other students complaining about the next class through a second thicket of trees.

"Ugh, I wish we could skip this one," one of the Santos Sisters said.

The mousey Stephen nodded in agreement. "Maybe Old Man Whittaker finally slipped and broke a hip."

"No way," she replied. "Elder Akande says he's built like a lion."

TJ tilted his head to Joshua. "Who's Old Man Whittaker?"

"Oh, if you thought Mr. D was bad, Old Man Whittaker is supposed to be four-times worse." The treeline thinned, revealing spots of the lagoon. "He's a miserable old dude. And he don't take no kind of nonsense."

"How do you know so much about this camp?" TJ asked Joshua.

TJ thought he did his homework thoroughly, but Joshua came far more prepared.

"Research, man. Research," he said. "Plus, a lot of my kind—erm, us Reeds—have been through here."

"Why aren't you at Ifa or one of the other academies?"

"I'll tell you about it later. What you *should* be asking is how to deal with Whittaker. We both know we won't do well with that drill sergeant this summer. And we can get better with Mr. D's class, that's just studying, but now we're gonna do some actual magic. We'll want to get on the old man's good side if we're gonna ask for extra help."

TJ imagined an old man with a large white beard, a humpback, bags under his eyes, and a few missing teeth—the kind of old man that looked like they never smiled in their life. He could almost hear the voice of the imagined instructor, reedy and gruff at the same time.

But when they arrived at the lagoon, there was no decrepit-looking elder. In fact, the other veteran campers seemed to be smiling, a few of them even hopping in place.

"See, he did kick it," Stephen squealed.

"That's rude!" Manny called out.

Stephen stopped his heel-toe skip and frowned.

Ayodeji pushed forward with his arms crossed. "So who's the instructor then?"

A rustling came from the treeline just off the lagoon. A few campers whooped, converging on the newcomer. When TJ finally got a good look at who they saw, he too couldn't help but beam.

"Mr. Bolawe? Is that really you?"

18

MR. BOLAWE

TJ STOOD DUMBSTRUCK FOR WHAT FELT LIKE A BRIEF ETERNITY. Mr. Bolawe just kept smiling with sweat on his brow and soaking through his white dashiki. Most of the other female campers didn't seem to know who he was, but some of the boys did, all of them nodding their approval.

"Excuse my tardiness, class," Mr. Bolawe panted. "Or, um—do you call it a class?"

Several campers shrugged.

"What are you doing here?" TJ asked.

"Yeah, where's the old man?" Ayodeji questioned.

Mr. Bolawe threw his hands to his side. "Sick, I suppose. I thought I'd only be volunteering for the opening day. I was halfway to the airport this morning when I got the call."

Whispers spread within the cluster of campers, each coming up with different theories of where Old Man Whittaker was.

"Maybe he finally retired?" Joshua mumbled in TJ's ear. "Heard he was here even when Louisiana was part of Mexico."

"No way, that guy would have died in the middle of a session if he had the chance," one of the Santos Sisters replied.

"Maybe Director Simmons heard my complaint last year," Ayodeji pushed his glasses up his nose and sneered to one of his friends. "The Old Man probably got fired."

"Okay, campers!" Mr. Bolawe raised his voice—and his hands— once more. "You can take it up with one of the elders if you want to get in contact with Mr. Whittaker."

Ayodeji let out a boisterous laugh, his nose sounding like it'd blow a wad of snot. "Hah! Talk to that old dude? You can miss me with that."

Mr. Bolawe frowned at the boy and crossed his arms. Ayodeji caught on quickly. "I-I mean..." he stuttered. "What I meant to say was... I hope he gets well real soon."

TJ shook his head and shared a look with Joshua, who mimicked the wide eyes on Ayodeji.

"So, what are we going to do first from the book?" TJ curled his hands behind his back, doing his best to remember the first few exercises.

"No need for books today," Mr. Bolawe said, waving away the copies of *A Guide for Everyday Diviners* most students were already pulling out. "I don't know what Elder Whittaker had planned for you all. I'll need a day before I figure out my own lesson plan—if I even need one." He scanned around the marsh casually, his fingers tapping at his thigh. "But maybe that's for the best. I can teach you all the old way, the oral way."

So I didn't need my book at all today, TJ thought with slumped shoulders. *What was all that stress for?*

Mr. Bolawe rubbed his hands together. "Um... right... okay..." It took TJ a moment to realize the man had no plan for them at all as his eyes traveled in a slow triangle between the murky waters, the treeline, and then the campers again and again.

Finally, he pointed near the lagoon's edge. "Oh, duckweed!"

The campers followed the path of his finger to a cluster of odd green plants. TJ would've likened them to tiny lily pads, but slightly thicker.

"Duckweed—also known as *lemnoideae* for you science fanatics— is a perfect representation of the philosophy followed within the Ifa community and Ifa Academy itself. Come, take a closer look."

Mr. Bolawe waved the campers over, encouraging them to inspect the strange wetland plant. "See how they group together? Their benefits are numerous. They provide food for the waterfowls." He nodded to a goose across the lagoon, which was picking and chomping at the duckweed. "They provide shelter for fish and frogs alike." He inclined his head toward a tiny bullfrog just before it ducked its dark eyes beneath the plants with a *plop*. "But perhaps most of all, it helps protect the lagoon from excess evaporation so that Olosa's Domain can remain strong and thriving."

As TJ bent low to the thickly bunched plants, he could see now how they worked in concert with the rest of the wildlife. Many fish-tails appeared and disappeared beneath the duckweed for cover as sparrows tried picking at them. And several birds were gorging themselves on the plants.

A set of giggles ran down the lagoon's edge. TJ tilted his head between the other campers to see Manny and the Santos Sisters playing with a friendly bullfrog which had apparently hopped into Manny's hands.

"I think he likes you," came the voice of one of the twins.

"Kiss him," the other twin said jokingly. "It could be a prince in disguise."

Manny shook her head, her thick curls bouncing to and fro. But she grinned and sniggered all the same as she placed the frog back into the lagoon. When she looked up, she caught TJ's eyes again.

How was she so good at knowing exactly when he was gawking at her?

TJ quickly wiped what was likely a goofy smile off his face and pretended he had been observing a trio of quacking mallards that landed at the far end of the lagoon.

"Yes," Mr. Bolawe continued. "Duckweed is essential for a healthy swamp. But leave it unchecked..." He walked farther down the treeline, where the duckweed huddled thickly. Here, TJ couldn't even see the lagoon under their green mass. "Leave it unchecked, and it can overgrow. And when new duckweed has nowhere to go, it goes down deep into the lagoon. Where before it protected the wildlife, it can quickly suffocate frogs trapped between its clumps. It also hogs the oxygen necessary for the swamp to thrive, killing the fish that rely on it."

He held his hand above the water, stretching his fingers like he was controlling a stringed puppet. And on cue, TJ saw that weird fog swirl between Bolawe's fingers and the swamp below. A few moments passed, and out came a tiny dead fish.

"Left to its own devices, duckweed quickly goes from nurturer to destroyer."

"Why not just get rid of it all?" Ayodeji picked up a clump and threw it into a bush. "That's what my father's doing in Lagos to make room for his development."

Mr. Bolawe's eyes tightened for a moment. Then he let out a long sigh before saying, "Campers, can anyone tell me what would happen if we did that?"

"We'd kill the swamp," TJ spoke up, eyeing Ayodeji as he spoke.

"Getting rid of the duckweed wouldn't help. You need some of it around to feed the geese or cover the frogs. If it was all gone, then…" TJ turned to Bolawe, who gave him a nod, a sign he was on the right track. "Then the balance would be broken."

Mr. Bolawe snapped his fingers. "Mr. Young's got it. That's the key. That's the foundation of Ifa… balance."

TJ had been so used to being wrong the whole day that being right for once felt like fresh air after a rainy day. And at the corner of his eye, he could see a scowl on Ayodeji's face—a very welcome sight.

"At its core," Mr. Bolawe went on, "Ifa, and what we do as diviners, is a struggle between the middle road: the balance between life's extremes. Take water, for example."

Bolawe shot his hand out to the lagoon, forcing the water at its edge to ripple magically. "Like Yemoja, she and it are the mothers of all life. Water sustains us, fills out most of our bodies, most of the world. But water can also be dangerous. It can drown us. It can force us into a sharp rock on the beach without warning or trap us in its white-water rapids."

Mr. Bolawe flipped his hand and spoke an incantation TJ had never heard before: "Ìtusìlẹ̀ òmi." When he said it, it sounded powerful, almost sinister. The gentle ripples cascaded into large waves that crashed against the mossy trees, and mist drizzled onto TJ's face. "So we must always know where we align between these two faces of water, or duckweed, or what have you. We must always be in search of our òrì tútù."

TJ knew what *that* one meant; he heard it from Mom enough. It meant "cool-headedness," the act of being neither too hot nor too cold in any given situation. Again, balanced, poised. Even Dad used that one phrase, though he always compared it to the philosophy of some famous basketball coach named John Wooden.

Turning to the other campers, TJ saw a group of faces he had not seen since the day started. They were… *actually* listening. Even Ayodeji seemed to consider Mr. Bolawe's words in a way he didn't in Mr. Du Bois's class. It wasn't like the kid was being a try-hard to prove himself as he did before, but he was actually interested in learning what he didn't already know. And to think Bolawe had seemed to improvise his lesson plan on the spot—not unlike the way he slapped together his counter against the Keepers at the funeral.

"How do you know so much about this stuff, um, sir?" Joshua asked. His side was damp from the after splash of Bolawe's wave.

Mr. Bolawe gave him a short chuckle, the smile lines on his face creasing deep. "I suppose I know it mostly as an instinct more than anything, a homage to Osain, the Orisha of the Wood. He's my closest alignment. I've always had an affinity for any form of his forests, and forests are the epitome of balance."

He gazed into the lagoon almost longingly, like he had just been speaking to someone or something deep within. "But enough about all that. I'm sure you all would like to learn a spell or two, right?"

The campers nodded vigorously; others gave a subtle "mmhm," while most, including TJ, exclaimed an old-fashioned "yes, sir!" TJ couldn't believe his own exclamation, almost forgetting his nerves altogether.

For the next few minutes, Mr. Bolawe explained how they all could help clear out the duckweed with a simple water-manipulation charm. He demonstrated how he used his fingers the same way someone kneaded bread as a way of parting the waters around the duckweed. Then he reminded them to repeat the phrase *"gbe omi lọ"* as he continued his motion.

"Gbe omi lọ," TJ repeated.

He thought back on Gary, the little boy from the first day, and how he'd done his little dance to manifest water. The boy had said he was doing it "wrong," but the result seemed right enough to TJ. So, maybe he should've done something similar. But what? What would be his own trigger, his own silly little dance?

"We are all differently endowed, Tomori," Mom called out in his head. *"Be secure in who you are."*

And then an idea struck him like a warm shower on a cold morning. Mom had put him through piano lessons back at home as a way to manifest magic out of him—something about music being magic in and of itself or some such. It didn't work then, but perhaps it could at that moment.

He tapped his fingers along an invisible piano, imagining himself playing the only song he had ever gotten right back in piano class: chopsticks. With each downward motion of his hand, he felt a tug on his fingertips, like there was a string attached to a line being pulled by a fish.

Sure enough, just there at the top of the water, a steady set of ripples bubbled to the surface. TJ realized that the benefit of miming the classic piano song was that its in-and-out motion helped pull the water from the bottom of the lagoon bed, where all the duckweed had clustered, and up to the top.

"Just like that, TJ. Great work!" Mr. Bolawe encouraged.

To TJ's surprise, he had been one of the few campers to pull the duckweed to the surface. A flutter came to his stomach, but for once, it wasn't a case of nerves... it was excitement, giddiness. But it didn't last long. Just as TJ was about to thank Mr. Bolawe for the compliment, Ayodeji butted in.

"This is baby stuff," he complained, even as he struggled to part the thick duckweed.

TJ turned back to his charm work. The only way to shut up a kid like Ayodeji was by proving him wrong time and time again. But, thinking back to earlier that morning, Miss Gravés had been right about one thing: Magic. Was. Exhausting.

Sure, Ayodeji wasn't completely wrong—the charm they learned was simple in execution—but the more TJ shifted the waters, the more it felt like something was being drained from him. After only a half dozen tugs of the duckweed, he felt like he had used his brain too much. Had it not been for the combined efforts of the class, he had no idea how someone could clear out the lagoon alone.

Another half-hour passed, and the campers continued to clean up the duckweed where the green mass was thickest, leaving pockets of the plants for the wildlife that thrived on them. When it was nearly time to break for lunch, Mr. Bolawe gathered everyone near a large tree, where they sat down cross-legged in a semi-circle around him.

Though some campers tried to hide it, they were all completely beat. Manny's hair looked like she had just come out of the shower, and Ayodeji's silly little man bun was coming undone around the edges. Surprisingly, it was Joshua who looked the least haggard; if TJ hadn't known any better, he would have thought the kid hadn't participated at all. But, like the others, there was a small mountain of duckweed next to Joshua.

The weariness that ran through TJ was not like the one he felt during that morning's Ere Idaraya Training, however. It was more depletion than exhaustion, like the drain someone felt after singing a song too long or when you shouted too loudly at a concert.

"Before I let you go," Mr. Bolawe started. "I'd like to end our session together with a question... A question I'd like you to think over until we meet again—*if* we meet again." TJ hoped they'd have Mr. Bolawe again. He was easily his favorite counselor that day, and he wasn't even an "official" counselor. "I'd like you all to ponder this... what does Ashe mean to you?"

Mr. Bolawe was a regular ol' hippie with all these questions about balance and the meaning of things, but TJ thought about it for a moment in earnest. For his whole life, the word meant something he could never attain, something that wasn't meant for *him* but meant for his sister, his mother, his brother. Now it took on new meaning. But he wasn't sure how he would redefine it.

Ayodeji lifted his hand in the air eagerly, perhaps keen to earn back points with Mr. Bolawe. With a short incline of his head, Bolawe allowed the boy to speak.

"To me, Ashe means freedom," he started. "It means *I* can be a change in the world. *I* choose my destiny no matter what anyone else says. With Ashe, I have the power to protect my family, my land."

Mr. Bolawe pinched at his lips as he considered the boy's words. "That's an interesting thought. I didn't mean you have to answer right now, of course. I was thinking tomorrow we'd—"

Another hand shot into the air. This one belonged to Manny.

"Family and connection" was all she said at first. Bolawe smirked, crossing his arms and leaning back on his tree. Clearly, he hadn't intended for this to be a conversation, but he seemed willing to hear the campers out anyway. "Ashe connects me, connects all of us together. Without it, we'd have no line to our ancestors, our loved ones."

TJ felt a rush go through his neck as he thought on Dayo again.

"The energy we feel from them... that's Ashe," Manny added. "I know that's not the exact definition, but... that's what I feel. And Ashe *is* feeling at its core, right?"

Through her curls, TJ could see that she had been biting her lips. When she finished talking, she bunched her knees close to her chin as though she expected Mr. Bolawe to debate her interpretation. The man sat there mulling over her response, though, no sign of disagreement on his face.

"And I'd say it's hope," TJ added, his heart pounding quickly as half the class, including Manny, turned to listen. He wasn't even sure how he came up with the word. He had been struggling with his own explanation. Manny's answer sounded right to him, and he couldn't just piggyback off her response. "Sorry, that's all I can come up with. Hope."

But hope made the most sense for him. It *meant* the most to him. Until a few weeks ago, he didn't think he'd amount to much; now, he could pull duckweed from lagoons without using his hands, run a mile under ten and a half minutes, and stare down giant alligators. But most of all, he had the hope he could be as good as his sister.

Mr. Bolawe glanced at the watch on his wrist. Instead of the standard clock hands, it had what looked like a floating galaxy. It didn't make sense to TJ, but it did to Bolawe, apparently, as he said, "And with those last words of hope, our session has ended. Enjoy your lunch break, young ones."

19

A LUNCH FOR TWO

THE TEEN CAMPERS LEFT THE LAGOON IN ENTHUSIASTIC conversation. The resounding consensus was that Mr. Bolawe's session was much better than Old Man Whittaker's ever were, even better than all the others they had ever had. TJ couldn't chime in and give his two cents, as he had never met Old Man Whittaker, but he didn't see how he could challenge any of their comments. He'd only been at camp half a day, and he wholeheartedly agreed that their substitute was by far the most engaging teacher by a long shot, especially against Miss Graves's grueling coaching and Mr. Du Bois's condescending instructions.

"I mean, Old Man Whittaker was grumpy and everything," Joshua said as he ducked under a low-hanging branch. "But the kids *did* learn with him—so I heard. With this Bolawe guy, though, we learned plenty, but it had actual meaning, you know? He's got that old school, classic vibe going on."

TJ ducked the branch as well. "Yeah, he's pretty cool. He was at my sister's fu—" He held his tongue. He hadn't told Joshua about Dayo's funeral, though he suspected, like with everyone else, that Joshua already knew. When TJ saw Joshua gulp and look away, he *definitely* knew he knew.

An awkward silence fell between them, each of them finding interest in the beetles crawling through the rotting wood on each side of the path. TJ could see the intermediate group stumbling from Miss Graves's obstacle course through the thick branches, each one more drenched in sweat than the last. One camper even tripped and fell. When his friend came back to help him, he threw up a hand, and TJ assumed he said something along the lines of "just... leave me here."

"I'm sorry about your sister," Joshua finally said. "I ain't want to say nothin' because I figured you'd heard it enough."

TJ waved a hand. "Don't trip. I get it. It's hard to talk about."

Joshua clutched at his stomach, and his face scrunched up.

"You don't have to be so dramatic," TJ said. "It's okay that you didn't want to say anything, for real—"

Joshua shook his hand "no," still gripping at his stomach.

TJ's eyes went wide. "Oh no, if you're finna let one go, tell me now. I was trying to be nice last night, but you really know how to stink up a—"

"Nah, nah, I think I'll be fine." But Joshua looked like he was about to turn purple as his stomach grumbled deep and low. "Okay, that was a lie. Maybe I'll have to skip lunch."

Coming from Joshua, that was a serious statement. The way he inhaled breakfast that morning was a feat unmatched by any competitive eater TJ had ever seen.

"I told you to be careful with those grits, man." TJ shook his head. "They just didn't look right."

"Maybe you're right." Joshua winced. "I think I'll go visit the healer. Maybe if I go now, I'll have time to get a po' boy." Joshua's eyes looked like they could water. TJ wondered if it was from the aches or the thought that he might miss out on French bread and fried fish. "Can you save one for me, man?"

"Yeah, dude, of course." TJ gave him a pat on the back, but that only made Joshua suck air into his teeth with another grimace. "Sorry, Josh. Didn't mean to—"

Joshua clenched his eyes, shaking his head as he turned off to the office cabins, his shoulders slumped. TJ hoped he'd be all right. His face had gone between purple and green and back again within the space of a few seconds.

☦

A FEW MINUTES LATER, TJ FOUND HIMSELF BALANCING TWO TRAYS of po' boys with sides of roasted Brussels sprouts, watermelon slices, and boxed apple juice.

The mess hall was loud and rambunctious, the complete opposite of that morning when most of the campers were still waking up.

With food in their bellies and three activities out of the way, their collective energy had culminated in campers rapping in a corner emphatically—using pencils as drumsticks, boys and girls shouting over each other like they weren't sitting right next to each other, and children running between the tables playing tag, to which Mr. Du Bois waved his staff to halt them in their tracks with a wind wall.

Without Joshua around, TJ wasn't sure where to sit. Besides the younger children and a few others in the preparatory group, TJ was too new to form any bonds with the other campers.

TJ surveyed his options. He definitely wasn't going to sit anywhere near Ayodeji. The boy sat among a group who seemed to find entertainment by humiliating the younger campers with fish sauce on their faces or whose shoes were untied. TJ wasn't in the mood to have the boy and his friends talk mess about his outdated Jordans or oversized digital watch.

Another moment passed as TJ's eyes continued to travel along the mess hall for a seat. A scratching overhead brought his attention up, and he saw a moving statue the size of a giraffe writing along an elevated chalkboard that spanned from wall to wall. The lines it drew were empty, but just above it read:

Camper Ranking & Assessment this Friday

For a moment, TJ could feel his heart in his throat. There was no way the elders would put campers' grades up there for everyone to see, would they?

Turning away from the board, TJ returned to his search for a table. It wouldn't be so bad if he found an empty table by himself, would it? But even that wasn't an option—every table had at least a dozen kids around it.

Just as TJ was about to give up and look for a spot outside, he heard a familiar giggle to his side. Like the other campers, Manny and the Santos Sisters laughed with raucous mirth. Another boy at their table was telling them a joke. TJ recognized him as one of his co-campers in the preparatory group, a tall, light-skinned boy named Lorenzo with curly hair and green eyes.

TJ racked his brain for a good intro. He remembered yesterday Manny liked comedy, the perfect in for TJ. He just had to think of a good joke or something that would catch her attention.

Shuffling closer to her table, still balancing a pair of trays, he tried to listen in on Lorenzo's wisecracks. But the boy wasn't speaking English. It was that strange-sounding Spanish again.

Perfect, I'll impress her with that.

TJ wasn't fluent, but the handful of times he visited Christian Flores' house back in Los Angeles, he picked up a few things. At one of the boy's birthdays, one of Christian's cousins even thought TJ was Dominican because he requested food from his mother entirely in Spanish.

Taking a deep breath, TJ walked by Manny's table casually like he wasn't listening at all. Then he turned on his heel and hit them with a greeting.

"*¿Oye, qué tal?*" he asked, impressing himself with what he thought was perfect pronunciation. "*¿Cuáles son las vacas más perezosas?*"

They all stopped laughing at once and turned to him with expressions of utter confusion. Maybe he got one of the words wrong, or his accent wasn't quite right. He tried again, but this time he attempted to emulate their strange accents, elongating the ends of his vowels as they did.

"*Vacaciones!*" Still, nothing but crickets. "You don't get it? It's a pun… because… *vacas* and… *vacaciones…*"

They stared at him with raised eyebrows. Lorenzo looked like he was close to another chuckle, only this time at TJ's expense. A rush of heat tingled through TJ's ears.

This wasn't going the way he pictured it.

"*Lo siento,*" he rushed out. "*Mi acento es malo. Todavía estoy aprendiendo.*"

One of the Santos twins cocked her head to the side, a revelation tracing over her eyes. "Hold up. Pause. Are you speaking… *Spanish?*"

"U-um…" TJ stuttered.

He wanted to say yes, but somehow that seemed like the wrong thing to reply. He must've sounded ridiculous for her to even ask a question like that.

The other Santos twin drew a hand over her lips to cover the smirk growing under it. "*Cara,* we're speaking *Portuguêse.*"

TJ was sure he had died right then and there.

Lorenzo burst out in a fit of laughter. The Santos Sisters followed suit, giggling uncontrollably, the freckles on their cheeks scrunching up their face. The only one who didn't seem to find the situation amusing was Manny. To TJ's surprise, she looked red herself as though she were... embarrassed for him?

"Oh man, that was a good one." Lorenzo got up from the lunch bench and smacked TJ on the back as he threw his tray away. "Thanks for that, new kid."

"His name's TJ," giggled one of the twins—TJ couldn't tell which. The strain in his neck released a bit after her statement. At least she knew his name, even if he didn't know hers... it could've been Antonia or Andressa. But the tension locked right back up when she said, "But yeah, man, that was pretty cringe."

She got up from her seat and followed Lorenzo, her sister not far behind.

"You coming, Manny?" she asked, still getting over her last few sniggers. "We're going to sign up for the crossover team right now, and Lorenzo thinks he'll actually make the dueling squad this summer."

"Hey," Lorenzo said, "third time's the charm, right?"

"Nah, I-I'm good," Manny said as she poked at the two remaining Brussels sprouts on her plate with a fork. "I'll catch you guys later, though. You still on for some pick-up crossover later, right?"

"You know it," Lorenzo said, waving goodbye. "Ayodeji was talkin' mad mess today. Can't wait to shut him up. And TJ, don't be a stranger. We'll teach you how to speak some *Portuguêse, sim*?" Lorenzo walked backward with the twins all the way out of the mess hall, laughing the whole way out.

TJ's arms felt drained of all feeling, numb. He wanted to think it was because he still held up two trays full of food, but he knew that wasn't the case at all.

"Don't just stand there like you're gonna bug out." Manny nodded to the empty bench across from her. "Take a seat, yo."

TJ dropped the trays onto the table, his shaking arms thankful for the relief.

"You didn't have to stay," TJ said. "Thanks for not laughing, but you could've gone with your friends."

"I'm still eating..." She flicked her Brussels sprouts like they were miniature golf balls.

For whatever reason, she didn't want to go with her friends. Or maybe, as far-fetched as it probably was, she actually *wanted* to stay to talk with him. But ever since he took a seat, she never looked him in the eye for more than a few seconds. Was she nervous? Or was it something else? TJ couldn't help staring at her parted lips, which had this cute uncertainty about them. She wore some sort of pink-ish purpley lip balm that made them look —

Focus, TJ.

He took a bite into his po' boy to stop himself from gawking. A few times, he would've sworn Manny was going to open her mouth to say something, but she always seemed to take one furtive look at him and then away again.

"So..." TJ started, sipping from his juice box. "You're a pretty good runner, huh?"

She shrugged. "I get by."

"Get *by*? You should've lapped me twice."

"You heard my dad. He loves soccer. You ever run up and down one of those fields before? It's mad exhausting."

TJ loved the way she talked. He'd only heard a handful of New York accents growing up — mostly through movies. The dialect suited her well, he decided.

TJ bit into half a watermelon slice, pointing the remaining half at Manny casually before saying, "I couldn't believe it when I caught up to you, you know. It almost looked like you exhausted yourself, like I did in the first lap. That, or you slowed down on purpose."

Manny's face, which had been softening the more they spoke, hardened to stone when TJ said that, and she went back to looking everywhere but to TJ's eyes.

"Hold up, did you?" he asked. "Why? You could've aced that run, easy. I'd give anything to be as good as that. And I saw you in Mr. Bolawe's class. Your Ashe must be really strong... or am I wrong?"

Manny took a deep breath through her nose. "You're not wrong."

"Then what's the deal? That Ayodeji kid told me the camper with the best grades gets an invite to Ifa Academy."

"I know."

"You know?"

"They invited me to go last summer."

TJ nearly spit out his apple juice. "And you didn't accept it?" Ayodeji was wrong when he said no one was picked last year. Someone was. Manny just... declined. "My mom would be over the moon if I got an invite like that. It's all I've been thinking of since I learned there was a chance for me."

Manny stiffened on her bench, fidgeting in her seat. "That's a lot of food for one kid." She gestured to the two trays in front of TJ.

"Oh no," TJ said through the last bite of his po' boy. "This other one is for Josh. He'll be here soon. He just had a case of bubble guts."

"Oh yeah. He seems like a nice kid," Manny said as she leaned into the table to avoid a pair of running children behind her.

"Yeah… when he's not snoring, breaking wind, or burping."

Manny laughed, her nose scrunching up as though she could smell one of his toots. TJ noticed she had a slight overbite when she pulled her lips from her teeth mid-giggle. In all his efforts to re-steer his earlier fiasco, he'd almost forgotten the whole goal for him that summer was to get her to laugh in the first place.

"Well, I should probably go," she said. "I'm the captain of the crossover team, and I should see who signed up. We got smashed last year in the finals by Camp Mandawaca."

"Yeah, yeah, I wouldn't want to hold you up." TJ rubbed the back of his head nervously.

He didn't want her to go at all, not now that he got her talking again. But he didn't want to seem clingy either. He'd done that one too many times in the past.

"See you around, TJ," she said.

It was the first time she said his name. He liked the way it sounded on her lips, the way it sounded in her slightly husky voice. Before she got even a few steps away, she turned and said, "And, uh… *tchau.*"

TJ smiled. He had a feeling she wasn't going to let him live that down.

"*Adios,*" he said back with a half-grin.

Sure, their conversation didn't go exactly the way he thought it would, but he felt good about the way Manny seemed to have a bounce in her step on the way out of the mess hall.

20

THE FORGOTTEN TALE

THE CAMP SCHEDULE REGULATED THE REST OF THE DAY TO FREE play in various forms. Campers were allowed to swim in the lake, play on the field, or attend various tutoring sessions with any of the counselors and elders until dinner time.

Joshua returned just before lunch ended—looking a normal color—and wolfing down his meal like he had never been sick to begin with. After eating, he asked if TJ wanted to play crossover on the fields, but TJ had other plans.

For most of his free time, he locked himself in the boys' cabin, reading and re-reading the first chapter of *A Guide for Everyday Diviners*. He thought about getting the book to read to him aloud now that he was alone, but he always retained information better when it was read, not spoken. However, all the reading left a strain on his eyes, and when it grew too much to go on, he went into the bathroom to fill a sink with water.

First, he plugged the sink with a stopper, then let the water flow until it was halfway up. When the water settled, he readied himself to apply what he learned in Mr. Bolawe's class.

"*Gbè òmi lo,*" TJ recited as a bubble billowed at the sink's base, pushing the water away like he was parting a very tiny Red Sea.

But it wasn't enough.

The bubble was too small for his liking. If there were duckweed he was supposed to pull out, his little water bubble would have been too weak and flimsy to hold it. He remembered how big Ayodeji's bubble was by the end of the session when the boy split the waters between the duckweed.

That's what TJ needed to shoot for if he was going to get an invite to Ifa.

So, telling himself he would not leave the bathroom until his water charm was just as good, TJ continued. He played his piano and said the words over and over again. Images of Mom, Dayo, and the campers all flashed in his mind as his bubble grew with each new effort.

But then a knock came at the bathroom door.

"Yo, I gotta drain the snake!" came the voice of Lorenzo. "Open up."

"Sorry," TJ said. "Give me a sec."

He slipped on the floor, which he now realized was wet with water from his practice... If only he knew the incantation to dry it all up. Rushing for the paper towels, TJ did his best to lap up as much of the water as he could. But when he opened the door to let Lorenzo in, the boy looked at the floor with disgust.

"*Cara*, did you have an accident?" he asked as he tiptoed around the pools of water.

"Oh no, nothing like that," TJ blurted as he grabbed for more paper towels. "I was just—" He stopped himself short of the truth. "The faucet wouldn't cut off. It just kept coming out."

Lorenzo stepped into one of the bathroom stalls, his voice muffled as he called out, "Yeah, Elder Wale says he'll always fix it, but he never does. Just wait for him to get back. He'll clean it up."

Oh good. He doesn't know how to clean it up either.

TJ could never be sure what magic he was and wasn't supposed to know at his age. He caught his own expression in the mirror and realized how bug-eyed he looked. He shook his head free of the shock and splashed water on his face before draining the sink. Then, after placing down a few more paper towels just to be safe, TJ left the bathroom as a rush of teen boys came barreling into the cabin.

It looked like each of them had been in a water fight, their dashikis wet and sticking to their skin. But a few of the long-haired boys looked like they'd just been through a drier, their hair plump and fluffy. It wasn't until TJ got a good whiff of one of them when he realized their clothes weren't sodden by water but by the glorious aroma of teenage boy perspiration. The blown-out hair must have been from all the wind magic they were using during a crossover match.

"Yo, did you hear the rumors?" Juice, the junior counselor, murmured to his younger brother Stephen as TJ let them pass into the bathroom. "People are saying Director Simmons is locking down the outskirts. *Divination Today* says there were Keepers spotted not too far from here."

Stephen sucked his teeth. "You lie!"

"That's what I heard."

TJ stopped his walk straight away and turned to the boys. "Keepers? Here? What for? Aren't they supposed to be in Nigeria?"

"*Supposed* to be," the pimple-faced Juice said. A few of his zits were already popping... maybe that's why he was called Juice. *Gross*, TJ thought. "Hey, I heard they were at your sister's funeral. Is that true? That's what it said on Evo that first day before it got taken down, anyway."

TJ almost forgot about the search engine Tunde introduced him to. With all the first-day activities, all he could think about was how he could pass and get accepted to Ifa Academy among all these magical kids, but without his phone, he'd forgotten about his little investigation.

"Yeah, they were there," TJ said. "They attacked us."

Juice and Stephen traded looks of astonishment, and in unison, they said. "For real, for real?"

"Yeah, it was messed up. Nobody got hurt, though."

"I knew that blog was bull." Juice sucked his teeth. "Said there were three unconfirmed deaths. Just clickbait, like always."

Stephen smacked TJ lightly across the arm. "Watch yourself, TJ. Looks like you're a Keeper magnet. First at your sister's funeral, now they're showing up in New Orleans."

He and his brother laughed as they walked into their respective stalls to "drop a deuce," as they said. Their chuckling did little to quell the nerves building in TJ's stomach. They had only been joking, but he wondered if what they said could be true.

At first, the Keepers just seemed like they were attacking the funeral, but what if they really were after him? No, that didn't make sense. What would they need him for? And if they had been, they could've come for him during the parade or even before he left for camp. It wouldn't make any sense. Besides, it's not like he was anything like Dayo.

TJ shook his head. This was all based on a blog with faulty information said in jest by the brothers. He was just paranoid and probably tired—no point in thinking about it.

"TJ!" came Joshua's bellow. The giant of a boy went for a bear hug, but TJ slipped his stinky pits and held out an outstretched hand.

"Bro." TJ plugged his nose. "After you go shower."

He hadn't even realized they were on hugging terms to begin with. TJ still didn't understand why the kid sought out friendship with him. Then he thought about it... He was probably the only one who tolerated the boy.

"Oh, right..." Joshua blushed. "Sorry. But, dude! You should have come out and played! We had a tournament. First day of camp, they let us do whatever we want after lunch. Tomorrow we'll have to choose tutoring. What've you been getting into all this time?"

TJ forced himself not to look back at the bathroom. "Oh, nothing. Just... studying."

"Oooh, you're looking to get that invitation from one of them academies, ain't you?"

"Yeah, something like that..." TJ mumbled as he rubbed at his eyebrow.

"Well," Josh said. He hobbled over to his bunk, probably sore from all the games, then snatched off his dashiki to put on a fresh one. "It's almost dinnertime, and then the first night's campfire."

"Josh, man." TJ facepalmed, peering through the cracks of his fingers as a new pool of sweat dampened the boy's crisp dashiki. "You gotta take a shower *first.*"

Josh's mouth opened in an "o" and he took off his already moist dashiki. His ears looked like beets. "Oops, sorry."

Joshua ambled to the showers and returned a few minutes later, clean and ready—only to put on the shirt he had already ruined before. TJ didn't say anything this time. They were already running late for dinner, which the schedule said was shrimp gumbo, cornbread, and a side salad.

Next to Mr. Bolawe's class, the food was without a doubt TJ's favorite thing about Camp Olosa.

After gulping down two bowls of gumbo and a heap of cornbread, TJ and Joshua walked down a path TJ had not yet gone down before. Past the lagoon and next to the lake, tucked between two oak trees that grew sideways instead of up, was a great firepit surrounded by a tiny amphitheater.

Everyone from camp was there, from all the counselors, campers, juniors, and elders. Stepping over the low-hanging branches, TJ ogled at the ten-foot-high fire, which didn't bloom orange as it should have, but a white-ish-purple. Even odder, TJ didn't feel any heat from it, as he and Josh took a seat in the second row of the slatted stone benches lodged into the shallow hillside. There might not have been warmth from the strange fire, but TJ felt as though he was filled with something else, something more... celestial.

"Let me guess," he whispered to Joshua. "Is that some sort of spiritual fire where one of the Orishas will come out and surprise us with a hymn?"

Joshua gave him an exaggerated pout. "Wow, that's half right."

"Wait, what? Really?" TJ was only kidding.

"Well." Josh jabbed a finger into his chin. "It would be fully right, but things with the Orishas have changed. Back in the day, they said it was easy to get an Orisha or two to talk to us. Nowadays, some summoners are lucky to get an ancestor of one of the counselors, but no one's ever actually seen an Orisha come out of the fire for a long while. Mostly it's used as a transport, though. Sort of like the one some adults use to travel through water with."

Suddenly the fire made TJ uncomfortable. The thought of some ghostly spirit coming out of the bizarre flames didn't exactly inspire awe for him. He imagined some giant specter coming out with a head the size of one of the presidents on Mount Rushmore.

"Seriously," Josh nudged him with his elbow, "it's not as crazy as it sounds. What, you've never felt an ancestor before when you pray?"

TJ's lips twitched as his mind wandered back to Dayo. It seemed like such a long time ago since the funeral when he thought he felt her. When Manny mentioned her family in Mr. Bolawe's class, TJ thought he sensed his sister again passing over his neck, but how could he really know?

It was easy to believe in a thing when he could see it. Bright purple flames, giant alligators, and people disappearing into lakes... *that* he could wrap his mind around just fine. Intangible sensations across his neck, though? Not so much.

"Hey, Joshua, can I ask you something?"

"Shoot away, friend."

"Ashe... can it be, you know, seen. Does it look like a mist?"

"Huh? What do you mean?"

"Sometimes I think I can *see* Ashe when other diviners use it." TJ waved the notion away when Joshua gave him a confused expression. "Ah, nothing, never mind."

"Hmmm, that's interesting. Never heard of that before. Maybe you should talk to Mr. Bolawe about it." He jabbed his chin over to where the counselors sat, Mr. Bolawe among them.

"Yeah, maybe I should." TJ turned back to the purple fire. As he continued his one-sided staring contest with the flames, TJ could have sworn he saw the impressions of a human figure within. He blinked and jumped a little in his log seat but stopped his jittering when Joshua gave him a side-eye.

It couldn't be. He'd only been joking about seeing to believe.

He watched as the fire seemed to spread around a set of shoulders and the outlines of a torso. TJ looked around to see if anyone else had noticed, but all the other campers were too busy talking amongst each other. Looking back, the more he stared, the more certain he was there was something more in the crackling white-purple blaze than fire.

Could it have been Dayo?

TJ's heart pounded as the figure solidified before his eyes. Then, from the flames, it finally emerged. But what came out was not some translucent apparition or ancestral spirit, but an ordinary and very solid woman.

A very solid woman who wasn't Dayo.

The campers clapped and hollered as the woman curtsied and patted off a stray flame that danced on her shoulder. It was just a transport portal, like Joshua had said, a performance, not some gateway to some spirit realm.

TJ settled back on his log, his heart shrinking. He'd almost convinced himself it was Dayo. How could he be so naive?

Trying to distract himself, he turned to the new arrival. For a moment, TJ thought the woman could've been a younger version of Elder Adeyemi. They had the same dark eyes, the same oblong face, and a certain fondness for sparkling eyeliner. Yet that's where the similarities ended.

Elder Adeyemi wore her hair natural and short in an Afro, whereas this woman had hair straighter than a horse's tail going halfway down her back. Instead of some elaborate skirt or dress, she wore simple, homey blue jeans, and she was much larger, her white dashiki wrapping around a plump and shapely figure.

"Is that woman related to Elder Adeyemi?" TJ asked Josh.

"Who's that?" Joshua whispered back. "That's Director Simmons."

TJ glanced back at the woman. Perhaps she just reminded him of the elder who was responsible for him being there in the first place.

He still couldn't shake the resemblance, though. As Director Simmons raised her hands to quiet the campers, her graceful gestures looked just like Adeyemi's.

A tap came at TJ's shoulder. He turned to see Manny smiling at him.

"You're half right again," she said.

How long had she been there? Was she listening to everything he and Joshua were talking about? He must've sounded like an idiot asking about spirits coming out of the flames and seeing Ashe moving around.

"The Director is Adeyemi's younger sister," Manny told him.

"I knew it—" TJ said but was cut off sharply by one of the Santos twins shushing him.

Manny froze in place, her shoulders going tight around her ears as she mouthed "sorry" to TJ.

"Welcome, campers!" Director Simmons said, her voice just as smooth as her sister's. "Sorry I could not introduce myself during the day. There were a few things I needed to attend to. But I am happy to see you all here for another summer." Her eyes roamed the campers. "I see many familiar faces and a few new ones." TJ tensed when Simmons lifted her hand in his direction. But she was gesturing somewhere behind him. "You. Young one, what's your name?"

Everyone shifted in their seats to get a better look at the kid. It was Gary, the little boy TJ had met the day before. The boy had his arms tucked tightly at his sides, and his voice came out low and meek.

"Speak up, honey," Simmons encouraged. "We're all family here."

A few sniggers came from down the way. TJ wasn't surprised to find Ayodeji and his friends hiding their laughter behind the collars of their dashiki lifted over their mouths.

"My name's Gary..." he mumbled.

"Nice to meet you, Gary." Simmons curtsied again, her sleek hair nearly touching her bent knees. "Tell us. What is your best talent?"

The little boy slumped on his log, his head dipping into his dashiki-styled hoodie like he was a turtle hiding from a seabird. At the far end of the amphitheater, Miss Gravés encouraged the young boy to share, but that only made things worse. The boy looked near to tears.

"He's great with water!" TJ spoke up. The boy's chin lifted just a bit, his eyes slowly recognizing TJ as they widened. "I met Gary yesterday at check-in. You all should see what he can do with his water manifestation. Way better than anything I can do. Go ahead, Gary. Show 'em what you got."

The boy's brows knitted together, and his chest heaved in and out. But TJ saw that the tight grip his hand had constricted into had loosened at his side already. The boy might've been nervous, but he knew he could do it. He just had to get over his stage fright.

C'mon, Gary.

TJ locked eyes with him, doing his best to convey a sense of security, of encouragement. After a moment, Gary nodded, sat up from his seat, and dropped into that strange sway he did when TJ first met him.

With the firelight reflecting off his arms and legs, the boy's unique version of water manifestation ushered in the first audible laughter from Ayodeji's group. Mr. Du Bois snapped his fingers so emphatically TJ could feel it in his chest, and the older boys stopped their chuckling.

But the damage was done.

Nothing was coming out of Gary's fingers, and the boy was already faltering in his little two-step.

A familiar tingle drifted to the tips of TJ's fingers, and he concentrated hard on Gary's hands. Like with basketball, TJ visualized what he wanted to happen, his mind's eye fixed on water coming out of Gary's hands just like they did when the boy squirted his father. The more TJ concentrated, the greater the tingle, and after a short moment, a fountain of water shot from Gary's hands, even stronger than yesterday's. The campers exploded into applause, and Gary cried, though this time his eyes were wet with elation, not despair or embarrassment.

TJ let out a long breath as he glanced down to his own fingers. Tiny drops of water fell from his nails to the dirt below in little pools.

"You okay there, TJ?" Joshua asked, a little worry in his voice.

TJ answered, "I'm good, I'm good. Thanks, man."

When TJ lifted his eyes, he caught the attention of Mr. Bolawe and Mr. Du Bois, whispering to each other at the other end of the amphitheater. Neither of them was looking at Gary but straight at TJ. And they didn't look away, even as TJ held their gaze. Did they know what he was doing? Would it be considered cheating?

"Very well done, Gary." Director Simmons clapped. "Very well done."

A group of the younger children huddled around Gary, giving

him slaps on the back and jumping up and down. When they finally settled down, Simmons spun her shoulders to TJ. "And what a perfect segue. As the preparatory group already knows, we have another new student this summer, Tomori Jomiloju Young. Most of you might know his older sister, Ifedayo."

A hush cut over the campers, which was only punctured by a few shrill whispers as TJ felt every head turn to him.

Great...

Now he'd be the center of all the attention.

"And as most of you know," Simmons said. "We lost Ifedayo this past month. We hope and pray she has found her way safely to the Orisha Plane."

"Ashe," the elders and counselors chimed together. A few of the students spoke the word in unison as well. Joshua put a tender hand to TJ's back.

"Now, the rules here are very simple," Director Simmons said after an appropriate silence passed. "Do to others as you would like to be done to you. Do not say any Orisha's name in vain while you are on these grounds. Listen to your elders, and treat them with respect."

Director Simmons clapped her hands together. "Well, tradition has it that we have our newest counselor lead the first night's story. At this time, I'd like to officially announce that Mister Joseph Whittaker could unfortunately not join us as an instructor this year. So please, everyone give a warm, Camp Olosa welcome to your new Ẹmi Guidance instructor, Mister Olufemi Bolawe."

A majority of the campers clapped and hollered. Some even stood to their feet to show their appreciation. Clapping along with everyone else, TJ wondered if most of the applause was for Mr. Bolawe himself or because Old Man Whittaker wasn't going to be there anymore.

Mr. Bolawe gave the crowd a small smile and a wave as he trotted over to Director Simmons. He embraced her in a long and warm hug. When they broke, the director continued her clapping and stood to the side to give Bolawe space before the great flames.

"Thank you, thank you," Mr. Bolawe said humbly with a hand over his heart and a short bow to match. "I'll be brief. I'm sure you all want to get to sleep as soon as you can to wake up early for tomorrow's activities."

A few of the teens groaned, and TJ knew they were already

thinking about the mile they'd have to run in Miss Gravés's session tomorrow.

"The *pataki*—sacred story, that is—I'll share is new to even me. I recently had a conversation with a very wise bàbálàwò. Forgive me if I don't get everything right. This is a very paraphrased version."

He took in a deep breath, closing his eyes and letting his chest fill until there was no more space to let in new air. Then he let it all out in one long exhale. When his eyes opened, they had lightened slightly, less a natural brown and more a silver-ish, almost white hue.

Every camper sat at the edge of their logs in anticipation. Then, Mr. Bolawe finally spoke, *"As we all know, our people come from the land of Old Ile-Ife. Long now has it been a place of peace… relatively."*

A few of the elders chuckled, and Bolawe smiled before continuing:

"This story is the tale of how we diviners earned our power. It started with a war between the River People and Mountain Dwellers."

Mr. Bolawe seemed to scan each face in the crowd, old and young alike. A few of the elders who sat near the white flames nodded in approval of the telling. The campers sat with wide, curious eyes, TJ among them as he sat forward.

"The River People," Mr. Bolawe went on, *"were done with the fighting. But their chief wanted nothing to do with the other humans, who had stolen his lands' healing berries. So he asked Oshun, the Orisha of Rivers, to carve him and his people a home. And so she did, creating the Benue and Niger rivers to give the Chief the protection he needed."*

Joshua, at TJ's side, crossed his arms.

"What's wrong?" TJ asked.

Joshua's eyes widened, and he fixed his expression. "Oh, oh nothing. It's just erm… my grandmother told the story different, is all."

Mr. Bolawe wiggled his fingers along the campfire, and an image of humans atop a mountain sprang forth. *"But the Mountain Dwellers pursued the River People, empowered by Ogun, the Orisha of Iron and War, who showed them the way across the new rivers, and war continued…"*

The flames transformed to show the acts of war: clashing swords, arrows through the air, famine, and bloodshed. The heat of the flickering war licked at TJ's chin. And his eyes watered at the image of emaciated children, who were more bones than skin. There was nothing to eat when everything else was on fire.

"When Oko, the Harvester, could no longer sustain the fields of blood, he

went to Olodumare, the Unseen Monarch, and begged him to intercede, to stop the scouring of their good earth."

Bolawe clapped his hands together. "Now, campers, this is where the story *really* gets interesting, so pay special attention here." A light twinkle shined in his eye—something beyond the reflection of the firelight.

"Olodumare decided then to turn to his most knowledgeable advisor, Orunmila the Wise, and asked what should be done."

TJ's focus sharpened. Orunmila was Dayo's Orisha.

"Never one to rush, The Wise pondered for sixteen days and sixteen nights. On the dawn of the seventeenth day, he answered his monarch. 'The Orishas should leave the humans to their own affairs without interference from the divine,' he said.

"The Unseen Monarch asked about the Coastal Folk of the lands, and Orunmila told him that, for the most part, they had kept themselves out of the fighting."

"Coastal Folk too? How many different people are there in this story?" Little Gary asked from within the crowd.

"Only three tribes." Mr. Bolawe beamed. "I assure you, there are no more. But these people, the coastal folk, are the most important. As they are the root of our ancestral path."

"Ooooh!" Gary stretched. "Okay, I think I understand now."

Mr. Bolawe continued, *"The Great One did not like this and said, 'I will give these Coastal Folk a sliver of my power to quell this war of the Mountain and River. These Coastal Folk shall be the mediators and the bridge toward a new age for the people. And if they do not slow this war, then we shall leave the mortals to their fate.'"*

TJ's rear end had become sore from how far along the edge of his log he was sitting. And his ears seemed to pulse with the strain of listening intently. This was the sort of thing he needed to know. A forgotten tale... something that he couldn't just look up on Evo or anywhere else. This was information that could only be learned from a diviner like Mr. Bolawe.

"But the Chosen Children failed the Great Monarch, Olodumare, in the end. Ogun's Mountain Dwellers won the war with the Chosen Children's help, who grew hungry with their new power. They forced Oshun's River People to surrender with more dead than even the Great Orishas could count. And Olodumare, shamed by the humans, tried to take their power away. But before he could, he disappeared, never seen again in the Sky Realm, the Aqua Realm, the Terra Realm, or even the Mortal Realm..."

"Oooooh," a few of the younger campers exclaimed in whispers.

Mr. Bolawe's eyes fell over TJ for a moment. The flames dancing around the man's arms started to dissipate. The lake and the amphitheater around them darkened.

"Orunmila the Wise gave us one message, a divination of the Unseen Monarch's return. The true details of his message are still debated to this day. But one thing the oracles all agree upon is the destined manifestation of a Promised Child who would uncover the Unseen Monarch."

TJ's heart dropped into his stomach. *The promised child*, TJ thought as the rest of the campers started mumbling to one another.

That's what they called Ifedayo at her funeral. But that Orunmila Orisha was wrong, the oracles and all the priests were wrong. Ifedayo might've been aligned with the Great Oracle, but she still died anyway...

"What's wrong?" Joshua asked at TJ's side.

TJ hadn't realized he'd been frowning. "Nothing. Really... nothing. Sorry, I just got a lot on my mind."

⚧

LATER THAT NIGHT, WHEN ELDER WALE CALLED LIGHTS OUT AND Joshua started up his snoring again, the last thought TJ could remember before he fell asleep wasn't about a mile run, or duckweed, or even the cute girl who didn't seem completely repulsed by him.

His last thoughts revolved around Bolawe's story.

If Dayo was supposed to be that promised child, what did that mean for everyone else? For him? Mom always said prophecies were misread all the time, and some were outright wrong. But TJ couldn't shake that thought of the Great Orisha going missing and a promise of his return.

He brushed his fingers on the back of his neck, remembering that day in his sister's room. What if Dayo was really with him now, just waiting for him to continue her work?

TJ's heart sank. *That couldn't be true.*

Director Simmons said it herself. She'd be with the ancestors now. Distant. Gone, like the Orishas had gone in the story.

But at least TJ still had her staff.

That week, it was time to find out more about the promised child and the missing Olodumare.

21

LIBRARY ON THE BAYOU

IT HAD BECOME EXCEEDINGLY CLEAR TO TJ THAT SIMPLY WANTING
something hard enough just wouldn't cut it.

Despite passing out after Miss Gravés's Tuesday and
Wednesday classes, he still couldn't break an eight-minute run.
Joshua had said diviners were supposed to have better endurance
and physicality than the clouded, but TJ's "diviner" legs seemed to
miss that memo.

Even when studying his textbooks well after lights out, he failed
to answer any of Mr. Du Bois's questions, even falling asleep despite
himself during some of the instructor's sessions.

And with Mr. Bolawe, though TJ enjoyed his classes, he couldn't
do any better with the water charms they were mastering that week.

It went without saying, but his desire to research more about that
forgotten tale and the lost Orishas was distracted by just about everything else the camp threw at him.

No matter how hard he concentrated his Ashe into his exercises,
he *still* couldn't keep up with the rest of the campers, not even the
intermediate group or the children at elementary levels. In fact, it
seemed like everyone—especially Joshua, who spent the most time
with TJ—did better than him at everything.

"I mean, I'm pretty good with magic as it is," Joshua had said on
the second day of camp. "But something about working with you,
man... It's like breathing in fresh air after being near smoke and fire,
you know?"

"You're a really good teacher, TJ," Manny had said on day three.

"I never would've thought of shifting my hands like that to pull the water away from each other."

"Heh, no problem," TJ had replied sheepishly, thinking that perhaps his future lay in a career as an instructor. Heck, maybe he could be Mr. Bolawe's assistant or something. That wouldn't be so bad.

He had to remind himself that that wasn't the goal, though. He needed to get into Ifa Academy, not be an assistant, and he needed to find out more about what really happened to his sister.

That was easier said than done, of course.

On the fourth day of camp, when TJ was partnered with Lorenzo in Mr. Bolawe's class, he almost dropped the broken branch they'd been tasked to mend when the boy said TJ was like a lucky charm.

It was regular ol' middle school all over again.

It only took a few days, and already his old moniker replaced his name for most of the students.

"*Jábọ̀ àfẹfẹ,*" TJ said with gusto after lunch that Thursday.

He was alone in the cabin again, which he decided would be his go-to for his free-play sessions. At the moment, a water lily he found outside laid at the foot of his bunk bed, and even though he held his sister's staff in hand, he still couldn't get the damn thing to move an inch.

"Come. On!" he shouted at the staff, looking at the face carved at its head like it was a real person. "I'm saying it right, aren't I? *Jábọ̀ àfẹfẹ!*" He thrust the staff toward the water lily. "*Jábọ̀ àfẹfẹ!*"

Nothing. The crystal lodged in the staff didn't even glow. He grunted and put the staff away beneath the loose floorboards under his bed.

Plopping onto his bed, he recalled something Mom would always tell him. Something about people trying to do too much at once and that sometimes it was a good idea to take a break from a difficult task for others.

Tunde would always say he never had an issue doing three or four things at once while giving TJ that knowing side-eye of his. At the time, it had pissed TJ off... but now, alone at camp, he sort of missed his little brother's jabs.

He laughed in disbelief. It hadn't even been a week, and he was already homesick.

It was, however, in thinking of his family that his thoughts returned to Dayo and Mr. Bolawe's story. Taking out his books, he scanned through every page in hopes he'd find something. Just as before, he found nothing about Olodumare being lost, let alone anything about a promised child.

He glanced at his watch and saw he had five minutes until snack time. If he skipped out on it, it would've been the best time to do some research at the library while all the campers were at the mess hall. So, he took in a deep breath, clambered out of his bed, and made his way toward the door.

Jogging across the patchy lawn and ignoring the afternoon humidity threatening to ruin yet another of his dashikis with sweat, TJ rushed to the camp's library, only slowing to a hurried walk when he saw a group of campers near the lake. He didn't need them asking him questions about where he was running off to.

"Hurry up and tell us already!" one of the camper girls shouted into the huddle she and the others were clustered around.

"Shhhh! If you stop hounding me, I could get a word in, fool. Like I was saying, I overhead the counselors saying they caught a Keeper near the Lafayette Cemetery, caught 'em with a Yewa mask."

"Shoot, that ain't too far from here," another older camper boy said, sounding worried.

"What you actin' scary for? Ain't no Keepers coming to a camp full of kids."

"My mom said they recruit kids all the time to do their rituals to bring back the Orishas. I ain't tryin' to be one of them kids."

"Fool, who want to kidnap your narrow-a—"

The worried boy punched the girl and nodded toward TJ. TJ acted like he wasn't eavesdropping at all and kept walking.

So there *were* Keepers in New Orleans. He'd have to find out if that was common or not. The little voice inside him told him it definitely wasn't. More reason for him to get to the library.

✝

THE PATH TO THE LIBRARY WAS SANDWICHED BETWEEN THE LAKE and the staff cabins, just behind a thicket of tupelo trees. The shanty that served as the camp's sole house of books sat on a tiny marsh island surrounded by thick green slush. TJ put his finger to his lips as he tried to remember how to get across. Elder Wale had mentioned it during his little orientation, but TJ could barely understand his slurred words.

"Afternoon, TJ," came a voice from the side.

TJ nearly jumped as he twisted to the image of a yawning tree, its barked lips stretched out wide.

"Afternoon, Monsieur Francois." TJ sighed with relief.

The tree chuckled. "Apologies, didn't mean to give you a fright. I was just catching up on my beauty sleep."

TJ still didn't know what Monsieur Francois looked like. He never transformed out of his tree form, and he surprised campers all over the grounds. He always apologized after giving the kids a scare, but there was always a hidden snigger under his sorrys. TJ wondered what he even did at camp to begin with or what his role was besides acting like an oversized scarecrow against non-magical thugs trying to sneak in.

"Oh!" he said. "Were you trying to get across? Did Elder Wale forget to explain it to you little ones again?"

Monsieur Francois cleared his throat, which sounded like scratchy husks being rubbed together. Then he sang roughly:

> *Below the thinking tree, you'll find your trails,*
> *Where the drinking flees, and the truth unveils.*
> *Under root tap a beat of one and three.*
> *If learning's what you seek, there's no other key.*

After finishing his short stanza, Francois did a little flourish with one of his branches and bowed. He opened one wooded eyelid as though he expected applause for his performance, but none came.

"Do you get it?" Monsieur Francois asked with a frown. "I can go again if that'll—"

TJ threw up his hands. "No, no, I think I got it."

He pressed his hand into his forehead as he recalled the first line. First, he just needed to find a thinking tree. Scanning the woods along the bayou, he couldn't help but pass over Francois' tree form over and over.

"I'll give you a hint." The tree man smiled. "You can stop acting like you're not looking at me. I'm not the thinking tree, though I can see how that can be misleading."

That's right. Monsieur Francois was always moving around. Whatever entrance led to the library had to be something stationary, something that looked like—

TJ's eyes settled on a cypress whose branches curled into the figure of someone hunched over in thought, the branches serving as an arm and the bulbous trunk as the head.

"Oh, good! You got it!" Francois clapped his branches together, casting off pieces of wood shavings as he did so. "I was so close to telling you, but you got it all on your own."

As TJ sloshed through the thick mud to the thinking tree, he wondered if Francois had many people to converse with. It must've been lonely having to be a tree all the time. Maybe he was stuck like that. Either way, TJ couldn't blame him. The other trees along the swamp didn't look like the best company.

TJ glanced at his watch again. He didn't have much more time. The campers would be getting their snacks by now.

Once he approached the thinking tree, he scanned along its edges to the roots where it dipped into the murky swamp. Bark and water met a strange ripple that ebbed away from the tree's base and flowed out toward the library's direction. TJ dropped to his knees, caking them with mud, and tapped a beat of one and then three along the long root that dipped into the water. After a brief moment, the tree rumbled, and several sets of thick roots sprouted from beneath the water, crafting a perfect—yet lumpy—bridge between the tree line and the tiny marsh island.

"Make haste!" Monsieur Francois chortled. "The roots don't stay up for long."

"Thanks." TJ waved to the tree, who saluted back.

A few hops and skips along the uneven path later, and he finally landed at the front of the library. It looked like the shanty was sinking into the muddy island like a stout, unfinished version of the Tower of Pisa, but when TJ opened the front door, the interior wasn't slanted at all; it was completely level.

He gazed between the threshold and the interior. The more he tried to make sense of it, the less he understood how the building could be lopsided on the outside and flat on the inside.

Unlike the musty and dingy libraries TJ was used to, this one looked almost otherworldly, with vines twisting around bookcases and strange-looking flowers sprouting from under the floorboards. He couldn't decide if it was because it smelled so fresh—instead of the mold he expected to inhale from outside—or because of the fireflies that flitted in between the aisles, but the room brought TJ calm and peace. Perhaps it was the shimmering light that flitted through the thin slats serving as windows, which added a serene nature to the library.

Besides the vines and insects, the library seemed to be empty.

There wasn't even the sound of indistinct whispers or the turning of pages. At the very least, there had to be a librarian, right?

"Hello!" TJ called out, his voice echoing off the high, open ceiling. "Anyone here? It's my first time."

No answer came.

Maybe the library was self-serving. *Or maybe I need to speak some proverb to manifest an ancient talking monkey with a monocle or whatever.* Oh, what TJ would give to have his phone to just look up what he needed.

TJ took another look at his watch. There were only ten minutes left before he needed to head out, and he wasn't even sure where to begin searching for information on Olodumare or promised children. Should he start down the row full of scrolls, the one with all the thick tomes, or the weird one littered with masks atop shelves? There were a bunch of miniature statues strewn about the floor and shelves like the elementary campers had had their way with them. Some upright, others overturned.

Elder Wale had probably told them how to navigate the library on the first night when he explained everything about the camp, but again, TJ couldn't remember anything he'd said. Not with Josh talking his ear off, anyway.

But a tingling at his fingers told him to go down the aisle with all the masks. And now that he gave them a second scan, he could've sworn that the one in the middle was the same design as the ones the Keepers were wearing at his sister's funeral, slitted eyes and all.

A nervous heat snaked down his spine, but he padded down the row anyway, reading off the labels under each mask. Each of them was propped up on displays and seemed regulated to certain Orishas. Sure enough, the design of the Keeper-looking masks seemed to be molded around the visage of Orunmila the Wise, his sister's Orisha. That was at least one connection he could make between the tale and the Keepers.

The masks ranged from small and large, iron and wood. The first mask TJ settled on was a simple stone one with cowries marking the eyes and mouth. But when he picked it up, cautiously as he did, nothing happened.

So he decided to ask it a question. It only seemed logical.

"Hey there, um, mask of Orunmila…" He sounded ridiculous to himself. "I was wondering if you could tell me about what you meant when you said a promised child would uncover what was lost, I mean, uncover the Great Monarch Olodumare."

The mask vibrated in his hand, not vigorously but lightly, like a cellphone barely vying for his attention. TJ's heart fluttered a little, hoping that he wouldn't drop it. It was working. He could see a faint fog casting off from the mask's cowries, and a whispered voice called out in his mind.

"A promised child will rise with the light of a dying, falling star, and the Lost Monarch will return once more." Excitement spiked through TJ's chest at the words "falling star," and he brought the mask closer to his face. *"Yet only at the behest of one of my chosen children. One must go to the Great Water of the Lagoons to start down the divine path. Find the light in the deep, heed its call, and you will have all you desire."*

Heart pounding, TJ asked quickly, "W-what is the falling star? And what Great Water? And what if you're wrong? What if the promised child died?"

"You do not have to take my word for it. I can show you..."

"Show me? Show me how?"

"You have to raise it to your face," a voice came from down the aisle.

For the second time, TJ nearly jumped out of his dashiki. Was it everyone's mission at camp to give him a heart attack?

"And you wouldn't want to put that one on. It'll just make you start seeing all kinds of—Tomori? Is that you?" TJ turned to see Adeola of all people walking down the aisle.

Without the funeral garbs, he forgot how thin she was, her sharp cheekbones framing her small eyes. She wore a new bull nose ring— an accessory Mom had always hated on her. Her stylish, long bangs still covered one side of her face, though she shaved the sides of her head. Usually, her hair was on point, but now it looked a bit disheveled, like she'd been sweating. Must've been that wonderful bayou moisture—no one was safe from its clutches.

TJ swallowed hard, putting the mask down like he hadn't picked it up at all. "Adeola? What are you doing here?"

"I thought it was still snack time for you kids. What are you doing at the library?"

"I asked you first."

"Oh, right..." Her eyes shifted to the side. "Well... I... work here."

Her words came slow, cautious. What was it? Did she think a job as a camp librarian wasn't good enough?

"What?" TJ's mouth fell open. "Why didn't you tell me?"

"Sorry, Elder Orji always has me running errands. She's the head librarian." She leaned in close. "But she's always napping. What's up with you?"

"This week has been the worst. I've been dealing with all these things I didn't even know that I didn't know—and there's this kid who won't give me a break—and the grades post up tomorrow, and I know I'll be last—and oh, you should meet this girl Manny—"

Adeola lifted her hands in the air. "Slow down, li'l man. Take a breath."

"Sorry," TJ said. It'd been a while since he could let out everything he wanted to say to someone he really knew. "I'm trying to find some information on—" He stopped short before going on, feeling a bit unsure. "On Olodumare and Orunmila. I'm trying to figure out why Olodumare disappeared and how he'll return."

Adeola tilted her head, and her bangs covered one of her eyes. "Information is sort of my job. Was the mask speaking to you in your head?" TJ nodded. "Which story about those Orishas did you want to know?" TJ didn't respond as he bit the inside of his cheek, but Adeola looked at the mask in his hands. "Though I'm surprised, I thought you were looking for information on Eshu..."

TJ lifted an eyebrow. "Eshu? I... I thought this was Orunmila. The label said—"

"It's a common mistake." Adeola opened her palm and waited for TJ to hand her the mask. He did, and she set it down further along the row along with the other masks labeled under "Eshu."

With a smile on her lips, she turned to TJ to say, "Don't worry. Even the elders make the mistake. Eshu is a trickster, so he likes to mimic other faces. But tell me, why are you researching Olodumare and Orunmila? Some project for that hard-ass Du Bois?"

"Yeah, something like that. I've... got a group project, and I was supposed to cover them."

"Group project, eh? Who are you trying to impress? Wait, pause... you did mention a name." She put her finger to her lips. "Someone with an 'M', right?"

"Deola..." TJ grumbled. "We were talking about the Orishas."

Adeola laughed, then led TJ back to the entrance, where a collection of plush pillows were laid out on the ground. "Well, I'm aligned with Orunmila like your sister, but I do know a thing or two about Olodumare as well, considering his energy is universal and all that." That made sense. And, if TJ remembered correctly, she was top two in her class, just under his sister when they graduated from Ifa. "Lay it on me. What do you need to know?"

"Mr. Bolawe told all the campers a story about Olodumare disappearing, and Mom said something about the oracles talking about a promised child." His fingers twisted together nervously. "Then everyone keeps saying Dayo was supposed to be that promised child, but she—" TJ couldn't bring himself to say the words.

Adeola blew out a long breath through her mouth. "Yeah, that's a lot... but I think I know what you're getting at. All that stuff has been debated between the oracles ever since Dayo came to Ifa Academy."

"So is it true? Was she some promised child? Mom said she was supposed to awaken a long lost Orisha."

"Funny thing about that." Adeola nodded back to the shelf they had just come from. "The elders and oracles debated if she brought back Eshu himself. In Nigeria, during her first years, the reports of Eshu sightings increased. Most think it was just coincidental, though, and the sightings sort of died out..."

"You knew her though... so, what do *you* think?"

"You mean do I think she brought back any Orishas?"

"Yeah."

A sadness crossed Adeola's expression. "I did... at one time... But that doesn't matter now."

She fixed her face when she caught sight of TJ's frown. Then she jerked, a thought seeming to strike her. "Oh! I forgot to give you this when I saw you at the funeral."

She flung out two fingers and twiddled them like she was skimming through a book. "*Iwe, wà ji mi,*" she said as a pocket notebook dusted from thin air. TJ waved a hand over his face and coughed away the dust cloud.

"Sorry about that," she said. "I forgot I left it in my closet for so long." She handed him the leather-bound book. "It was your sister's. She gave it to me before—" She dropped her eyes from TJ's.

"It's okay," TJ said, keeping his eyes fixed on the brown and weathered cover. It looked like it had been black once.

"Oh no, I mean she gave it to me before—before something else." TJ gave her a look that said she needed to go on, but she didn't, instead saying, "There's a bunch of stuff in there about her own theories about the promised child. You'll see a few scribbles of mine in there too."

TJ thumbed through the first pages. His sister had written about everything from her idle thoughts on trivial television theories to the deep mysteries of elemental magic. There were five whole pages dedicated to stafflore, including her own Orunmila staff—TJ's thoughts pulled back to the old piece of wood under his bunk.

As he continued skimming, he couldn't ignore the sensation of his chest swelling with joy. It was nice seeing his sister's handwriting again. He could almost hear her voice through the jagged chicken scratch Mom always complained about.

"Thanks," TJ said. "But you're still not off the hook for not telling me you work at the camp. I thought I was all alone here."

"I'm sure you'll hold me to it." She patted his shoulders and grinned. "Now, get out of here. Go impress that girl of yours."

"I never said anything about wanting to—"

"Don't worry. I'll hold *you* to that the next time we meet." She winked. "And watch out. Someone's about to come through that door."

As predicted, the library's entrance door swung open to the figure of Mr. Du Bois, who held a tattered mask under his arm. When the instructor saw where TJ's eyes had landed, the man tried to hide the coral-looking mask behind his back.

"Good afternoon, Mr. Du Bois." Adeola inclined her head with what sounded like a forced tone of friendliness.

"Miss Washington," he intoned. "A surprise finding you here."

"I'm full of 'em," she replied.

Both of them held stilted and strained grins. TJ didn't even want to get in the middle of whatever story was probably between them. Though no matter what it was, he was sure he'd side with Adeola. Mr. Du Bois gave him all kinds of bad vibes.

"You wouldn't happen to know where Elder Orji is, do you?" Mr. Du Bois asked Adeola.

Adeola thumbed behind her. "Just in the back. Taking her mid-afternoon nap like usual."

"Thank you." Mr. Du Bois gave her a short bow then shuffled to the back of the library. Adeola watched him all the way down the aisle.

"Dude, what are you doing here?" She turned to TJ. "Get to your next session."

"Oh, right!" TJ straightened, remembering where he needed to be. "Catch you later, Deola."

22

POP QUIZ

"ARE YOU GOING TO EAT THAT BEIGNET?" JOSHUA ASKED
through a mouthful of his own powdery pastry, ignoring what TJ
had just told him about the library.

TJ casually gestured for Joshua to have at it, and the boy stuffed
the sweet bread into his mouth, dotting his lips with sugar. Joshua
moaned as though he had never had something so delicious before.
TJ still hadn't gotten used to how excessive the boy's tones came
after a particularly good meal.

"I don't know how you people don't eat this every day," Joshua
said as he licked his fingers.

TJ gave him a look. "What do you mean by *you* people?"

Joshua pushed his lips together like he'd said something wrong.
TJ looked down to the bony bump at his wrist, then to Joshua's,
which was non-existent under his thick skin. "What? You mean like
skinny people or something?"

"Yeah…" Joshua trailed off, looking almost relieved. "So what
were you saying before?"

"I was saying I saw my sister's friend in the library, and Mr. Du
Bois had this weird mask made of coral, like from the ocean or
something."

"Oh yes, yes. And you mentioned something about an Eshu and
Orunmila mask?"

"That too." TJ hadn't told him why he was at the library or what
the mask had told him. Now that TJ recalled it, he wondered if the
message was even real or if it was all a trick. The mask was Eshu

acting like it was Orunmila, after all. Its words could've been entirely made up.

"What did the mask say to you, by the way?" Joshua asked.

"Some pointless gibberish," TJ answered offhandedly as he looked out into the mess hall, which had nearly cleared out for the night. At the far end, only a few children were left at their table, over-watched by Miss Gravés, who made sure they finished all their peas. "Why? You've studied enchanted masks before?"

"A little. Just like with staffs, we're not allowed to use masks until we get older. All I know is that they can boost Ashe and provide messages sometimes, depending on the mask and its properties. Whatever that mask told you, Eshu or not... you should listen to it."

"When I get the chance, I'll go back there." TJ opened his book to an exercise he was reexamining. The section was titled *Work Smarter, Not Harder: Efficient Concepts for Most Water Charms*. "But with all this work loaded on us... I don't know when I'll get back."

"Or you can just do the tutoring classes after lunch, so you don't stay up at night."

"And embarrass myself in front of Mr. Bolawe or Mr. Du Bois? Nah, I'm cool on that. I'd rather they think I'm just a late bloomer, not a complete dud."

The next day, however, Mr. Du Bois's Ogbon instruction killed him.

The old man slammed the preparatory campers with a pop quiz on Olokun, the Orisha of the Ocean's Depths.

TJ should've seen it coming. Throughout the week, Mr. Du Bois kept hinting that the class should brush up on their knowledge of "the great and deep blue." Despite the obviously cryptic reminders, TJ simply didn't have the time to keep up. If he put too much time into his Ogbon Studies, then his mile run the next day suffered, or if he put too much effort into retaining new spells from Bolawe—like he had been doing the night before—he had no time to reread the chapters on "the deep blue."

But he couldn't make any excuses when everyone else seemed prepared and ready.

Ayodeji rifled through his quiz, answering each question with such ease that it seemed like his pen never lifted from his paper. And though Manny's paper only had a few half-sketched lines, TJ was sure it was enough to at least pass like she always barely did. Joshua, on the other hand, had already leaned back in his chair and looked like he was fighting off the urge to fall asleep. When TJ took a peek at his paper, it surprised him to find every *inch* of it was filled with words.

TJ glanced up at the U-shaped crown-masks of Olosa, as though the artifacts lined over the blackboard could give him the answers he was searching for, like the masks in the library.

They didn't.

Just as TJ lifted his pencil again to add more guesswork to his essay portion, Mr. Du Bois called time. Each campers' paper whipped from under their hands—whether they were still writing or not—where they flitted through the air and stacked themselves neatly atop the counselor's desk. A tall wooden human-like statue with a too-long neck and disproportionate limbs sat behind the desk, correcting the papers with a reed pen. Its bark creaked as it marked quiz after quiz with a mechanical precision TJ's eyes couldn't keep up with.

Mr. Du Bois lifted the first of the corrected papers as he twisted the edge of his thin mustache. "Ah, Mr. Reed. You have some very specific answers here."

Joshua straightened in his seat. "Yes, sir?"

"These answers here were correct," Mr. Du Bois started. "You got the threshold of Olokun's Domain right, the Mid-Atlantic rift. And you're correct in saying sailors would offer cowries to Olokun before they set sail. But those were freebies, of course." TJ's throat went dry. Neither of those was his answer. "But your essay here is quite interesting. Care to explain what you wrote?"

Mr. Du Bois turned the paper to the rest of the class, revealing what looked like a novel down the page. A few of the campers gasped. Stephen even shouted an elongated expletive that would've slammed him with an automatic R-rating, which he apologized for straight after.

"I don't think I need to explain much, sir." Joshua shrugged. "I think I was pretty thorough there."

Mr. Du Bois rose the paper to his nose and squinted. "On this third line here, you seem to think Olokun was entrapped in his own fortress because Orunmila had a... bad attitude."

"That's right." Joshua blinked like it was a matter of fact.

"Did you forget that Olokun was set there to contain his great rage and power against we mortals?"

Joshua pursed his lips. "Depends on who's tellin' the story, I reckon."

"Right..." Mr. Du Bois narrowed his eyes. "And I suppose a teenager knows better than generations of elders and bàbálàwò."

"Well, I wouldn't call myself a teenager, exactly."

"Oh? What would you call yourself, then?"

"Uh..." Joshua gave TJ a sidelong glance. "What I mean is that... I'd prefer to be called... a young man, is all."

"Whatever it is you'd like to be called, your very long-winded bit of fiction is still incorrect."

"What?" Joshua threw up his hands. "You can't be serious. That's the way it happened. Orunmila just didn't listen to—"

Mr. Du Bois held up an open palm. "That's enough, Mr. Reed." He snatched a second test floating in the air. "And you, Mr. Young." TJ hid his face under his hand. Now he was going to hear it. "You have an interesting response I'd like to dig deeper into."

"I wouldn't," TJ mumbled under his breath.

Mr. Du Bois turned sharp eyes on TJ. "What's that?"

TJ looked up. Had he really said that out loud? The other campers stared at him like he'd just poked a lion. Ayodeji was on the edge of another one of his despicable sneers.

"N-nothing, sir." TJ dropped his head, readying himself for whatever embarrassment would be slung his way.

Mr. Du Bois narrowed his eyes a second time. "In your first response, you bring up the notion of good and evil. It's a common misconception, especially here in the West." He turned his voice to the rest of the class. "When speaking of the Orishas, you'll not find the concept of a devil or demons. The Orishas are no more evil than a hurricane to a bayou or a panther hunting an antelope. They simply... are. They exist outside of the realm of morality in the sense that we, as human and divinerkind, understand it. While it is true that mankind can be good or evil, the same cannot be said for the Orishas. Do you understand?"

"Y-yes..." TJ muttered.

"Can anyone tell me the correct answer to this question?"

Like clockwork, Ayodeji's hand sprang into the air, his gold-framed glasses nearly falling from his face, and Mr. Du Bois nodded to the boy.

"He commands the gate where souls cross between the realm of the living and the spirits."

"That's correct," Mr. Du Bois said as he pulled out another paper. "And it seems like you've received a perfect score on your quiz. Well done, Mr. Oyelowo."

"No, thank *you*, Mr. Du Bois." Ayodeji tilted his head toward TJ and gave him a cheeky wink. TJ had half a mind to flick him off, but he kept his fist clenched, instead digging his nails into his palms.

For the rest of the class, TJ checked out and doodled little stars and planets modeled after the ones hanging from the ceiling. Mr. Du Bois explained the history of Olokun and something about the Orisha's relationship with the other water deities, like Yewa, Olosa, and Yemoja. TJ probably should have paid attention, but he was afraid the moment he appeared interested, Mr. Du Bois would've called on him to answer another question he didn't know the answer to.

☦

WHEN THE SESSION ENDED, TJ WAS ALREADY READY WITH HIS packed bag. He was almost halfway out of the door when Mr. Du Bois called him back.

"Mr. Young," he said flatly, "can I have a quick word?"

TJ pinched his eyes shut as the rest of the campers shuffled around him to get to Emi Guidance with Mr. Bolawe. The last thing TJ wanted was a private conversation with Mr. Du Bois, especially when Bolawe promised they'd be learning about hearing voices on the water.

Ayodeji brushed against TJ's shoulder. "Oh, my bad, bro," he apologized—nothing about his tone said he was genuine. "Good luck in there. At least you can tell your momma you lasted a week at camp before you got kicked out."

TJ lunged at Ayodeji, but a meaty hand clenched around his wrist. TJ twisted to find Joshua holding him in place. He figured the kid was strong but hadn't realized how firm his grip could be.

"Fighting's no fun," he said with a joking murmur. "Don't let him get to you."

"Is there a problem, boys?" Mr. Du Bois asked.

TJ finally freed himself from Joshua's grip. "No, sir."

"Then come over here. I don't want you late for your next session."

"Thanks, man," TJ said to Joshua. "I'll catch up to you later."

"Yeah, sure thing." Joshua saluted TJ and turned on his heel to follow the rest of the campers.

TJ shifted toward Mr. Du Bois but didn't move from his rooted position at the door.

"Please, sit." Mr. Du Bois slumped into his seat as he rubbed at his temples. TJ kept his feet planted like stones. "I don't bite, Mr. Young. Come, sit."

TJ dragged his feet a few inches forward and waited.

He didn't sit.

"Listen, young man..." Mr. Du Bois started. Then he raised his voice, interrupting himself. "Mr. Reed, I don't believe I invited you to stay. Please, move onto your next session and give the privacy of our conversation some *respect*."

"Sorry, sorry!" came the sound of Joshua's voice from the porch outside, followed by the plodding steps of the retreating boy's feet in the mud.

Mr. Du Bois didn't speak again until he was sure Joshua was gone. "Mr. Young, I know you've started late, and you've a lot to learn... but this..." He lifted TJ's paper, which was marked with a big fat zero in bright red ink. "This I cannot accept. If you don't put in the effort, there are other young diviners who'd love your spot. When your sister was here, she never had an issue. She was quite astute. I don't know why you're not applying yourself."

I am applying myself!

"Is there anything you need from me? Are there concepts that are not clear for you?"

Anything not clear to me? Let's see, let's start with chapter one...

"Your sister did so much better when she —"

"Enough about my sister!" TJ shouted despite himself. Mr. Du Bois lifted his eyebrows, then dipped his chin into his hand. But he made no move of retort; no change came to his face to say TJ was about to be in trouble.

"Sorry. I'm just tired of hearing about her, is all."

Mr. Du Bois's posture remained stoic and unmoving. To TJ, it looked like he was being examined, but he couldn't tell. And when the stare down grew too uncomfortable, he cast his eyes to the ceiling where the child campers' planetary projects hung.

Mr. Du Bois was the first to break the silence. "If you will begrudge me this. I think it's important for you to know... Your sister was one of our best juniors. She even taught me a few things."

"A junior? My mom said she was at camp, but I thought she was, you know, a camper..."

"Oh no, she was much too talented for a place like —" Mr. Du Bois stopped himself and swallowed hard. TJ had found some solace in the thought that Dayo needed a little extra help too. But if she wasn't even a camper to begin with...

"That's not the point I'm aiming at." Mr. Du Bois's thin mustache twitched with his lip. Clearly, TJ had been putting on a sad face. "What I mean is that she helped campers get better. But those campers put in the time. So I will ask... Why haven't you been going to any of the tutoring sessions?"

TJ shrugged. Sure, he knew the answer, but he wasn't about to confide that in Mr. Du Bois.

"If you cannot keep up with the workload," Mr. Du Bois went on, "then perhaps I should tell Director Simmons you should be placed with the intermediate class... perhaps even the elementary group. Like I said, there is no shame in starting from the basics."

TJ imagined himself among a huddle of six and seven-year-olds. He was already tall among his peers. Among *real* kids, though, small ones, he'd look like a giant. And how ridiculous would it be if the other campers saw him learning how to cure bean sprouts with children barely out of kindergarten? He could already hear Ayodeji's laughter, could already see Manny's kind but disappointed look.

No, he couldn't have that.

Clearing his throat, Mr. Du Bois glanced at his watch. "I can block off my second tutoring session for a private one if that works for you."

TJ couldn't believe it. One of the main reasons he didn't want to take on a session was because other campers would be there. It was like the old dude really *could* read minds. But TJ couldn't remember anything about diviners being able to do that. Maybe he'd ask Joshua about that later. Whatever the case, he couldn't break face and let on that Mr. Du Bois had hit the mark.

"Okay... sure," TJ said, feigning a casual tone as the echo of the next set of campers came crunching down the path outside.

"Show up on time." Mr. Du Bois gathered the quizzes and straightened them on his immaculate desk. "I don't give my campers many chances. If you 'ghost' on me, trust that I will be even harder on you for the rest of the summer. Now, get on to your next session. You're late."

23

VOICES ON THE WATER

"Ah, TJ." Bolawe clapped his hands together as TJ tried to sneak between the treeline leading to the lagoon. "So glad you could join us. Next time, please let Xavier know I need to have my campers here on time."

"Yes, sir," TJ mumbled.

He tried his best not to look up at the other campers, Ayodeji in particular, who he could already hear sniggering. Instead, he focused on Joshua, who had left a spot open next to him near a patch of grass off the lagoon where a trio of butterflies flitted about.

Taking a seat next to Joshua, TJ asked, "What did I miss?"

"Nothing much. We got grouped together."

"Great, what are we doing?"

"Sorry. I should have clarified… *we're* not grouped together. I meant a more relative we."

"Oh, right…" TJ watched as everyone listened intently to Mr. Bolawe's lesson plan. The counselor was saying something about Olosa and the lagoon's power to carry messages. "Who are you grouped with?"

"One of the Santos twins and the girl with the pink glasses." Joshua tilted his head toward TJ. "So what did Mr. Du Bois want?"

"And who am I grouped with?" TJ ignored the question.

"Um…" Joshua pressed his forefinger into his temple. "That one girl who runs really fast and that guy with the man bun."

"Manny and Ayodeji!?" TJ asked a bit too loudly. Half the class snapped their heads to him.

"Yeah, those are the ones," Joshua answered, completely unaware of all the eyes that had shifted to them.

Mr. Bolawe cleared his throat. "May I continue, Mr. Young? Mr. Reed?"

"Yeah," TJ blurted before he realized that was the complete wrong thing to say. "I mean, sorry, sir. I didn't mean to..."

He settled on just not talking altogether. That seemed to be the best play. Getting on Mr. Bolawe's blacklist was the last thing he wanted or needed at the moment.

The counselor didn't press the issue, settling for a stern look, then turning back to the rest of the class. "As I was saying, there are different interpretations of magic around the world. What is taught at Ifa Academy is but one of many."

TJ thought back on the foreigners who came to his sister's funeral. They were diviners too, but they had entirely different cultures.

"For example," Bolawe continued. "Ashe as we know it can be loosely translated to *qi* in Far East traditions. Greeks and Indians have their own interpretations of the gods and their folklore. Heck, even Norse mythology's Thor seems to be next of kin to our own Shango. And our own neighbors in Nigeria, the Igbo have their own yet closely related beliefs. But really, it's all connected, more than we care to admit sometimes. And what connects us most to the heavens —the bridge—are our ancestors and the spirits."

Mr. Bolawe knelt at the edge of the lagoon and scooped a handful of water. "Our best way of communicating with those long gone is through water itself, may it be the ocean, a lake, a river." He let the water drip through his fingers. "Or a lagoon."

TJ leaned forward to hear better, recalling the message from the mask.

"One must go to the Great Water of the Lagoons to start down the divine path."

"This is the reason Camp Olosa was built where it is now," Mr. Bolawe continued. "It has strong ties with her lagoon, which at one point was jointly ruled with her sister, Oya. And as you know, because you did all of your reading," he swayed his head across the mass of campers, giving them a wink, "Yewa now helps preside over the dead. Today, we will channel both of these Orishas in an attempt to commune with our ancestors."

A sharp drumming ran through TJ's chest. Could something like that really be true? Why hadn't Mom ever mentioned anything like that? He always thought the most a diviner could do was speak and commune with animals... not the dead.

"Of course," Bolawe said, "I don't expect any of you to communicate to anything or anyone but each other. Only the most experienced diviners have the right ear for communicating with the ancestors, and even then, the messages they receive are vague and muddled. But it's great practice to expand your 'divine palette,' as it were." He clapped his hands together like he always did to begin and end his speeches. "All right, you all should know your groups. Let's get started."

The campers broke off into their respective groups: Joshua with his partners and TJ with Manny and a very disgruntled Ayodeji.

"All right, let's get this over with," Ayodeji grunted. "I don't know how we're even going to be graded on this session. I need to make up for Gravés's run this morning, and TJ sucks, so he ain't gonna help the group."

"I see some very unenthused faces," Mr. Bolawe said before making his rounds between the groups. TJ could've sworn he was eyeing Ayodeji in particular. "I expected as much, so I brought these along." He withdrew three gilded bangles that clinked as he showed them off. The light through the swamp's canopy shimmered along the objects' braided design. "These are Brass of Olosa."

"No way..." TJ heard Ayodeji gasping behind him. "Those aren't real, are they?"

"The enchantments on them are a little old," Bolawe pursed his lips, "but they should serve you all well if and when you get your staffs. The brass will allow you to channel your ear to voices on the water more easily. It only seems appropriate that a winner earns them. So, what we'll do is this... I'll make my way to the far end of the lagoon, where I'll speak a riddle. The first group to decipher it — and provide the answer to it," he lifted the bangles in hand once more, making them sound like music, "will earn a trio of Olosa's Brass."

Splashes of water sloshed as each camper rushed into the water, ready to listen to Mr. Bolawe's riddle, some pressing their ears *into* the water, others simply wading.

Andressa Santos—TJ could *kinda* tell them apart now—nearly tripped over Joshua as she said, "Come on, come on. Don't think I haven't noticed you're the best with your Ashe. You better win this for me."

Joshua blushed and gave TJ a sheepish smile as he allowed himself to be pulled into the lagoon's shallows.

The other campers turned immediately to the strongest in their groups. TJ was doing the same thing. But he couldn't decide who between Manny or Ayodeji would be better at listening to voices on the water.

It didn't matter, though... Ayodeji was already wading into the water without a second look over his shoulder. He was obviously going to try and win the thing all on his own.

"It's obvious, isn't it?" Manny said as she rolled up her jeans to her knees. "We'll never be able to commune with Orishas or whatever, but we can listen for Mr. Bolawe's voice. Like he says, he wants us to sort of... you know..."

"Be shapeless, formless," TJ finished for her. She looked at him with a blank stare. "Like water." Still, nothing. "You know... Bruce Lee."

"Oh, you mean like how Isola says in our book," Manny said. "We have to accept Ashe to use it."

"Yeah, something like that..." TJ sighed. He couldn't expect her to get *all* his references. "Maybe the best way to be open to Mr. Bolawe's voice is to, well, be like the water."

"Okay, are you two done?" Ayodeji crossed his arms. "I can't concentrate with y'all running your mouths like that."

"Well first," Manny dipped her toe into the water, "maybe we should all get in *together* and just, I don't know, put our ears close to the water?"

Ayodeji sucked his teeth, ignoring her. "Bolawe's cool and everything, but I hate it when he forces us to find our own way. Can't he just tell us what we're supposed to do for once?"

"I actually like the way he teaches," TJ retorted.

"Oh, shut your mouth. That's because you don't know the difference between *ṣúrú, ẹ̀rọ*, or *ètùtù*."

TJ opened his mouth in an automatic rebuttal before he realized he had no idea what the difference between whatever it was Ayodeji just said.

"Okay, that's enough," Manny said. "I don't think we'll get anywhere unless we work *together*."

Ayodeji didn't seem to hear Manny because he kept to his wading through the water, crouching low as though the voices would bubble to the surface for him to hear.

TJ took off his shoes and socks, rolled up his jeans, and dipped his toe into the waters. It was warmer than he expected, and duckweed stuck between his toes. There must've been some chapters about hearing voices on the water, but all he could recall was Yemoja being the overseer of salt waters. What he was stepping in now was fresh... well, if anyone could really call it fresh with its putrid greens and dingy browns.

"One must go to the Great Water of the Lagoons to start down the divine path."

Today couldn't just be a coincidence.

TJ thought back on his fundamentals. All Ashe came from the Orishas, and almost all the Orishas required offerings. While all the other campers moved around the waters, shushing each other to stay quiet, TJ tried to recall what it was Olosa required in offering. That would be what would start this whole thing, right?

There was an image that came to mind every time he thought on Olosa, just on the edge of his memory. It was something furry... no... wooly. Something that walked on four legs.

"A sheep!" he blurted, but then he got his own shush from Ayodeji, who now had his eyes closed and was humming to himself.

TJ lowered his voice to Manny before saying, "We have to offer Olosa something so she'll help us, yeah? We just need a sheep."

Manny peered over each of her shoulders, then back to TJ with a skeptical expression. "I mean, you're not exactly wrong, but... where we gonna get a sheep around here?"

"I don't know." TJ shrugged. "I just remember in the camp's brochure it mentioned a factoid about Olosa liking sheep as offerings."

"Maybe a long time ago," Manny said as she shuffled deeper into the puke-green lagoon. "But the Orishas haven't helped us diviners in, like, forever. Before we were even born. You know that story Mr. Bolawe told us the first day... some of the elders at Ifa Academy think it really did happen. Offerings like that don't happen much these days, though."

TJ glanced over to Joshua, who was still being pushed by Andressa Santos to get started, but Joshua didn't seem like he was up for it. Maybe this kind of magic was difficult even for him.

"So what do we have to do?" TJ asked.

Manny threw her hands out like a melodramatic actress on a stage play. "What I've been telling you gents all along... we have to work *together*!" She raised her voice in Ayodeji's direction.

"Be quiet," he spat back. "I think I got something."

Manny pinched the bridge of her nose and sighed. TJ was beginning to sympathize with Ayodeji's earlier musings. How the hell were they supposed to hear voices on the water without even knowing how they were supposed to do it in the first place? They needed some kind of direction, *any* kind of direction.

Should they have dunked their heads under the water and listen for voices that way? No, even TJ knew that was wrong. Among non-diviners, even they could hear voices across the water. How did that saying go? Voices carry or whatever? Maybe diviners could just hear at greater distances. But what did they need to tap into to even start hearing voices?

"Find the light in the deep, heed its call, and you will have all you desire."

What does that even mean, though?

"Yo, Ayo," Manny said, wading over to him. "There's a reason we're grouped up. Listen to me."

She grabbed at his shoulder, but he shoved her off, and she slipped on a wet stone and went tumbling into the lagoon with a splash.

"Ooo," Antonia Santos called out near a bundle of duckweed with her group. "They always say the boy who hits the girl likes her!"

"Shut up, Santos!" Ayo spat.

"I have a first name, you know!"

Ayo didn't seem to care, still intent on picking up voices.

Without thinking, TJ rushed forward and tried pulling Manny. It didn't help much; they both ended up tripping over another wet rock and splashing into the lagoon again. Their dashikis were soaked through, and Manny wore a scowl.

TJ lifted her upright properly this time and asked, "Are you all right?"

"Yeah, I'm good," she said, then whispered, "That kid is such an a—"

"I know, I know." TJ tried to steady her on her two feet.

She had started to shiver under his grip, and he barely noticed that he had started to rub her arms to warm her.

Turning to Ayodeji, who didn't even seem to care what he had just done, TJ scolded with a harsh voice, "You should apologize to her."

The earnestness in his voice shocked him. He wasn't even trying for such a deep and serious tone. He wasn't going to complain, though. It got Ayodeji's attention... Manny's too. She blushed, and a sliver of a smile flickered across her lips.

"Yeah, yeah, sorry for the pushing," Ayodeji said almost offhand-edly. "But I gotta have those bangles."

A shiver that shot from foot to spine rushed through TJ's body as he continued to stroke heat into Manny's now goosebumped-skin. There was a faint whisper in the air like the wind was speaking.

"Did you hear that?" he asked Manny. She looked up to him, her cheeks still rosy, and TJ realized he hadn't stopped rubbing her. "Oh, sorry."

"I-It's okay," she stammered, still shivering. She almost said it too quickly, and it brought a flutter to TJ's stomach.

Another splashing of water broke their shared gazes as Ayodeji waddled over to them to ask, "What did you say, Young? You heard something?"

"I don't know... maybe. It was probably just the wind, though."

"Well, go on. Try again, bro. You might pick something up."

TJ threw an eyebrow up at Ayodeji's use of "bro." He never said anything like that to TJ before, definitely not in a training session. If it weren't for the prize, he probably wouldn't have changed his tune like he did. TJ couldn't say he blamed Ayodeji, though; TJ wanted one of those bangles too.

There was a certain voice he'd love to hear.

Listening to the lagoon was like listening to a void, though. Silence beyond silence, except for the other campers who were whispering instructions to their respective groups and the intermittent croaking of a frog and a bird's squawk overhead.

"What was I thinking," TJ opened his eyes to see Ayodeji shaking his head, "Asking a chump like you to pick up voices. 'Lucky charm' my ass." He turned, giving his back to TJ.

There wasn't a comeback TJ could come with. No retort that would make any sense. Ayodeji was right. His first week at camp was a total dud. He didn't deserve to be there. Like Mr. Du Bois said, there were others more worthy, others more fit, others who could prosper because they had the talent, not because they had some famous sister.

A hollow pit deepened in TJ's stomach as he watched the others. Some of the campers were already working out what Mr. Bolawe's riddle was; TJ caught snippets, the telltale eagerness that said a few of the others were close to figuring it out. Even Joshua seemed to be getting into it, to the utter delight of Andressa Santos, who jumped and clapped.

"Try touching me again," Manny suggested after a while.

The double-take that shook through TJ's head brought him all the way out of his stupor. "Come again?"

"You heard whatever you did when you held me, right?"

"I mean… I guess?"

"So…" She stuck out her arm. "Don't make it weird, and it won't be weird."

TJ felt his face flush. "Nah, it's okay. We'll just let one of the others get it. We'll never get it in time now. We're too far behind, and—"

Manny rolled her eyes and snatched TJ's wrist. The moment her skin wrapped around TJ's forearm, the same shiver shot through him, and the whisper came again. It was still distant, otherworldly, like it was being filtered through a funnel, but it was there.

"Okay, I'm *definitely* hearing something," TJ said breathlessly.

"Me too, me too." Manny held his wrist tighter. "But it doesn't sound like Mr. Bolawe." She squinted in concentration. "Maybe we just need it to be clearer—Ayo, get over here. We can hear something."

"I'm not going over there. I think I got something right now."

"Boy, stop lying. You ain't got nothin'. Come over for a second. Grab TJ's other wrist."

Ayodeji turned around so fast his designer glasses nearly fell off the bridge of his nose. "Hell nah, I'm gonna touch that dude's hand."

TJ tried to tune the two of them out. The whisper was becoming clearer, less a filtered voice and now something with weight behind it.

Manny was right though.

It wasn't Mr. Bolawe's voice.

This one was female.

A lightness came to TJ's chest, and his pulse quickened. Could it really be her? Could it really be Dayo? He hadn't felt something like this since… since the funeral.

"Stop trying to act cool and grab my wrist, man." Again, TJ surprised himself with his own tone. Even Lorenzo and Antonia's group, which was closest to them, turned their heads like peacocks to see what was going on.

If TJ had the slightest chance to hear his sister…

It's all he wanted ever since that day in her bedroom. It was half the reason he came to this camp in the first place. He wasn't going to let some punk wannabe "thug life" guy get in the way of that.

So TJ emphasized, with more force, "You want those bangles or not?"

Ayodeji sucked at his teeth again, but he didn't come any closer. "What you hear anyway?"

"A voice, like we're supposed to," TJ said irritably. The voice was already receding to a whisper. "Come over here real quick, or we'll lose."

He peered over to another group who looked ready to jump out of the lagoon and announce they had it.

They didn't have time, so TJ lied. "It's Bolawe. I think he's reciting some prayer..."

"Which one?" Ayodeji asked skeptically. Still, he refused to come forward.

"I-I don't know." TJ couldn't even think of a prayer he could come up with.

Manny, however, did. "It sounds like a prayer to Olokun... or maybe Yemoja." Her eyes pinched shut in faux concentration. "You know, actually, it might be Yewa. What do you think, TJ?"

It took TJ perhaps a beat too long to catch on and continue the charade, but Ayodeji didn't seem to notice. The boy was nearly on the tip of his toes. "Oh, oh... it definitely sounds like something about Yemoja, for sure. Yeah, yeah."

"That would make sense since... since..." Manny stammered. "Yemoja is Olosa's mother."

"Right...?" TJ shot her questioning eyes. "Right!"

Ayodeji snapped his fingers. "What's the first line you hear? Is Bolawe saying, 'Yemoja, mother of the fishes?' He probably wants us to recite the prayer back to him. That's easy."

"Well, come over here and help us figure it out," TJ said.

Begrudgingly, but surely, Ayodeji trodded over and grabbed TJ's free wrist.

The voice boomed out then. Loud and clear.

It was chanting.

"*Come to me, come to me,*" it said. It was Yoruba, but for once, TJ could understand it without issue.

"What the hell is this?" Ayodeji said. "This isn't some prayer."

TJ ignored him. *Come to you where?* he thought. *Dayo, is that you? Where do I have to go?*

"We're supposed to be hearing a man's voice, Bolawe's voice, not a female, idiot." Ayodeji snatched his hand away, but TJ grabbed for it again.

"No, no wait," TJ said. "T-this is part of it or something. I-it's what Bolawe wants us to hear."

Ayodeji tried to pull away, but TJ wouldn't let go. "Let go of me, man. Get off me."

"Come to where?" TJ shouted to the lagoon, desperate for a response. "Come where?"

A sharp pain impacted his chest, and the connection was gone. The voice petered out like a delicate gust giving way to peace and quiet. Next thing TJ knew, he fell back into the lagoon once more with a splash.

Through the current Manny's voice wavered through, saying, "What did you do that for, you jerk?"

"He wouldn't let go of me!"

"You didn't have to elbow him like that!"

A hand clutched at the collar of TJ's dashiki and pulled him from the waters. Through the lukewarm water dripping down his Afro and over his head, he could make out Lorenzo's loose curls and green eyes. "You all right there, *cara*?"

"Nah," TJ grunted through the bruise swelling between his chest and ribs.

TJ's vision was too faded to properly see Ayodeji just ahead. Black and red spots threatened to take his conscious thought. A warm stream came from his mouth, and he could only assume it was blood.

"He didn't have a clue what he was doing," Ayodeji was saying to Manny.

"You heard that voice too!" Manny shot back. "Why would you want to stop it?"

"Because he doesn't know how to listen," TJ grunted.

His legs were like noodles beneath him. He would've fallen if Lorenzo wasn't still holding him up.

The blurry figure of Ayodeji turned and spat, "At least I'm not here on a pity ride because my sister went and got herself killed."

And with that, TJ forgot about his weariness, forgot about the blood pooling from his mouth, forgot about the ringing in his ears.

All that mattered now was making Ayodeji bleed.

TJ pulled back his hand and flung it out with as much Ashe as he could muster. From the tip of his fingers, a concentrated wind gust shot forth and thumped against Ayodeji's chest, hurling the boy back into a spin that sent him head over heels. Even the trees near them pushed out against the manifested wind, and the long hair of certain campers blew back like they were hit with a leaf blower.

All energy drained from TJ's body as Ayodeji bolted up from the ground, the boy's top knot coming undone. "Okay, so you want to play like that, then?"

He cracked his knuckles and stepped forward, though TJ could tell he was shaken up by the way he wobbled. He was just protecting his pride at this point.

"Fight! Fight! Fight!" one of the campers called out.

"Damn, TJ..." Joshua said from the side. "I didn't know you could do that."

"C'mon." Ayodeji gestured TJ forward. "Try that again, òlòsí."

TJ didn't have to understand to know that was an insult.

"That's enough." Manny stepped between them. "Both of you."

"Nah, let 'em go," Lorenzo said. "Sometimes you just gotta let it happen."

"Lorenzo!" Manny chided him with the tone of a mother. "Mr. Bolawe!"

At the far end of the lagoon, TJ saw Mr. Bolawe making his way hurriedly over. But TJ didn't care. He limped forward and pushed his way past the both of them. "He talked about my sister. And someone needs to teach him a lesson."

"You already did that." Manny's eyes pleaded with him to stop.

TJ halted his steps and gazed at her. She was right. He didn't need to keep fighting. He'd made his point. But just as he turned to Ayodeji to call the fight off, an invisible force wrapped around his ankle and flung him around like a loop on a rollercoaster. His spin ended in a harsh splash in the lagoon, but he landed on his feet, thankfully.

TJ lifted his hands to defend against the next gust of wind, but he was too exhausted, too inexperienced to even know how to counter it. Like Ayodeji before, a wind gust caught him in the chest and he flew back, but instead of landing in the dirt, his head smacked against a tree.

A third blow came for him, a huge gust that brought leaves with it in its wake like a whip. It came down fast and harsh, aimed to slap across his chest.

"I said no!" Manny shouted as she outstretched her arms in a protective orb of wind that shielded against Ayodeji's attack.

"Stop! Stop!" Mr. Bolawe called out.

Wobbling to his feet, TJ stumbled over to Ayodeji again. He was barely three steps from the boy when two meaty hands came over at the edge of his vision, and he was clutched in a giant bear hug.

"Let go of me." TJ kicked limply, too exhausted to really muster any fight against the hold. "Get off me..."

Joshua's voice came to his ear. "It's not worth it, friend. It's not worth it."

Despite himself, or perhaps it was something in Joshua's smooth timbre, TJ stopped fighting back. He let his tense muscles hang loose, but Joshua still held him firm.

"What's going on over here?" Mr. Bolawe hustled over to the commotion, pushing through campers who were trying to get a better look between Joshua, who was holding TJ back, the Santos Sisters, who were holding Manny back, and Ayodeji's jackass friends, LaVont and Jimoh, who were protecting him like they were part of a king's guard.

"TJ wouldn't listen to me," Ayodeji blurted. "He kept saying he heard a woman's voice when we were supposed to be listening for your voice, sir."

"But we should have listened to TJ," Manny shot back. "I could hear it too." She twisted to Mr. Bolawe. "Didn't you say it takes a great diviner to hear voices? Maybe we *were* hearing an Orisha? Communing with that voice seemed more important than some class assignment."

TJ felt a little embarrassed with the whole class knowing that he was hearing voices he wasn't supposed to. Chatter started up and rippled out along the lagoon's edge, the waves of murmurs and whispers like wasps to his ears. He didn't know why it bugged him. After all, like Manny pointed out, Mr. Bolawe said only very esteemed diviners could hear anything at all. But what he heard felt like it was for him *specifically*. He didn't need everyone asking him questions, least of all a counselor.

It took TJ a minute, but he finally met Mr. Bolawe's eyes. The man fixed him with a curious expression, not unlike the way he did at the funeral when TJ came to or on that first day of camp when TJ was looking into the enchanted bonfire. The stare should have made him uncomfortable, yet somehow, he knew if he told Bolawe the truth of what he heard, he'd believe his every word.

Instead of speaking to him, Mr. Bolawe looked away and out to the greater class, his odd expression gone as soon as it came. "Well... I hadn't expected this to happen as it did. You three." He waved his finger between TJ, Manny, and Ayodeji. "I need you to apologize to each other."

"But Mr. Bolawe..." Manny started but was swiftly cut off.

"No excuses. There seems to be fault on all sides. Do it now and put this to bed."

"I apologize for my actions, TJ and Manny," the words came so quick out of Ayodeji's mouth, there was no way Mr. Bolawe would believe it. It was beyond disingenuous. "I should have never raised hands and put them to either of you. I hope you can forgive me and we can move forward from this."

TJ wanted to puke. Manny looked like she could've thrown something at Ayodeji. And Mr. Bolawe totally bought it. "Thank you, Mr. Oyelowo," he said, then turned to TJ and Manny.

TJ bit the inside of his cheek. He wasn't going to say a damn thing. Manny seemed like she was definitely thinking the same thing, her nostrils flared, and her skin flushed purple-red. Her lips were moving, but TJ couldn't hear what she was saying.

"What's that, Miss Martinez?" Bolawe asked, canting his head.

"Sorry." Her voice barely came above a whisper. In fact, if TJ hadn't been anticipating what her next words would be, he wouldn't have known what she said.

Mr. Bolawe, seemingly satisfied, brushed away a loose leaf on his shoulder. "And you, Mr. Young."

TJ kept his mouth shut and his face fixed with a grimace. He didn't look at anyone, not even Ayodeji. He just stared out across the lagoon where a trio of cranes balancing on one leg each seemed to wait in anticipation for his response.

"Mr. Young…"

Mr. Bolawe could've been talking to a tree, and he would have gotten more of a response — Monsieur Francois notwithstanding.

"All right then." Mr. Bolawe clapped his hands together. "Session dismissed. Everyone is free to go to lunch. Everyone, save for TJ."

A stream of "ooos" trickled throughout the group as TJ swallowed long and hard.

Great. The week was turning out just perfect. If he were lucky… he'd be sent back home without any of the other campers having to see him.

24

FIASCO FRIDAY

It took a long while for Mr. Bolawe to speak at first. For a few moments, the man knelt next to the tree TJ had slammed into. He said some words, and the scar that was left there started to knit itself back to health. Words seemed difficult to cross Mr. Bolawe's lips, and TJ suspected that he used the time to heal the tree to figure out what to say next.

TJ stood there, not knowing what he should do. But he knew he wasn't going to speak first.

That was for damn sure.

"You know," Mr. Bolawe finally said, rubbing at his deep pores. "Your sister loved coming to this lagoon."

TJ scoffed. "Don't do that."

"Do what?" Bolawe's eyebrow lifted curiously.

"Try and let me off easy. Just tell me how it is. Straight up. I know I'm getting kicked out for fighting and not apologizing."

Mr. Bolawe rubbed dirt free from his hands with a hint of a smirk. "Look, I like you, Mr. Young. But right now, your behavior is unacceptable."

"Then you have another reason you should kick me out."

"It's not my intention to kick you —"

"Why are you always being so easy on me? Why don't you tell me I need to push harder and to focus like Miss Gravés?"

"There are enough hardships in your life. I don't need to pile them on." Mr. Bolawe drew his hand to TJ's lips. TJ jerked back. "Your lip is cut. Let me heal it for you."

"I can do it myself," TJ whined as he dabbed at the wound. Blood was already coming down his chin. "Àrá mì n dù mí. Gbin àwọ àrá mì."

"*Awọ*," Mr. Bolawe corrected his pronunciation.

TJ recited the healing spell again, but he was still butchering it. Mom had warned him about the intonation, but he couldn't do it right for the life of him.

"Mr. Young, just let me—"

"I told you I got it!" TJ didn't have it.

Mr. Bolawe lifted his hand again. "TJ..."

"Look, if you're not kicking me out, could you stop coddling me?" TJ retreated to the lagoon to wash his cut. Then he thought better of it. Lagoons were sort of filthy, and he didn't have the ability to manifest fresh water. Add another failure to his resume. "Why can't you tell me I'm not applying myself like Mr. Du Bois? You can't keep letting me off when I'm not even half as good as the other campers. I couldn't even defend myself against Ayodeji. I need to learn this stuff by the end of the summer. I have to—"

"Ifa isn't going anywhere. It's only the first week, and you're new to all this."

"More coddling!" TJ scoffed. "Were you like this with my sister? Is this how you treated her?"

"Well, no... but she *did* come to this camp."

"Then why with me? I bet she didn't need to be carried like this. What happens if I don't get into Ifa Academy? What other options are there?"

"If it comes to that, we'll think of something. Don't worry about it."

"Why can't you get mad at me? This whole time you were supposed to discipline me. Tell me I had detention or some shit. I don't need this." TJ stormed off toward the treeline; it was obvious Mr. Bolawe wasn't going to stop him. "And you know something. Mr. Du Bois told me about Dayo. She didn't even come here as a camper. She was a junior helper herself. She always had the talent. I don't. To be honest, I just came here to find out more about—" In his anger, he almost let it out. "Forget it. Just forget it, okay..."

TJ brushed a vine to the side to open a path back to camp. But Mr. Bolawe's gentle baritone slowed him. "TJ, about your sister..." TJ halted his march but didn't turn. "There's more to say."

Someone cleared their throat farther along the path around the bend. They both did a little jump.

It was Mr. Du Bois. "Something's come up, Olufemi. You're needed in the offices."

"Just give me a moment. I wanted to tell TJ—"

"Don't mention it. I've heard it all with my sister. She's perfect. I get it. She did everything right. I *get* it. For the rest of the summer, I don't want to hear any more about my sister, got it?"

TJ didn't wait for Mr. Bolawe's answer, or rebuttal, or whatever he had ready in response. He barely even registered Mr. Du Bois reminding him of their tutoring session later.

All TJ wanted was to be away from there. Far away.

⚰

THE MESS HALL WAS SUPPOSED TO BE WHERE A TEENAGER COULD relax, have some fruit juice, or scarf down some chips. Lunchtime was meant to be carefree, thirty minutes of no adults, no instruction, and no stress. It was exactly what TJ needed just at the moment.

Yet, he felt miserable.

Legs quivering atop the wooden floor, he stared at the large seventy-five written next to his name on the blackboard over the chow line.

A seventy-five that was near at the bottom of a very long list.

The tray of food in his hands looked like a toddler had placed it. He had paid no mind to the ketchup he squirted over his mashed potatoes or the Italian dressing he had poured over his double-fudge brownies.

He couldn't help it, not with that seventy-five ranking taunting him from above.

While the rest of the campers enjoyed their lunches and chitchatted about what they'd do during their free time over the weekend, TJ stood transfixed at yet another living statue writing down the week's grading scale. Unlike Mr. Du Bois's statue, this one had hands that were too long for its body, tall enough to reach high along the fifty-foot blackboard.

For the entire week, the board was empty, and TJ had wondered what it was there for. But the moment the statue—which had stood in the corner like a decoration—came to life and started writing on the board with chalk, the entire camp had gathered around to see where they ranked. All the other teens rated in the top forty and had long gone to their benches to finish their meals. TJ had stood there for several minutes wondering if his parents registered him in the camp at all until the statue chalked: *SEVENTY-FIVE. T. YOUNG. AGE 14* on the board just under SEVENTY-FOUR. Z. BRISKER—a seven-year-old.

Do they really have to put the ages next to the names?

It was one thing to sort of know you were the worst in your class, but to see it in large print for all to see was a different thing entirely. The closest teen to TJ, Marie Wilson, was at the thirty-eighth position on the list—a whole thirty-seven position gap between him and her. At this rate, he'd be lucky to overtake the pre-teen intermediate group, who huddled around the middle of the pack.

After a few minutes, the statue finished off the last name: *B. OLALOYE. AGE 6*, who ranked ninety-third on the list.

What would Mom say when she found out? A sick acid burned down TJ's chest at the thought. This was worse than getting a "C" in Algebra with a Nigerian mother at home. This stuff *should've* come easy. He was learning magic tricks, for crying out loud!

A light tap came at TJ's shoulder. He turned to find Joshua giving him a cautious look. "You okay, bud?"

"Yeah." TJ tried to sound casual. "I was just daydreaming."

"For the *whole* lunch period?"

TJ peered over his shoulder. There were only a few pockets of campers left, including Manny, who glanced over at him with doe eyes.

"I had a lot on my mind, I guess..." TJ brushed past Joshua and headed toward an empty table. A pair of feet tapped against the wooden floor behind him.

"Listen," Joshua said. "What do you have planned after your... lunch?"

TJ looked down at the soggy mess he concocted and groaned internally. Could the day get any worse? He slammed his plate down, and his food exploded in a spray of ingredients never meant to mix.

"If you're going to tell me to do some tutoring," TJ said through an awkward mouthful of ketchup'd mashed potatoes. "I already got a lecture from Mr. Du Bois and Mr. Bolawe—"

"No, no, nothing like that. I was just going to give you some pointers about fighting. That was a good air-punch you had, but you gotta be trickier. Throw a few feints or two, you know?"

"Joshua, not right now." The topic of him getting beat down was the last thing he wanted to discuss.

"I'm just sayin'. You coulda had him if—"

"Shut up, man!"

Joshua clamped his mouth shut, his ears reddening a little. "Hey, man," he said, "don't sell yourself short. You knocked him back pretty good."

"And then Manny had to come rescue me," TJ mumbled.

"Ah, come on. It wasn't like that. She just didn't want you in trouble."

Joshua could've been talking to a wall. Or perhaps a sledge-hammer was a more apt description, as TJ started slamming his head onto the table.

"You feel better?" Joshua asked.

TJ stopped and planted his head onto the table like a magnet drew him there. "Marginally."

"Look," Joshua pulled out a brass bangle from his pocket. "I was gonna use it for myself, but I swiped this from Bolawe... Here, take it." He slid the metal along the table. "Maybe this will help you next week or for whatever else you might need it for."

TJ rolled his head along his arm to peer at the brass. It twinkled against the overhead fluorescents. "Nah, man. That's yours. I'll just go to Mr. Du Bois's tutoring or something. He'll have a field day chewing me out."

Joshua took the bangle and stuffed it into TJ's dashiki pocket. "Look, dude. I heard what you were screaming in class. If the bangle can help you with..." He glanced over his shoulders, then murmured, "Your sister. I'd be a jerk not to give it you, you know? Plus, what are friends for?"

TJ sighed, but he accepted Joshua's gift. "I appreciate it, man. Really. Sorry for gettin' mad."

"Don't mention it." Joshua gave him a little shove. "Now go find out if that was your sister talking to you or not."

☨

INSTEAD OF GOING TO THE FIELD WHERE ALL THE OTHER CAMPERS were working off their lunch with a game of crossover, TJ limped his way to the boys' cabin. He stumbled to the bathroom to clean his face. He almost didn't recognize his reflection in the mirror. Half his right cheek was swelling like a grapefruit—and the cut on his lip ran with blood again from the inside of his mouth and midway down his chin.

A buzzing came to his ear, rumbling to his right like the electric lantern outside, and with it, a familiar brush against his neck. A heat baked at his thigh, and he slipped his hand into his pocket. The brass seemed to beckon him with its warmth.

Well, Joshua didn't give it to him for no reason. So he slipped it on.

The sensation along his neck redoubled, and the buzzing in his ear grew louder.

"Who is that?" TJ spun, screaming at nothing but empty bunks, and that familiar brush along his neck came again. "Dayo, is that you? Can you hear me?" His speech was broken up through lumps of snot. "I can't do this. I can't be like you. I never could."

The buzzing persisted, rolling out into a low drone. It didn't sound like a typical buzz in his ear. It sounded more like it was coming from the middle of the cabin.

Tiptoeing against squeaky floorboards, TJ edged closer to the sound that grew louder and louder until finally, he settled his weight in front of his bunk.

The buzzing stopped.

TJ knelt and squinted to the dark shadow under his bed. A glow of dirty emerald emanated there. TJ uplifted the floorboard, reached out, and dragged his baseball bag toward him. Then he unzipped it to reveal his sister's staff, its faded green crystal shining brightly.

"Dayo, is that you?" TJ asked it. "Dayo, can you hear me? Just give me a sign. Anything." The crystal pulsed at the same rhythm of a heartbeat, *his* heartbeat. TJ ran his hand down its shaft, and a whisper came to his ears, distant and otherworldly. It had to be Dayo. But he had no way of communicating with her, except… he did—the brass around his wrist.

"Hang on, Dayo. I have an idea."

25

LIGHT IN THE DEEP

AFTER THE NIGHTLY CAMPFIRE, TJ WENT STRAIGHT TO THE BOYS'
cabin without a word, where he threw himself to his bed and under
the warmth of his blanket. When the boys filed in, he heard a few
mocking whispers from Jimoh and LaVont.

"Aw, look. The chump's going to bed early," Jimoh jeered.

LaVont made kissing noises in response. "Maybe he'll call his
momma so she can take him home."

"At least he lasted a week." That voice belonged to Ayodeji. "That
was longer than what you said, Jimoh. What was your guess? Two
days?"

"Nah, one," Jimoh answered, and they all laughed.

One of them shoved against TJ's feet. He ignored them and
pretended to be asleep. And he continued to pretend even after Elder
Wale snuffed the lanterns out, even after Joshua's snores filled the
room.

He had to be sure no one would catch him. Not now.

A half-hour after Joshua's first series of snorts and wheezing, TJ
was satisfied he could make his first move. Throwing his blanket
from his feet, he gently pressed his feet into the cabin's squeaky floorboards. During the day, TJ never noticed how many loose boards
there were, and that night it seemed like every single one screamed at
every light tiptoe of his feet. There was no real way to avoid them, so
he ground his teeth and hoped for the best as he leaned down to
retrieve his staff. The moment he touched its smooth wood, Joshua's
snoring stopped.

TJ froze. He knew he should've hopped back into his bed and put the staff back in its bag. In fact, he kept pleading with his body to move but it wouldn't, fighting against reason, too petrified to move an inch. But after a short moment, Joshua's snoring rumbled on.

Before his body locked up on him again, TJ snatched the rest of the staff's length from under his bed and shuffled along the bunks. He disregarded if anyone saw him walking by. For all they knew, he was going to the bathroom. Technically, he was—he just wasn't going to stay in there.

TJ crossed the threshold and locked the door behind him, then turned to the shiny faucets and luster stalls that gaped at him in the dark. He stared straight ahead at the single window at the back. Most of the time, it was used for airing out any stinky dumps, but that night it would be TJ's exit.

With light feet, TJ moved to the window, opened it, and dropped his staff gingerly through it. The wooden shaft rustled against the bush below after it fell. Then he jumped up and forward, leveraging his weight on his wrists and sliding forward on his forearms until he squeezed through the tiny window. Once he fell into the bush next to his staff, he snatched it up and turned around to see if anyone would follow.

There was no one, save for the carving just under the roofing depicting Olosa and all her animal companions—who were all staring straight at him.

TJ locked up, thinking Olosa would cry out and sound the alarm, yet surprisingly she only smiled and winked. It even looked like she was egging him on, and the fish next to her wiggled their little flippers. Waving back nervously, TJ backpedaled very slowly. The whole thing was sort of creepy.

If Olosa is okay with me sneaking out, TJ thought, *maybe I shouldn't be so scared.*

Once he reached the treeline, he turned around and headed for the lagoon, a smidge more confident in his midnight endeavor.

He had to admit, though, the camp at night was an entirely new beast, with its loud crickets, croaking frogs, and dark trees that looked more like dark specters in the night. Twice he stopped short because he thought he saw movement through the shadows. On his third halt, he realized there actually *was* something skulking through the night.

Wood creaked like the inside of some old pirate ship or like a spooky door frame of an old mansion. But that didn't make sense.

The part of the swamp he was sneaking through didn't have any structures that would sound like that. There were no boats on the lakes or the lagoon, and he had left the cabins at least a hundred yards behind him.

Then he saw it.

A pair of bright red lights revealed themselves between dark tree trunks and hanging leaves half a football field away.

TJ drew behind the first bush he could find large enough to hide himself behind. But he didn't see the large puddle it sat in, and his foot splashed in it. The red lights lifted and focused on him. They grew bigger through the dark, and that strange croaking of wood came with it.

A violent pulse raced along TJ's throat as he realized what he was seeing: one of the statues on patrol with ruby crystals for eyes. It was like a wooden Terminator stomping forward, and its crimson glare was locked onto its target. In the space of a few seconds, it had gone from the far end of the forest to a mere few yards from TJ's hiding spot. With each creaking step, TJ's legs drained of feeling. He needed to run, and he needed to do it now, but fear fixed him in place.

A loud snap cracked from somewhere off to TJ's right, and the statue stopped its march and turned its head to the sound. Without as much as a second glance at TJ's bush, it redirected its long strides toward the disturbance.

TJ blew out a silent but long sigh and thanked the Orishas for his good fortune—something he didn't often do. But it took a while, a long while, before TJ could get his legs moving again. Fear rolled through him in waves as he expected to see another pair of red eyes glaring at him.

It must've been fifteen long minutes before he pressed on, though this time at a much slower pace than before, his hurried walk traded for a measured step befitting a US Navy SEAL.

Each sound and dark corner seemed to amplify tenfold from what they appeared to be just a few moments prior. Biting down on fear, he overlooked all that as he shouldered through weeds and branches until he arrived at one of the most beautiful landscapes he'd ever encountered.

During the day, the lagoon looked a sickly green with its lumpy duckweed and tree branches that twisted like the fingers of a nasty witch. Even with all the wonderful wildlife ducking in and out of the bushes, its foul appearance couldn't be helped. But at that moment in the night, with a cluster of fireflies hovering over the black water majestically, TJ could call the lagoon nothing short of marvelous. The awe of the sight sent him keeling back onto his butt.

For a longer while than he intended, he just sat there among the dazzling light of the fireflies and a soothing melody of crickets, his run-in with the red-eyed statue nearly forgotten.

Dad had always talked about camping his entire childhood, that typical stuff you saw on TV where a son learns how to fish in one of those rickety old boats. But Dad was always so busy, and he never got the chance to fulfill his promise. TJ thought one of their camping ventures would have looked just like this in some forest—with far less mud—as his father told him stories about the cosmos or some such. Or maybe that role would go to Mom, who'd make mention of the wisdom he could divine from Orunmila's stars.

The thought of Orishas brought TJ back to his reality at Camp Olosa. He turned his gaze from the heavens and to the staff lying next to him in the mud. He ran his finger along the bottom where it narrowed to a point, then up the middle where the wood broke out into the figure of a helix, then up to the crystal and the figurehead that rested atop it. As his finger drew closer and closer to the top of the staff, it seemed to bring forth another glow from the crystal, and with it, a whisper.

But again, the whisper was faint, barely a murmur over the croaking frogs and singing crickets. He withdrew the bangle Josh had given him and gazed upon how it shined against the green hue of the staff's crystal. Slipping it onto his wrist, he expected the whisper to grow loud, but nothing happened. So he recalled Mr. Bolawe's lesson about voices on the water and how it felt when Manny and Ayodeji were channeling through him before their exercise turned into a fiasco.

Fate—or the Orisha—seemed to tease him, though. He gave them his energy, yet he received nothing in return but the lagoon's natural music—whatever good that would do him. Yet he persisted, squinting his eyes and concentrating his ears to decipher the words of the water.

It was like trying to speak a foreign language he knew existed, one he knew what sounded like but without the experience to understand its vocabulary, its nuance. He *knew* what Ashe felt like. It was just there at the tip of his fingers and the curl of his toes. He just couldn't grab it, harness it.

Why would it not listen to *him*? Why wouldn't it let him communicate with his sister? It was so easy before. He wasn't even trying the first time he heard her.

Frustrated, TJ clutched the largest rock in reach and hurled it into the water. It thudded into the center of the lagoon with a large splash. Once all the ripples settled, a *thwack* came from the forest behind him, like someone had snapped a twig in a bush.

Once was just a coincidence, some rodent or other animal in the night. Twice in the space of a few minutes meant someone else was there, someone watching him.

Without thinking, TJ hid his staff between a thicket of reed plants and twisted on his behind, his heart thundering in his ears. He suddenly remembered how Director Simmons warned them of the dangers of Olosa's Domain. What if Ol' Sally was stalking him to finish the job? Perhaps she was already full when she saw him that first day. Or maybe that statue had returned to loom over him again.

"Psst," hissed a voice from the shadows. "I didn't mean to scare you."

Through the dark, Adeola materialized with a wide smile.

TJ let out a deep breath as his previous fear turned to mild annoyance. "What are you doing here? I almost pissed myself."

"I was in a late meeting with Mr. Du Bois about joining the camp."

"I thought you said you were the librarian's assistant?"

"Oh, I am. I am." Adeola cleared her throat. "But I was seeing if I could have a position as a counselor. That Mr. Bolawe guy seemed to beat me to it, though."

It seemed odd that a meeting or a job interview would be held so late at night, but TJ decided to let Adeola off. After all, he'd just been caught out of bed, and she could've had him kicked out if she wanted.

"You know, it's dangerous out here," she said as she knelt next to him. "Sally's just on the other side of the bank."

TJ whipped his head in the direction she pointed. "Really?"

Adeola laughed and threw her head to one side to reveal her second eye that was often hidden under her bangs. "No, but she could be. She protects this place, you know."

"Right, right." TJ tried to play off his fear with a straightening of his hoodie.

"What's going on? You must have a good reason for being out here so late. Is everything okay?"

TJ was about to open his mouth in an automatic lie but stopped himself short from the first utterance. This was Adeola he was talking to, possibly the closest thing he had left to his sister. She deserved the truth, and he needed to be honest with at least one person.

"Nah." TJ shook his head. "Things pretty much suck right now."

"Your sessions aren't going well?"

"They were going fine like I told you yesterday... well as fine as failing is concerned. But we were doing this exercise with voices on the water when—" TJ stopped himself. "It doesn't matter. I saw the rankings at lunch today. There's no way I'm getting accepted to Ifa. I'm not even better than some of the little kids."

Adeola nodded to the thicket next to TJ. "And that hasn't helped you at all?"

TJ didn't have to look to know she had seen the staff. Instead of trying to deny it or hide it, he slid it out from the tall reeds. "It doesn't matter. It doesn't work right. Maybe it only worked for my sister."

"Did you read that notebook I gave to you? Your sister's notebook."

"I, um, skimmed it." TJ felt his face go red. "Most of it's in Yoruba, and I can't understand it. Plus, I've had so much on my mind, I haven't dived deep into it or anything."

"You know what I'm going to say now, right?"

"To read it?"

Adeola smiled. "And take extra care with the stuff she says about her staff. By the way... you have to be careful with that thing." She jabbed a finger at the staff. "You shouldn't have it at camp. Kids your age aren't allowed. Maybe I should keep it for you until summer is over."

TJ found himself clutching at the mahogany tighter. "No," he blurted. "I mean... it's the only thing I have that's hers besides the notebook—thank you, by the way."

Adeola looked between the staff and TJ as though she were deciding if she should overrule him and take it anyway. "First, you're very welcome. And second..." TJ was ready for it. He was already working on several reasons he should keep the staff instead of her taking it. "Second... I won't tell anyone, but you have to promise me one thing."

"What?"

"Promise me you'll keep it hidden, keep it safe. No one can know you have it." Her tone came with an edge of earnestness TJ had not expected. "I mean it, Tomori Jomiloju. No one."

"Okay, okay, I promise," he said with his hands held up, trying to lighten the dark mood. "Don't get all Gandalf on me." He looked to the staff once more. "What? Do I have the one true ring in my hand or something?"

Adeola shook her head and cracked her first smile. "Of all the teenagers I know, you're the only one who would make that joke." Her lips flattened again, eyes narrowed. "But do as I tell you."

Another rustling came at the treeline. This time TJ and Adeola jumped in unison. No one appeared from the dark to greet them, though. Still, it could've been the statue coming back, or worse.

"I think it's time for us to go," Adeola said with more fear than TJ expected from her.

"Don't worry," TJ said. "If it's Ol' Sally, you should have seen me with her last week. We're best buds at this point."

"No, I really should take you back to your cabin."

"Please, Deola. I'm out here to find my sister. I swear I heard her voice in the water today. If there's any chance I could hear her again... hear Dayo again. I want to at least try. You of all people could understand that?"

Adeola looked unconvinced.

"Give me half an hour. If you still find me here, then you can drag me back to my cabin."

Adeola took in a long and deep sigh, but she relented. "Don't tell anyone I was here, okay? I was supposed to head straight out to my... cabin."

"Sure thing." TJ nodded as he watched her retreat back into the swamp and back toward camp.

For the next few minutes, he recanted the primary prayers to Olosa. He started at a whisper, and nothing happened, just the typical void he'd always felt whenever he tried to speak to the Orishas.

A small voice came to the back of his mind, another encouraging memory from his sister.

"*Just because you can't spark a candle with your fingertips doesn't mean you don't have Ashe, TJ,*" Dayo had said to him once. "*You just need to find what works for you.*"

What *did* work for him, he wondered. If not the staff, if not the prayer, then what could he do? His mind pulled back to Dayo's parade, how the performers and the others seemed to generate energy through song and dance. There was just one issue with that...

TJ hated both singing and dancing.

But he resolved to make an effort, dipping his heel into the dirt and turning around in an awkward pirouette as he sang the prayer instead of just speaking it. By his fourth attempt, all he managed was to silence the croaking frogs, who seemed struck dumb by his terrible singing voice. On his fifth attempt, he held up his sister's staff over his head like he was doing a rain dance but ultimately was met with no fanfare.

He flicked the brass around his wrist twice, then thrice. And still nothing.

After his dozenth try, he relented. Something wasn't right. Whether it was the butchered prayer, his borrowed staff, or he himself that was the problem, he couldn't tell. He tried his best. Like Dad said before TJ left, that's the best he could hope for. Despite the thought, it didn't help fill the emptiness panging at TJ's insides.

"Well, it was nice knowing you, Olosa," TJ said to no one. "I'm tapping out. I'm done. I'll go back to Los Angeles and be a plumber."

TJ was about to turn on his heel, dejected and defeated, when a glowing orb blossomed beneath the center of the black lagoon. The orb grew brighter and brighter as it climbed to the surface, and when it broke through, it brought with it both light that washed against the banks and...

A voice.

Not a human voice, not exactly. It was something more ethereal and airy, making the hairs on TJ's arm lift. But the voice was unmistakably female. It had to be Dayo. The voice was too distorted, though. He couldn't be sure. The orb fell again, its light dimming as it sank back underwater.

Was the magic failing? Had TJ done something wrong to make it go away?

"One must go to the Great Water of the Lagoons to start down the divine path." TJ recalled the mask's message. *"Find the light in the deep, heed its call, and you will have all you desire."*

"Dayo!" he shouted. "Come back! Wait! It's me, TJ!"

TJ didn't have time to think. He couldn't let that orb get away, couldn't let that voice be snuffed out when it took him so long to get there.

With hoodie and jeans still on, he dived into the lagoon and swam after the light. When his head broke the plane between the misty night air and the cool, thick waters, he could hear the voice clearly as though it permeated throughout the entire lagoon, like surround sound speakers.

"Come to me, come to me," it kept repeating—*she* kept repeating.

TJ dug deeper and deeper through duckweed, loose branches,

and fishes alike. Nothing would stop him from getting to the light. Nothing at all.

I'm coming, Dayo. I'm almost there.

At the corner of his eye, he could see something shadowed against the light. In the back of his mind, he thought it might've been Ol' Sally protecting her celestial maiden.

It didn't matter.

Not now.

TJ was so close.

Just one more push, one more stroke, one more breath, and he'd be there.

But his energy left him. He couldn't hold his breath any longer, not when he was pushing so hard. Water forced its way up his nose and through his lungs.

No, I'm almost there. I'm. Almost. There...

A tight tug came at his elbow. Was his arm in the clutches of Ol' Sally's mouth? He didn't have any fight in him left; there was no more air in his lungs. He let himself be pulled as the edges of his vision darkened.

☥

TJ COUGHED UP WHAT FELT LIKE TWO GALLONS' WORTH OF WATER onto mud as snotty liquid spilled from his nose like a water hose. Someone next to him was coughing, too, as he realized he was being patted vigorously on the back.

"I knew I shouldn't have left," came the voice. It must've been Adeola.

"Sorry. I should've listened to you. I should've just gone back."

"Huh?"

TJ turned on his back to see that it wasn't Adeola but Manny who stood over him, her curly hair matted down in wet clumps. "Manny? What are you doing here?"

"I heard a noise outside the girls' cabin," she said, settling herself into the mud next to TJ. "Thought the boys were trying to prank us. Ayodeji getting payback or something. When I followed the noise, though, I saw a big light. Then I found you..." She paused a moment, then frowned. "TJ, you weren't trying to..."

TJ didn't understand what she was suggesting at first. Then the grave frown on her face, the way her eyebrows bunched together made it clear. "Oh, no, no, I wasn't trying to—do you really think I would—no, I was trying to—" He cut himself off at the truth. "I just needed a swim. It helps me clear my head and all, you know."

Manny gave him an unconvinced look. "You wanted to swim in a pair of jeans and a sweatshirt. Really?"

Water was coming down around her cheeks like tears, and duckweed stuck between her curls like some mermaid. TJ felt butterflies in his stomach. She didn't even have to try to look pretty, even when she was wet and covered in swamp gunk.

"Fine, I'll tell you," TJ conceded. "But promise not to make fun of me."

"Why would I make fun of you?" The genuine tone in her voice caught TJ by surprise. Her eyes were so gentle, so caring.

"I thought I heard my sister, okay?" TJ peeked up to Manny, expecting her to look wide-eyed with disbelief. She simply waited for him to continue, and TJ decided not just to tell her the truth but the whole truth.

"Not just today," he started. "Ever since she passed away. The first time I was in her room, something weird happened. There was this sort of brush on my neck. I thought it was the wind, but all the windows were closed. And then at the funeral, when I touched her, something happened to me. I wasn't able to do any magic before then. I mean, I've always felt like there was *some* Ashe in me, but it always felt like it was distant, like it was behind a curtain, if that makes sense."

TJ waited for Manny to interject, but she continued to listen. "And then I came to camp, and today in Mr. Bolawe's, I heard a voice... no, not a voice, more like a whisper, but not like a whisper either. It was like it was in my head, *directly* in my head. You heard it too. You said you did. So I came out with my sta—" TJ twisted his head to look for where his sister's staff had gone.

"Don't trip. I got it right here." Manny lifted it from her side. "How did you smuggle one in?"

Once more, the crystal pulsated a dirty green hue. TJ jabbed his finger at it, ignoring Manny's question. "See! That's what happened today. It glowed like that, and I heard that strange voice again. I was tired of not knowing what was going on, so I came here to see if I could hear more voices again, and... well, this ball of light came out of the lagoon. It was like it was calling to me, so I sort of... followed it."

"Sort of?" Manny raised an eyebrow. "You nearly got yourself killed."

"Yeah, well… that wasn't my intention." TJ fell back into a lump of grass, suddenly aware of his aching muscles and the fatigue in his body complaining about rest. "I was just trying to get to my sister, was all."

For a long moment, they both let the music of frogs and crickets fill the space between them. Eventually, Manny plopped next to TJ, her hair like a big pillow for her head.

"I lost my older cousin this year, too," she said out of the blue.

TJ rolled his head to her. She was looking up at the stars, her face placid as the lagoon was now. "She went to Ifa too. Knew your sister. I hated how everyone kept telling me how sorry they were, like it would help, like it would bring her back. And I'd give anything to have her back. Even if it was just to talk to her again one more time, you know."

TJ waited for a long enough pause before saying, "Manny… I didn't know."

"I haven't told anyone at camp." She turned to him, and they locked eyes.

TJ knew what that meant. He knew that kind of confession didn't come lightly. But why him? He had barely known her a week, and even then, they'd only spoken a handful of times.

Manny must've been thinking the same thing because she said, "I can't imagine what it's like for you. Your sister is so well known. I can tell you get mad pissed when people bring her up."

"Yeah, I need to work on that—"

"Don't," she shot back. The curtness of her words seemed to take her aback as well. "I mean, that's why I like you." TJ's eyes widened at that; Manny blushed. "No, not like—you know what I mean. Don't make it weird. You always make it weird."

TJ threw his hands back against the dirt in retreat. "I didn't say anything."

Manny turned away from him and directed her eyes skyward again. TJ would've sworn he saw the impressions of her dimples betraying valleys in her cheek.

"So." TJ sighed. "What happens now?"

"You said you could hear your sister, right?"

"I think so. I'm not really sure it was her, to be honest."

"Well," she lifted on her elbow, leaning her head on her palm, "don't you want to find out?"

26

THE WHISPERING TREE

MANNY ALREADY HAD PLANS THAT WEEKEND. FIRST WITH HER crossover team, who were taking on Camp Loa from Haiti on Saturday, and second with some family she had in New Orleans on Sunday. But she promised TJ the moment she returned, and they had free time, they'd start work on finding out more about Dayo's voice and what she might've been trying to tell him.

So for most of the weekend, TJ kept to himself, skimming, reading, and re-skimming Dayo's notebook as much as he could.

By Sunday, he had nearly finished reading it, although he didn't understand half of the material, notably the notes left in Yoruba. Dayo's theories and concepts when it came to Ashe, and the Orishas was well over his mystical reading level. He couldn't even answer Mr. Du Bois's "easy" pop quiz last Friday, let alone her musings on the importance of *ètùtù*.

Mr. Du Bois! TJ thought as he remembered he had indeed ghosted the instructor's offer for tutoring.

When Ogbon Studies came about on Monday morning, TJ didn't have to wonder why the man had been giving him thin lips that matched his skinny mustache. The two or three times TJ braved to meet the instructor's eyes, he immediately regretted it.

TJ couldn't say he cared all that much about Mr. Du Bois or the big bold fat "D" he received on that morning's pop quiz. He'd barely even registered the crimson-writing that read, *"this is what lack of accountability earns you."* The only two things on TJ's mind had been his plans with Manny after lunch... and his sister's notebook hidden under his notes about the different types of offerings to the Orisha, Oya.

He and Manny had seen each other briefly the previous night when she returned. They didn't talk about much, just light conversation about how she was visiting with her aunt and uncle, who were also diviners—her Aunt under Ifa and her uncle under Candomblé.

"My *tia* got me these," she had said, flashing a new pair of burgundy earrings in the shape of coins. "They're Oya earrings— that's my Orisha alignment, in case you didn't know. The earrings aren't enchanted like the bangle Josh gave you, but they're mad cute, though, right?"

TJ had wanted to say, "yes, they are very cute." He even wanted to mention how well they matched her new lip balm, but then he second-guessed himself and just ended up staring.

"There you go again." Manny pushed him. "Stop makin' stuff weird, yo."

Luckily Manny's cabin leader had called her in, saving him from further embarrassment. And from that night until Monday morning, he studied up on Oya, where he found out that burgundy was her ordained color, and offerings like coins, red wine, and cloth were her favorites.

He and Manny agreed to meet to further investigate the mysteries of stafflore—Dayo's staff in particular—and how they could commune with the dead. He wanted to give Manny something special for helping him but had no clue what he could offer. They were too young for wine, he had no cloth, and her aunt already gave her some coin earrings.

"You okay, man?" Joshua asked, bringing TJ back to Mr. Du Bois's droll about some old-school diviner who got caught between an earth portal. "You thinking about Friday night again?"

TJ's quirked an eyebrow, then murmured, "What about Friday night?"

"I didn't want to say nothin', or I could've given you away. But I saw you leavin' with a staff."

"I don't know what you're talking about, man."

"C'mon, don't do me like that. Can you at least tell me what it looks like? Can I see it?"

TJ jerked around to the rest of the class, but none of them were paying them any mind. Plus, they were giving Joshua his usual three-seat buffer. TJ hadn't even realized how accustomed to the boy's body odor he had become.

When TJ was positive that no one was listening to him, most half asleep from Mr. Du Bois's boring lecture, he turned to Joshua and murmured again, "Not right now."

"But I know a *ton* about stafflore. I can help you."

TJ then changed the subject to that morning's breakfast menu of sweet potato biscuits—which diverted Joshua's attention as desired.

Things didn't get any less awkward in Mr. Bolawe's sessions either. TJ kept to his promise of keeping his distance and leaving his relationship with the instructor on a strictly teacher-student basis. He didn't hang around after class or anything like he used to.

When they were dismissed for lunch later, TJ scooped up a single warm piece of bread, ran into his cabin to retrieve his baseball bag, and dashed out to the spot where Manny said to meet just near the treeline next to the amphitheater where a tall line of totems depicting the water Orishas stood.

After a few minutes of waiting, a sharp hissing came at his side. He turned to see Manny's head hovering between a pair of trees. She beckoned him with a waving hand.

"Where are we going?" TJ asked.

She shook her head, looking down the way TJ came. "Follow me before anyone sees us."

TJ shuffled forward, avoiding the boy and girl who had made the amphitheater their make-out spot. He hefted the bag at his back over his shoulder and ducked into the trees with Manny. As he crossed into the thicket of the swamp forest, cool air wafted across his face. He'd never been into this part of camp, a far cry away from the main grounds. It seemed the wind persisted here, never letting up against the leaves that ebbed atop its current despite the lack of any real gusts.

Manny pushed forward, occasionally stopping at a tree or a bush to seemingly gather her bearings.

"C'mon, tell me where it is," she kept whispering to herself.

"What are you looking for?" TJ asked as he nearly tripped on a large root.

"The whispering tree. I always forget where they are in all this. It don't help that they keep moving."

Oh, great. Another living tree…

"But usually," Manny continued as she rounded another bend, "Usually, Oya has my back, tells me where to go, you know?"

"Oya? You mean your Orisha?"

"Of course. Doesn't your Orisha talk to you?"

TJ frowned. "I don't know that I have one."

"Everyone does, even the clouded."

"So you're telling me you have full-blown conversations with Oya?" TJ asked as they passed by a bush that looked almost like it was dancing the samba against the winds.

"Not exactly. No one communicates with the Orishas like that anymore. Me and Oya... we don't speak with words but more with... feeling." Manny edged her chin over her shoulder curiously. "You really haven't felt anything like that?"

"I guess I did Friday night. Maybe Olosa is my Orisha, then?"

"Maybe." Manny shrugged. "Oh! Wait, they're over there."

She pointed across a small clearing to a tree TJ had never seen before. It looked like its branches hung from branches, growing off each other, and its trunk had deep cuts within it. One of its gaping holes looked like it could fit a small child, maybe even a teen.

"Just stand right there." Manny held out a hand to TJ. "The whispering tree can get kind of shy. I've never brought anyone else here before. They're kind of my secret."

TJ shot an eyebrow up at that. "Not even the Santos Sisters or Lorenzo?"

Manny shook her head sheepishly, her ears going a bit red. It wasn't lost on TJ how special this moment was, but he didn't want to make the situation any more awkward than it needed to be. Manny had made it plenty clear how "weird" he made most situations between them. She had brought them there so they could do their research in peace—and so no one could snoop on them working with a forbidden staff—not for any other reason.

Though that didn't stop TJ from thinking about that couple at the amphitheater.

"How did you find this place?" TJ asked idly as Manny took her first steps forward.

"There's a bunch of whispering trees at Ifa Academy. Me and the other Oya students had classes among them all the time—hey! Enough with the questions. I know how you can get started up real quick. I've gotta get us in here."

Manny approached the tree like it was some sort of dangerous animal that required caution. She held her eyes low and her hands out to her side.

"Hey there, it's me again," she started. "I brought a friend with me today, if that's okay."

The tree twisted to one side to get a better look at TJ behind the bush he stood next to.

"He's nice, I swear. We just need to hide away for a bit to figure some things out, again, if that's all right with you."

The whispering tree fluttered its leaves. Was that its form of speech? Manny looked over her shoulder and gestured for TJ to come.

Taking a few cautious steps forward, TJ held tightly to his baseball bag and mimicked Manny's deferential posture from before. He kept his eyes low, but he wasn't exactly sure what gaze he was avoiding. Where would a tree's eyes even be? At least Monsieur Francois' bark had the impressions of a face.

"Thank you, Mister... tree." TJ could almost hear the eye roll underneath Manny's groan. "Misses... tree?" TJ tried a second time, though he was only met with another even deeper groan.

The tree's leaves sputtered again. This time the fluttering chorus almost sounded like laughter.

"You're lucky they think you're funny," Manny said out the side of her mouth.

TJ mumbled back without looking away from the tree. "Who's 'they'? You keep saying 'they'. Isn't it just one tree?"

"Well, 'it' doesn't quite fit, does it? I don't know. English doesn't have the right word for it. Yoruba works a lot better for that kind of thing. You can speak it, right?"

Yeah, terribly, he thought.

It had been bad enough he'd been butchering Yoruba incantations all last week. Still, he did his best as he stammered, "*I hope they can accept me as a friend,*" in Yoruba, tapping the ground and bowing for added effect. That's what Mom always told him to do when he greeted elders. But then he wondered if the whispering tree required a full prostration. TJ was about to bend down again when another flutter from the branches came.

This time it was unmistakable.

That was *definitely* laughter.

Manny chuckled too. "Yeah, they like you for sure, for sure."

The gaping hole at the tree's center expanded, welcoming them inside its bark.

"What can I say." TJ gave her a wry grin. "I bring the best out of people —" He stopped himself short. "I mean... nature?"

"Okay, stop talking before they change their mind." Manny grabbed his arm and shoved him into a gap in the tree.

TJ tumbled headfirst into what he had expected would be a very dark and wooded area. Instead, he and Manny had been transported into a tight green and yellow clearing with twisting branches overhead whose gaps let in the afternoon sun through lines of rays. The packed earth below them, covered by loose leaves, began to shake. Two structures that looked like makeshift wooden chairs rumbled from the ground and a canted stump that looked like a table sprouted from below.

TJ's mouth fell wide and open. "I mean, I knew stuff like this exists, but I've never actually seen most of it."

"It still amazes me too," Manny agreed as she threw herself into one of the wooden chairs. She hooked her leg over one of the armrests before saying, "So, bring out that staff of yours. Let's see if we can get it to light up again."

"Oh, right." TJ slung the baseball bag from his shoulder and dropped it onto the stump. He unzipped it from the top and pulled out the staff, whose dingy green crystal remained clouded. "I haven't heard anything else all weekend. It hasn't glowed at all."

"You said it glowed only three times?"

"Once during the funeral. Friday after lunch. And then by Olosa's Lagoon that night."

Manny pressed her hand into her chin in thought. "What's the common denominator between all those?"

"Real talk. I couldn't say. They all seem to be so random."

"Maybe not." Manny sat forward and stretched out her hand. "Crystals glow when magic is activated. Can I see that?"

Without thinking, he held it out for Manny to examine. He was surprised by how willing he was to give the staff up to her. She took it in her right hand and ran her left hand over the face carved at the head.

"The connection, it seems," Manny said, "is your sister. The funeral was the first connection. Then after lunch, you said you were calling for her. And then by the lagoon, you thought you heard her."

"I've been trying to speak with her for weeks now, even before camp, though."

Manny pursed her lips in thought. "Yeah, you're right."

A short silence sat between them before TJ said, "Maybe we should just go back to the lagoon tonight. I'm telling you, I was close. Just a few more moments —"

"And what? Have you drown? That's what happens when the brain lacks oxygen, TJ."

"I'm not crazy."

"I'm not saying you are. But there's got to be another way to communicate with your sister without killing yourself."

"Maybe that's the only way," TJ said in a cavalier manner.

Manny gave him a sharp look and a sharper strike across his arm. "Don't talk like that. *Ever*. Not around me."

TJ threw up his hands. "Sorry, sorry. I didn't mean to."

The first real awkward silence between them hung heavy in the air. Despite his joking, TJ honestly couldn't think of what would bring his sister's voice back. Perhaps a near-death experience was really the best thing.

But Manny was right. That was too dangerous, too stupid. There had to be another way to make the connection without such extreme methods. What could they use to communicate? What would he even ask if he did get in touch with Dayo?

Ask which of the Keepers killed her, for one, TJ thought.

Then a thought dawned on him. "What about the water?"

"Huh?" she asked with a canted head.

"Remember how you, me, and Ayodeji were listening for voices on the water?"

"Yeah."

"Well." TJ lifted on his knees, the new thought giving him a surge of energy. "I was trying to recreate that feeling when I was at the lagoon. And the staff seemed to help. And there was a lake right next to my sister's viewing. Maybe we just need to learn the proper water ritual, so I can speak with my sister. Maybe that's what that white orb thing was… her spirit or something."

A light fell across Manny's face. "Maybe that bright light works the way water bowls do."

"Yeah, something like that… maybe."

Manny tapped at the staff. "We gotta learn more about this. We just don't know the first thing about using a staff for a ritual like that. We don't get that kind of training until we're sixteen—and that's if we even pass Ifa's exams for Senior Secondary School."

"So that means you're going to try for Ifa again this year?" TJ smiled.

Manny frowned. "I was just talking out loud. And I told you I don't wanna talk about that."

"All right, have it your way," TJ relented. "So, where can we learn more about this staff? I was just at the library recently. Maybe there first? I could introduce you to Adeola."

"No, I got a better idea," Manny said. TJ raised his eyebrows in anticipation of her response. "We should speak with Elder Akande this weekend. She's a master of stafflore and all."

"Great, but why not right now or tomorrow?"

"Crossover practice. You should watch our game this Friday. We're hosting Camp Mandawaca."

"I'll be there." TJ smiled, happy to come to anything Manny invited him to.

27

STAFFLORE

"NEITHER OF YOU IS OLD ENOUGH TO BE ASKING QUESTIONS ABOUT staffs," a pajamaed Elder Akande said that Saturday morning as TJ and Manny stood bug-eyed outside of her bayou cabin. The delicate scent of incense wafted briefly from inside of her home-office before she slammed her wooden and rickety door in their faces.

"We only wanna know about the magic behind it," TJ shouted as he cast a sidelong glance to Manny, who shrugged. He took that to mean she thought his answer was good enough, so he continued. "So... so we can tailor our studies to better prepare for the day we make our own staffs."

Manny looked very impressed, throwing a thumbs up and mouthing, *"tailor our studies. Good touch."*

"It's after tutoring hours," the elder's hoarse voice came from within. "You campers had all last week to come and see me during my allocated hours, but you neglected your visiting sessions on that silly crossover game."

TJ and Manny exchanged cringey grimaces. While TJ had spent most of his free time trying to learn how to do magic without any help, Manny had spent hers out on the crossover field with her team almost exclusively.

"But TJ thinks he heard his sis—" TJ nudged Manny at her side. "He thinks he heard the voice of an Orisha on the water."

The door swung open, casting out that stark herbal smell once more. Elder Akande could have given a court jester a run for their money, with her sleep cap half off her forehead and sleep in her eyes.

TJ did his best not to stare at the dried drool coming away at the corner of her mouth.

Maybe it was better if they just came back later.

Eyeing TJ up and down, the woman asked, "You're that Young child, aren't you? Ifedayo was your sister."

"That's me." TJ nodded.

"And you think you've heard Orishas, have you? You do know they've been quiet even before *I* was born?" That was saying something—the radio was probably just invented when she was a newborn. "Wasn't Counselor Bolawe teaching you about voices on the water? Perhaps it was his voice you heard."

"This voice was female, and..." TJ took a breath. "And it didn't sound... human."

"Then speak with Bolawe. I don't see how this has anything to do with stafflore."

Manny leaned forward before TJ could answer. "TJ just found out he's aligned with one of the water Orishas, and he's applying for Ifa at the end of the summer. We got a test coming up in Emi Guidance, and we think it's best if he knew some of the advanced magic surrounding the water magicks... so that he's better prepared."

Elder Akande turned a sour look on her. "Why don't you help the boy, then? You were at Ifa last year. And if memory serves, you were our top student last summer, eh?"

Manny got real quiet, real quick, the same way she always did when she and Ifa were brought up in the same sentence. TJ figured it was his turn to come up with an excuse, but Manny was ready with her own. "I'm aligned with Oya. I don't know a whole lot about Yemoja, or Olokun, or Olosa, ya know. TJ's been going to tutoring with Mr. Du Bois and Mr. Bolawe, but nothing's been stickin'." She drew her head forward and lowered her voice. "To be honest, the other instructors don't have the same wisdom as you, Elder. If TJ has half a shot—and you know he does with his family line—*you're* the best bet he's got."

Manny was gassing her up. TJ couldn't believe it. It was genius.

"I'm sorry for not coming to your sessions, Elder." TJ bowed his head. "Please, with everything going on with... you know. It's been hard for me. And my grades are so low. I need *your* help."

A short silence filled with the cacophony of buzzing flies. And then...

"Fine, you can have half an hour." She waved a hand into her home. TJ and Manny were too shocked to move, which beckoned a finger-snap from the elder's hand. "Well, do you want my instruction or not? I'd much rather be sleeping on my day off."

The pair of them jolted in place then shuffled forward as Elder Akande grumbled something about finally retiring one of these years and that Whittaker had the right idea.

Of all the cabins TJ had been in, Elder Akande's space felt the most lived in. The cabin was a single room split down the middle by wooden slats which separated her living quarters and her office. Shelves of staffs—some iron, some wooden, and others hybrids—littered the back of the room. On the left rested traditional African masks, and on the right, older weapons of axes, spears, and shields.

"Have a seat just there." The elder pointed to a dusty and dingy brown couch to the side. "I'll only need a moment."

TJ fell onto the couch without a thought.

That was a mistake.

The moment his butt fell onto what was likely once a fancy suede, he sank straight into its wooden base, his tailbone suffering for it. Manny took a different approach, dusting off soot at the armrest before taking her seat. It looked more like she hovered than sat.

A short moment later, Elder Akande returned from the half of the cabin that served as her bedroom wearing a simple robe of blah green. Unlike most bùbá and ìró TJ had been familiar with, the elder's bore no intricate design or shimmering braids between its lining.

With a great heave and a few cracks of bone, the old woman fell back into a rocking chair opposite TJ and Manny. "So," she said, patting and rubbing her knees. "What can I do you for?"

"Right," TJ started. "Well, you see… Like we were saying, last week, we learned about voices on the water. And we were wondering if there was a specific technique to… hear them." Manny coughed. "To hear them with a staff, that is."

Elder Akande interlaced her fingers over her lap. "That exercise doesn't require the use of a staff. That brass around your wrist should do the trick just fine, child."

TJ covered the brass with his hand, completely forgetting he still had it on.

"In theory, would an Orunmila staff work, though?" Manny questioned as TJ put the brass in his pocket.

The elder gave Manny an inquisitive look that bunched her eyes between her brows and bags. From all the reading that TJ had done over the weekend, he gathered that his sister's staff was made in alignment with Orunmila, her primary Orisha.

"I suppose so…" The elder hummed. "That specific staff does have a particular affinity for such things. But I thought you said the boy was finding alignment with an Orisha of the Aqua Realm? Orunmila is primarily concerned with divination and the Sky Realm."

"Oh, well…" Manny's voice cracked a little. "I thought water and divination were interconnected somehow…"

Akande grunted. "Depends on who you ask. What books do they have you reading in Emi Guidance? Not that wretched book from Amos Isola, right?"

Manny swallowed deep. "Um… Yes. Is something wrong with what she says about staffs in that book?"

Akande chewed on her lips so harshly it looked like she was biting down on tough jerky. "She *thinks* she knows a thing or two. She doesn't even fully understand the difference between staffs fashioned from trees fertilized in goat manure and those planted with banana peels. I keep telling Director Simmons we need to switch it up, but she never listens. You see, the difference between the tree development is…"

As the elder explained more about the different benefits of tree cultivation and then onto the debate between wood versus iron builds —she highly favored wood—TJ couldn't help but let his gaze wander just past her folded cap to a shelf full of jars. They were filled with clear liquids, like ice cubes that had just started to melt. And at each of their centers was a crystal of changing colors.

"What about crystals that go from green to red and back again?" TJ asked when Elder Akande finally took a breath. "Does that happen when different magic is cast?"

Elder Akande lifted an eyebrow. "That's not usual at all. Do you mean the crystal changes color entirely, or the hue is slightly different? Change of color can mean several things. None of them good."

TJ exchanged a side-eye with Manny before asking, "When you say not good… how bad do you mean?"

"I'm sorry." The elder looked between the two. "This conversation has gone from water Orishas to staffs and now to changing crystal colors. What is this all about, really, eh? How do you even know to ask some of these questions? Did you come by a staff with a changing color? Did someone tell you to come and ask about this?"

"What? No, nothing like that."

"Oh, I knew I shouldn't have run my mouth…" She slapped her

knees. "Those United Council folks were here last week asking about changing crystal colors, and the Keepers sighted in the French Quarter—"

TJ cut in. "So, there really are Keepers near the—"

"You don't have any test, do you?" Elder Akande squinted darkly.

Manny sat up suddenly, then bowed. "Sorry for disturbing you with our silly questions. We'll just be going now."

"Yeah, maybe it was a bad idea to come here," TJ agreed, following Manny without protest.

They were already out of the door and down the porch when they heard Elder Akande calling, "Don't go around talking about crystal colors changing. That's Keeper talk, that is! Dark stuff! Tricky stuff!"

TJ turned on his heel at the sound of "Keeper talk," but Manny grabbed his arm and forced him to keep walking. "Don't look back; don't turn back. She's gonna get us in trouble."

"But Keepers…" TJ trailed off as they made a turn at a bend where the bayou cabin disappeared behind a thicket. "Manny, I gotta tell you something." He made his arm dead weight and forced her to stop.

"What? What is it?"

"I didn't tell you about what happened at my sister's funeral."

"What do you mean?"

"When I went to go for her staff, when those Keepers attacked us, the crystal in her staff… well… maybe I imagined it, but her crystal was red for a moment. And then it went back to green. Do you know what that means?"

Manny shook her head. "No idea. I didn't learn much about staffs. That's still a few years away. But if Elder Akande said it was bad…"

"Then it's probably something bad." TJ threw his head back down the path, half his mind thinking he should go back and ask a few more questions, but if Manny said it was a bad idea, it probably was. "Well, we can't go back there. You were saying something about the library, right?"

A pair of figures mumbled from somewhere farther down the treeline leading up to Elder Akande's. Then, around the bend came Mr. Bolawe carrying a wine bottle under his arm and Mr. Du Bois bearing a wrapped box with a bow.

Mr. Bolawe gave them an awkward half-smile while Mr. Du Bois settled for a curt nod.

"What are you youngsters doing here?" Mr. Bolawe asked amicably.

TJ still wasn't all the way okay with speaking with Bolawe, so Manny, thumbing over her shoulder, answered, "Just visiting the old lady." She lowered her voice. "Careful, though. She's a bit grumpy."

Mr. Bolawe lifted the bottle from under his arm. "Ah, but we've come prepared with gifts."

"You shouldn't disturb her so early, though," Mr. Du Bois said earnestly. His tone dampened the friendly mood that was building among them. "In fact, the both of you should be studying if your first two weeks' results were anything to go by."

A pang of guilt shot through TJ's chest as he felt his lips curl down into a frown. Manny's face didn't change at all. After all, she didn't seem to care about her mediocre grades. Must've been nice to be so carefree.

"Well, we were just headed to the library, in fact." TJ tried for a forced half-smile of his own, though in the direction of Mr. Du Bois, not Mr. Bolawe. He was hoping his response would earn an approving look from Mr. Du Bois at the very least. It didn't.

"Good, then we shouldn't keep you," he intoned darkly.

TJ grabbed Manny by the elbow and tugged her along the path before either Mr. Du Bois hit them with another glare or Mr. Bolawe tried to make nice with him. Both were awkward situations TJ would rather avoid. However, when they were out of the sightline of Elder Akande's cabin, Manny locked up like stone.

"Hold up a minute." She turned to peer through the trees. "Do you hear that?"

TJ glanced over her shoulder, where he could barely make out the counselors' shoulders through the foliage. It sounded like they were arguing about something.

"We diviners got what was coming to us," Mr. Du Bois was saying. "Our gifts and blessings have been squandered for too long. But Olokun was foolish to oppose the Monarch."

"Olokun gets a bad rap," Mr. Bolawe replied. "He was only trying to protect diviners from the clouded."

"By drowning an entire country?" Mr. Du Bois gave Elder Akande's door a knock.

"You're not wrong, friend. Olokun went too far then, but his intentions were sound. Whatever the case, we need to be ready. The oracles predict his return is imminent."

"Just like they predicted with that promised child. The oracles have been wrong more often than not these days. And with Keepers finding a new home so close to the camp... I wouldn't hold my—"

Akande's cabin door swung open again. "If you li'l children don't get off my porch and—Oh! Xavier, Olufemi. What do I owe this pleasure to?"

Manny tapped TJ on the shoulder as Elder Akande invited the men inside. "C'mon, we really should go to the library like we said."

"Yeah, right behind you," TJ answered, but he hung at their hiding spot a little longer.

What was all that talk about the promised child and Olokun? Mr. Du Bois had *just* tested them about the Orisha, but TJ couldn't decide what all of that could've meant. Then he remembered one of the Keeper's mantras... to bring back the power of the Orishas. Last week, there was a sighting at that cemetery, reports of a Keeper found with a mask, and then Mr. Du Bois showed up with a mask at the library. What for?

Maybe Adeola at the library would know something. He hadn't seen her since the lagoon.

"TJ, what are you doing?" Manny whispered harshly behind him.

"Sorry. I mean... I'm coming. I'm coming."

28

MYSTERIES & MOCKERIES

TJ and Manny searched for the most undisturbed corner of the library they could find. But it seemed like half the camp had chosen to spend their Saturday afternoon to study, tucked away between the vines snaking out of the bookshelves and tables.

"What!?" TJ exclaimed. "When I was here, it was empty!"

"That was the first-week slump," Manny explained as she pushed her way through a trio of intermediate-level campers. "Once everyone sees where they are in the standings, it motivates them to put in the work."

Well, I definitely can relate, TJ thought.

"It's like everyone is applying to an Ivy League or something," TJ said as he caught sight of Ayodeji's man bun in the corner of the library under a lantern filled with fireflies. For once, he wasn't shadowed by the tall LaVont or Jimoh. Instead, he traded his lanky companions for stacks of books piled on chairs next to him.

Manny saw him too and led them in the opposite direction. "Well, Ifa Academy sort of is an Ivy League. Its acceptance rate is lower than Yale's, ya know."

TJ stopped himself before he brought up that Manny had been accepted, though.

"Is there something I should know about the academy?" he asked curiously, not wanting to stoke Manny's ire. Instead, it seemed he only brought forth confusion as she turned a raised eyebrow his way. "I mean... would there be a reason why someone *wouldn't* want to go there?"

The stern look from Manny told him he'd crossed the line, and she started pulling down books and scrolls into her library cart. "I don't know," she said. "And I know what you're doing. Stop it. Seriously."

Despite good sense, TJ simply couldn't relent. "I'm serious too. If there's something I should know, you'd tell me, right? I mean, with my grades the way they are now, I don't have a chance to get in, but let's say by some miracle I do. I should know if it's some sort of twisted front for human trafficking or something like that, right?"

"No, it's nothing like that." Manny shook her head, and she set her eyes on an empty table. "It's just…"

"What? Not for everyone?"

"Yeah, something like that…"

Manny took her seat on a rickety old chair. TJ sat down as well, but he felt something poke him.

"*Watch where you're sitting, boy,*" said a tiny wooden statuette speaking Yoruba. Unlike the giant statues that roamed the swamp at night or the others that graded papers, this one had a round belly and a comically large head that was twice the size of its body.

"Oh, sorry," TJ said back in English as he set the little guy atop the desk.

"*No, no, no. The desk is too cold. Put me back on the seat where it's warm.*"

"Suit yourself."

TJ obliged and set the figure back down where he found it and instead took the empty seat closest to Manny instead of across from her. When TJ looked up, Manny was already hiding between the pages of a large tome. Did that mean she didn't want to talk to him anymore? It was a wonder why she put up with TJ at all. And he had always been bad at keeping a lid on it when he was advised to, but he couldn't help it—not when everyone else he ever spoke to said that Ifa was the greatest thing ever. He decided not to push the subject further, though. He'd been able to get Manny to spend almost half a week with him. No need to go spoiling it all now over something so small.

Then it occurred to him suddenly that they were in the library!

He turned to the tiny statue again, who laid flat on its back like it was on a tanning table, and asked, "Have you seen Adeola today?"

"*Ade-who?*" it asked irritably without opening its eyes.

"Adeola. She's an assistant or something. I just saw her last week and—" He stopped himself from saying he saw her in the middle of the night. "Oh, I'm sorry. You might know her as Miss Washington. She's got short hair, real thin."

"*Never heard of her,*" the statue answered through a snort. "*And are you gonna keep running your mouth, or do I need to ask you to move off to another table?*"

TJ kept his mouth shut this time. He glanced back to Manny and almost asked if she ever saw Adeola in the library, but she was still covering her face. TJ scanned around to see if he could spot her anywhere helping the other campers or maybe restocking one of the top shelves, but all he saw were students. In fact, it seemed like the only assistants in the library were other tiny little statues like the one beside him—who already started into a creaking snore.

That was odd. If the little guy didn't know Adeola was around, maybe she wasn't involved with the library at all. Now that he thought on it, even Mr. Du Bois seemed surprised to see her. And she did look super skittish the last time he saw her. What was that all about? TJ shook his head and put the thought away. He was sure Adeola had some sort of explanation.

Keeping his mind focused on the task at hand, he unwrapped and flipped open his sister's notebook and turned to a new page where he could draw. Though Dayo's notebook had been riddled with all kinds of notes and annotations, there were very few doodles, a far cry from TJ's own school papers.

There were maybe two or three little sketches of Dayo's staff illustrated in the book, nothing with nearly enough detail. TJ couldn't just go back to his cabin and pull out the staff for examination, so he started sketching it from memory, from the smooth shaft at the bottom to the braided wood at the center and the face at the head with its wide nose and wide lips, and the crown it wore on its dome, topped with what looked like a bird and what TJ assumed were branches and leaves.

"Hey, this page here says Orunmila staffs glow brightest of all other staff types," Manny said so suddenly TJ nearly ruined the finishing stroke on his sketch. "It says that the crystal at the mouth glows in the presence of recessive magic."

"Recessive magic?" TJ frowned. "What's that?"

"It means passive magic," came an unwelcome voice from behind. TJ and Manny turned dark eyes to Ayodeji, who stood over them with a stack of books under his arms. "And what's that you have there?"

TJ covered his sister's notebook instinctively. "None of your business."

"You said something about Orunmila... that staff you was drawing wasn't no Orunmila staff."

"Like he said," Manny interjected. "That's none of your business."

Ayodeji shrugged, pushing his silver-plated glasses up his nose with his elbow. "Whatever. Just thought I should help him get *that* right, at least. It's not like it'll help him where he's at on the standings and whatnot. For your information, Orunmila's face is more wizened and slender like an elder. That wide nose and mouth you were drawing belongs to Eshu, the Gatekeeper, the Trickster." TJ couldn't begin to understand why Ayodeji felt the need to tell them this. "It's an amateur move, honestly." And there it was. The boy just wanted to make TJ look bad. "You should cut this dude loose before you lose some brain cells, Manuela. I've got a seat open at my table for you. I'm a pretty good study partner."

TJ couldn't bring himself to look up to see Manny's reaction, instead casting his eyes downward to the desk. After all, he had annoyed her with his questions. Maybe she would sit with Ayodeji and ditch TJ there.

But when Ayodeji smacked his lips, TJ looked back up. To his surprise, Manny stuck out a finger at Ayodeji—the most wonderful finger she could've flung up in that boy's direction.

"It's *Manny*," she said coldly, still holding up the gesture to make the point.

It didn't seem to faze Ayodeji at all. In fact, he only smiled with infuriating confidence. "A'ight, bet," he said as he trotted off back to his desk.

Once he was a comfortable distance away, Manny glaring at him all the while, she turned her shoulders to TJ. "Let me see your drawing."

"It might not be right," TJ said quickly, holding his sister's notebook close to his chest. "I was drawing from memory and all... but I'm pretty sure I got the face right. The big nose and big mouth sort of reminded me of Joshua, so I just thought of him while I was—"

"TJ!" Manny hissed, holding her hand out expectantly.

TJ gave out a great sigh and handed her the notebook, hiding his face with his free hand. Through the darkness of his palm, he could only hear the intermittent humming of Manny's voice. After a few moments, she finally breathed out a "damnit."

"What?" TJ asked, still covering his face.

"The jerk is right. It is an Eshu staff. Are you sure your sister wasn't aligned with him instead?"

TJ finally withdrew from the security of his blinding hand. "I'm *pretty* sure she was aligned with Orunmila. I'm not that dumb when it comes to the Orishas."

"He could still be wrong." Manny rubbed at the edge of her eyebrow. "Hey, little guy."

The statuette groaned, then answered in English this time, "Name's Woodsworth."

"Woodsworth," Manny corrected herself, "can you help us find something about Eshu staffs?"

"Right on it." He didn't move. "All right, done."

TJ and Manny exchanged looks of utter confusion.

"Um…" TJ trailed off. "If you don't want to get it, we can go ourselves."

"I don't need to," Woodsworth flung his little arms behind his head and lounged again. "There's no such thing as Eshu staffs unless you mean the Trickster's counterfeits."

"Huh? That doesn't make sense." He turned his voice to Manny. "Does it?"

Manny flipped through the pages in her book. "Oh, wow. There really isn't anything in here about Eshu staffs. That can't be right… ugh, and I do *not* want to ask Ayodeji." She planted her palm to her forehead in frustration. "Let's go back to Akande's cabin real quick and ask her the different properties between an Orunmila staff and an Eshu staff."

"Ugh," TJ grunted. "Let's make sure we bring a gift or something for her before we go… or else she'll tear our heads off."

But after a short trip to the mess hall where they picked up some jelly-filled donuts as a greeting gift for Elder Akande, there was no answer at her cabin door.

"Maybe she went away?" TJ shrugged. "Could be somewhere on the campgrounds."

Manny shook her head. "Maybe. We can always just come back."

TJ knocked again with more force. "Elder Akande! It's TJ and Manny again. We brought donuts this time." On TJ's fourth set of knocks, he nearly fell forward as the door opened inward.

But Elder Akande was not there to meet them.

Instead, it was Mr. Du Bois.

"Elder Akande is not here," he said darkly. "What did you two say to her? She just quit."

29

M.I.A.

EVERYONE AT CAMP HAD A DIFFERENT OPINION ABOUT ELDER Akande's swift departure. She was the second counselor to leave a long and tenured position with little to no word. At the very least, Akande left a note detailing her desire to visit the Caribbean, which apparently had long since been one of her bucket list items, according to Director Simmons.

"Maybe she has cancer," Chanelle Williams, one of the preparatory level campers, said the following Friday during Ere Idaraya Drills. "When my great aunt got diagnosed, she up and left for Peru without telling us nothin'."

Lorenzo shook his head. It had only been the first lap, and pit stains already soaked his dashiki tank top. "Nah, I heard she was into some weird shit. You ever been in that shanty of hers? Super creepy. I bet the Keepers spotted in New Orleans had something to do with it. Maybe *she* was a Keeper, and somebody was about to uncover her. Who knows."

TJ and Manny exchanged worried looks as they jogged beside one another. Though it'd been nearly a week since the elder up and left, they hadn't told anyone that they were the last to see her. Neither of them believed in the theories of her going off to the West Indies, or falling into the wrong crowd, though.

"All of this is crazy, ain't it?" Joshua said, waddling behind them on their second lap. "Do you think all that stuff is true?"

TJ hadn't been the best friend to Joshua the last week. Hell, the last two weeks even. His newfound bond with Manny and all the craziness with lagoon voices and missing elders had him spending less time with the boy. That didn't stop Joshua from always trying to butt in whenever TJ and Manny shared in their private sidelong glances and musings.

"Oh, I'm sure it's nothing." TJ waved him off—the gesture had almost become a habit at that point. And on cue, Joshua put on that little pout he got whenever TJ was short with him.

"Listen," TJ added hastily. "It's hard work taking care of all these kids—and for so many years, too. I'm sure wherever she is, she's all right."

Despite TJ's guilt, he and Manny agreed not to tell anyone about their involvement with Elder Akande, which meant keeping their distance from Joshua, in TJ's case, and the Santos Sisters, in Manny's.

"Yeah, yeah, she's got her reasons…" Manny added as she tapped on TJ's shoulder. He had come to know this as their signal to go faster and pull away from Joshua. TJ picked up the pace, following alongside Manny, and as planned, they were out of earshot after only a few long strides.

"How was your search yesterday?" Manny asked as they turned into their third lap.

"Nothing," TJ whispered back. "There's nothing about Eshu staffs at all, except that they are tricky to use and haven't been seen for centuries. If that's true, then I'd never be able to use my sister's staff."

"Unless, of course, you're aligned with Eshu."

"I doubt it. The Great Trickster. Guardian of Gates. Master Communicator." TJ shook his head. "I'm not exactly a class clown, and my scrawny butt isn't guarding anything, and I don't know if you've noticed this yet… but I'm an awkward speaker most of the time." He sighed. "If I could just get my hands on my phone… My brother showed me how to look up diviner stuff like this. It'll only take me five minutes. Tops."

"They've got our stuff locked up mad tight," Manny said. "Doesn't matter anyway, there's no reception in this swamp to begin with."

TJ glanced through the trees to Olosa's Lagoon, which laid just on the other side, where a pair of beavers frolicked and barked at one another. Both of them suddenly stood stock still as a huge alligator tail whipped out from the lagoon's water. It wasn't long before Ol'

Sally's head sprouted from the depths to eyeball them. Her glare said it all: *y'all better stop all your tom-foolery before I make you my breakfast.*

"Maybe we don't need to know the specific properties of the staff," TJ said. "Maybe we can just use it to hear my sister's voice again. I've done it before. I just gotta figure out how to do it on purpose."

Manny's eyebrows bunched together. "Nah, that's too dangerous. There's a reason we aren't allowed staffs. They require official licenses and stuff. Even some adults never get 'em. We have to know the difference between an Eshu staff and an Orunmila staff, or any ritual or spell we may cast could backfire. Plus, as far as we can tell, your sister's staff is aligned with Orunmila."

"Are you talking about Eshu again?"

TJ and Manny nearly jumped out of their sneakers, tripping over themselves like newborn ducklings. Behind them, somehow, was Joshua.

"Holy shit, dude!" TJ blurted. "How long you been there?"

Joshua beamed, looking proud of himself. "It took me a while, but I managed."

The boy was barely sweating.

"Where did this ball of energy come from?" Manny asked as she regained her pace and balance. "You haven't even broke a ten-minute mile yet."

"Great work, Joshua!" Counselor Gravés shouted from her lead position on the opposite end of the track. "You see, with a little effort, you can improve!"

Joshua waved with zeal, the back of his bicep flopping like jello. "Thanks, Miss G!"

TJ still couldn't fix the shock from his face. He always figured if Joshua was properly motivated, he could get to moving. But he always figured there would be a donut at the end of the track, not a conversation he was clearly being left out on.

Keeping pace with TJ and Manny, the boy went on, "You know... I'm quite familiar with Eshu and all that. What's your question? His origins? His roles? His favorite colors? The etymology of his names. The Brazilians have over a dozen different names for him. There's Akessan, Bara, Elegba, Inan, Lalu—"

"Okay, okay, take a breath," TJ cut him off. "So you know a thing or two about him. But we don't have any questions about Eshu. Mr. Du Bois barely quizzes us on him, for one thing."

"And what a shame that is." Joshua closed his eyes dramatically.

"But, thank you," Manny said. "If we ever need to know anything more, we know who to come to."

✠

AFTER THEIR DRILLS, TJ HAD TRIED TO CONVINCE MANNY THAT Joshua was harmless. And, after all, he did seem to know quite a lot about Eshu. Maybe it was okay if they let him in on what they knew and what they were trying.

"Let's think on it today," Manny said as she walked down the muddy path leading to the girls' cabins. Unlike the boys' cabins, which rested over a shallow pool of marsh, the girls' was up on a hill between a clearing of willows. And the rules were clear that absolutely no boys were allowed on said hill.

Manny turned halfway up the slope to say, "We need to vet him more before we have him in our li'l squad."

"If you say so." TJ waved goodbye to her and headed off to his own cabin.

As he walked by some of the straggling girls who were making their way to their cabins, he heard a few of them whispering, giggling, and pointedly avoiding his eye contact when he glanced at them. What was that all about? TJ's hands shot to his face to feel for any hanging boogers or sleep in his eye, but his hand came away clean.

Then he heard one of the girls passing by murmur, "I mean, I guess he kinda cute."

Were they talking about *him*?

Nah... they had to be talking about Lorenzo or someone else. That would have been the first time a girl would have called him anything but goofy, weird, or different.

Halfway to the boys' cabins and well away from the last huddles of giggling girls, TJ heard a voice he'd never expect calling after him. "Yo, TJ, hold up."

TJ turned to see a sweaty Ayodeji jogging up to him. The boy wore an uncharacteristically wide smile that TJ assumed was meant to be disarming. It only made TJ's guard go up all the stronger.

"How's it going, man?" he asked once he caught up.

"Um... good?"

What was Ayodeji playing at? Something here was wrong. Very wrong. His smile looked like it was plastered on an action figure's

face before he casually replied, "That's what's up, that's what's up...
Not too hot today, right?"

"Uh... I guess..."

Was the boy *really* trying for... small talk?

"Hey, man. Sorry about how things started between us a couple
weeks back. I can let myself get a bit too angry sometimes. My mom
says I get it from Shango. Us types can get a bit too heated, you
know?" Ayodeji smacked TJ across the shoulder. For once, it wasn't
to cause him pain but to show some contrived form of camaraderie.

TJ didn't like it.

"All right, dude, this is just weird. What do you want?"

"So... that Manny girl," Ayodeji started, his fixed smile finally
falling a little. This must've been the real reason he'd wanted to talk.
"You two are pretty close, right?"

TJ threw up an eyebrow. "I guess..."

"She never talks to anyone outside of class—wait, let me get that
for you." Ayodeji nearly tripped over himself trying to get the boys'
cabin door open for TJ. "After you." Ayodeji held out a hand, his
tone trying for that whole butler shtick.

"Um..." TJ trailed off.

"Oh, right." Ayodeji stood up straight. "All right, I can go first if
you want." He pushed into the cabin where a lineup of boys already
stretched from the showers to the bunks.

"Like I was saying," Ayodeji went on. "You two gotta be close,
right?"

"She hangs out with the twins and Lorenzo all the time."

"Right, right, but the twins don't count, and Lorenzo... well, you
know. He don't count either."

"What's that supposed to mean?" TJ asked coldly as he caught
the back of Lorenzo's curly hair at the front of the line.

Ayodeji sucked at his teeth. "Ah, you know what I mean."

Despite his best efforts to be "friendly," Ayodeji still managed to
grate on TJ's nerves.

"Oh, I didn't mean anything by it," Ayodeji let out quickly. "It's
just... Manny never talks to... boys, you know."

"What? You have a crush on her or something?" TJ had only
meant to say it to get a rise out of Ayodeji, but he didn't expect to see
the boy's cheeks flush.

Oh damn, he does like her...

For a moment, TJ pictured Manny and Ayodeji hand in hand,
and a heat rose within him he didn't expect to feel so fiercely.

Jealousy.

Ayodeji must've thought he and Manny were together or something. That was probably what those girls were whispering about too. It must've looked like TJ was walking Manny safely back to her cabin, but he was just caught up in their conversation, was all.

Ayodeji was just trying to confirm it all for himself. And then what? Was he going to use TJ to holler at Manny? She wouldn't even like him. They were always at each other's throats.

But then TJ thought about it in another light. So many times in school, he saw it happen. The boy and girl who were always fighting tended to end up together. Maybe that was Ayodeji's play. Maybe Manny was flirting with him without even realizing it.

Or worse, she *did* realize it.

TJ turned a scowl on Ayodeji. He'd never seen the boy wait so patiently for answers before. Ayodeji was crazy for thinking TJ would tell him anything, though. But TJ had to admit the position he was in was a lot nicer than getting bullied. He could definitely see himself stretching this out.

"How did you get her to talk to you?" Ayodeji finally asked after the long silence between them became too much.

TJ responded automatically with, "By nearly drowning in the lagoon."

"Oh," Ayodeji said, clearly not taking it as humor. "Is that where you two are always sneaking off to?"

"It's a joke, dude."

"Oh, yeah, yeah. Right, right. That's what's up." Ayodeji kept chewing on his lip like there was a question he was mulling over. "She's pretty, though, right?"

TJ shrugged. "I guess."

"You guess?" Ayodeji's face seemed to brighten a little.

"I mean, I never really noticed," TJ lied. "But now that you say it... I guess so. Yeah, she has a... a good nose..."

"Nose?" Ayodeji laughed. "Bruh, I'm not lookin' at her nose."

"Well, I mean, she's—why am I even talking to you right now?" TJ's tone turned cold. "Two weeks ago, weren't you the dude saying I didn't deserve to be here?"

Ayodeji started stuttering another response, but TJ didn't hang around to listen, already backpedaling to the end of the line where Joshua waited. The stout boy had been doing a good job of acting like he wasn't eavesdropping this time.

"So Eshu," TJ said. "You know a lot about him, right?"

The boy beamed. "Tons."

"All right, lay it all on me. What do you know?"

30

IN THE SHADOWS

LATER, AFTER LUNCH, AS TJ AND MANNY SAT INSIDE THEIR whispering tree, TJ debated to tell her about his conversation with Ayodeji. Part of him thought it was hilarious how timid the boy had been when he beat around the bush about liking Manny. But another part of him was afraid of her response. What if she blushed when he told her? What if she actually liked him *back*?

So, he decided to say nothing at all as he, for the dozenth time, stroked the gnarled edge of his sister's staff.

For the past few moments, he and Manny had taken turns straining their eyes at the face carved at its head. TJ apparently hadn't drawn it from memory correctly. Instead of a pair of wide-set eyes, bulging nose, and thick lips, the face had indeed been the slender visage of Orunmila. But every so often, the face seemed to change when TJ stared long and hard enough. TJ thought he was crazy, that it was his eye strain that was playing tricks on him at first until Manny swore she saw the staff change too.

"Josh said Eshu staffs are very rare," TJ said as he rubbed his eyes after yet another strained examination. "But when I showed him my sister's staff, he said it definitely wasn't an Eshu staff. Maybe we should have Josh join us. We aren't getting anywhere new on our own."

"You may have a point," Manny commented, closing the book in her hands with a sigh. "A third brain is better than two, I guess."

TJ slumped back into some moss. "Awesome. If we have any specific questions, I'll ask him to come with us. He was so excited when I asked about my sister's staff. He's like a fiend for that Eshu stuff."

"That's his alignment, right?"

"I never asked, but I wouldn't be surprised."

Manny lifted the staff in her hand and took her hundredth look at it. "That could be your little mission this weekend. I won't have any free time to help you again."

"Another visit to your aunt's?"

"Nah. The Camp Olosa crossover team's got an away game in the Amazon with Camp Mandawaca. They'll need me. It's a big game. And those Mandawacans don't play around."

"Oh, yeah." It wasn't the first time TJ had been jealous of her crossover teammates.

TJ hadn't been chosen for any of the teams, not for crossover, not for dueling, and not even for debate. He couldn't say he exactly cared—outside of not seeing Manny—he'd been so preoccupied with everything else. Plus, he needed to catch up with his regular studies as it was, so it wasn't like he'd have the extra time to begin with.

"You know what's been weird lately, though?" Manny asked.

TJ lifted his head from the collection of scrolls at his side. "What?"

"That Ayodeji kid… I feel like he's been hounding me all week." TJ gulped. "I thought he was on me 'cause I didn't pick him on the crossover team, but he's never even asked me about it. Besides, he got chosen on the dueling squad, anyway. But it's still weird. Did you notice he was following us today after Mr. Du Bois's session?"

TJ's mouth went crazy dry. "Nope," he half squeaked, then cleared his throat. "Definitely not."

TJ couldn't decipher the impassive expression curling across Manny's face. Instead of sitting there trying to make sense of it, he changed the subject. "It's still crazy what's going on with Elder Akande. Leaving is one thing. But without warning like that? I didn't even know Old Man Whittaker, but it's not ordinary for *two* elder counselors to up and leave, right?"

"Very unusual." Manny nodded. "It's gotta be foul play."

TJ's thoughts spun back to the funeral. "You mean like the Keepers? You believe Lorenzo's theories?"

"Maybe… probably. Just this morning, Lorenzo was saying Monsieur Francois saw a few too many suspicious cars rolling down the highway near the camp entrance."

"Why take out the elders at some little camp? Shouldn't they be attacking Ifa or New Ile-Ife or something?"

Manny shrugged. "Besides what happened at your sister's, everything they've been doing has been in Nigeria. But it's possible they've got someone on the inside here to check up on things. Some of us campers are the 'future of divinerkind' and all that. Maybe they want to shake up who's running things."

"Then why not attack Director Simmons?"

"She's mad powerful. If I was a Keeper, I'd want to take out her support before I'd take her down."

TJ shook his head. "This is crazy. We're talking like conspiracy theorists."

"Better safe than sorry, like my *papai* always says."

TJ threw up his hands. "Fine, let's go down this rabbit hole. What would anyone want with Elder Akande?"

"All that knowledge... anyone who's amassing small militias would definitely want someone like that on their payroll—or servitude, however they do it. Some famous mask maker in Abuja went missin' a few months before I left Ifa. The whole school was on lockdown then. And you said something about those Keepers having distinct masks, right? Bet they got those from someone."

"Okay, sure. But the timing... The timing is so weird. Do you think someone got to Akande because of what we said to her? Maybe she knew something about the staff."

TJ reached out for it, and Manny handed it to him. He rolled it around in his hands, feeling the smooth mahogany on his skin. "What if my sister's staff is special? What if that's what the Keepers were going for? This is going to sound conceited, but I thought they were after me when I heard the rumors of them being nearby. But going after the staff... that makes *way* more sense."

"Sure, but who else knows you have the staff with you besides me and Josh?"

"Mr. Bolawe let me through with the staff the first day."

Manny tucked her hair behind an ear in thought. "Mr. Bolawe's new. Perfect candidate. Maybe the Keepers smuggled him in. Why are you making that face?"

TJ held his neck firm, not realizing he'd been shaking his head or that he had sat upright. "Oh, was I? No, no... Bolawe... Bolawe makes sense."

"Don't do that."

"Do what?"

"Don't just agree with me because we're friends."

The use of the word "friend" always took TJ aback. Manny had used it a few times at that point, but he still wasn't used to hearing it. He supposed they were. If Mom asked him if he'd made any friends, Manny and Joshua would've been at the top of the list. To hear it out loud, though, was another thing. It was true what Manny said. He'd been far too deferential to her, too afraid to lose whatever favor he was able to curry with her.

"Speak your mind," she challenged him, ending the beat of silence.

"I don't know," TJ said. "Mr. Bolawe's been nothing but nice to me. I even got mad at him about it last week. And at the funeral, he helped defend my sister's casket. He's the one who turned the tides against the Keepers, if anything. And if the Keepers do want the staff, why would they let me in with it?"

"Oh, you see... I didn't know all that," Manny said. "But who else knows you have a staff?"

There was definitely someone TJ could think of. "Well, I don't know. Maybe I know someone... but it just doesn't make sense... or maybe I don't want it to make sense."

Manny drew closer to him, her voice low. "C'mon, you can tell me."

She had a way about her that was so disarming. Though she was demanding for him to spill it, TJ didn't feel at all pressured to respond. He knew if he chose not to, she wouldn't hold it against him. Maybe that's why he was so open with her.

"I wasn't completely honest with you that night you found me at the lagoon," TJ started. Manny didn't seem to take a breath, but her eyes were still patient. "Before you came, I met with someone... someone who I think might *actually* be a Keeper."

TJ explained everything that happened with Adeola, who she was, and how her actions could've been less than wholesome.

"So you think it could be her behind all this, then?" Manny asked.

TJ shrugged. "I don't know. She was my sister's best friend. I don't think—"

"It's the ones who are closest to us who can do us the most dirty."

"I mean, there was this one Keeper at the funeral..." TJ's voice caught in his throat for just a moment. It was like he was suppressing something he never wanted to say out loud, like vocalizing it would make it true. "I can't be sure, right? All those Keepers were wearing masks, but… one of them had these ìdẹ beads that were red, pink, and burgundy. When Deola said 'what's up' to me before the funeral, she was wearing them too." TJ shook his head as though to shake off where his thinking was going. "But plenty of people had those beads on at the funeral."

"Hmmm." Manny pressed her hand into her chin. "And you said she was the library assistant?"

"That's what she told me."

"I've never seen anyone like that. The little wooden ones take care of keeping that library together. And Elder Orji, of course, though she's always napping."

"Deola said the librarian gave her all sorts of errands and that she was always —"

"Busy," Manny finished for him. A great sinking feeling caved to the bottom of TJ's stomach. How could he be so stupid, so gullible? "Sounds like she has something to hide," Manny went on. "That story she fed is a load of crap. Bet she's not there if we go by the library right now."

"No, you're right." TJ sunk his head deep into his chest, hiding the shame on his face. "And the little walking statues you were talking about… they were all on the floor and shelves. She must've stunned them. I thought the elementary-level campers were playing with them and left a mess. But one of those things should have greeted me or given me some sass like that other one, right?" TJ smacked his head. "I was looking for her that day we were researching. Dang it."

"Do you think she's still on the campgrounds? Did anyone else not see her?"

"Just…" TJ lifted his head with a new thought. "Just Mr. Du Bois! When I ran into her at the library, Mr. Du Bois was there too. And he was holding this mask in his hands. He even tried to hide it from me when I looked."

"Wait, what did the mask look like?"

"It was um…" He snapped his fingers, trying to recall the image. "Coral. It looked like it was made from coral."

"The Keeper at the cemetery, the one that got caught. Rumor was they had a Yewa mask with them —"

"And Yewa uses coral with her crown." TJ facepalmed, and his heart dropped. "And… oh my goodness! When I saw Deola at the funeral, she had these Yewa beads with her. Damn, that all fits."

"Okay. So we'll need to talk to this Adeola chick, then. Why not just... ask her, ya know? Or if she's watching you or whatever, maybe we can get her to come at you again."

"Or we can have her think we know more than we do," TJ said. "If I can speak to her again, I can say I know something about the Keepers or that I need help with them. Or I can make some excuse that I can't trust anyone here but her."

"But we don't have our phones," Manny reminded him. "Except..."

"What?"

"Except the Director. She's got a water bowl in her office for emergencies and stuff. I had to use it last summer because..." she trailed off.

TJ figured whatever she was going to say related to Ifa Academy or some other subject she got bottled up about. Instead of pressing, he said, "Oh great, so let's just ask her to use the water bowl and talk to Deola. My mom uses one to speak to my grandma in the kitchen all the time."

Manny shook her head. "One problem. We have to be supervised when that happens. So that means sneaking in..."

"Well, we're pretty good at doing that. Not an issue at all." TJ rocked on his stump, excitement guiding his giddy movement. "So after we get in contact with her, what then?"

"Catch her in a lie, of course," Manny said.

"And how do we do that?"

"Listen closely." Manny clapped and rubbed her hands together. "This may get a little complicated."

31

IN THE NIGHT

FOR THE REST OF THE WEEKEND, TJ SAT THINKING ABOUT WHAT Manny had told him about "the art of subtly." How he needed to look, sound, and even think as they attempted to trick information out of Adeola.

But he couldn't help the slicing guilt rifling through his gut.

Though their discussion made sense as they talked it out, he still couldn't believe that Adeola was a Keeper. Worse yet, he couldn't figure out a scenario where she wasn't either. Not with all her sneaking around, the Yewa beads, and the Yewa mask. And they couldn't exactly tell any of the counselors at camp, as they weren't sure who could be trusted, especially when they figured Mr. Du Bois was in league with Adeola and the Keepers.

"So... you excited to see Manny tomorrow?" Joshua asked that Sunday night a few minutes before lights out, his body slumped over his bunk like always. "I know her and the crossover team just got back tonight. And you been doing a good job of avoiding your favorite bunkmate."

"Sorry, man," TJ sighed. "I don't mean to ignore you... there's just a lot going on."

"Oh, the woes of puppy love," Joshua said in an almost sing-song voice.

TJ threw out a stiff hand in front of his face as he turned to look to see if anyone was listening, namely Ayodeji. But most of the other boys were tucked under blankets; Ayodeji already snoring out a loud blubber.

"No," TJ hissed. "It's not like that. We're just..." TJ couldn't bring himself to divulge he was sneaking out again. Granted, he and Manny had almost agreed to bring Joshua into the loop about the staff and everything else. Was it so bad to get his advice? In a few hours, Manny would meet him outside the boys' cabin, and TJ didn't know much about breaking locks or activating water bowls. Joshua probably knew all that tricky stuff, being aligned with Eshu and all that.

Something on his face, the twitch of his lips, or the way he opened and closed his mouth several times must have been enough for Joshua because the boy plopped down from his bunk.

"Don't be so nervous, dude," he smiled. "You can tell me anything. I'm your boy. If you can't talk to me about girls, then what the heck have I been doing talking to you all summer?"

TJ couldn't help but laugh. He'd almost forgotten how funny Joshua could be. It really had been some time since they'd *really* hung out. Sure, they'd had lunches and class together, but TJ's head had been distant with everything else going on. He owed it to Joshua to give him *something*.

"Tomorrow," TJ began. "Tomorrow, I'll tell you what's been going on. I'm exhausted. Just give me some time to sleep it off. Then I'll let you know what we've been up to." He really wasn't all that tired. He just wanted to make sure Manny was okay with it all.

Beaming, Joshua stuck out his hand a few inches from TJ's face. TJ flinched and took a moment to realize the boy was offering a handshake. Taking Joshua's palm into his own, he squeezed hard as a way to say he meant what he said.

"Deal," Joshua said after dropping TJ's hand. Then he made an awkward half jump and spent the next few very loud moments struggling to get into his top bunk.

"Just use the ladder, man," LaVont grunted sleepily.

"All right, boys, lights out!" came Elder Wale's voice.

TJ turned his head to watch the wily old man lift his staff to snuff out each light one by one.

An hour later, TJ listened for Manny's signal. And the moment his watch hit "23:00"—his father had a preference for military time— a long, low trill broke through the constant chirping of crickets. It was Manny's call, a perfect whistle against the wind. TJ would've bet she was using some sort of Oya wind magic to make it sound so delicate.

Like before, TJ took the bathroom exit, tossing his sister's staff out the window and wiggling through the tall and thin slit of the bathroom. After falling into the bush after his staff, another trill came from the treeline.

"Psst, it's me, Manny. Follow my voice."

TJ tip-toed to the collection of trees closest to the boys' cabin, avoiding the swamp puddles that pocketed the path. When he made it to the trees, he could finally see Manny, who was wearing rough cargo pants and a combat long-sleeve shirt with her hair pulled back in French braids free of any hair dye. TJ gave her a wry half-grin.

"What?" Embarrassment laced her voice. "Do you think I over-dressed?"

"Nah, you're fine." He sniggered. "You even got the hair on point and everything."

She hit him across the shoulder. "Oh, shut up. We might need to do some climbing or whatever. I didn't want to get my knees all scraped up. In the last week, Gravés makes us hike through the entire swamp, you know. So maybe you should have brought some gear too."

TJ tugged at the padded shoulders on her shirt. "Where did you even get this? It almost feels real."

"That's because it is. My mother was in the military for a few years."

"Hey, my dad too! Fort Lewis. Where was your mom stationed?"

"Fort Drum. She was a... wait —" She went stiff and gestured for TJ to get down low. "Who's that coming through your window?"

TJ dropped to his belly and narrowed his eyes to the window leading into the boy's bathroom. A lumpy figure was trying to squeeze its way through the tiny hole feet first, like the last bits from a toothpaste tube.

"Oh, no..." TJ breathed out.

"Who is it?"

"I have one guess."

Joshua jostled against the window frame, banging against it loudly. TJ lifted himself from prone and went to help the boy get out. Tugging at his feet, TJ heaved and heaved, but he only made the banging louder. TJ curled his feet and clenched his stomach with each bang. Someone was going to wake up soon with all the racket.

"Step back, step back," Manny hissed as she set her hand against the window frame. Then she uttered the incantation, "*Èpó, wà ji mi.*"

The window frame glistened with an oily substance which was

just enough to help slip the stout boy flat on his back and into the bush. TJ and Manny went over to help him up.

"Buddy," TJ said as he lifted his friend up, putting his back into it, "I told you, I'd speak to you tomorrow."

But when he lifted the boy, he realized Joshua must've lost a fair few pounds. Then the moonlight shined down on the boy, and TJ didn't see the friendly round face of Joshua but the sharp, broad scowl of Ayodeji. TJ took a backstep instinctively, like he had just seen a roach scurrying underfoot.

"What the hell are you doing here?" Manny spat, speaking for TJ when he could not.

Ayodeji brushed off leaves from his chest and hair. "I should be askin' *you* that question."

"That really ain't none of your damn business." Manny's hands clenched into fists, and the contortion on her face said she'd use them.

"Just go back to sleep," TJ added bitterly.

He realized all that snoring Ayodeji was doing was for show. The boy must've known TJ was sneaking out with Manny.

"Fine, then." Ayodeji jumped back into the window frame. "On my way back, I'll be sure to tell Elder Wale that I saw you two sneakin' off while I was takin' a piss."

Manny grabbed Ayodeji's shoulders and brought him back down into the bush. TJ expected her to start wailing on him until he promised to shut up, but instead, she held the side of his arms in an almost gentle way.

"You can't do that, Ayo." Her voice came out softly too.

Ayodeji canted his head. "Yeah, why's that?"

"Because..." Manny gave TJ a sidelong glance. "Because TJ is trying to communicate with his sister."

"Ifedayo? Isn't she..."

"Yeah, yeah, she is, but TJ heard her. And if you go back and tell Elder Wale, he won't be able to hear her again. But then TJ ran into this woman named Adeola and—"

"Hey, wait, wait," TJ cut in, but a single finger pressed into Manny's lips silenced him.

This felt very wrong. Even if it meant shutting Ayodeji up he didn't want to talk about Dayo like this.

She continued, finishing her story with the explanation of them wanting to use Director Simmons's water bowl to speak to Adeola. TJ couldn't help but hang his jaw low, flabbergasted at Manny's candor. And here he was debating if he should tell Joshua what was going on. Someone far more trusting than Ayodeji ever could be.

What was this girl playing at?

"To sum it all up," Manny said, holding onto Ayodeji's shoulders, which he did not protest at all. "We need your help. *I* need your help."

Ayodeji considered her last words for a moment. That confident grin traded for a genuine and inquisitive rubbing of the peach fuzz above his lip. "Well, when you put it like that," he said. "I think I'm in."

TJ cleared his throat and stepped between the two. "Excuse me." He pulled Manny away. "I just need a short word."

When they were outside of Ayodeji's earshot, TJ tried his best to sound calm and collected as he said, "What in the *world* do you think you're doing? Do you remember this is the guy who hates my guts? Or did you forget that he kicked my ass two weeks ago? And what were you doing talking to him all sweet and stuff? It was like you were—" TJ stopped himself short of the word "flirting."

Manny stood there patiently as she waited for TJ to get it all out. TJ peered over her shoulder to Ayodeji, who examined under his nails casually, that smug grin plastered on his face.

"It was like you were being his friend," TJ finished.

"Right now, that's what he is."

"What's that supposed to mean?"

"Tell me, TJ. What's the other option we've got?"

"He can—well, we would just—" TJ didn't have anything. He glanced over to Ayodeji again, who had turned his head up to give TJ a full smile. "Okay, you're right. He has to be a friend."

"Or else he'll snitch." Manny put a hand to TJ's shoulder. The same gentle one she gave to Ayodeji. "Don't worry, a guy like that would never be my friend. After today, we won't have to talk to him again. The only leverage he has is if we get caught red-handed right now."

"But did you have to tell him *everything?*"

"Hey, I didn't mention the funeral or the crystal changing color. But if I didn't say all that other stuff, he wouldn't believe me."

TJ inhaled through his nose deeply, then stormed past Manny into the treeline, away from Ayodeji.

"Welcome to the team, Ayo," she said from behind.

"Nah, that's not good enough," the boy replied. "I want *him* to say it."

TJ spun on his heel. Now it was him with the clenched fists. "You what!?"

"We're ain't a squad unless the *whole* squad agrees."

TJ couldn't believe it. Wasn't it okay that Manny wanted him in? It was bad enough they didn't have a choice in the manner; now the jerk wanted to rub that into TJ's face too.

Manny gave TJ a sincere look. They were in this deep, and what was this one more thing?

"Fine, you're on the team," TJ forced himself to say.

For now, you jerk.

32

THE WATER BOWL

AGAIN, TJ GRUNTED LOW AS HE SHUFFLED OFF TO THE FOREST thicket where he retrieved his staff. When Manny and Ayodeji caught up, the man-bun-wonder called out, "Woah, woah, woah. Hold up." Manny and TJ turned. "You were serious about the staff? No way a scrub like this kid smuggled it in without someone noticing."

"Don't sound so surprised," TJ gave him a smirk of his own. He relished in the perplexed expression playing across Ayodeji's face as he and Manny left him in their wake.

"What about spirit water?" Ayodeji asked.

Once more, TJ and Manny twisted to him, and Manny was the first to ask, "What about it?"

"Did you bring some with you?"

"No," TJ said defiantly, thinking Ayodeji was about to show off again.

"So, how did you expect to talk to this Adeola person after breaking into Simmons's office?"

TJ and Manny looked at each other and shrugged. TJ figured there would be enchanted spirit water in Director Simmons's office. His mom always had her own tucked between the salt and pepper in the kitchen back home. Without it, water bowl communication wasn't possible, or else anyone could speak via any source of water. If water bowls were like someone's phone, enchanted spirit water was like their own personal phone number.

Ayodeji facepalmed. "All the counselors keep their spirit water with them. We're not just going to find some laying around. But tonight, you two are in luck. Mr. Du Bois might have taken my personal water bowl, but I was able to use a bit of sleight of hand to hang onto my spirit water." TJ thought he couldn't hate Ayodeji's nonchalant tone any more than he already did, but every time the boy spoke, he was proven wrong time and time again. And each time he spoke, he seemed to direct his words to Manny exclusively, not TJ. "While Mr. Du Bois was busy confiscating half my bag, I took a few things off him. It was easy, really."

That's because he was too preoccupied with all your other stuff you tried sneaking in, TJ thought bitterly.

Ayodeji pulled out a vial of spirit water from his shirt pocket and twisted the little thing in his hand. The moonlight caught the unnaturally bright blue liquid that almost looked like a hotel pool lit up at night.

"As you can see," Ayodeji said. "I'm more useful than you thought." Again, his words were only for Manny. He wasn't there to help the "team," he was there to help himself rub shoulders with Manny. Ayodeji must've read something on TJ's face because he added, "Don't look so surprised, my dude."

"You keep that stuff with you all the time?" Manny asked.

Ayodeji rolled the vial along his knuckles and tucked it back into his pocket. "I don't trust any of them boys in the cabin. Anything can be found when we're away at our sessions."

TJ thought back to how poorly hidden his staff was under the floorboards.

With a confident little jaunt, Ayo made off into the night and the dark forest.

The rest of the way to the office was left in relative silence, save for the four or five compliments Ayodeji gave Manny, most of them about the "impeccable practicality" of her outfit. TJ kept his rolling eyes forward, keeping his ears open for any creaking wood or low growls. He and Manny had snuck around the swamp long enough to start figuring out the habits of the red-eyed statue sentry, Ol' Sally, and Monsieur Francois, but he could never be sure.

When they arrived at Director Simmons's cabin door, TJ tugged on it only to find it was locked, as expected. The cabin was slightly exposed in a relatively wide clearing in the swamp, and it made TJ nervous. Anyone or anything could see them from the treeline.

Cracking his knuckles, trying to forget how vulnerable they all really were, he set into a lock pick incantation he had discovered in the library earlier that day. But each time he said the words "*ṣí fun mi*" the door did nothing more than jostle. By the fifth attempt—a cold sweat brewing at the back of TJ's neck—he gave it up.

"Hold up, hold up," Ayodeji piped in, pushing TJ away from the door. "You're not getting through the Director's door with a spell made for toddlers. Let me show you how it's done."

Ayodeji twisted his neck and stretched his arms and legs.

TJ settled back onto his heels next to Manny, who whispered to him, "It was a good try. Maybe next time."

Her words were meant to make him feel encouraged, but he couldn't help feeling belittled like he really was a toddler trying at something elementary. No wonder he had mastered the spell so easily during the day. He'd learned it from one of the library masks after putting it on and getting a demonstration, and now that he thought about it, the mask did look like it was made for a child's head.

"*Bí ikú bá tilẹ̀kùn, ebi ni ńṣí i,*" Ayodeji said, his Yoruba clear and confident. He was clearly a native speaker. As he spoke the words, he moved his hands around in what looked like a ceremonial, almost ritualistic dance, his fingers drawing an invisible figure. To TJ, it looked ridiculous, but in just a few seconds, the door swiveled inward, inviting them into the office space.

"If you're so good with your Ashe, why are you here?" TJ asked defiantly.

"'Cause I was *too* good." Ayodeji stretched his hands out casually. "Officially, they said I had a behavioral issue and whatnot, but I don't see it, do you?" Ayodeji waved a hand out like a butler, and he adopted an almost perfect British accent in Manny's direction, "After you, my lady."

Manny curtsied. "Why, thank you, my fine gentlemen."

TJ rolled his eyes as she walked in first. Despite what she said before, he still didn't like how she was playing into Ayodeji's hand. Not one bit.

As TJ followed behind Manny, Ayodeji blocked his way and went ahead. TJ grunted but suppressed the urge to make an outcry against the boy. That's what Ayodeji wanted, any excuse to start another fight that TJ knew he'd lose. So he bit his tongue and gazed upon the items within the low-lit room.

"And let there be light," Ayodeji said as he snapped his fingers to manifest a fire in his palm.

Manny did the same.

TJ snapped his fingers a few times before giving it up. They weren't supposed to be learning fire with Mr. Bolawe until the following week.

"Here, take some of mine," Manny murmured to him. "Just focus your Ashe into the flame. Channel Shango."

"Thanks," TJ said sheepishly, taking Manny's flame into his own hand, which shrunk from a few inches to just one upon transfer.

"Can you see the Ashe like you told me before?" Manny asked.

"Yeah, but just 'cause I can see it don't mean much. I'll keep it lit up, though. Don't worry."

Unlike Elder Akande's office and just about everything else at the camp, white covered almost every surface in Director Simmons's modern-looking workspace. The walls were minimalist, with every angle cut sharp at ninety-degree angles, from the bookshelves, the light fixtures, and the single marble table at the center. The only flare to the room, and perhaps it was by design, were plush chairs in Nigerian pattern designs, squared photos with colorful abstract art, and several curious Hulk-sized statues that lined the back.

The statues were oddly familiar to TJ. They were the same ones who roamed the grounds during the day. Now, seeing them stacked side by side and nearly touching the ceiling, TJ could tell they were all different from each other. And when his eyes crossed over a familiar slender-looking face and a wide-nose one just beside it, he realized they all represented different Orisha. TJ had come to know these two well over the past weeks: Orunmila and Eshu, respectively.

TJ peered down to the staff in his hand, and an idea sparked in his mind. He lifted it between the two statues, hoping the crystal in his staff would glow again. But nothing happened. The crystal remained cloudy and dull, and there was no vibration between his palm and the staff's shaft.

"The water bowl is hidden in one of these statues," Manny said, pointing at each of them. "I know she said something about water being important for Yemoja, Olokun, and Oshun, so I'm thinking either of these three might hold the water bowl."

"Could be any of the water Orishas," Ayodeji said, looking between a different set. "Don't forget about Olosa, maybe Oya."

Manny whipped her head to him in confusion. "Oya? But she's all about wind and the dead."

"Nowadays." Ayodeji touched the cheek of the Oya statue. "But she used to rule the lagoon with her sister Olosa."

TJ was ready for Manny's retort. After all, Oya was her Orisha alignment. She knew everything about her. But the rebuttal never came. Instead, she looked down and mumbled something to herself. "I forgot about that. You're right. Okay, pretty good, Ayo."

Ayodeji shrugged like it was nothing, then winked. "Hey, I'm only here to help. A child of Shango is always there for a child of Oya, you feel me?"

A lump caught in TJ's throat. *That* definitely wasn't an act. It was true that Oya was known to be Shango's favorite wife. Did that mean those with their alignments were also connected like... connected-connected, that kind that turned "like" into "like-like"?

A dark cloud filled TJ's heart. So far, he had done nothing to contribute to the group, nothing to impress Manny with. He had just one job... and he couldn't even do that.

Manny stuck her tongue out against her upper lip as she hummed in thought. "So... which statue do we pick, then?"

Ayodeji leaned in close to her, nearly touching her shoulder. "We'll need to be careful. If we pick the wrong one, I'm sure there's some sort of alarm system in place."

TJ rifled through everything he knew about the Orishas in his mind, but he drew blanks. He needed to say something. He needed to show *some* kind of value.

Then it sprang to mind.

"It's Oshun!" he blurted in a whisper.

He walked over to the statue of Oshun, running his hand over her beaded U-shaped mask that came down around her eyes and the wooded waves that came at her feet like a waterfall. "She represents both flowing water and divination. Flowing water fits because, well, that's what it looks like when you use a water bowl to communicate. And, this might be a stretch, but divination is a bit of a form of communication. I mean, communication with time itself. It's like Mr. Du Bois was saying about old diviners who did it. And like Mr. Bolawe taught us, voices carry over water."

"Oya communicates with the dead," Ayodeji reminded him, pointing to the Orisha's statue with her sword and whip. "That's more solid than divination, which is more foretelling than anything else."

Manny shook her head. "But Oya is missing the water element. Even if she did preside over lagoons at one point, lagoons are often still water, not flowing. TJ makes a good point about the flowing element."

"And I ruled out Yemoja and Olokun because of the ocean bits,"

TJ said. "Water bowls can't use salt water, right?" He turned to Manny, who didn't have an answer for him. TJ shifted his gaze begrudgingly to Ayodeji, who, after a long moment, nodded.

"Then I think Oshun is our best bet," TJ said with a confidence that was only partially solid.

Ayodeji shrugged and shuffled next to him. "Well... if you're wrong, we know who to blame."

He started up his little dance again and uttered the lock pick spell phrase. Like the front door, the statue jostled but didn't open. Ayodeji fidgeted with his hands before saying nervously, "Give me a minute. I just need to loosen up after that first door."

And again, he went into his little dance. Slowly, very slowly, the door parted. Ayodeji's strained face turned confident again, and TJ knew he'd do it—and then he'd have to suffer his conceit again. TJ didn't want to see that face for the rest of the night if he could help it. He wanted Ayodeji to get lost, go back to bed, and forget he ever saw anything.

As TJ watched the statue part farther apart, he could see the magic like a thick smoke in the room. The energy was being pulled between the essence locking the statue in place, and the magic Ayodeji used to pull it apart. TJ's fingers tingled as he pictured the statue closed once more as he continued to plead for Ayodeji's failure.

The chest of the statue smacked shut in a cloud of dust and wood shavings. Ayodeji flew back bodily as though the shutting motion had blown him back with a gust.

"What the hell?" he bellowed, quickly getting back to his feet and dusting himself off.

"Well, looks like TJ's right," Manny said. "That's definitely the right one. Here, let me have a try at it."

TJ traded a look with Ayodeji. This time it was the other boy who couldn't hold the eye contact as he glanced away, embarrassment reddening his cheeks.

TJ couldn't be sure, but by all reasoning, it was his fault Ayodeji couldn't get the statue open. The middle flaps at the statue's chest were already heeding him. Hell, he almost had the thing open all the way before TJ wished him ill.

But how could he? It'd clearly been established that Ayodeji was his better. How could he ever do anything against that?

TJ stared down at his hands in slight awe, and he would've sworn Ayodeji's mystical fog was drifting into his fingertips.

Manny started her own dance and incantation, mimicking the exact moves Ayodeji had done. But unlike Ayodeji, she didn't even get the statue to crack an inch. This time, however, TJ wished for her to do better, to open the hidden door, to succeed where Ayodeji had failed. He glanced back down at his hand, and the mystical fog pushed out toward Manny and swirled around her dance like a cyclone.

And just like that, in almost the next moment after the fog touched Manny, the statue opened wide to the shelf, housing a simple but weathered water bowl carved with wavy designs of fish and boats on its side.

"That was easy," Manny said. "I didn't even break a sweat."

Ayodeji looked beyond flabbergasted. "That's *exactly* what I just did."

Manny giggled. "It's okay. You loosened the jar for me." Then she gave him a playful smack against the arm. TJ frowned and went for the communication bowl to keep the task in focus.

But as TJ shot his hand forward, something blocked it. He tried to push against the invisible wall again and again. Yet each time the tips of his fingers drew forward, a blue hue rippled around the bowl — not unlike the color of Ayodeji's spirit water.

"Damn," Ayodeji said. "It's got a protective enchantment. Sort of like a lock screen on an iPhone."

"So we need a password?" TJ asked.

Ayodeji nodded. "Ideally. But there are other ways to get through it. We just need to, you know, part the waters."

"Like in Bolawe's class with the duckweed?" Manny asked.

"Yeah, something like that could work. One of us can part it while the other takes the bowl out. But the magic holding it is bound to be strong, very strong. It could take hours…"

"We didn't come here to turn back now." TJ looked down to his watch, which now read "0:04." Then he looked back up to Manny and Ayodeji. "We've got the time."

Ayodeji stepped forward. "All right, I'll take a crack at it."

Manny put a hand to his chest to stop him. "Let's give TJ a shot at it first. You and me should take a break and rest up in case he needs us to tag in soon."

"Fine by me." Ayodeji shrugged as he walked toward the mini-fridge tucked in a sharp white box that looked like something straight out of a sci-fi movie. Inside were tiny bottles of water, juice boxes, and sports drinks.

TJ started work on the enchantment, thinking back on the day he learned to clean the duckweed by separating the water around it to the tune of his piano song. At first, he tried using his own Ashe, but he could barely make the water bowl encasing shudder. So he pulled up his sister's staff and worked his Ashe through the wooden shaft.

Still, the protective enchantment resisted him.

And there was no fog, no mist that he could see.

TJ dug deep, concentrating inward, thinking not of the task of pulling the protections away but of his sister and the lightness he felt during the funeral. His insides roiled as that memory resurfaced to his mind, and for a moment, he was back in that strange cloudy abyss with those colossal figures looking down on him.

"*Woah, woah, TJ, are you okay?*" Manny asked distantly, though TJ knew she was just there at his side.

"*Yo, his eyes are going nuts,*" came Ayodeji's voice, just as distant.

TJ latched onto their voices and the fear that pulsated from them. He pulled on their Ashe in the same way he did with Manny, then he pushed it back out through his fingers, along the staff, and straight out to the protected water bowl.

"*Let go, TJ!*" Manny shouted. "*You don't look so good.*"

"*I can't... stop... right now,*" TJ strained, his voice sounding like it was underwater as he clenched his grip tight around Dayo's staff. "*We'll lose it if I let go. Almost... there.*"

TJ's legs started to give from under him, the magic resisting him too much. Manny and Ayodeji held him up by each of his armpits as TJ opened a hole large enough in the enchantment for them to pull the bowl out. But neither could as they spent their time trying to keep TJ from falling over and knocking his head against the hardwood.

"*I gotta go for it,*" Ayodeji called out.

He let go of TJ to grab for the bowl. He had a hand on it just as TJ let out the last of his reserves.

But Ayodeji was too slow to rip it out.

The protective water enchantment came down around Ayodeji's wrist in a constricting grip. The boy screamed at the top of his lungs as the Oshun statue protecting the water bowl came to life and clutched him in a bear hug. Like the sentry statue out in the swamp, this one's eyes flared red.

TJ fell to the floor as Manny's support on his shoulder gave way. When he looked up in an odd upside-down angle, he could see the Orunmila statue also trapping her in a wooden grasp. TJ tried to shuffle to his feet and get out of dodge, but before he could step out of the cabin, one of the remaining statues pulled him into an unbreakable hold.

TJ dropped his sister's staff near the white table as whatever statue was holding him gripped harshly around his chest like a living straitjacket.

Ayodeji tried using his feet to beat the Oshun statue that had him, but he couldn't even make a dent, flapping around like a fish on a deck. The red-tinted glasses on his nose should've fallen with all his erratic movement, but TJ suspected they were held on with magic.

Manny filled her cheeks like a balloon and blew out a gust of magical air, but her wind was weak and did nothing to break her free. In fact, to TJ, it seemed as though her wind was being enveloped in a shadowed sphere, suppressed by some unseen force.

TJ's eyes went wide as he realized it was the statues themselves that held all their magic down.

Ayodeji tried to heat his fingers like hot rods beneath the blue orb locking his fingers, but the moment they lit up, they dissipated in the next instant.

Whatever magic was at play here was the same TJ used against Ayodeji earlier. But where something was taken away, TJ knew, something else was given.

Focusing his Ashe inward once more, he sensed for the magic at work in the room. The aura around Manny was, as he suspected, a faint bubble around her, keeping her locked into an invisible cage. With all his might, he sank deep into his Ashe, letting it flow through him freely and out again as though it were sweet air being inhaled and exhaled on a spring's day. The cycle funneled through him. He pushed it out toward Manny. And little by little, her cage dwindled and dwindled until it was no more.

"Now, Manny, now!" TJ choked out in an exhausted shout.

Once more, Manny filled her cheeks and blew them out. She went flying out the statue's grasp, going in one direction and the statue in the other. The statue smashed against the pale wall where its back splintered into wood pieces. Manny dashed for the cabin door where the statues didn't seem to follow.

"Great!" Manny said excitedly. "Can you do that trick again?"

Fatigue took hold of TJ, gripping around his heart. "I've got one more in me, I think. And that's it."

Ayodeji didn't even plead. From the resigned expression on his face, TJ knew what that meant. He was going to be left behind to fend for himself. TJ put in a second effort and exerted his will over the next barrier. A few moments later, to Ayodeji's apparent surprise, it was he who was freed.

"Go, Ayodeji. Go!" TJ shouted.

"Yo, you didn't have to. You should've —"

"Stop talking! Go!"

Ayodeji lit his hot rod fingers again and forced the statue's arms away. He sprang up and dashed for the cabin door.

TJ tried working on his own hold, but he was beyond exhaustion. All he wanted to do now was fall down, take a nap, and not wake up until next week.

But he couldn't get caught either.

So he started the cycle again. He inhaled, filled himself with Ashe, then let it out again. Yet it wasn't a magical release that came forth, but the release of the bottom of his stomach as his dinner splattered all over Director Simmons's desk in a disgusting collage of orange and brown mess.

Though his mind seemed to be up to the challenge, his body was not.

At least his throw-up matched the room's secondary color palette.

With dribbles of vomit caking the side of his mouth, he rolled his head to one side and murmured, "Y-you guys go... y-you both have higher grades than me. If I get kicked out... it won't matter."

"No, TJ. We can't leave you!" Manny cried.

She balanced on the balls of her feet like she was psyching herself up for double-dutch, too afraid to cross into the cabin again where she'd get snatched, but steeling enough courage to try for it, anyway.

The look of genuine shock on Ayodeji's face surprised TJ. Ayodeji wasn't so vocal as Manny in her proclamation, but his expression said it all. TJ never thought he'd see the look on him: one of utter respect.

The boy nodded, long and slow. Both of them knew what had to happen. Ayodeji tugged at Manny's arm. "C'mon. We gotta bounce."

"No. I told you. We're not leavin' him."

"It's either him or all of us. Don't let what he's doin' go to waste."

The tears that finally spilled from Manny's eyes told TJ that she understood it too. They'd have to leave. There was nothing they could do, and TJ's Ashe was all spent.

Lights from somewhere behind Manny and Ayodeji lit up, casting them in silhouettes.

"Who's there?" came a woman's voice, and the other two bolted for the trees.

TJ tried one last time to exert his will over the statue that held him firm, but there was simply nothing there. He just needed more time to recoup his energy.

He dropped his tired gaze to the floor where his sister's staff lay just against Director Simmons's desk, half of it layered with his throw up. They'd take that away too when they found him. He'd get kicked out all before the first session even ended. He could almost hear the disappointment in Mom's voice, the quiet and disappointing looks she'd give him on the return trip.

The light outside grew wider and brighter as whoever approached came nearer. TJ released the tension from his arms and legs and waited for his destiny to come down on him like a scythe.

Suddenly, the room filled with a thick gray smoke the same moment the woman entered the room.

"What's that? Who's there?" The woman coughed. TJ recognized the voice as Director Simmons herself.

With renewed energy, TJ reached his hand out to the staff he knew was just feet from him. "*Wà ʃi mi,*" he called out to it. And again, "*Wà ʃi mi.*"

On the third command, the staff snapped into his hand like a magnet, and he felt its energy rush through him like a breaking dam. With another effort, he pushed against the statue until its magical grip fell away like chains had been binding him.

And like that, he was free.

He had no clue why or how, but he was free.

It took a moment longer than it should've to get to his feet and find his bearings, but he did it, somehow. He found his balance just as Director Simmons lifted her staff in the smoke. The crystal at the head of her iron staff was sucking it all up like a vacuum. TJ didn't wait for her to clear the room as he dashed for the open door and straight out in the piercing cool air.

As he ran, he couldn't believe his luck. Then he realized it wasn't luck at all. The smoke came from someone. It had to be Manny or Ayodeji coming back to give him more time. TJ barely noticed where he was going as he turned around a corner between two trees in the direction of the boys' cabins. Had he been paying attention, he would've seen a great mass of a man blocking his path. Instead, he went headfirst into the figure's chest and fell straight onto his back into mud and muck.

"What are you doing sneaking around at night?" It was Mr. Du Bois. "Director Simmons, he's over here!" he called out.

TJ rolled his head in the dirt, defeated. Just to his right, not fifty yards away, he could see Manny helping Ayodeji slide back into the boys' cabin restroom.

At the very least, those two would get off okay.

33

PAST DUE

MR. DU BOIS STOOD OVER TJ LIKE A SHADOW AGAINST THE starry night—literally, the *worst* adult to find him on the grounds.

Mud rubbed into the back of TJ's neck as he laid there defeated, the cool early morning air through the swamp trees nipping at his cheeks. He and the counselor stared at each other until Mr. Du Bois's cold eyes narrowed at what lay at TJ's side.

"I don't know how you got that in here," he said deeply. "But... *Wà ṣi mi.*"

Dayo's staff vibrated for a moment, snapped upright, and then soared straight into Mr. Du Bois's hand with a soft *smack.*

"*Kùró lọdọ mi,*" he said, and the staff disappeared. TJ didn't even make a sound of protest. "Don't worry. You'll get it back at the end of the session... if you last that long."

Du Bois stuck out his thin hand to TJ. Even if TJ had the will to take it, he didn't have the energy. His whole body felt deflated. The man, however, didn't wait for TJ's go ahead, lifting him to his feet from the mud, then nodding his head back in the direction of Director Simmon's cabin. "After you, Mr. Young."

TJ sighed heavily, lifted slowly, and turned with low shoulders and lower spirits as he took the walk of shame straight back to the scene of the crime. But his feet didn't agree with him. In three steps, he slumped back into the muddy grass, and Mr. Du Bois had to lift him by the waist to keep him steady until they returned to the Director's cabin.

"This is why Counselor Gravés has you run your little hearts out," Mr. Du Bois said. "Magic isn't easy to hold, is it?"

Through the treeline, the outline of Director Simmons took shape. She wore an oversized bathrobe, which at first looked like a billowing witch's robe. A patterned headwrap enveloped her head, and fluffy slippers hugged her feet.

"Tomori Jomiloju Young," she said when she got her first look at TJ. Unlike the teachers back home, she got his name right. "I'll admit, I didn't expect to see you out here tonight." She turned to Mr. Du Bois, her long headwrap whipping with her. "Thank you, Xavier. I'll take it from here."

"There's no trouble in me staying." Mr. Du Bois bowed. "The boy probably wasn't alone and—"

Director Simmons held up a flat hand. Mr. Du Bois got the message, then turned to TJ as though to give him a look that said: *"Nice to have known you."* With a spin on his heel, he headed off back into the dark trees.

Why hadn't he said anything about TJ's staff? He would've sworn that was the next step of the conversation.

When Mr. Du Bois was thirty feet away—likely in search for TJ's partners in crime—Simmons cleared her throat. "Well, I'm plenty awake now. I'm sure you are as well. I've already cleaned the mess you made, so come right in, and we'll figure out what's what."

She waved him inside, and TJ followed suit. He dipped his head back into her now fully lit office. The space looked far less haunting without the dim light. Even the statues which had looked like dark specters in the shadows seemed serene and calm, though the Orunmila statue that Manny escaped from still had a deep chunk split out of its cheek and an angry expression to match.

"Sit," Simmons commanded gravely.

TJ took long and sluggish strides to one of the Nigerian-patterned plush seats across from her desk—one smothered under papers. For a moment, TJ thought he and the others had made all the mess before the Director said, "No, that wasn't you. This just happens when I'm doing finances, is all." She waved her hand across the table like a casino dealer. "But I know where everything is… mostly."

"I was homesick," TJ blurted, though his voice was hoarse. "I wanted to speak to my mom, and I know we can't have our phones, so I figured I could just use the water bowl real quick."

"Oh, is that so?" Simmons said, her elevated pitch telling him she was unconvinced. "And you didn't think it wise to ask one of the elders, or myself, to use it?"

In truth, TJ and Manny had thought of that. But to use the water bowl properly meant they had to be over-watched by one of the adults. And that wouldn't do when their plans involved practically interrogating a potential Keeper through the Director's very own water bowl.

TJ wished Manny was there to do the talking. She was much better at it. His whole homesick opening didn't get him off. It just pushed him into a dead end. So he just sat quietly and bit his tongue.

"You couldn't wait another week for the midsummer break?" she asked him, offering him an out. But TJ knew better than to lie again.

When the Director shook her head, a *clack-clack* rang out from under her head wrap. TJ assumed she had hair rollers under it. "I'll have to mark you down for this," she said sadly. "By a lot. *And* you will be disallowed from all rec time for the rest of the summer, too. Detention, in other words."

TJ shot her a questioning eyebrow. "Wait, you're not gonna kick me out?"

Simmons waved a dismissive hand. "Oh no, no. This isn't Ifa. And this is your first offense. But before I cut you loose, I do have a question." She got up from her chair and moved to the front. When she got there, she swung the squeaking front door back and forward. "How did you get past the lock?"

"Um... a spell."

"Well, yes, of course. Which one is my question, child."

"Oh, right. Well, the one about um... death's door and um... hunger?" His words couldn't have rung any more false.

Simmons considered him a while, then looked back to the door and then back to TJ. When she was satisfied with her back and forth, she moved onto her statues, pointing at the three that had trapped the children. "And what's your story with these? I assume you tried to get away, but each of them grabbed you."

TJ told her the story, editing out the bits that involved his accomplices and making it out as though he did it all his own. As he spoke more and more, he found himself waning, even nodding off halfway through his own explanation. It was like a wave of exhaustion had stormed through him, and he decided it was best if he just knocked out then and there. He'd never used so much of his Ashe all at once and so concentrated before. He could've never guessed it would've left him *this* drained.

In his debilitated reflection, it only then washed over him how insane the Ashe he manifested was. Director Simmons herself must've enchanted the statues, yet somehow he freed himself. He, TJ, who all summer had an issue manifesting the simplest of magic, could suddenly fight against powerful magic molded by a senior diviner.

It made little sense.

That recycling fog from the others—Manny, Ayodeji, and the statues, funneled through his mind the same way it funneled through his own body. It was magic unlike any taught all summer.

Something entirely different.

"That must have been difficult for you," Simmons said almost to herself. She moved to her sci-fi-looking mini-fridge and pulled out a can of espresso. "Here, take this." She handed the cold can to him.

TJ didn't like coffee, but he couldn't control his lolling head anymore. So he cracked it opened and downed it in a dozen gulps.

He couldn't believe how easy he was getting off. At this point, he was expecting to have his head torn off, but instead, Director Simmons seemed to be giving him a post-game interview with only a tiny detention as a consequence.

"I saw the vomit," she went on. "You must have pushed yourself past your limits—and without a staff on top of it all." She looked away as though something caught her attention. She was so unlike her sister. Where Elder Adeyemi seemed regal, almost too calm, Simmons was casual in a more laid-back way. "TJ, can you give me a moment? There's something I'd like to try. Just… don't fall asleep on me."

TJ gave a very slow nod, more out of a head swimming in confusion than fatigue. Simmons clapped, making TJ jump, and then she hurried out of the cabin.

TJ sat in silence for what felt like several minutes. The only thing to break the quiet was the crickets chirping through the windows. One of the many papers strewn across Simmons's desk caught TJ's eyes. Against its white paper and black ink, a great big blotch of red was stamped over it. TJ couldn't see it at first—part of it was covered by a Manila folder—so he slid the page out to get a better look.

When he read the top of the page, his spine locked up tight, and his breath caught in his throat. It was a past due notice that was supposed to be sent to his parents the following week. From what he could read, it didn't seem like they'd paid for anything, except for his meals. But everything else was marked with red ink:

**Lodging Fees. Unpaid. Facilities Fees.
Unpaid. Personnel Fees. Unpaid.**

Clattering feet against wood came stomping around the corner as TJ tossed the bill, letting it land where it may atop the desk. A moment after the paper settled, Director Simmons came shuffling into the room with an assortment of herbs, flowers, boards, and whatever else. Then she flung them all along the desk.

"If I'm not mistaken, you have not yet been identified to have an alignment with any of the Orishas, correct?"

"Nope," TJ answered.

"Very well, very well." She stuffed a handful of cowries into TJ's palm. "Throw these just inside here."

TJ glanced down as the director placed a cup of water and an *Ọpọn Ìfà*—a divining board—onto her mountain of papers. It was a small and circular thing made of wood, bordered by wiggly designs of animals and faces. At the top was the long and slender head of Orunmila.

"Um, is this part of my punishment?"

"No, no, nothing like that. Just doing a few tests is all." Excitement bubbled at the edge of her dark eyes. "Go on, try it out."

A little confused at the bizarre request, TJ shifted the cowries in his palm to see they were cut in half, the outsides an earthly red and the insides a paler, gentle pink. It was clear Simmons wanted him to perform a divination, but he couldn't recall the first thing he had to do. He remembered his sister using her own board during her summer breaks... all he could think of was her blowing on her cowries before letting them go. So, TJ drew his hand to his mouth and blew.

Simmons slapped his hand. "What are you doing that for, eh?" In her scolding, a bit of an old Nigerian accent slipped through. "You're not using the sixteen cowries, and you are certainly not at the level of a bàbálàwò."

"Sorry, sorry," TJ apologized. "Just a um... habit."

The questioning glance from Simmons looked wholly unconvinced. "Take this cup of water, sprinkle them onto the nuts, and then cast them to board, please. But make sure you ask Orunmila specifically."

"Ask Orunmila what?"

"Whatever it is you'd like to know, so long as it can be answered yes or no."

Anything he wanted? He didn't have to think on that long at all. He dipped his fingers into the cup of water and sprinkled the nuts.

"Wait, wait, don't let them go," Simmons blurted. "You haven't done your prayer, your knocks, or your shifting." She shook her head. "Did you learn none of this?"

In truth, TJ probably did at some point. But with everything going on, he couldn't keep up, plus none of it seemed to matter in light of recent events and past due bills.

The Director explained how he should have properly done the divination, the prayer to obi, the honor to Orunmila, and then the final question. "Okay, now you may proceed," she said.

Holding his hand over the board, TJ thought, *Great Diviner, will I see my sister again?*

His fist came loose, and he let the shells fly free. They tumbled and rolled briefly, then settled to show a clear picture of each of their dark backs. Even TJ knew that was bad. His chest caved. He knew he'd never see his sister again, but with the voices, the staff, the funeral, all of it, he thought perhaps there was at least some chance.

"Hm," Director Simmons hummed. "What did you ask?"

"If I'd get into Ifa Academy," TJ lied.

"Oh my, don't ask something like that! There are too many variables in something like that. Try for a more simple thing, child. Like if it will be overcast tomorrow or anything like that."

"Oh… right."

But that didn't work well either. TJ asked if there would be a thunderstorm the next day, expecting the answer to be an obvious "no," but the shells read "definitely."

"Right, so you don't have the eye, then," Simmons pulled out a new set of objects: seashells, seaweed, and coral.

"So I was wrong then?"

"Considering we've been going through a heatwave, I would say it's very unlikely. And there are no clouds in the sky at all."

So then his prediction about his sister might've been wrong too. The thought warmed TJ a bit, if only just.

"Okay, how about this…" Simmons led him through more tests, some of them the same as what Priest Glover gave him before he'd come to Camp Olosa. And just like then, all the tests seemed to bring no sense of encouragement from the Director, same as her sister. At one point, TJ asked why he was being tested at all, to which the Director said, "strong magic is best tested straight after its use."

Really, she was probably trying to figure out how he got through her door and free from her statues.

"Well, it was worth a try," Simmons huffed as she gathered her divination board, herbs, seaweed, flowers, and all the rest again. Then she looked at her table for too long a moment. TJ swallowed deeply.

"You know," Simmons cleared her throat. "There's a reason the phrase goes 'organized mess.' Yes, my desk may look a bit like clutter to some." She lifted the past due bill. "But I know where most everything is, and more importantly, where I placed them."

"Sorry." TJ dropped his head into his chest. "It was just sitting right there; I had to look—I had..." The lump in his throat stopped him from going on.

"You weren't meant to see this. I didn't want to worry you when you were studying so hard—"

"Studying so hard?" TJ shot back. His outburst took both him and Simmons aback. But TJ got over it first, continuing on. "I'm about to flunk, and my parents can't even pay my way? How pathetic is that?" TJ launched out of his seat.

"Tomori, we already said we'd work something out with your mo—"

TJ didn't want to hear it. "Can I be excused to my cabin, please?"

Director Simmons's eyes looked devoid of the hope they had before, darkened seemingly by TJ's mood. It seemed she had more to say, but every time she met TJ's hurt and fierce gaze, her lips pursed. Eventually, she settled her shoulders back and took a deep breath. "Yes, Tomori, you may be excused. I'll walk you back now."

34

SUMMER'S BREAK

TJ WOKE UP THE NEXT DAY WITH THE WEIGHT OF THE PAST-DUE bill still pressing on his mind. As the first break of morning light slithered through his window's wooden slats, almost on cue, Joshua dropped his head over the top bunk, and, with a groggy yawn, he asked, "So... about what you were saying yesterday. What do you have to tell me?"

TJ had completely forgotten his promise to Joshua, but he wasn't up for the boy's jovial spirit. It wasn't like it mattered if he wasn't coming back for the second half of the summer.

"Give me until breakfast at least, Josh," TJ answered, rolling out of bed as Elder Wale and Juice started magically pulling covers off of boys. Like a zombie, TJ gathered his towel and toothbrush and slumped to the bathroom.

"Rise and shine, little diviners," Elder Wale wailed. "Let's start the last week of session one on the right foot!"

"What's wrong?" Joshua asked as he waddled behind TJ.

"Nothin', man," TJ said irritably. "Just wait until I've got some food in me."

But even after breakfast, TJ gave Joshua the cold shoulder. Technically, he never lied either, as he didn't touch his breakfast, therefore never filling his stomach with food, which had been his prerequisite for conversation.

As he made his way to Miss Graves' morning session—ordering Joshua to go ahead and stop bothering him—he was pulled behind the outhouses stacked between the mess hall and the rest of the campgrounds. TJ lifted his fists in defense but lowered his hands when he saw it was Manny and Ayodeji.

"Bruh, I can't believe you're still here," Ayodeji said with a surprising tone of honesty. "We thought they would've sent you packin'."

"You couldn't have told me in the cabin?" TJ asked.

"And have LaVont and Jimoh see me talkin' to you?" Ayodeji scoffed. "C'mon, man. You know how it is."

TJ rolled his eyes. "Director Simmons seemed more interested in how I—uh, we—broke into the office at all." Both their eyes went wide. "Don't worry. She doesn't know you two were there. She did give me a bunch of tests though."

"She was probably trying to find out how you broke her enchantments," Manny said knowingly. "I mean..." She looked to Ayodeji. "We was wondering how too."

"Yeah, that's what I thought too. I couldn't even begin to tell you how I did any of that."

An awkward silence fell between them as they looked everywhere but at each other.

Ayodeji punched TJ lightly across the shoulder. "Hey man, what you did back there for us—for me—it was pretty dope."

"Wasn't good enough. I couldn't get myself out."

Ayodeji sucked his teeth. "I was bankin' my little smoke trick would've helped."

"It did," TJ assured him. "And I would've made it away, but I ran into Mr. Du Bois. He took my staff and everything."

"Damn..." Ayodeji said.

"What's even stranger is that when he took my staff, he didn't tell Director Simmons."

Manny stuck out her neck. "What? Okay, that's mad suss. Should we tell someone he did that?"

"I don't know." TJ shrugged. "Simmons let me off, but if she knew I smuggled a staff in, I might get in *real* trouble. Forget about getting more coral rubbed against my skin or throwing cowries on a board."

"Man..." Ayodeji said. "I'm telling you... if it was me, I'd be kicked out, no question. It really must help to have a famous sister."

Manny punched Ayodeji straight in the gut, and the boy keeled over, wheezing. "That was fair," Ayodeji said as he placed a hand on one of the outhouses. "Oh, he knows I didn't mean nothin' by it."

"So is that it?" Manny asked. "Is your staff gone for good?"

TJ shook his head. "I'll get it back at the end of the session."

"Oh, good! Then we can still figure out what's going on with the voices and Adeola when we get back from break."

TJ didn't have the heart to tell her that it was very likely he wouldn't be coming back. And despite the fervor she and Ayodeji spoke with over the next week as they went over different theories and possibilities surrounding the staff, Adeola, the missing counselors, and Mr. Du Bois's suspicious behavior, TJ only participated halfheartedly, his mind halfway home already.

The Friday before the last day of session one, it was Joshua, not Manny or Ayodeji, that he confided in. He felt like he owed Joshua after keeping him in the dark for so long. The boy had been nothing but nice to him. There was no reason to ignore him.

"Listen," TJ said as they gathered their things from Ogbon class. His hands were still sticky from the paste they were using to make their own divination boards. "I'm not coming back to camp next session."

"What!?" Joshua asked so loudly it turned the heads of Ayodeji and his friends at their desks.

"Jesus, man," Ayodeji said mockingly. "Say it, don't spray it."

Though TJ and Ayodeji had been on friendly terms the past week, in front of Ayodeji's friends, it was business as usual. And when it came to Joshua, things didn't change at all.

"Sorry," Joshua apologized, his face scrunched up bashfully.

Ayodeji led his friends from the instruction room, and Joshua leaned in close to listen to TJ's next words. "Yeah. My folks can't pay my way. Unless I come into some money, I can't come back. Plus, Mr. Du Bois might be right." He peeked up at the counselor, who was examining everyone's boards at his desk. "I'm taking up space for another diviner kid who actually deserves to be here."

"Then take my place. This camp is a drag, anyway."

"Is that genius talk? Top five in the rankings too boring for you?" TJ looked at Joshua like he had grown a second head. "You're insane, dude."

"I'd like to think I'm more... misunderstood."

"Nah, I can't do that, man." TJ lifted a fist to dap Joshua, but Joshua didn't move to reciprocate. "Come on, Josh. Your parents would never go for it."

"You don't know how persuasive I can be, friend."

"Thanks. You been a good friend, but you barely know me. I've been keeping things from you." TJ sighed deeply and told him every-thing about the staff and the water bowl and all the rest.

Joshua's mouth fell agape, dropping farther and farther the more TJ confessed. "You should have told me all that stuff. I told you I could help!"

"I know, I know. And maybe I should've. Maybe then we wouldn't have gotten caught up like we did. But real talk, it was nice knowing you this summer, Josh. If you're ever in Los Angeles, just hit me up."

☥

ON THE LAST DAY, AS ALL THE CAMPERS PACKED UP FOR THEIR one-week break, TJ asked Manny and Ayodeji if they would ride with him back to the airport. Manny said yes straight away, but TJ made the mistake of asking Ayodeji in front of LaVont and Jimoh.

"Get out of here, scrub." LaVont laughed.

TJ changed tack and droned, "Sorry, what I meant to say is that we've been assigned to the same boat back. Miss Gravés wanted me to let you know you need to be there by nine o'clock."

Ayodeji played his role well, rolling his eyes and disparaging Miss Gravés's name before he agreed to come with TJ.

On their way across the dock, TJ crossed Mr. Bolawe, who was seeing the campers out. TJ had half a thought to apologize and even tell Mr. Bolawe he wasn't coming back, but he decided against it. Sometimes it was better to just ghost instead of meeting a situation head-on.

Following Ayodeji onto the airboat where Manny waited alone, the cab driver nodded and said, "All right, then. We off!"

As they scuttled across the bayou, wind whipping through Manny's hair, water speckling Ayodeji's glasses, and TJ holding his baseball bag tight—his sister's staff returned to him as promised—Manny and Ayodeji spoke, once again, about everything they'd do when they returned.

"Maybe we need the time off to get our heads right," Ayodeji shouted over the roar of the bayou boat. "When I get back to Lagos, I'll ask my parents about it."

"Me too," Manny agreed. "None of my family are diviners, but I might find something at the New York Library. It's so huge, and I always find hidden little gems there. We should focus mostly on how to work TJ's staff with the lagoon."

Ayodeji turned to TJ, holding down the stylish dad hat threatening to fall from his head. "And TJ, try your best to get in contact with Adeola. Keeper or not, she's the one who gave you that journal. She's bound to know something about it."

"I'm a fluke, just like that bàbáláwò said," TJ said suddenly.

Manny held her hair out of her face to peek at TJ curiously. "What are you talkin' about?"

TJ had to prep them for what was to come. They had to understand where he was coming from before he just laid it all on them at once. "Did you see the rankings on the board this morning? I'm never gonna get accepted to Ifa or any magic school. What's the point?"

"I still can't believe Joshua got top five in grades, actually," Manny commented.

Ayodeji frowned. "Look, man. That stuff I told you before... I was just trying to, you know, get you off your game. You don't even need to be a top student grade-wise to be considered. It just helps in the final interview, is all. I was top three last year, and I didn't even get an interview anywhere. But then again, no one got an offer."

"That's not exactly true..." Manny trailed off, looking away from him. "I got accepted."

"What!?" Ayodeji blurted, nearly tipping over in his seat and into the river. "Then what in the hell are you doing here?"

"She doesn't like talking about it," TJ cut in as he saw that familiar shadow drop in front of Manny's face. "And it doesn't matter. I'm not getting an interview *at all*. Not when I'm a joke of a diviner."

"Listen." Manny sat closer to him on the seat they shared in the back. "I know jokes. I got jokes. You... you are not a joke."

Ayodeji slumped his arm over his seat. "A joke couldn't have done what you did with those statues, man. Don't trip. When we get back, we'll get your grades up, *no wahala*, man."

"That's not everything." TJ rubbed at the back of his naps. "My family can't afford my tuition..."

"Oh, that's it?" Ayodeji scoffed, then pointed at his glasses. "I got these gold-plated out of my own pocket. My parents give me a forty-K *naira* allowance per month—I think that's a thousand a month in U.S. dollars. I could just—"

"Nah," TJ cut him off as well. "I'm not taking your money." He turned to Manny. "Either of you."

"Don't look at me," Manny said. "My parents are broke. We don't pay a dime for my tuition, you know." She dipped her head low, her thick hair like blinders on a horse. It was like she was speaking to him and only him. "You can apply for scholarships, maybe even a grant."

"Again, my grades are abysmal. That type of stuff isn't gonna work for me."

The boat shifted underfoot as it transformed back into a cab, bumping against the muddy banks leading back out to the highway. Monsieur Francois waved a jolly goodbye with his tree branch arm, but none of the kids waved back, stunned in their silence. For a long moment, the only sounds through the cab were the clanks of the car's shocks as it crunched against the dirt road below.

"I can't believe you're telling us this just now," Manny said, her eyes away and out the window. "You've known since Simmons spoke to you, huh?"

TJ must've imagined it, he had to have imagined it, but through the faint grimy reflection of the window, it looked like Manny's eyes were... watering.

TJ's heart fluttered a sorrowful beat before he said, "You all were so excited. I didn't want to mess that all up."

"But I'm your *friend*, TJ." She turned to him so suddenly it made him flinch. "You don't just lay this on someone two seconds before we're about to leave."

TJ looked to Ayodeji out of the corner of his eye. The boy had absolutely no intention of getting in the middle as he turned to look forward and out the front window.

TJ glanced back to Manny. "Manny, I'm sorry. I wasn't even going to say anything at first."

"That's even worse!" she blurted, her cheeks flushing red.

TJ cleared his throat twice, but the lump in it simply wouldn't go away. "Well, I wasn't really going to do that," he mumbled. Then he tried for a joking tone. "Couldn't let y'all think I went on some extended vacation like Old Man Whittaker or Elder Akande." A smile crested around the last of his words, but neither of them laughed, nor did they look at him.

The rest of the ride to the airport was left in a weighted and uncomfortable silence.

35

BACK HOME

MANNY'S LAST WORDS PRESSED ON TJ'S MIND ALL THROUGHOUT his plane ride home. Halfway through the trip, he cursed himself as he remembered he never asked for her number. And when he searched her name on social media, she didn't seem to be on any of them. Plus, there were about 3,691 people named "Manuela Martinez."

Yeah, he counted.

There was a time during the first few days where TJ thought he could go back to camp, that he deserved it. When he returned Dayo's staff to her pedestal at his family altar, he was able to fill the water glass with no issue—to Mom's delight. When Tunde made fun of his abysmal grades, TJ imagined his dog Simba biting Tunde, and in the next instant, it actually happened. And when Dad set TJ to the glorious chore of pulling weeds from the garden, TJ didn't realize he'd been pulling them with magic until they were all gone.

It seemed like, without the pressure of talented overachievers, TJ really had made progress in a short amount of time, remembering incantations and rituals he didn't realize he had retained. But the past-due bill was still on his mind, and the thought of some other kid being overlooked *because* of him. And all of it was made worse when he brought in the mail one day from a real estate agent. The envelope had a headline that read:

Thank you for reaching out to Square One Real Estate. We have priced your home and think you'll like its value.

Shame filled TJ as he read the words, and his body tensed as the worst thoughts came to mind. Were his parents really thinking of selling the house? He knew they had come onto some hard times, but did that really mean it had come to this? And why now? The timing was too convenient for it to be a coincidence. He couldn't allow them to sell the house to put him in a program that he wouldn't even succeed in.

With the letter half scrunched in his hand, TJ stomped to the kitchen, where a waft of spicy red chicken and jollof rice filled his nose. Were he in better spirits, his stomach would have grumbled. Afrobeat music in Yoruba reverberated against the kitchen walls. His parents did their typical little shimmy as they turned around each other, Mom tending to the oven and Dad chopping garlic. Each of their turns was punctuated with a kiss.

"What's this?" TJ flung up the letter.

Dad squinted, and TJ knew what he would say before he did. "Boy, you know I can't see that without my glasses."

"Give it here, baby." Mom turned off the music, her skin looking flush. "Tomori Jomiloju, I said give it here." She raised her voice.

TJ let her snatch the letter from him, and Dad stopped his chopping, looking far more interested. Mom turned her back on the both of them as she read the envelope.

"What is it?" Dad asked.

"Oh, it's nothing," Mom answered as she stuffed the letter into a drawer and turned back to the oven. "Just some junk mail, is all."

"No, it's not," TJ said. "Mom's trying to sell the house."

Dad dropped his knife; Mom chewed on her lip. Then she turned back to the oven to check on the chicken. "I'd say it needs ten more minutes. What do you think, honey?"

"Show me that letter," Dad intoned with crossed arms.

Without looking, without even moving her head, Mom dragged her hand along the paint-scuffed drawer, took out the wrinkled letter, and handed it to Dad. TJ watched as his father brought the paper close to his eyes, then walked off to the dining room where his glasses lay next to a Phil Jackson book. He put on his glasses, sat in his favorite chair, and read.

The room seemed to grow darker then, weighed down by the quiet that was only punctured by the slight sizzle of the frying pan in the kitchen. None of them shifted. The only thing betraying movement were the curtains billowing softly behind Dad.

"When were you going to tell me about this?" he finally asked as he turned the letter over. "You know how I feel about this. I'm not tryin' to be run out of my neighborhood so whoever can take the house we worked for."

Mom cut off the fire on the stove and shuffled over to the dining room table. "I was going to tell you when I got a good offer... you know, one you'd agree to." Dad pressed his chin into his fist. "I wasn't going to go forward with anything. Not until talking to you, of course."

"Why?" Dad asked with a husky voice.

"Because it's too expensive to have me in camp," TJ cut in.

"No, it's not just that," Mom said. "When you get into Ifa, we'll need to cover those costs as well."

Dad rubbed the back of his head. "Costs? There weren't no 'costs' with Dayo."

"That's because she got grants, scholarships," TJ blurted before Mom could stammer an excuse. "But you saw how I'm doing at the camp. I'm not getting accepted. It'd be a waste to go selling the house on me." He swallowed hard, revving up for what he was about to say. He wasn't sure when to tell his parents, but if he didn't do it now, they'd get a pretty bad surprise come Sunday when TJ was *supposed* to leave. "That's why I'm not going back to camp for the second session."

Nothing but stale shock hung heavy in the air. Then it was quickly cut by a stream of uncomfortable laughter from Mom. "And what makes you think you're not going back, eh?"

"Because you're trying to sell the house!"

"I thought TJ was covered at that camp," Dad said. "Didn't that Simmons woman say not to worry about paying?"

Mom shook her head. "No, we have to pay. An Abimbola always pays. I already sold ìyá àgbá's coral beads to cover Tomori's meals."

TJ recalled that was the one expense covered on Director Simmons's past due bill.

"You didn't..." Dad rushed over and wrapped her in his arms. "You should have said something. I could have taken some extra hours at the gym. They've got after-school programs and —"

"No!" TJ bellowed. "No one's taking more hours, no one's going to sell any more family heirlooms, and we are *not* selling the house. I'm not good at this magic stuff. And let's face it," he turned his glare from Mom, "I'm no *Ifedayo Young*." Mom's deep frown cut TJ to the core, but he went on. "Just because I can fill a cup with water or set Simba on Tunde if I want doesn't mean I'm good enough. All those other kids are leagues ahead of me. You see this." He pointed at the scab along his lip. "This is 'cause I didn't know how to defend myself because some kid wanted to make it clear I didn't belong."

"You're getting into fights?"

"Who's bullying you, son?"

TJ ignored them both. "Director Simmons did her tests on me, but it didn't matter. I'm ranking behind seven-year-olds. *Seven-year-olds*. I'm not going to let everything fall apart just so I can go back and fail. I suck. Just say it, Mom. Just admit it." Mom was near to tears. "No amount of money, no amount of training will change that. I'm just an ordinary kid with barely passable magic. Not every bird is equally endowed or whatever... but some of those birds need to know their lane. I'm not some hawk or some peacock or whatever else you'll call me. I'm a pigeon, and you know what? That's fine. I may not be the best, but I make everyone else around me better. That I can live with."

TJ stormed off around the corner and slammed into Tunde, who had obviously been eavesdropping. He didn't even think as he shoved him down. "You liked that, didn't you? Now you can be the only diviner in the family." TJ shoved him again, even though Tunde had a genuine look of hurt. "Get out of my way."

"Tomori Jomiloju Young!" Mom bellowed, her Nigerian tongue in full effect. "You can be mad all you want, but you do *not* walk out on your parents like that, and you do *not* push your brother."

"Sit down, son," his father added with a voice so low, TJ could feel it in his chest. "You know how you're supposed to act. We raised you better than that."

Mom dropped her head as TJ took his seat and sighed. "We all just need to take a minute. Everything is just... coming at once."

TJ was more than surprised. He fully expected Mom to be the one to start shouting him down in a duet with Dad. But then he understood it. She had pushed too hard, and she had been keeping her own secrets. Her guilt was just catching up with her.

"Plus," Mom said, brushing a hand over Dad's shoulder, "We got a thing or two to talk about ourselves. I should've told you about those bills. I just... I didn't want to put that on you, was all."

If it weren't for the ice cream truck rolling down the street outside with its joyful music, the dining room would've been left in a heavy weight of silence. Tunde glanced between Mom and Dad. Mom and Dad looked at each other like they were coming to some sort of understanding. TJ just sat twiddling his thumbs, unsure who would speak up first or what they would say.

It was his father who opened his mouth before anyone else. "Now, with all these emotions coming at once, we'll give everyone time to settle down. But tonight... tonight, we'll *discuss* this."

36

A SIMPLY WHOLESOME GUEST

THE NEXT MORNING, TJ FOUND HIMSELF LISTENING TO THE SAME audio message he'd heard since he got his phone back: *"Hello... Hello, I can't hear you. Can you speak up? Hah! Got you... you're talking to my voicemail. Leave a message at the beep."*

It was Adeola's voicemail.

The first couple of days of the midsummer's break from Camp Olosa, her phone rang for a little while before cutting to her automated message. In the last few, it went straight to voicemail. TJ closed out his phone app and swiped over to his text messages. There was a long column of text after text — all from him.

> *TJ: Deola u there?*
> *TJ: Y u lie about workin the library??*
> *TJ: U kno I can see that u read my texts?*
> *TJ: Turning that feature off isnt going to help.*
> *TJ: Just talk to me. Im sure u have ur reasons.*
> *TJ: Deola???* 😳

The rest of his texts were a stream of GIFs ranging from silly pouts to full-on rage. TJ might not have wanted to go back to camp if it meant his family going on welfare, but when he thought about it, maybe he didn't have to go at all. He could learn on his own in between algebra and life skills. Most of his best magic happened naturally, anyway. If he finally found a Keeper or an Ol' Sally who wanted to fight, raw instinct would just have to kick in when he needed it, just like in Director Simmons's office.

At least, that's how he rationalized it all.

That's how it always worked on TV and the movies with all those superheroes who just discovered their powers. And except for the X-Men, none of them went to school to learn to do what they did.

The only thing that got to him was that he wouldn't see his friends again if he didn't go back. But he tried to distract himself from that thought as best he could, diving into his investigations further. Specifically looking at Adeola and who she associated herself with.

Despite his conversations with Manny and Ayo, TJ didn't want to think Adeola was some bad person. He'd known her for a long, long time. She came over just about every summer once Dayo started at Ifa Academy. She was always so funny, the real kind of funny that was effortless, a free spirit who never made fun of TJ for still watching cartoons even though he was too old for them back then.

It wasn't like Adeola was ever trying to do him harm, either. If she wasn't supposed to be at camp, maybe she was… he didn't know, watching over him or something? Why would she help him in the library? Why did she give him his sister's notebook? But then his thoughts always circled back to Mr. Du Bois and how he was always talking about accountability and "the right way to do things," and yet he didn't say anything about Adeola when she obviously wasn't supposed to be there. Or the fact that he was hiding a mask, or even that he took TJ's staff without telling the other adults.

A knock came at TJ's door.

"I'm not hungry" had been his automated response the three other times Mom, Dad, and Tunde asked him to come down. This time he said, "I'm naked, give me a second."

"Well," came a familiar baritone. "That was far more information than I needed."

TJ's eyes shot wide, and he rushed to the door, swung it open, and revealed Mr. Bolawe, who was shielding his eyes. "Sir… what are you doing here?"

Slowly, Mr. Bolawe pulled his hand from his face—which had been covering his eyes—and, with a slight smile, said, "Your mother said I should probably come and speak to you. Would you care to join me for brunch?"

☨

SIMPLY WHOLESOME WAS A FAVORITE RESTAURANT OF TJ'S parents. People ranging from all hues of brown from deep umber to light redbone mingled between images of Malcolm X, Zulu shields, or signs that read "Black-owned" along the walls.

It was the weekend, so there was live music playing—jazz that day. Fashionable teens with hooped earrings and baseball caps bobbed their heads to the music while the older crowd with long gray dreadlocks or bald heads tapped a beat with their fingers along linoleum tables.

It was a convergence of Black culture: music, food, and community. And there was no wonder Mom suggested TJ and Mr. Bolawe go there alone to chat over shakes and Jamaican patties. It was a much better vibe than the house.

Though TJ felt like he could breathe for the first time in a day, he still couldn't meet Mr. Bolawe's eyes fully. The last time they spoke, it didn't end well, and TJ never really made things right before he left. Outside of answering a question or two during class, they hadn't really interacted. Even their drive over to the restaurant was mired in a thick quiet that neither seemed comfortable to break.

"Kwesi special and jerk chicken patty?" a woman with sunbaked locs and a kind smile asked.

TJ raised his hand like he was in class, and the woman handed him a pink shake and a plate filled with a smoking pastry of deliciousness. Not thinking, TJ went for the patty but remembered what Mom said about eating before everyone at the table got their food.

"Go on." Mr. Bolawe gestured with a light chuckle.

The woman who served TJ shared in Mr. Bolawe's laughter, then said, "Give us a few minutes, Olufemi. Your order will be right out."

"Thank you, Apryl." He nodded, and the woman walked away to check in with another table.

TJ bit down into the first flakey gob of allspice, cayenne pepper, and brown sugar-flavored chicken and breading. Though hot on the roof of the mouth, the whole thing melted on his tongue as he chewed, and his whole body warmed. Perhaps it was the food, or maybe it was the strawberry shake he slurped up, but his previous reservations at conversation evaporated.

"How did you get here so fast?" TJ asked Mr. Bolawe, whose pore-ridden cheeks pressed high into the bags under his eyes in a smile.

"I took a water portal from Olosa's Lagoon straight through to the Kenneth Hahn Park Lake. Only took a few seconds, though I needed a quick nap right after." Mr. Bolawe smiled as his order of a Hercules shake and veggie burger came out. Before taking his first sip or bite, he measured TJ with a curious expression. "I meant to speak with you before you left camp, but with everything going on..."

"Don't worry about it," TJ said through his food. "I didn't mean to say all that stuff."

"You did. And I needed to hear it. I *have* been going easy on you. I shouldn't have let you bring in that staff, for one."

"About that." TJ finally set down his patty long enough to speak clearly. "Mr. Du Bois took my staff but didn't tell anyone."

Mr. Bolawe leaned forward with his elbows on the table. "Didn't tell anyone? What do you mean?"

"I mean, he took it, made it disappear like you adults do, but then when Director Simmons found us, he didn't say anything about it. Don't worry, he gave it back like he said he would, but I was wondering if that was... normal."

"No, it's not." Mr. Bolawe pressed a curled hand into his head in thought. "I'll speak with him. I'm sure he has his reasons. Is that why you don't want to come back?"

"Nah, Mr. Du Bois I can deal with. It's just..." TJ bit his lip. "I'm not cut out for this stuff, even when I was using my sister's staff, and, you know... other reasons."

Mr. Bolawe might've already known about his family and their financial situation, but if he didn't, TJ wasn't about to share *that* with him. The creeping of that familiar awkward silence was coming again. So TJ turned away but saw a pair of teen girls in line, one in an ordinary gray pullover and the other with a loud multicolored workout getup with bright yoga pants and a tank top. The two of them laughed about some private joke, their giggling so familiar.

They looked and sounded just the way Dayo and Adeola used to be with each other.

Perhaps TJ had been staring too long, perhaps Mr. Bolawe could read his thoughts, or maybe the man was simply thinking the same thing, but he cleared his throat and said, "You know, the very first time I saw you at that funeral, TJ, I knew you instantly, that Ifedayo was your sister. Oh, no... You look nothing like her. Yes, you're both tall, but you wear your height more like a newborn horse, and she was more... graceful. Your auras, however, are quite the same."

TJ turned away from the girls who had veered into the adjoining market. "Back at camp," he said. "You said you knew her... knew her well. What did you mean by that? Were you, like, her mentor or something?"

Bolawe snorted. "I might have *thought* myself her mentor, but a brilliant girl like that... she didn't need one. Every few generations, there comes a diviner like her who simply thinks differently. Sure, you can guide someone like that, but you can't teach them, not really. Their minds are too unique for that."

"I never knew *that* Dayo, not the one everyone talks about on *Divination Today* in those memorials. She was nice to me, always nice. But she never seemed like some genius."

"She's quite good at that, didn't flaunt her talent. You know, she didn't have many rivals at the academy, even after she got out. She was very giving with what she knew, gifted as she was. Many times she would tell me how she would've eventually gone back to Ifa to teach. That was always her premier passion."

TJ swallowed hard, thinking what it would have been like if Dayo were one of his counselors at camp, just like at home—except now he'd *actually* have Ashe for her to work with. Instead of Mr. Du Bois breathing on his neck, it could've been her nurturing him along but not letting him get away with anything less than his best.

"Olugbala and the Keepers didn't get that memo, though," TJ said sadly.

Mr. Bolawe's eyes darkened. "No, they didn't..." A silence. The man pressed a fist into his head as though a headache pained him. "There are a lot of dangers out there—diviners who don't always agree with one another and would stop at nothing to shut the opposing side down."

He sighed deeply, and his frown drooped farther down than TJ thought anyone's could ever go. TJ knew Mr. Bolawe knew his sister, but he hadn't realized how deep that connection might've gone. The man's words were just filler, though, TJ could tell. He was working to say something else but couldn't bring himself to do it.

"Tomori, listen. I was not completely forward with you last time we discussed your sister. I didn't just know her well. I didn't just serve as one of many unnecessary mentors. I was there when... I was there when she passed. In part... no, in large part, it's my fault she isn't sitting with us today. She and I fought alongside each other when things went bad. Very bad. She wouldn't have been with me if I could've just done it myself... but I told you, she had a big heart. She would've never left me alone."

TJ's thumb dug hard into the side of his finger. He was expecting this sit-down to be about him going back to Camp Olosa. But a turn like this? Bolawe was there with his sister when she passed? A tightness pressed into TJ, a deep sense of hardening that wouldn't quite let him breathe.

"What are you talking about?" he asked. "Fighting against what? The Keepers?"

"I can't get into any of it, not now, not while everything's still under investigation."

Images sprang to mind of the most savage fight he could imagine between his sister and faceless Keepers. Blood coming away from deep cuts on her face, flame enveloping her clothes, and screams, terrible screams. It made his heart drip like acid tearing through his veins. But weeks of waiting, hours and hours of wondering the truth, forced the questions from his mouth: "Did she... when she was... did they hurt her bad? Was she in pain?"

"I couldn't say, to be frank." He rubbed at his jaw. "It's a lot to explain, and I'll be sure to tell you when the time is right. But what I need to make clear is how important it is that... that I get it right this time." Bolawe closed his eyes and took a breath before continuing. "I made a promise to myself that day never to let something like that happen again, to any diviner. And you, you Tomori, are that second chance, if you'll allow yourself to be."

"Second chance at what? I've already proven I'm not my sister."

Bolawe shook his head. "No, you're not your sister. You are not a child of Orunmila. You are not a child of Eshu. And you are not a child of Shango or any of the others. I spoke with Director Simmons and her sister Elder Adeyemi, and I've been observing your progress. It's obvious none of the Orisha align with you or your Ashe..."

TJ slumped back in his seat, his half-eaten patty and shake forgotten now. Mr. Bolawe gave him the cold hard truth. No sugar-coating like TJ had gotten mad at before. For once, the man was being honest with him, and TJ didn't feel any better for it.

In fact, he felt worse.

"But," Mr. Bolawe threw up a light finger, "this does happen from time to time, rare as it is. During the transatlantic trade, Ogiyan—venerated now as the Orisha of Cassava—was not recognized until that time. Even Olokun was merely known as a famed merchant until they ascended. Every few generations, there's an entirely new Orisha that sprouts up. Not just a diviner, Tomori... an *Orisha*..."

TJ lifted his eyes to the man, to Mr. Bolawe's lips, which were on the edge of a smirk. "So, are you trying to say I'm an Orisha in a teenager's body?"

"Well, not exactly. It works a bit differently than that, but essentially... yes. And your family line has been known to be quite powerful."

TJ glanced down at his hands and thought about how they so often tingled. In his short time studying as a diviner, he never read anything about a sensation like that. And the wisps he sometimes saw when people manifested Ashe failed to be mentioned by any of his books, or those old masks, or any instruction from the elders.

"Seeing Ashe isn't normal, is it?" he asked.

Mr. Bolawe quirked an eyebrow. "Seeing?"

"After the funeral, I started to *see* Ashe like a faint fog. Every time I brought it up, someone would correct me. Does that mean I'm... like you said... different?"

"That could certainly be it. I've seen the other students with you," Mr. Bolawe leaned forward, "how well they do when you're around. Think about it, think on what the Orisha do, what they give us. We channel through them to make the extraordinary possible. Just as your fellow campers seem to funnel through you."

"I don't understand that, though — wouldn't I be good at at least one thing?"

"Listen, I know what happened in Simmons's office. Just think back on what you did there."

TJ shook his head. "I had Manny and Ayo with me, to be honest. I probably couldn't have done half that stuff if they weren't with me."

"Hmmm." Bolawe leaned back in his chair, then ran his hand through his naps and curls. "There may be more to it than *just* your friends."

Mind racing back to that night, TJ wondered if something special had been going on. He thought it was just another inconsistent use of his magic, some tap that he sprung because of desperation, something any kid could've done in the same situation. But now, Mr. Bolawe was suggesting something else, something far more unique.

"*A power that only popped up every few generations,*" he had said.

Bolawe laughed and said, "It's like Einstein said, 'if you judge a fish by its ability to climb a tree, it will live its whole life believing that it is stupid.' What's your nickname at camp? I think I heard that Ayodeji boy say it."

TJ rolled his eyes. "Don't make *me* say it."

"I don't want you just to say it," Bolawe chided. "I want you to *own* it."

TJ sighed. "Lucky charm..."

"That's right. And what does a lucky charm do?"

"Bring good fortune to others."

"And you're more than that. Think back to what you did in that office again and tell me what you're capable of."

"I... I... made the statues stop. I focused so that the Ashe could basically, like, pause. So that Manny and Ayo could get away. I... made the Ashe stop, and before that—in camp, I mean—I could make others do things they thought they could never do. Like that little boy Gary, or Manny and Ayodeji during your sessions..."

Bolawe snapped his fingers and turned to the flowerpot at the center of the table. "I may not have told you, but I am aligned with Osain, the Orisha of Harvest. This flower is on its last legs. I could cure it now, bring it back to life as if it just bloomed for the first time."

He looked around at the other customers in the restaurant. They were all engaged in their own conversations, and if not, they were watching the band play a new song many of them seemed to recognize. "Give me a few hours," Bolawe continued, "maybe the afternoon, I can get the dull petals to shine, I could get the roots and the soil to look rich. But with you..." He put a hand to TJ's shoulder, and TJ could feel that familiar tingle at his fingertips once more. "Concentrate, just like you've done time and time before."

With his free hand, Bolawe pinched the root of the flower and began to chant low. Like TJ did during basketball, like he did with Manny and Ayodeji at the lagoon, he focused on that current that drove in and out of his chest.

The cycle swirled from within him and out again into Mr. Bolawe's hand where the wilted flower, once a lame, hanging thing, slowly lifted, cycling through its life in reverse. The sharper TJ made his focus, the more he could see, really see, the Ashe at work, the way it flowed around and about them both.

In only a handful of minutes, the flower blossomed as though it had just sprouted for the first time, a healthy hue of yellow and a stem of vivid green. Mr. Bolawe dropped his hand from TJ, and the connection was severed, that brilliant energy gone.

TJ gazed down at his t-shirt, now drenched in sweat, and wetness trickled down the side of his face. It was like he'd just run up a sand dune with ankle weights. His chest constricted, his breaths coming up short. But when he looked up at Bolawe, who looked unphased, free of any sweat or labored breaths, he was met with a knowing smile.

"Now," he said, turning the centerpiece around to show one hidden petal that slumped to the side. "I left you one petal. Go on. Finish it off. The incantation is the prayer to Osain."

TJ put a finger to the drooping petal and recited the words. Like a residual aftershock, like Mr. Bolawe's hand was still on his shoulder, that same Ashe flowed and revolved in and around TJ and back out to the last petal, which slowly, but surely, stood to attention like all the rest.

This time it was all TJ, no help at all.

They never learned that one at camp. It was his first time doing it —the first time that wasn't an accident, at least. His lips parted in amazement, and he might've had a bigger reaction were he not utterly deflated.

"Tell me," Bolawe said, "what's more powerful than being able to control Ashe itself, eh?" He canted his head with a hum. "Others can siphon from you, and you can siphon from others. You've been right all along, Tomori. You're nothing like your sister. She had a curriculum to follow, but she had a ceiling—one you do not have. For you, the book hasn't been written yet."

TJ let his mind wrap around the nebulous concept of being able to *really* control magic itself, to manipulate it to his will. It was a lofty notion, one that would take a long while to come to grips with.

Maybe it was because he worked up a sweat, or maybe it was his disbelief, but all of it made him nauseous.

Then, with harsh breaths, he said, "That… that sounds nice… and everything, but the camp grades us… individually. If I don't fit in the curriculum… how do I even show… my worth?"

"Leave that to me. Promise me you'll return, and I'll make sure you'll get your due."

37

BACK TO THE BAYOU

WHEN TJ TOLD HIS PARENTS HE WOULD RETURN TO CAMP OLOSA under the condition that they didn't sell the house, Mom blared a *"good, 'cause I was going to force you on that plane either way"* in her thickest use of Yoruba.

The trip back to camp was just like the one before. TJ's family ran late like always, with him and Mom barely making it to his flight on time, Mom spending too much of the flight encouraging TJ, and the cab driver rolling through with his clunky and mildew-smelling cab just as before.

The only difference was that Manny wasn't there to share the ride.

TJ found himself frowning a little, peering around Mom to see if Manny might've come out the automatic doors from the airport terminals. Then TJ figured she must've had an earlier or later flight and wouldn't show up.

TJ had spent much of his time staring out the plane window over the American south, pondering how he could make up for what he did to Manny. Her sad eyes still stuck to the inside of his mind, and the hurt in her voice made his insides turn every time he thought of it.

Perhaps it was a good thing she wasn't sharing a cab with him, though. It was packed that day, with five campers pressed shoulder-to-shoulder. TJ's face was almost plastered to the car window like he was on an overflowing bus during rush hour. All the rest of the kids were no older than eight, and TJ's eardrums suffered for it as they rattled off excitedly to one another about what they had done over the past week.

"My mom took us to Disneyland!"

"My cousin got a bouncy house and a slide on his whole street!"

"I ate a scorpion!"

Couldn't someone tell them they were all sitting right next to each other? And why weren't their parents saying anything?

TJ craned his neck to the bench in front of him. None of the adults seemed to even hear the storm of voices roiling behind them. TJ could see Mom's lips moving, but no sound was coming out. An inward chuckle took TJ's chest. They had set some sound barrier between themselves and the rambunctious campers. TJ wondered what magic was at work and if he could do it himself—it was probably advanced magic he wouldn't learn for years, knowing his luck.

Then he remembered his sit-down with Mr. Bolawe.

Staring down at his fingertips, TJ concentrated hard on the flow of Ashe billowing through the cab as they bumped over every pothole on the highway. Against the violent rocking, against the loud conversation, TJ settled into himself. When he lifted his gaze, like all the other times he dug deep, he saw the wisps of Ashe around him, saw how it created a barrier between the cab like a web of mist stretching from roof to floor.

He wasn't sure how the magic worked or what maintained it. It was one thing helping Mr. Bolawe along with a wilting flower—TJ at least knew the foundations of that magic—but this? This was something else.

Then again, he didn't know what he was doing against those statues either, and he made that work somehow.

Maybe I just need to pull on it, he thought.

And so he did. As though he were pulling a plastic wrap, he visualized the sound barrier drifting away from the side of the passenger window closest to him and tugged it around himself. For a moment, he had it. The rowdy kids' shouts turned to murmurs, their grating voices no more than whispers.

But it didn't last.

TJ could only hold the Ashe barely a minute before exhaustion took him, and the noise came back in full force. The inside of TJ's cheek was not having a good time as he chewed on it to quell his frustration. He had to remind himself that that was *much* better than anything else he had done. It also proved that Mr. Bolawe was right... He had some sort of direct control over Ashe that he didn't realize he had before. He just needed to learn how not to get fatigued so easily while using it.

Until then, regular ol' headphones would have to do.

He flipped on his favorite, upbeat playlist, a strange assortment of remixes from a foreign plunderphonics artist that always got him jazzed. As the first song's beat kicked in, TJ bobbed his head happily.

Yeah, this next session's gonna be great.

☥

After TJ went through three more of his playlists on blast — two of them being hardcore rap and the other classic rock — they arrived at the docks of Camp Olosa.

The moment TJ was free of the other kids' pinning shoulders, he let out a huge breath like he'd been submerged underwater. Though he couldn't prove it, he was almost certain two or three of the little kids were having a farting contest.

Staring up at the leaning and half-sunken Camp Olosa sign, TJ grabbed his things. His gaze fell from the two "Os" that looked like eyes glaring at him and watched the congregation of kids coming together. Each of them was more excited to see one another than the last. But one, in particular, made TJ's eyebrows jump.

"Bruh!" Ayodeji shouted across the deck. He kept cocking his head to one side, his man bun like a pointed finger in the direction of a crooked cypress. "I didn't think you were coming back."

"Well, well, well," Mom said at TJ's side as she handed him his backpack. "I thought you said this place didn't have anyone who cared about you. Go ahead. I've got to speak to the Director, anyway."

TJ didn't take much time to consider why Mom was meeting with Director Simmons. Thinking of it only made him want to turn around and head back to the airport.

Ayodeji waved TJ over some more, pointing behind the large cypress, and clearly indicating he wanted to talk away from the crowd. TJ gave Mom a swift hug, hefted his bags over his shoulder, and made his way over to Ayodeji. Before TJ could say as much as a "hello" or "what's up," Ayodeji contracted a case of verbal diarrhea.

"So my uncle says diviners speak to the dead all the time," he blurted. "We just need the supplies. Obviously, we can't get nothin' in, but the library's got stuff and Akande's old office does too — but not just that, we'll need to practice this one ritual my cousin said worked for his girlfriend—oh, and we'll need a specific mask made of pure iron—oh, and an offering for your sister, you know her favorite food, right?—oh, and—"

"Okay, okay, okay." TJ waved his hands in front of Ayodeji's face to get him to stop. "Take a breath. We can't even think about any of that stuff until I can get my staff in." He shifted his baseball bag over his shoulder.

Ayodeji sucked his teeth and waved a dismissive hand. "Just do what you did last time. Actually... how did you get it in last time? I never asked."

"Mr. Bolawe," TJ explained. "But that's not gonna work this time. Mr. Du Bois gonna be mad-doggin' the whole time. Guaranteed."

"It's a good thing I'm here, then."

"Huh? What you mean?"

Ayodeji pulled off his glasses and set them into his palm, a smirk stretched across his face. Then he closed his eyes, took an inhale and said, "*Kuro lọdọ mi.*"

His dark metal glasses frame, which looked like they were lined and inlaid with tiny dots of sterling silver in the design of Shango's axes, shook in his hand for a moment and then vanished.

"I don't believe it," TJ gasped.

Teleportation of objects was supposed to be *very* advanced magic. At least, that's what his book said.

"Believe it." Ayodeji lifted his chin, his gaze locked on something behind TJ. Following his eye line, TJ saw that Ayo's glasses had transported to a rock near the river's edge. "Been working on it all week. Can't tell you how many of my frames I jacked up. One's still stuck in my closet wall."

"Ayo!" TJ gasped, "we're not supposed to learn this until right before getting staffs."

"Damn, bro. Don't act so surprised. There's a reason I'm top ten in the camp. *Wà ọ́i mi.*" His glasses jumped from the rock to his hand, and he put them back on. "But I'll admit, I don't know if I can do something like a staff. Magical objects are harder to move because they got a 'heavier' weight. But if we do it together—"

"Heavier weight? My sister's staff isn't all that heavy."

"It's more than that. Anything enchanted has that *itis* effect, ya know? It's like eating the same weight of kale and then that same weight in cake. One of them is going to weigh you down more than the other. But that's okay, we can all do it together and it should work. There's a communal version of the spell, a tiny ritual we can do. But..."

"There's always a but."

Ayodeji pressed his chin in his hand. "There's the problem of the silent alarm. Plenty of the older campers try to manifest their stuff into the camp, and they get caught, or their stuff gets taken away for good. Anything that tries to pass magically through the campgrounds gets picked up by Simmons's and Du Bois's border enchantments."

TJ didn't have a clue how they'd get around some alarm system. He couldn't even think of how they'd get the staff into camp in the first place. Sure, he could boost Ayodeji like he did with Mr. Bolawe, but going from glasses to a "weighty" staff seemed like a tall order.

As TJ scratched his head, the loud rumble of another bayou boat coming in interrupted his thoughts. Both he and Ayodeji turned to look at it. It wasn't as loaded as TJ's boat, but there were a few campers inside. One of them had a great mass of curly hair bundled into a ponytail.

"Perfect, let's go talk to Manny," Ayodeji said. "She might've found something herself."

As Ayodeji started forward, TJ stopped him with a long hand. "Give me a minute. I should talk to her first. She's probably still mad at me."

"Oh yeah, right, right. She did get real quiet when we was going back to the airport. Go ahead, I'll be over here. Just don't let anyone see you when you come back."

TJ nodded and stepped away.

"Oh, and... TJ."

TJ stopped walking off. "Yeah?"

"I'm glad you're back, man. I never apologized for what I did—not for real. I was out of pocket for fighting you and laughing at you and whatnot. My bad, man. That was messed up."

TJ smiled. "Don't trip, man. You an alright dude. I had you all wrong."

Ayodeji shook his hands in front of his face. "All right, all right, enough of all that. Go over there and get your girl."

TJ held his automatic response of "she's not my girl." But he understood what Ayo meant. And that meaning went a long way with a guy like that. With a little clap to his chest over his heart, TJ lifted his chin in respect and Ayodeji did the same. In that moment, TJ knew Ayodeji—Ayo—would be a friend.

Turning on his heel, TJ made his way for the other side of the dock where Manny's bright yellow shirt seemed to glow against the blob of swamp green around her. Despite her radiant look, she wore a frown, though the Santos Twins, who flanked her, spoke with wide grins. As soon as the sisters saw TJ coming over, however, they immediately stopped their cheerful chatter in trade for scowls.

"She don't wanna talk to you," Antonia said.

Andressa stepped in front of TJ. "Get lost."

"Andressa... Antonia," Manny murmured. She interlocked her fingers nervously, then shifted her eyes to one side. They took the hint and walked down the deck with the other girls waiting in line to get their bags checked.

Despite calling them off, Manny didn't meet TJ's gaze. She didn't even turn her body to him.

It wasn't up to Manny to break the silence first, and TJ knew it. So he said, "*Oye, que tal? Está ocupado este...* um deck." Her lip quirked just at the edge of a true smirk. Almost as soon as it came, however, it diminished into another flat line. She didn't try to blow him off, though, so he tried something else.

"My name's TJ. I'm new here. I heard the first session was pretty good. Did you enjoy it?"

She didn't answer, didn't even move her body to him.

"Meet any nice people?"

"Well... there was this one guy who I thought was a friend, but he didn't even tell me he was leaving."

"He sounds like the worst. Good riddance. I probably wouldn't be here if he hadn't left."

Manny looked at him, her eyebrows knitted together in confusion.

"I don't think that kid is coming back," he explained.

She frowned and fully turned to him. "But I *want* him to come back."

TJ's heart fluttered a little. "Sorry, Manny. I should've told you how I was feeling. I just didn't want to see you looking all sad and stuff, and well—"

Manny rushed TJ and wrapped her arms around him. She smelled like one of those flower shampoos, and her body was warm. "Or maybe you were too scared I'd convince you to stay," she said into his shoulder.

TJ was reeling. He was hugging Manny, actually hugging her.

Their first hug.

It was nice and tight, not a half hold or without life. A *real* embrace. And without breaking, holding tighter even, Manny said, "I knew your ass couldn't stay away."

TJ didn't break either. "You know there are a lot of 'Manuela Martinezes' on social media."

"I was thinking that too the moment I got on the plane. And hey," she broke away, though she kept her arms around his shoulder, "there are plenty of 'TJ Youngs' out there too."

TJ laughed. "When did you give up?"

"After the thousandth TJ. I even looked up your full name."

"You would've never found it. I don't go by my real name online." Finally, they parted as TJ pulled out his phone. "Quick, let's swap right now before they take our phones."

They exchanged information—TJ's hands shaking badly from nerves as he passed his phone. After putting his number in Manny's phone, grabbing his own, and putting it away, he saw his text thread with Adeola.

"Oh, yeah. I didn't get to tell you about this." He showed his screen to Manny, who read over it carefully.

"Yeah, she's bad news, man," she said with a frown.

Before TJ could put away his phone, a flustered Ayo came stomping between them. "My dude, how you gonna leave me over there like that. I didn't think you'd take an hour talking to her." He twisted to Manny. "By the way Manny, you're lookin' real cute. Nice little shirt, I see you with that yellow. I mean that respectfully, of course. Not trying to come between you and TJ, or anything like that."

"Don't make it weird," TJ and Manny said in unison and they both blushed.

Before an awkward silence could settle, TJ said, "Sorry, Ayo. Manny, follow us."

As they walked over to the leaning cypress, TJ and Ayo explained their plans for getting the staff onto campgrounds. As Manny listened, the last boat came in and the line getting back into camp grew shorter. Eventually, someone would start looking for them, whether it was a counselor or one of their parents.

"Oh, that's mad easy," Manny said as they finished their recap. "We just have to use the whispering tree."

"There's whispering trees here?" Ayo asked. "I thought only Ifa Academy had those."

"Nah, there's one here too. Between the lake and lagoon. We learned about them during my Oya electives."

"Right." TJ lit up. "No one could find us when we were in the tree."

"Exactly," Manny replied. "The whispering tree is like a void of Ashe, at least that's what the teachers said at Ifa."

Ayo rubbed at his temples. "If that's the case, then why haven't campers tried to sneak stuff into the tree all the time?"

"Well, 'cause you have to be *actual* friends with the tree. And the whispering tree knows TJ's staff. They wouldn't do anything about it when it appears."

"Oh, fine," Ayo scoffed. "You gotta be friendly with the thing. But there's still an issue with that. I have to know where I'm transporting the staff. That's the most important part of the magic, you know. I can't just drop it off anywhere."

"TJ and I know where it is, shouldn't that be enough with the communal magic thing?"

"Nah, it has to go through me cause I'm the one working the Ashe."

"About that…" TJ trailed off, looking down at his fingers. He could already feel them tingling, ready for what he knew would have to happen. "I had a lunch with Mr. Bolawe over the break and well… I can probably help with that issue."

He explained everything he and Mr. Bolawe had discussed, ending his story by saying, "And he thinks I *might* be a new Orisha or something."

Ayo blinked twice, mouth agape. "Come again?"

"I mean, he's not really sure, and I'm not really sure. It was just a theory of his, really."

"TJ," Manny looked just as flabbergasted, "that's a *huge* thing."

"Yeah, I figured, but it's not like we could verify any of that."

"So that's how you were hearing voices?" Ayo said half to himself. "Maybe you'll be the Orisha of Voices or something… You know, that's not too unbelievable. You know that Ogiyan very recently got venerated as—"

"The Orisha of Cassava," TJ finished for him. "Yeah, Mr. Bolawe mentioned that too."

Manny gazed up into the trees, her voice also coming out like she was speaking to herself. "And that's why I've been doing so well when we were partnered up during our sessions."

"Lucky Charm is starting to add up, right?" TJ said a little sardonically. "I mean, I can't say for sure this will all work out. I get really, really tired when I'm doing it, like, more tired than after going through a session with Miss Graves, and I need a lot of people to sort of, like, feed off of. But it shouldn't take long, right? Ayo's pretty fast with the transport. I saw him do it with his glasses."

"That won't work either," came a voice from behind their huddle.

TJ couldn't tell which one of them looked more shocked, Ayo who froze up like a statue, or Manny whose eyes bulged, or TJ himself whose feet curled in his sneakers. But when they turned, they all let out a synchronized sigh of relief. It was only Joshua standing there with a bag of chips between his meaty fingers.

"We really need to do a better job of keeping stuff secret," TJ gritted over his shoulder.

Joshua rushed forward. "Oh, I didn't hear nothin' really, just about your staff, you all trying to get it into the whispering tree, and TJ possibly being an Orisha. By the way, congrats, if that's true."

Ayo facepalmed, and Manny hung her head low.

"You heard everything then, Josh," TJ said flatly.

Joshua blushed. "Oh... my bad."

"Go ahead..." TJ sighed. "Tell us why it's not going to work."

Ayo stepped forward and between them. "Wait, wait, we can't just let him know everything. He'll just go and tell Mr. Du Bois or whoever."

"Actually..." Manny threw up a finger. "He's been sort of eaves-dropping on us all summer. And well..."

"He hasn't said much to anyone," TJ finished for her.

Ayo grumbled and gave them all a look before he let Joshua continue. It wasn't like he or any of them had a choice. The last of the campers were being checked in. It was now or never.

"Listen to me real careful-like," Joshua said, putting on an exaggerated Bayou accent. He was almost too giddy as he hunched over on one knee and rubbed his hands together. "This is only going to work one way."

38

THE REVERSE CAPER

A FEW MINUTES LATER, TJ COULDN'T TELL WHICH OF THEM WAS sweating the most. Manny, who was getting her things checked by Miss Gravés, and couldn't stop peeking over her shoulder to the boys, Ayo, who wouldn't stop breathing hard on TJ's back, and TJ himself, who clutched his baseball bag so hard against his chest he thought he'd snap his sister's staff in half.

Joshua, who led them, was the only one who seemed not to care, the bounce in his step basically a jolly skip.

"Mornin' Mr. D... Mr. B," he said as he tossed three large bags onto the check-in table. "You know, it's a fine day for a dip in the *lagoon*, don't you think? Would love to take a big ol' *stick* and jump into it."

"We get it, Josh. We get it," Ayo whispered harshly from behind.

It was Josh's attempt at small talk. The line "dip in the lagoon" was their collective sign to enact their scheme. It was the reason TJ held onto his bag so close to his chest. In part it was nerves, of course, but it was also because that was the best way to know if the transport worked or not before he showed the counselors his bag.

Mr. Du Bois, at the far end of the table, didn't seem to take kindly to Joshua's attempt at chitchat. He responded with a knitted brow over slitted eyes as he started checking Joshua's first bag. Mr. Bolawe, however, responded with a friendly, "you know, it is a nice day for a swim," as he checked Joshua's other bag.

A heat tickled at the back of TJ's neck — Ayo was already concentrating on his incantation. It was almost like Ayo's Ashe, which filtered through the staff, was passing into TJ and out through his chest and back again on a loop.

TJ stole a glance back at the girls' table, and like Ayo, Manny was squinting in concentration as Miss Gravés spoke to her. As always, he could see Manny's Ashe's casting off from her body and drift toward TJ and the boys a few yards away. Her energy filled TJ with a warm sensation.

"Are you okay, Manuela?" TJ could hear the counselor ask.

After a while, the counselor waved her fingers in front of Manny's face. TJ couldn't hear what Manny said in response, but he assumed she had some excuse, and Gravés went straight back to talking again.

TJ could feel the moment Manny broke her concentration as she replied to Gravés, the gentle heat that had been coursing through him diminishing into a cooler sensation.

Ayo had tried to explain as much as he could about the magic before they were corralled back into line, but a few minutes just wouldn't help. TJ tried to funnel as much of his own energy into the communal incantation they were all secretly enchanting, but he just didn't know the spell well enough. Ayo at least had a whole week of practice.

"TJ, it's good to see you with us again," Mr. Bolawe said, snapping TJ out of his mystical stupor. "Aren't you hot in that thing? You're sweating bullets."

TJ became very aware of the droplets coming down around his eyes and soaking through his Camp Olosa dashiki. It didn't help that he wore a zip-up hoodie over it. But he knew the sweat hadn't been generated from too much clothing or the weather... he couldn't let Mr. Bolawe know that though.

"No, I'm fine, I'm fine," TJ assured him. "It's just the humidity. I'm already cooling down."

"Concentrate, man," Ayo seethed behind him.

TJ locked up his neck and put more focus into Ayo's Ashe. Talking about the weather wasn't helping anyone. Another stolen glance over his shoulder showed him that Manny was completely out of it now. Miss Gravés just kept talking and talking and wouldn't let her get away. Manny lifted her gaze and caught TJ's eyes. Her look was a clear message of "*I'm sorry.*"

"Well, hand over your bag," Mr. Bolawe said, gesturing for it.

"Hold up Mr. B," Joshua lifted another large bag. "I've got something for you to check right here."

"He already checked that one, Mr. Reed," Mr. Du Bois stared over his thin-rimmed glasses.

TJ's hands went clammy and his breath caught in his throat. If he got caught with his staff *again*, he couldn't even imagine what would happen. He didn't have to give up his baseball bag right away, though. So he swung over his backpack and set that on the table. Mr. Bolawe started checking it and mumbled a detection incantation under his breath.

"Just a little more," Ayo whispered behind TJ.

TJ could feel it getting closer too. The heat through him rose to a simmer. Even without Manny's assistance—and despite TJ being very little help—Ayo was putting in the work. More than that, Manny's energy seemed to be replaced somehow. Then TJ raised his head to see Joshua too was mumbling under his breath.

This just might work...

"All right, you look good," Mr. Bolawe said, setting TJ's backpack aside. "Next bag, please."

TJ swallowed so hard, he thought Ol' Sally would hear it—wherever she was in the swamp. He had to give his bag up. He couldn't just keep it plastered to his chest, though that was the only way he could tell if Ayo and Joshua managed it. Giving it up felt like giving away a part of his soul.

"I'll check the next one, Olufemi," Mr. Du Bois said. TJ's stomach bottomed out. "I've finished Mr. Reed's belongings, I'll take Mr. Young's next bag. You can start checking his though." He pointed to Ayo. "Careful with him, though, he tries to sneak in anything he can—"

"Good to see you too, Mr. Du Bois." Ayo saluted; Mr. Du Bois just frowned.

Even though TJ turned over his carry-on bag for Mr. Du Bois to check first, the counselor took his baseball bag instead. There was nothing TJ could do now. Either their plan worked, or it didn't.

Mr. Du Bois dug his hand into the main compartment of the bag as he said, "An interesting design... I don't think we have baseball here."

His searching hand halted. TJ knew he must've felt the staff inside.

"Hmmm," Du Bois hummed. "What's this we have here."

He tugged to get a better hold of the part of the bag that was supposed to house a bat.

TJ bit the inside of his mouth. Was it even worth it bringing the staff back? He might not have needed it at all now that he knew he had that newfound power of his. All he really required was Olosa's Lagoon, the will to hear voices on the water… and his sister's spirit.

He had compromised everything.

Now he wasn't going to be allowed in camp at all.

A flash of mystical smoke plumed from TJ's bag, the biggest one he'd seen since the funeral. It left a trail from his baseball bag, through Joshua at the head of the table and into the swamp, straight for where the whispering tree must've been.

"What's wrong, Xavier?" Mr. Bolawe asked as Mr. Du Bois sank his arm deep into TJ's bag.

Mr. Du Bois's lips were pursed so hard that his pencil mustache replaced his upper lip. He clearly seemed to think he had felt something. Yet… there was nothing there.

TJ let out an enormous sigh when he realized the staff wasn't in the bag anymore. And when he saw Joshua giving him a wink, he knew they were in the clear.

"Yeah, Mr. Du Bois, are you okay?" TJ asked, now feeling a lot more confident.

Mr. Du Bois grunted deep and long. "Yes… everything seems to be in order."

One of the little girl campers screamed at their side. Everyone whipped their heads to see her pointing to the treeline where a giant statue with red crystal eyes stood tall.

"There has been a breech," it said with a reedy voice.

"All campers and junior counselors," Director Simmons bellowed, jogging just behind the statues. Mom trailed at her heel. "None of you will leave the dock area. Counselors and elders, on me. We'll do a sweep. Yolanda, you'll take your obstacle course," she ordered Miss Gravés. "Xavier, you'll sweep the Ogbon cabin. Olufemi, stay with the campers."

"I really hope y'all's search is quick," Joshua said loudly. "I would really like to go to the *lagoon* before the sun goes down. I got my trunks ready and I want to jump off one of those *trees*."

"Yo, Josh, relax," Ayo said. "The lagoon will be there tomorrow."

"But I want to go to the *lagoon* today and drop off a nice *quiet tree*!"

Mr. Bolawe turned on his heel. "Mr. Reed. Keep your voice down. I think we can all hear you. I'll make sure everything is searched so you can go… *tomorrow*." Then he turned his voice to Director Simmons. "With respect, Director. Elder Wale and the juniors can watch over the campers. Let me help with the search. I can take the whispering woods near the lake."

"Very, well." She turned to the rest. "All right, counselors, let's get a move on."

☫

THOUGH THEY WERE ALL LOCKED DOWN TO THE DOCK AREA, THE campers were allowed to group freely. Ayo went back to LaVont and Jimoh who came rushing to him, asking if he had anything to do with the tripped alarm. Ayo acted like he hadn't just been speaking with TJ and Joshua before going off to the edge of the dock. Manny, who had been huddled up with the Santos Sisters and Lorenzo, came over to where TJ and Joshua stood near the Camp Olosa sign.

"You think they'll find it?" TJ asked before she could even sit down.

She didn't look confident. "I can't be the only one who's friendly with the whispering tree. I bet at least one of the elders knows about them too."

"They won't find the staff," Joshua said. "I have this on lock."

The campers waited in anticipation as counselor after counselor came back with nothing to show from their searches.

"You think it could be the Keepers?" Stephen whispered to his older brother Juice near the bent cypress. TJ couldn't help but lean an ear into their conversation. "I heard their leader Olugbala was sighted near the Mississippi River."

"Nah, no way," Juice replied, sticking out his chest and the "JC" stitched in his dashiki. "Director Simmons made all the junior counselors check the perimeter *three times* last night. It's probably just some kids sneaking stuff in like always."

"Yeah, maybe you're right. Those sightings were a couple weeks back."

After a while all the counselors returned to the docks, with Mr. Du Bois being the last one to return from a "properly thorough search" as he called it.

Director Simmons stood up on a pedestal at the rear of the registration table. As short as she was, she still commanded a grand presence as she spread her arms wide to call for everyone's attention. "Campers and parents! Please, attention forward and to me. We know one of you tried to get something inside the campgrounds. It's important that we know what that was."

TJ couldn't tell whose knees were more shaky, his, Manny's, or Ayo's. Joshua, however, was a picture of complete and utter smug indifference. It was like he was daring the director to uncover him.

"Know that we do this to protect you all," Director Simmons continued. "And if the culprit doesn't fess up, we'll do bunk checks morning and night until whatever got in is found."

"Maybe there was a mistake," Joshua suggested with his cheeky grin. He really needed to stop that, TJ thought. "Maybe a sparrow got in and tripped the alarm?"

Mr. Du Bois scoffed. "Impossible. My shield would know the difference between a sparrow and not-so-friendly entities. A *bird*? Really, Mr. Reed?"

"Mmhm. It's very simple. A lot of shield enchantments overcompensate like that."

The counselor licked his lips and stepped from the registration table to the dock. The campers and parents spread for him like he was a proton and they were electrons.

"What in the world is Josh doing?" Manny murmured at TJ's side.

TJ shook his head, his heart thrumming. "Showing off. He better cut it out though."

Mr. Du Bois stood inches from Joshua. Their stare down would've put one of those boxing movies to shame. "You seem to know a lot about shield enchantments," Mr. Du Bois said with heat. "Is there something you'd like to share with Director Simmons?"

Joshua shrugged. "You're not suggesting a kid like me can penetrate your defenses, are you?" He dropped his bag on the ground. "You want to check my things again? Maybe you missed something."

TJ did his best not to crack a smile. Well, he was already smiling. What he really was trying to suppress was a full-on chuckle.

An angry-looking falcon didn't have anything on the wicked stare Mr. Du Bois was fixing Joshua with. But what could the counselor do without evidence? TJ had to admit, though... It would've been *really* sweet if they could let him know it *was* a bunch of kids who tricked his little shield enchantment. But Joshua was doing a great job of doing that himself.

"All right, Xavier," Director Simmons called from her pedestal. "I think we made ourselves clear. If something turns up, we'll retrieve it."

Mr. Du Bois backed off and returned to the other counselors and elders. "Everyone will make their way to their respective cabins where a second search will commence."

The crowd swayed silently as the girls went down their own route and the boys went down their own. TJ shook his head in disbelief as he caught up to Joshua who sauntered with *way* too much swagger. "Bruh, I do not understand how you did that. I saw this huge bit of Ashe rush from my bag and through you."

Joshua shrugged. "I have my ways."

"Yeah, but how?"

"I think the saying goes... 'a magician never reveals his secrets.'"

39

WITH PROPER PREPARATION

THAT FIRST WEEK BACK FELT LIKE BEING AT AN ENTIRELY different camp.

For one, all the counselors seemed on edge. Though the silent alarm going off was explained away as faulty magic, counselors like Mr. Du Bois paid multiple visits to the boys' cabins each night, with Director Simmons doing the same for the girls.

A few UCMP officials even got called up to protect the camp boundaries, not so much because of the tripped alarm but because there were more reports of suspicious Keeper activity in New Orleans, including a few sightings from clouded city dwellers.

That first night, Mr. Du Bois checked under TJ's bed straight away, right where TJ had hid the staff during the first session. It was almost like the man knew exactly where to look, exactly which floorboard to overturn. Despite his scrupulous search, however, the counselor didn't find a thing. Dayo's staff was safely tucked away inside the hollow bark of the whispering tree on the other side of camp. Still, that didn't stop Du Bois from giving TJ a wicked glare whenever he made his nightly raids.

TJ couldn't say he really paid him much mind after that first night, though. The second and more important reason camp was different for him was for an entirely different reason. Each of his sessions, which had previously been more abysmal than the last, now felt like he was inputting cheat codes.

"I'm sure you all didn't do any running during your break," Miss Gravés had said as she lapped the campers that first day back. "I anticipated this. But it's a good thing. Sometimes we need to let our muscles rest so they can properly grow. And look at all your improvement — Mr. Young in particular."

It wasn't just his physique that had changed, but his stamina as well. In Mr. Bolawe's Emi Guidance session, TJ held onto magical attachments longer than he had before, and he didn't ruin his clothes with perspiration within five minutes — now it took around ten.

But he couldn't tell who benefited more from his improvement — him, Manny, Josh, or Ayo, who always found an excuse to partner with him. TJ didn't mind them hanging around. Within that first week, he discovered that they were a benefit to him as much as he was to them. They didn't just sap from him, but he siphoned off them as well in something like a superconducting loop of Ashe.

TJ would've thought he was well on his way to high grades at camp, and the merest semblance of a chance to get accepted to Ifa Academy, but, unfortunately, pure magical talent didn't quite translate to Mr. Du Bois's Ogbon Studies.

In truth, TJ was having an easier time of the sessions now that he wasn't up past lights out trying to cram in the intricacies between water-pulling and weed management charms, or taking midday naps that ate away at his tutoring time because Miss Graves's sessions were too tiring. However, despite that, TJ was still struggling to keep up. It was like Mr. Du Bois was giving them twice the amount to study, and some days he doled out two pop quizzes, one after the other.

"Some of you might feel above your studies now that you have…" Mr. Du Bois's eyes had lingered over TJ a touch too long, "come into new talents. But I can assure you, the theory of Ashe work and the history of the Orishas will be of the most importance once you get into your advanced classes. For example, Mr. Young," TJ sat bolt upright, determined to answer whatever came his way, "besides the scent of flowers to cover up the stench of the dead she guards, what does Yewa consider a favorable offering?"

"Fruit!" TJ blurted, happy to know the answer for once.

"What kind of fruit?"

"Um…" TJ trailed off and tried his best not to give Ayo a sidelong glance. He could almost feel the boy trying to tell him the answer telepathically. But if TJ even shifted his eyes an inch, he knew he'd bring on Mr. Du Bois's signature venom-like ridicule. So TJ stammered, "D-delicious fruit… sir?"

Mr. Du Bois pursed his lips and shook his head. "Wrong again, Mr. Young. Anyone else? Yes, you, Mr. Oyelowo."

"Virgin fruit, sir," Ayo answered.

"Correct. And can you tell me why this is so?"

Had this been a week or two prior, Ayo would have flashed a cocky smirk, but now TJ was only met with a half shrug—though LaVont and Jimoh, who sat just beside Ayo, gave TJ their usual sniggers at his expense. Still, Ayo went on and answered, "Because Yewa venerates modesty as one of her core values."

"As ever," Mr. Du Bois intoned, "It seems Mr. Oyelowo is the only one who takes particular care to detail."

Caring about detail was all well and good, but finding the right details to search for in the first place was a different thing entirely. One week later, TJ swore that the founders of the library designed it deliberately to confuse its visitors.

After complaining to the little library statues, Elder Orji, the librarian, who had been awake for once, told TJ that, "It's in the journey to knowledge where wisdom takes its mold. You children and your 'smart' phones got all the information and none of the retention."

Designed to train wisdom or not, the library's layout made no sense to TJ at all and was a pain in his side. What he could've discovered in a few minutes sometimes took a pair of days. Navigating the library required a familiarity of how each era of magic was ordered just to reference the right aisle, let alone the right shelf.

When TJ returned to his table with a scroll and book on the properties of different masks, where Manny, Ayo, and Josh sat within a mountain of study material, Manny said, "I've never heard of a diviner who can actually boost Ashe before. How does that even work? It felt mad OP in Mr. Bolawe's today."

"Yeah, I guess it could be a bit overpowered." TJ sat down next to her. "Well, I do get nerfed by getting super tired real quick."

Manny was sort of the best. It wasn't just that she was kind and compassionate, but she and TJ spoke the same language. Anytime TJ let himself slip out one of his usual geek references, he was surprised to find that Manny never judged him for it. More than that... most of the time, Manny knew exactly what he was talking about and would echo with her own reference.

"Talented diviner, new age Orisha, I don't give a damn how it works," Ayo said from behind an iron mask he was wearing. TJ had noticed his Nigerian accent leaked into his words more often than not when he hung around them. TJ wondered if Ayo had put on his American one mostly for the benefit of LaVont and Jimoh.

Today they had been investigating the best masks they could use to commune with those who'd passed away in the library. "I'm just glad Lucky Charm isn't just your nickname," Ayo went on. "It's got me up in the top ten."

Joshua, who had been looking over a scroll detailing different combinations of magical accessories, lifted his head and shrugged. "I don't know, y'all. Yeah, I feel better around TJ, but not like how everyone describes it."

"Maybe because you're already too good," TJ suggested. "And you've been looking at the scroll forever now—which Orisha combo looks like it'll work best, Mr. Number One?"

Joshua had been listed as the top student of the camp earlier that day at lunch. He had always maintained a position in the top ten percent of the camp since the beginning of summer, though, so it wasn't a surprise. The only reason he probably wasn't at the top then was because of Mr. Du Bois's pop quizzes or their daily debates about the Orishas and their history, which knocked him down a few points.

"I don't know." Josh rolled up his scroll. "A lot of the information in these seem… misguided. Divinerkind really have fallen short." He threw the parchment over his shoulder and one of the tiny statue assistants grumbled about littering. "Give me a few more days. I'll put together something for the ritual we found last week to speak to your sister. It'll be way better than anything we'll find in this place."

"And who went and made you leader of this little operation?" Ayo questioned as he tried on another iron mask.

Joshua thumbed to himself. "Who was the one who came up with the plan to get the staff in?"

"You did," TJ, Manny, and Ayo droned.

"And who's the one who got TJ that brass around his wrist?"

"You did," they mumbled again.

"And who's number one in the camp right now?"

"You are," they intoned one last time.

"I rest my case."

"Remember," Manny said over her own enormous book. "That still leaves the mystery of that white orb you saw in the lagoon, though, TJ…"

"The one with the voice saying '*come to me, come to me*'?" TJ asked in a spooky voice.

"Yup, that one."

"It's probably a portal," Ayo explained. "My cousin was telling me all about it. White orb. Diviner feels a pull like nothing else matters. Mystical voice in your head. It fits."

"What would we find on the other side, I wonder..." TJ mumbled idly.

"It's more likely something, or someone in the case of your sister, will come out," Ayo answered, "but we won't be able to go into it. No diviner has in a while. Some woman did it, I forget her name, but she came out a little loopy."

Manny shot up in her seat and slammed her book on the desk with a cry of, "Aha!"

The library was mostly empty, but a few "shhhs" shot from between the rows of shelves. Manny lowered her voice before going on. "Look here. It says that portals back in the day were common, but even ancient diviners had a hard time finding them—even when the Orisha were messing around with the Mortal Realm. See there." She pointed to a page inked with images of a moon cycle, a total planetary alignment, an equinox, and a solstice. "It says that portal openings are most receptive to showing themselves during nature's milestones."

TJ got up and peered over her shoulder to read a line of his own:

The last time planetary alignment was approximately inline was in 949 CE. And the planets will not replicate this phenomena again until, at the soonest, May of 2492 CE.

TJ sighed. "Great, so now all we need to do is build a cryopod, sleep in there for half a century, then wake up when the planets align."

Manny rolled her eyes and responded with yet another geek reference. "Keep reading, Sole Survivor."

Though such phenomena are uncommon. Divinerkind of the past have often put more trust in the more frequent patterns of nature: such as solstices, equinoxes, and most commonly, full moon cycles.

Ayo's second iron mask clanged against the desk as he rummaged through the piles of other masks, tomes, and scrolls around him. His fingers flew like a pianist's until they settled on a calendar. "There's a full moon on the Friday before Camp ends. That's our best shot."

TJ turned on Joshua. "Two weeks from now. That's enough time for you, right? Does the full moon help with whatever you were thinking of packaging for the ritual?"

"I got a few ideas." Joshua stroked his nonexistent beard like some sage wizard. "Yeah, the full moon should be perfect…"

"Great!" Manny beamed. "That'll give us plenty of time to practice and train up for the day."

"But there wasn't a full moon when I saw the orb and heard my sister's voice," TJ said.

"It doesn't have to be a natural phenomenon, man," Ayo said as he bounced in his chair a bit in excitement of new and solid information. TJ noticed he did that a lot, realizing that that whole "cool" thing was an act for Ayo. "Full moons and all that are just the easiest to replicate—if you don't count the pain in the ass of the timing. I mean, you nearly had to drown yourself for all that work, right? That ain't exactly your average night on the bayou."

"Yeah, no more drowning would be good." TJ nodded, feeling admittedly good about their chances in a couple weeks.

He surveyed each of his friends around the table with a smile, taking in the excitement as Ayo fist pumped, Manny quietly cheered, and Joshua smiled to himself. It had only been two weeks back at camp and they had made more progress than TJ could have ever hoped.

This was going to work.

He was going to speak with his sister again, find out who killed her, and then… well, he hadn't thought about what he'd do after he found out what happened to her. One thing at a time was fine for now. Their first order of business was getting that portal open.

"All right." TJ clapped his hands together like Mr. Bolawe always did. "We know what's what, we all know how to prepare. Let's make this happen."

40

AN ARRANGEMENT OF ACCESSORIES

WHEN OPERATION FULL MOON FRIDAY ARRIVED, TJ WOKE WITH a cold sweat. His dreams had been insane, all sorts of strange images: a world with trees that glowed vivid greens and oranges, floating mountainsides larger than they had any right to be, all backdropped by a purple sky.

At one point, he found himself deep under the ocean, but it wasn't quite an ocean. It was clearer than it should've been, and the coral and seaweed shined in bright hues like the trees above, yet the ocean floor had been backdropped by rusted and muted chains.

TJ laid in his bed a long while, processing the dream before it slipped into the typical abyss of forgetfulness like all his others. It almost felt like the same vision he had back at the funeral. Did that mean he was on the right track, that he and his friend's ritual to speak to his sister would *actually* work? He sure hoped so.

"Finally, you're awake!" Joshua came stomping into the empty boys' cabin. Slits of light leaked into the room from the thin window slats. "I actually just got back thinking I'd have to stuff smelling salts under your nose. I've got some good news!"

TJ rubbed at his eyes and lumbered out of bed. "Oh yeah, what's that?"

"Mr. B is doing one of his storytelling sessions at the fire pits tonight."

"Okay..." TJ yawned. "Great for Mr. Bolawe."

"He's doing it at 8 PM..."

"And the full moon is supposed to be at its peak at 8:09 PM..."

"Exactly! I mean, not everyone will be there, but at least a majority of the camp will be halfway across the grounds. We shouldn't have any interruptions."

"What time is it right now?"

"A quarter past six… in the afternoon," Joshua said.

"What!? No way I was out that long."

Joshua shrugged. "You were up until six in the morning, dude. And it's typical for diviners to feel drained before a big ritual. You know, magic stuff. When I saw you sleeping this morning, your eyes looked like they could pop out your lids." He put a gentle hand to TJ's shoulder. "Don't worry yourself. Plenty of time to do one more practice run. Hold on."

He hefted himself into his top bunk, making the whole cabin shake. After a short while, he threw down his huge duffle bag.

"Wait, don't open it." TJ led a groggy walk to the cabin door. Opening it a crack, he peered through to see a small group of intermediate campers playing crossover near the swamp's edge.

Then, with a hand outstretched, TJ said, "*Afefe.*" And a series of miniature windmills started to turn along the porch.

Without knowing it, it would look like the windmills were nothing more than a school project, but in reality, they were connected to an elaborate security system of Ayo's design. Once activated, they magically hoisted up a set of cans under the boys' cabin, and once someone walked onto the porch, breaking the gust line between the little windmills, the cans would drop and warn them that someone was coming.

"Dude, nice!" Joshua exclaimed. "You got it on your first try!"

"Don't sound so surprised." TJ grinned before closing the door behind him.

When he turned back to his bed, Joshua already had a spread of robes, bangles, earrings, cufflinks, bracers, rings, and some talisman, all along TJ's crumbled sheets.

"Oh, hey!" TJ exclaimed. "So you were able to get that… um… what is that exactly?"

TJ peered down at what appeared to be a crown with several necklaces hanging from its bottom.

"This here is the key." Joshua lifted the old brass crown and fit it over his head. The necklace beads hung over his face, looking something like a blue and white beard that covered most of his face. Only his nose protruded freely from the bunching of beads. "This is an Olosa mask!"

"Olosa?" TJ asked curiously, transfixed by the shimmer of the brass. "But we're trying to communicate with my sister… shouldn't we be trying to speak to Yewa? Or maybe Oya? Manny said Oya's the Cemetery Queen or whatever."

Joshua lifted a single, heavy finger, and the mask's beads clinked together like music. "This is true. But who's domain are we going to use tonight, eh?" His eyebrows lifted in question, and TJ understood what he was getting at. "I figured it wouldn't hurt to pay homage by having you fitted with this instead of an Oya mask or something else. In fact, most of the gear I got for you is favorable to Olosa. Trust me, this is going to work perfectly."

TJ shrugged. "Sure thing, Number One. I couldn't argue with you either way." Then he took the crown from Joshua's head and put it on his own. He could barely see a thing through the beads. "Where did you find this from, anyway?"

"Oh, you don't recognize it?" Joshua chuckled as he threw a blue and white aṣọ òkè robe over TJ's shoulders. "I mean, we only see it five times a week…"

TJ pulled the crowned mask from his head and examined it again. Then his eyes shot wide in fear. "This is from Mr. Du Bois's class? Let me guess, he has no idea you took it."

"Of course not."

"And you slipped in and out without anyone noticing?"

Joshua inclined his head, then echoed, "Don't sound so surprised." They shared in a laugh before he went on again. "Hurry up and get this stuff on. Gotta see if it's a good fit for you. I want you to try on these enchanted rings and this silver talisman. You still have that brass I got you, right?"

"Yeah, yeah." TJ did as directed, putting on and taking off everything Joshua had laid out for him, including Olosa's Brass.

"Hmmm," the boy would hum as they tried on new items. "That necklace doesn't quite suit you, try this one instead."

"How can you even tell?" TJ asked. Both of the necklaces he tried on looked and felt almost identical.

"Number One knows these things," Joshua would always reply, and TJ would roll his eyes and regret giving Joshua that nickname. But the moniker suited him. Over the past few weeks, TJ, Manny, and Ayo gathered items from here and there, mostly "borrowed" trinkets from the library. But it was always Joshua who came up with the best stuff—ancient robes from this famous warlock or an amulet from that noteworthy diviner. Whenever they asked him where he found the stuff, he'd mumble about breaking in here or asking for favors there.

After a few minutes, TJ was bedecked in a black and blue heavy robe meant for someone much wider than himself, the Olosa mask, which obscured his vision, an old hair comb that raked into his Afro, a necklace with coral hanging from it, and the Brass of Olosa, which was secured around his wrist. He gripped a hand mirror in his left hand, and in his right, his sister's staff.

In short, he looked like a ridiculous mess.

Joshua shot him two "a-okay" hand signs. "We're gonna kick that ritual's butt while wearing all this enchanted stuff."

"Thank you, Josh," TJ said. "Really, I mean it."

Joshua beamed. "Don't mention it, anything for a friend."

TJ took a seat and sighed as he surveyed the crystal in his sister's staff. Just a few more hours. A few more hours and he'd finally speak to her, finally find out what *really* happened to her. And he knew he couldn't have done it without Manny, or Ayo, or Joshua, especially.

"What are you thinking about, man?" Joshua asked him, taking a seat next to him on the bed.

"My sister," TJ answered. "The last time I saw her was a while back. We didn't see much of her once she graduated from Ifa. I've been reading about people who've communed with their family members. I was afraid she'd be different, you know… like some entity instead of a person. But she's supposed to be just like the way she was when she was alive."

A shadow seemed to hover over Joshua's face, even the dark wood about them seemed to darken until Joshua said, "I hope she's how you remember."

"Yeah, me too." TJ tilted back in the bed and stared up. "You know… I never told you why I'm doing this. Why I'm *really* doing this. I'm sure you heard, but the Keepers paid my sister's funeral a visit. My sister didn't just die, she was killed. By them." Joshua turned his chin to TJ but didn't move his eyes to look at him. "So I really appreciate what you and the others are doing. For real, for real. I won't forget it."

"Awww." Joshua smacked him across the knee. "Enough, dude. Too sappy."

"Hey, this is a rarity for me." TJ laughed. "I don't talk about this kind of stuff a lot, and—"

CRASH!

Someone was coming!

TJ shot up and Joshua spun his head to the cabin door. Heart racing, TJ glanced down to himself. There was no way they'd hide him and all the stuff they had tried on.

"Quick, TJ, under the bed," Joshua said with an earnestness he rarely adopted.

TJ dove under the bed, but his mask slipped off and tumbled just out of reach under another bunk. He outstretched his hand, but the boys' cabin door flung open, and his hand went right back under the shadow of his bed. All TJ could see were a pair of slacks and loafers at the threshold of the cabin. Before the voice spoke its first words, however, TJ already knew who it must've been.

Mr. Du Bois.

"Mr. Reed," he said. "Why am I not surprised to find you here?"

41

THE MOONLIGHT'S PORTAL

"Afternoon, Mr. D," Joshua said casually, though TJ could hear a hint of shakiness in his tone.

"Mr. Du Bois," the elder corrected.

TJ tried to call his fallen mask over to him with his sister's staff, but he only made things worse. As it dragged along the floor with his wind magic, it clipped against one of the bunk bed legs with a *thunk*.

It would've been better if he did nothing.

"What's that beside your foot?" Mr. Du Bois asked suddenly.

Joshua's feet jerked, and TJ knew he was putting on a face of mock confusion. "Beside my foot? What do you mean, sir?"

"*Wà si mi.*" A sharp gust of wind cut through the room and the crown-mask snapped into Du Bois's hand. "*This*, Mr. Reed. What is *this* doing in the boys' cabin? It should be hanging in my room of study."

TJ mouthed a stream of swears; they were totally busted.

"Beats me, sir. Maybe you should ask LaVont, considering it was under *his* bunk."

Silence came then. Neither Joshua nor Mr. Du Bois moved an inch and TJ knew they were staring each other down: Joshua probably with his bright, round face and slight smirk, Mr. Du Bois almost certainly with his knitted brow and pinched lips.

TJ's heart thumped against his chest, and he feared that Mr. Du Bois could hear how it drummed against the wood under his bunk.

"Very well, young man," Mr. Du Bois said coldly. "We'll get to the bottom of this before the night's through."

Then Du Bois turned on his heel, made for the door, opened it and closed it again in what seemed one fluid motion. Just as the door slammed shut, TJ let out the breath that was held captive in his chest the entire time.

"Wait, dude." Joshua whispered as he moved to the door to crack it open. "All right, he's halfway across the porch already. We're good."

TJ rolled from under the bed and looked up. "*That* was too close." Joshua lifted him up with a helping hand. "Too bad about the mask. Does that mean we'll go back to the original plan? Pull out the Oya mask like Manny said? What? Why are you smiling at me like that?"

"Because," Joshua said, "Mr. D didn't take the real mask. He took a fake."

"What are you talking about? I was trying to call it to me and he took it. I saw it."

Joshua hit him with another grin, then said, "*Ìbojù, wà ɔi mi.*" The mask popped out of thin air and settled in the boy's hand. "I saw what you were trying to do. So I switched them."

"I didn't see you with another mask, though."

"I didn't have time to show you all the stuff I got. I told you, dude. I got this on lock."

"Josh, you really are Number One!" TJ grabbed for the mask and ran his hand along the beads and the weathered brass. A flashing 19:06 — 7:06 PM — on his watch face caught his attention, though. "Oh shoot. We gotta go meet with Manny and Ayo."

He rushed to gather the magical accessories from under his bed. Joshua helped him, his hands working fast.

"Do you think Mr. Du Bois knows what we're trying?" TJ asked.

"I don't think so."

TJ bit his lip. Joshua had shown his loyalty; he could be trusted. "Manny and I think he might be a Keeper. He's been on my case all summer and well... there's this woman named Adeola. She was a friend to my sister. Her best friend. I ran into her last session and we found out she wasn't supposed to be here. Her and Mr. Du Bois saw each other in the library, but Du Bois didn't say anything to anyone."

"Why didn't you tell one of the elders? Or Mr. Bolawe?"

"I don't know who to trust at this camp. Well, maybe I should have told Mr. Bolawe, but I wasn't talking to him then."

Joshua put the last of their items in his duffle bag. "Damn, are there any more secrets I don't know about?" His shoulders slumped and his chin hung low.

The look made TJ feel a bit guilty. So he did what he always did in times like these. "Uh, let's see. I lied about lunch yesterday. I *did* get an extra dip. I just didn't want to share. But c'mon, man. Mr. Windell's secret sauce is too good."

Joshua's lips battled against a smile. "That's... understandable. Windell's secret sauce is pretty bomb." He smacked TJ across the shoulder. "C'mon, before Mr. D figures out the mask I gave him was a fake. Let's link up with the others and get to the lagoon. The quicker we do it, the sooner I can get the real mask back in place and Mr. D can't say anything against me."

☥

TJ'S WATCH READ 19:45 — 7:45 PM — BY THE TIME THEY SNUCK away to the lagoon.

"There you are!" Manny exclaimed as she came walking along the bank of the lagoon. "What took you so long?"

"A little run-in with Mr. Du Bois," TJ told her. "Did you make sure we're alone?"

Ayo answered for her. "Yeah, we double checked the lagoon and the whispering wood. We're alone. Even that Francois tree guy was at the amphitheater."

As expected, a majority of the camp had gone to the fire pits and amphitheater to listen to Mr. Bolawe's new stories. TJ wondered if he should've let Mr. Bolawe know what they were going to do. He would've helped them too, probably would've wanted to talk to Dayo as well.

"Hurry, put these on." Joshua stuffed his hand into his duffle bag and handed robes, bangles, and masks to Manny and Ayo.

Manny scanned her robes with a raised eyebrow. "Blue and white? These are Olosa's colors. What happened to all the Oya stuff?"

"Trust me," Joshua assured her as he pulled on his own robe. "This is going to work better."

As they dressed, TJ stared up into the darkening sky. As he gazed up at the moon, which shone bright and full against the dying twilight, TJ for the first time in months, felt light, good. He knew it was going to work. He was decked out like a wizard; he had his friends to help him, the moon to empower him, and his sister's own staff to call her. It didn't matter that he'd finished the camp only in the top forty. It didn't matter he wouldn't get the invite to Ifa Academy. It didn't matter he wasn't sure what to say to Dayo when she showed herself again.

And it didn't matter that he was nervous.

He was going to *see* his sister in just a few minutes, actually *speak* to her.

In his mind, he painted her face, her little chin, her upper lip that was slightly bigger than the bottom one, the wide nose she got from Mom, the thin and almost pointed ears from Dad, her almond-shaped eyes, deep brown but always bright in their unique way. But most of all he heard her voice in his head, her laughter. So kind. So gentle.

"TJ, you ready?" Joshua snapped his fingers in front of him. "It's 8:00 PM on the dot. We should start the ritual. You okay?"

TJ turned to him, then to Manny, then to Ayo. They all were dressed in heavy robes meant for adults, with necklaces hanging with coral like TJ's, and beaded masks that swayed left and right. Clowns. That's what they looked like. Clowns in some bizarre show.

But TJ didn't care.

"I can't tell you how much this means to me, y'all," he started. "You didn't have to do this." He looked at Ayo in particular. "None of you." Then to Manny. "But I'm glad I've met you." And last to Joshua. "None of this could have happened without you."

"Of course, TJ," Manny said. "We'll always be here for you, especially for something like this."

"Ah, man... you're not going to cry, are you?" Ayo murmured. He was swiftly met with a smack across the shoulder from Manny.

Joshua tapped his watch. "Come *on*, we'll do all the appreciation stuff after. There's only a few more minutes. Get in the water, TJ."

"R-right!" TJ stood up straight and rubbed his eyes with the back of his hand. They were indeed watering.

The first step into the lagoon was cool, but not chilling. Even his robes, which had been heavy against his shoulders, were then no more weighty than feathers once the waters touched them. With a hand mirror in one hand, and his sister's staff in the other, he raised both high over the water and began his chant.

The words were rehearsed so often, he didn't even have to think about what he said, like a favorite song he'd never forget. Behind him, Manny, Joshua, and Ayo parroted his hymn in near-perfect harmony. Their energy filled TJ and that familiar tingle he had known all his life swirled through his limbs, out through his fingers, and into the power of the staff. Only this time he knew what his power was, he knew what to focus on, and each of the magical items hanging from his wrists, neck, and head filtered that power and boosted it. It was like breathing the crisp air after fresh rainfall.

And then, very quickly, the lagoon began to bubble.

TJ repeated his verse faster and with more strength. This time, the crystal in his staff shone brighter than it ever had before, though instead of its typical muted brownish green, it transformed into a brilliant hue of scarlet. When he and Joshua had practiced the ritual, Joshua said this might happen. He said it was a good sign. Excitement filled every inch of TJ as the glow spread wide around him.

The third time they recited the hymn, this time with even more fervor, a luminous orb expanded at the bottom of the lagoon. At first it was no larger than a pea, then, quickly—very quickly—it ballooned to the size of a tire. It hadn't looked like that before when TJ saw it weeks ago.

But then he was on his own.

Now he could feel it, really feel the energy of it, like it was some miniature pure-white sun giving him life. And despite the aggressive light, it didn't sting his eyes, and he didn't dare blink.

His grip around the staff magnetized as it always did when he felt his Ashe course with such fierce strength. Nothing short of a bull ramming into him would have made him drop it—and even then, that wasn't a sure thing.

"*Come to me,*" a voice rang out from the bright orb. It was loud this time, almost like a shout in TJ's head. But he didn't stop chanting. He wouldn't stop. "*Come to me, come to me.*"

The orb—now the size of a person—broke the plane of the water. As it climbed up and up, it reformed to look more like a doorframe, and a shadow passed behind it. TJ was on the edge of calling out Ifedayo's name, but he kept to his chanting. He couldn't break the connection, not as the shadow formed into the figure of a woman.

"*Sweet, sweet, Tomori Jomiloju,*" the voice said. "*There's so much power imbued in you now, young one.*"

Young one? TJ thought idly. *Why would Dayo call me young one?*

And finally, the figure stepped out.

Ifedayo looked so different. Her ears weren't pointed anymore, but flat, almost nonexistent. Her eyes weren't almond-shaped but wide-set and overlarge. And her hair wasn't matted but long and flowing all the way down her back. But most of all, her body was covered completely in shimmering fish scales of blue and white.

Is that what happened when someone died? Did they take on a new appearance in the Orisha Plane? But Dayo hadn't been aligned with any of the water Orishas. Orunmila was associated with the sky, the stars.

It didn't matter.

It didn't matter how much she changed. She was smiling at him lovingly, benevolent... happy.

"TJ!" Joshua shouted. "The final word. Say it now so she won't go away!"

TJ shook from his reverie and, slamming the bottom of the staff into the lagoon, he shouted, "*Dùrò tì mì!*"

A ripple shot out from the bottom of his staff. Its red glow swelled and blossomed, bathing the duckweed, the cypresses, and the water in its blood hue. TJ, soaking through with perspiration and breathing heavily, uttered a strained but greatly relieved, "Hey, Dayo. I finally found you."

But Dayo gave him a curious expression, a slight tilt to her head. Then, without warning, her faint, inquisitive grin turned into a full scowl. Her scaled brow caved into an angry "V", and her mouth flew open, exposing several rows of sharp teeth. The scream loosed from her throat blared like a giant sea creature. Inhuman. Savage.

She threw out her webbed hand at TJ, but before she could clutch at his robes, she broke down into blue and white mist—a mist that drifted right into the crystal of his staff. Her shrieks died as she was sucked up little by little until there was nothing left.

Then there was silence.

Nothing but stark and naked silence.

TJ stared down at the staff in utter shock, his heart full of ice and horror. *What did I do?*

The staff crystal's red hue had returned to that dirty green again. It pulsated like the lump welling in TJ's throat. The well that tried to keep vomit from spilling out from his mouth.

"Dayo," he whispered.

He swallowed hard, his stomach churned, and his head became light and dizzy.

He messed up the ritual. He... he had *destroyed* Dayo. His knees buckled, and he would've splashed into the water had Manny not caught him.

"Give me the staff, TJ," Joshua demanded. "Let me check, let me check."

TJ didn't protest, didn't even lift a finger as Joshua took up the staff to examine it. The boy ran his hand up and down its length and he placed his ear to it like there was something to listen to.

He must've felt terrible; most of the ritual was his idea.

"Did I do it wrong?" TJ asked weakly. "Did I hurt her? Did I hurt Dayo?"

"It's okay, TJ," Manny murmured in his ear. "It's okay. Josh'll take care of it." She flipped her head to the boy with narrowed eyes. "Won't you?"

But Joshua just kept staring at the staff. He stroked the crystal like it was some precious diamond. And, very slowly, he laughed. But it wasn't a laugh that should've come out of a teenage boy's body. It wasn't exactly a man's laugh either. Like Dayo's scream, it was befitting of something... otherworldly.

"I got her!" Joshua bellowed, still cackling. "I got her! I finally got her!"

"Yo, what's wrong with you?" Ayo asked, pulling off his mask for a better look. His eyes darted between Joshua and TJ in utter confusion. "What's the matter with him? Yo, Josh!"

"My name's not, Josh," he chuckled through a new Nigerian accent.

"What?" TJ breathed out. "What does that mean?"

"Come now, child." Joshua faced them. The glow of the green crystal fell over his face like wicked acid. Even still he kept to his chuckling, and his words were almost sung through his laughter. "You're a sharp one. You don't recognize me?"

Ayo took a cautious step back and looked Joshua up and down.

"The Master of Mischief," Joshua said. "Overseer of Crossroads. Lord of Communications. The Owner of all Roads. The Guardian of Gates. Go on... say my name, child."

Ayo stood, horror-stricken, the green glow contouring his face in a bizarre look. "No... you can't be. All the Orishas are gone. Not even my parents—not even my grandparents have seen one."

"Ah, but the same rules do not apply to the One who holds the Keys." Joshua beamed.

As he spoke in that sing-song voice, he did a little two-step with the staff like some kind of jester. TJ didn't know what to think. What *could* he think? This was too much.

"C'mon, kid," Joshua said. "I'll take the Yoruba pronunciation, please, seeing as that is your mother tongue. Go on, say my name."

Even as Ayo shook his head, as though in disbelief of what this all meant, he still said, very softly, "Eshu."

"Eshu!" Joshua sang brightly. "Eshu! Eshu! Eshu!"

"No way..." Manny trailed off in a shocked murmur, still holding onto TJ tightly. "This can't be real."

This was all a dream. It had to be a very bad dream, TJ thought.

"Oh, yes! Our Eshu's crossover champion!" He bowed his head to Manny. "Definitely one of my better inventions back in the day. Though Oya had a hand in that one too, you know. Credit where credit's due. And can I just take this opportunity to point out you diviners are playing it wrong!"

TJ couldn't believe this. It didn't make sense, but it all fit: Those debates between Joshua and Mr. Du Bois, the reason Joshua always wanted to be around, the way he talked funny sometimes...

"Did you hurt him?" TJ asked darkly.

Joshua canted his head. "Pardon me?"

"Joshua Reed... was he a real boy?"

"Oh, heavens no. I had this body custom ordered by my old friend Obatala! No boys were harmed in the making of this skin."

"Why?" TJ asked as he pulled off his own mask. "Why trap my sister? Is she an Orisha now or something?"

Joshua took a step back in genuine confusion. "Excuse me? Your —" He glanced at the staff. "Oh! Kid... No, no, no. *This* one was not your sister. *This* was Olosa. Sorry, I thought that was obvious by now —" He smacked the staff head against his own like he was a dummy. "My mistake, I guess. You see, Olosa and I have a very old feud and she needed to be taught a lesson about why one cannot take shortcuts when they cross Eshu's paths. Admittedly, a trapping isn't my go-to. Too simple. No finesse. More a scolding than a lesson, eh? But this all serves dual-purposes."

"But my sister's staff." Anger boiled within TJ. "You made my sister's staff do all of that?"

"This isn't your sister's staff." Eshu wiggled his fingers across the mahogany and the figurehead turned from a slender one to a wide one, just like the way TJ drew it before. "Thanks to one of my mortal friends, we made the switch back at the funeral. Nearly screwed it up too. You seemed to notice the change in the crystal colors when I copied the original."

"Elder Akande told us changing colors was dark stuff," Manny gritted bitterly.

Joshua rolled his eyes. "Pfft. Even your elders are lost. There's nothing 'dark' about me or my magic. Nothing 'light' either. Didn't you pay attention to Mr. D? The Orishas just... are." He turned to

TJ then. "But worry not, your sister's staff is safe. It's being kept with Elder—"

A shadow sprang from the treeline. The dark figure wrapped around Joshua's girth and shoved him into the wet earth below. The two of them wrestled in the mud, kicking up the stink of the lagoon. TJ couldn't quite see who had sprung from nowhere. The robe they wore was a dark emerald, though sometimes the staff's green light glinted against the edge of their metal mask. A Keeper's mask. Every time they twisted and turned, the staff shot off sparks that fell into the water, flung into the trees, and shot high in the sky.

TJ wasn't sure what to feel... relief? Fear? Confusion was probably the most apt.

"Should we do something?" Manny asked.

"Looks like our savior's got it covered," Ayo answered.

Grunting, the masked shadow got leverage on Joshua, lifting the boy up off his feet and then pinning him against the bark of a tree with the staff at his throat.

"Oh, these mortal bodies are oh so limited, aren't they?" Joshua said. "*Kò ṣi àrá, kò ṣi iṣòrò.*"

And with those words Joshua... slumped.

He fell into himself like a rag doll.

A translucent wisp slithered through Joshua's eyes. The same wisp TJ often saw when he watched Ashe at work. It swirled and molded itself into a new figure just above Joshua's head. Then it solidified into an old-looking man, who wore loose fabrics of black and red and a hooked hat that sloped behind his head. His face was jovial, boyish, and plastered with a clown's eerie grin. And his large, round, exposed potbelly folded over in a second smile.

Eshu. The Gatekeeper.

TJ's stomach churned. It was magic, he knew, but seeing one of your closest friends crumble like a paper mache warranted the reaction. Everything in his body felt hollowed out.

"Over there! It came from the lagoon!" A voice TJ barely registered bellowed through the trees.

"I'll be taking that, thank you very much." Eshu wiggled his finger, and the staff sprang upward from the shadow's hand. The staff drove up with such force, it caught the bottom of the robed figure's mask and knocked it clean off into a bundle of shrubs.

The figure—a woman—swung back into the water. She had short hair, protruding cheekbones, and a nose ring: Adeola. So she never did leave the camp! She'd been spying all that time. All those reports of Keepers made sense now, and another wave of sickness threatened to invade TJ's stomach.

"Hand it over, Eshu," she said as she rubbed her jaw. "*Wà ḍi mi.*"

A wooden staff of her own popped and snapped into her hand. She angled it at Eshu's head.

But Eshu didn't seem to care, giggling. "Oh, sure, I'll do that. But there's a giant alligator behind you."

"No more tricks, Eshu."

"Well, it's *your* funeral." Eshu floated over Adeola's head.

She followed his arc just in time to see the maw of Ol' Sally, who sloshed through the lagoon shallows with preternatural speed. Adeola twisted her staff into the waters deftly, then a gust of wind shot from its tip and sent her hurtling straight up in the air.

TJ, Manny, and Ayo gasped. Ol' Sally was barely inches away from taking Adeola's whole leg.

Adeola continued air-stepping along the tops of trees even as Ol' Sally, still mid-run, went for the next best target: Joshua's body.

It happened so fast. One moment, Joshua's slumped body was pressed up against the tree, the next, it was swallowed whole by the great beast. A sharp pain pierced through TJ's chest as bones crunched, as though *he* were the one being eaten. Bile attempted to force its way out of TJ's throat. This was all too much to take in.

"I think the ol' girl is after this." Eshu lifted the staff in his hand. He floated above the middle of the lagoon with crossed legs. TJ thought he could hear the whisper of Olosa's screams inside.

"I think that's my cue to make like a tree." He shot the staff down at the black water below him and another portal, this time colored in red, opened up. "*Au revoir, Louisiana.*" And then he flipped in the air and dived into the portal like a corkscrew. Just as he passed over the threshold, the portal started to shrink.

"*Dìmu ḍàndàn ní!*" barked a voice from the treeline. A flash of blue filled the swamp and the portal's shrinkage slowed.

"Xavier, is that you?" Adeola asked through a cough.

Mr. Du Bois rushed from the treeline and picked her up. "Yes, it's me. Hurry, we have to follow the Trickster in before the portal closes."

"Behind you!" Adeola shouted.

"What's that?" Mr. Du Bois turned just in time to see Ol' Sally stomping for him. Du Bois lifted his iron staff and a tall sheet of fire manifested between him and the giant alligator in a jerk that must've been pure, raw reaction.

"Go!" Mr. Du Bois commanded. "Before it closes."

"Wait!" TJ shouted, but his voice was lost within the roar of the fire. "Adeola, wait!"

Adeola swam and slipped into the portal. Mr. Du Bois backed away slowly, keeping his fire shield between himself and Ol' Sally as he did his own backstroke into the portal. Even though he slipped in, and his fire with him, that didn't stop Ol' Sally from chomping away. She managed to lodge her snout into the portal, stopping it from shrinking farther like a cork to a wine bottle.

"C'mon." TJ pulled off his robe; it'd be too heavy for the swim. "We have to go after them."

"Right behind you." Manny already had her robe half off.

Ayo didn't look like he had any plans to move his feet. "Yeah, um... Keepers, rituals, maybe I can manage that. Ol' Sally, though? That's where I draw the line."

"Ayo!" TJ gritted. "If you don't get your scary-ass over here—"

"Ahhh!" Ayo yelped as a branch wrapped around his middle and pulled him back into the dark forest.

Manny ducked as a second branch came for her chest. But she wasn't fast enough for the third. With a loud smack across her arms, a branch wrapped around her and sucked her into the darkness as well. TJ rolled into the mud as a fourth and fifth branch flung out like a pair of jabs. But like his friends, he couldn't juke the branches for long, and he too was snatched by the ankle and then made to hang upside down.

"I've got them!" a smooth voice said; Monsieur Francois' voice. "The children are safe."

From the woods, Mr. Bolawe came tumbling out. Blood ran down half of his face. "Xavier attacked me... where did he run off to?"

Monsieur Francois dipped his trunk to one side, making TJ feel like he was about to do a loop.

"Oh, sorry, children." He stopped his dip. "They've gone into the portal, sir. Just one problem..."

They all turned to see Ol' Sally still doing her best to squeeze her way into the portal, but it was too small for her.

"I'll handle it." Mr. Bolawe stepped forward with his staff in hand.

"Sir!" TJ shouted, still hanging from his ankle. He felt like his stomach was going to drop through his mouth. "It's Adeola. She's working with Mr. Du Bois. They're Keepers. They've got my sister's staff—well, it's not really my sister's staff it was—"

Mr. Bolawe waved a hand of understanding. "No time, TJ," he said as he waded to Ol' Sally. "Sally, Sally... shhh, shhh, it's okay. It's me, Olufemi." The giant alligator stopped at the sound of her name. "No, keep that open for me if you can. Don't raise your head too quickly. Easy... Easy, girl. Yes, I'm going to get her back; I'm going to get *Olosa* back." Bolawe kept to his awkward one-arm breaststroke until his hand met the alligator's scaly back where he could balance. "*You* can't fit in there, but *I* can. On the count of three, you're going to lift your head and I'm going to go after them. Is that okay with you?"

Ol' Sally flipped her tail in the air and let it fall back into the lagoon with a splash.

Mr. Bolawe chuckled. "I'll take that as a yes. All right. On one. Two. Three." The alligator jerked her head back, and Mr. Bolawe dropped in. The portal closed behind him with a little *ding* befitting a jester's bell.

"Never fear, children," Monsieur Francois said proudly. "I've summoned Director Simmons. We'll get you back to safety."

"Not to be *that* guy, but," Ayo grunted as they were tugged along through the woods by the all-too-proud tree man. "I *did* say something about that staff head lookin' like Eshu, didn't I?"

"Ayo." Manny sighed. "You're allowed to shut up sometimes. You don't have to make a comment about every little thing."

TJ didn't have the energy or the care to piggyback Manny's chidings. The past half hour was a nightmare. He didn't know what to think, but he felt like he deserved to be hanging upside down. He'd been tricked, hoodwinked. Joshua—Eshu—*knew* he couldn't speak to his sister.

Now the staff was gone. Mr. Bolawe was alone with two Keepers and an Orisha. TJ would never see or hear his sister.

And it was all his fault.

42

A WHOLE LOTTA TROUBLE

"YOU HAVE TO BELIEVE US. JOSHUA IS AN ORISHA," AYO SHOUTED as they were set down in Director Simmons's office cabin.

"He's *actually* Eshu," Manny added. "The Trickster! The *real* Eshu."

The pair of them had never stopped belting as Monsieur Francois pulled them along from the lagoon to the Director's office.

TJ was completely deflated. His cheeks burned, his shoulders were sandbags, and his stare was blank. He had been so stupid. So *stupid*. It was like Ayo said... that picture he drew of his sister's staff looked like Joshua because it was the face of Eshu—albeit thinner and more wizened. The reason the head on the staff seemed to change was because it was the Trickster's face showing itself every now and then. Eshu's color was red, and Orunmila's was green. That's what the color change was all about. And that time when Joshua caught up to TJ and Manny in Miss Gravés's class... a kid his size should've never kept pace with them.

Ayo and Manny continued talking over the other, their words sounding like gibberish as they were moved into the Yoruba-patterned plush seats beside Director Simmons's white-marbled desk. The statues were still there, all staring at them like before. They wore angry expressions along their wooden brows. Clearly, they hadn't forgotten when TJ and his friends had last come to visit.

Each of them, save one.

TJ stared at the statue behind Director Simmons's desk. There he was, staring at him with that wicked grin: Eshu.

TJ stared at it because he still couldn't believe it. He stared at it because maybe the features would change.

But they didn't.

It was clear on the unblemished polish of the wood, the fine contouring of the wide face, the Gatekeeper was looking straight at him. And the Orisha statue mocked him with that goofy expression. TJ could see how Joshua shared in the round wide nose, the love handles, and those jovial wide eyes.

"Miss Martinez, Mr. Oyelowo," Director Simmons said with a hand to her forehead, "Take a breath, please. Let me get everything in order and then I'll take down your stories."

Manny pressed on. "But Director—"

"I'll only be a few minutes!" Director Simmons twisted her hand and Manny was planted into her seat magically. Ayo was halfway to his own protest, but the same happened to him. TJ didn't have to say anything at all and, like the others, an invisible force pressed him down into his seat. Then the Director stepped out onto her porch and into the night, where she closed the door to her single-room office behind her.

On the other side of the door, her voice could still be heard as she said, "Do you know what happened?"

"I only saw the tail end of it, *madame*," came Monsieur Francois' voice. "But Olufemi was in a fight with Xavier. Olufemi told me to go ahead and help the kids, to help young Tomori Jomiloju. When I got to the lagoon, Ol' Sally had her head stuck inside a portal."

"You don't mean an *actual* realm portal, do you?" That resonant voice belonged to Miss Gravés.

"Realm portal?" Manny asked Ayo. "Like a transport portal?"

"Sorta, except instead of traveling, you go to one of the Orisha Planes."

TJ strained to hear more of what the adults said.

"I can't be sure where the portal led," Monsieur Francois said, "but in all my three-hundred years I've never seen one like that, though I heard them described just like that when I was a child."

"Portals or not," Director Simmons said. "We had a breach. Do we know if that Keeper was alone?"

"The elders only saw the one," Miss Gravés answered. "The elders and the juniors are shepherding the children back to their cabins."

"Good... Good... let them mind that. But you. I want you to take the Cypress Guard and a few of my own to make sure the grounds' perimeter is airtight. We may have more unwelcome guests soon. I've already contacted my sister. She's informing the UCMP and should be here soon. Monsieur Francois, can you help with defense as well?"

"Of course, Director," he said.

"Ò ∂ābo, Director," said Ms. Gravés.

And Director Simmons returned to them both, "*Ìpàdé wà bi óyin, Olúṣọ.*"

Footsteps pounded away against the cabin porch, and Monsieur Francois' signature creaking of wood shuffled away until their sounds receded into the steady rhythm of crickets.

Simmons rushed back into the room from the porch, tapped the forehead of each of her statues, and waited. Each statue's eyes flared red, and they all sprang to life like wooden robots off an assembly line.

"Camp Olosa may be in danger," the Director told them. "Maintain the perimeter of the grounds. You know what to do if any outsiders try to cross over. But allow Elder Adeyemi and her cohorts to pass when they arrive."

A series of creaks crunched as the statues inclined their stiff necks to Director Simmons. Then, one after the other, all except the Oshun statue, which housed Simmons's water bowl, exited the room. TJ never took his eyes off the Eshu statue. Even with its rigid gait, it seemed to skip.

TJ felt himself mumble something, though the words didn't quite seem to reach his own ears.

"What's that, Mr. Young?" Director Simmons asked as she plucked the fine comb still lodged in TJ's Afro.

"Joshua," TJ croaked. "Who were his parents? Where did he come from?"

He didn't quite believe the story Eshu told them about having his body fashioned for him. If he lied all summer, he could've still been lying then.

Simmons frowned, dropped the comb on her desk, then took a seat. "That's not my business to divulge, young man."

"Manny and Ayo are right... he's not a real kid. Or maybe he was. Eshu was using his body."

Director Simmons shook her head. "Impossible. An Orisha hasn't been seen for many, many —"

"Call Elder Wale. He's watching over the kids, right? Joshua isn't going to be there."

"Elder Wale would have informed me if —"

"Wale doesn't remember what he had for breakfast..." TJ trailed off at Simmons's raised eyebrow. "M-Ma'am... Sorry, but... just make the call. Please."

Director Simmons unlaced her fingers and held them flat against each other as though in prayer, as though she were measuring the truth in TJ's words.

"TJ's telling the truth, Director," Manny added.

Ayo nodded in earnest. "The Orishas are back."

Director Simmons took a deep breath. Then she pulled out her water bowl from the chest of her Oshun statue. From a pocket in her dashiki, she withdrew a phial of vivid blue spirit water, poured it into the bowl, and watched as the water lifted and cascaded like a stationary waterfall. Soon, Elder Wale's face filled the ripples.

"Director Simmons?" his hoarse voice rang out.

"Evening, Wale." She gave him a half smirk. "Do you have a full count of your boys? Any missing?"

"Missin' boys? My junior told me you had Ayodeji and that Tomori Jomiloju boy."

"Yes, they are with me now. But do you have a full count of the others?"

"Let's see, hmmm..." Elder Wale's face dipped out a view for a moment. "There's Lorenzo, Stephen is just over there with his brother, yeah, yeah, and then there's that Jimoh boy right there—I'll tell you what, that one is taller than a mother—"

"Joshua Reed," Simmons cut him off. "Is Joshua Reed there with you?"

"That big-boned one? Let me check right quick..." Again his face disappeared as he shouted, "Reed! Joshua Reed! Is you here? Hey, LaVont. You see that big boy anywhere?"

"Elder Wale!" Director Simmons swallowed, then kissed her teeth. "I've told you before... we always double count."

"He here, he here... I'm sure of it. That boy lives in the bathroom, I bet he's there. Hey, Juice Man! Any of them boys in that bathroom?"

"They're all in bed, sir."

"Ah, don't pay that no mine, Director," Wale started. "The boy's probably—"

Director Simmons dipped her phial into the water and cut off the rest of Elder Wale's excuses. Then she grumbled, "That man's gonna be the end of me. Yemoja, help me." She rubbed her temples and TJ noticed properly for the first time how disheveled she was with bags under her eyes and her headwrap half done.

TJ maintained his blank stare. "Joshua's getting broken down by Ol' Sally's stomach acids right now. So, Director Simmons, please tell me you know where he's from."

With her hands over her face, Simmons lumbered back in her chair. "That would make sense..."

Manny tilted her head forward slightly. "What would make sense?"

"Mr. Reed... he doesn't have any family. His papers said he was from New Home Orphanage. I never heard of it before, and it took some time to verify it, but I did. He had all the paperwork, and he never gave me any trouble, so I didn't think much of it..."

"He told us he had his body made by an old friend," TJ said.

"Old friend making bodies? You mean like Obatala?"

"That's the name he used, yeah." The tightness in TJ's chest released a little; at least Joshua wasn't a real person.

"I can't believe it..." Director Simmons said lightly. She peered at each of them, realizing they were telling the truth. "This is... very heavy stuff." She eyed Manny and Ayo. "What were you two saying about Mr. Du Bois? He was speaking with the Keeper you said?"

"Yeah, he was working with—" But Manny stopped herself short. Her eyes hovered just outside a sidelong glance toward TJ.

"He's a Keeper. He's working with my sister's best friend, Adeola," TJ started. Then he explained everything that had happened that summer, from his run-in with Adeola in the library and by the lagoon, how she ignored him, why they had broken into Simmons's office, and what had just happened that night. He even recounted the ritual, Olosa turning to mist, and his sister's staff.

"You're telling me Olosa is *trapped* in a staff?" Director Simmons finally asked after she let it all process. She said the words with gravity and the color in her skin paled.

"Yes," TJ answered. "I think so. Is that bad?"

Simmons rocked her head from left to right. "Depends on who gets their hands on it. A staff imbued directly with an Orisha like that... it would be quite powerful. There are theories of how much power, but no one's ever managed to do something like that before."

"That's what the Keepers want," Manny said, more to TJ than Simmons. "That's what Adeola and Mr. Du Bois are after. They want the staff for themselves."

"To do what, exactly?" Simmons asked.

"We don't know," Ayo chimed in. "Keeper stuff! Does it matter? They shouldn't have something that powerful!"

TJ's heart sank. Director Simmons was right. He couldn't imagine what they would do with something like that. Standard magic was crazy enough... magic on the scale of the Orishas, though? Unfathomable.

"You should probably call the elders, Mrs. Simmons," TJ said, "give them a heads up before they catch up to them."

Director Simmons tilted her head. "What do you mean?"

"The other counselors are going after Adeola and Mr. Du Bois, right? I remember how Mr. Bolawe fought at my sister's funeral. And we already saw him bleeding bad a few minutes ago. He's going to need help."

"Heavens... Mr. Young, no one goes into a realm portal and comes out." TJ looked to his friends with a questioning and slightly fearful expression. Manny shrugged, but Ayo gave him a haunting nod.

"Past diviners *have* tried when they've barely managed to get a portal open," Simmons explained. "We mortals are not meant to be there... not before our time, not before we're ready."

TJ knew she was referring to death, and a chill ran through him, his sister on his mind. Then it occurred to him that that day in the library when he was researching the forgotten tale of the lost Orisha and the promised child was probably all fake. Adeola said he had an Eshu mask in his hand, a trickster's mask. That stuff about falling stars and divine paths leading to lagoons was just a way to get TJ obsessed with the lagoon and the voice within it. Not his sister's voice, but Olosa's herself.

I'm such an idiot...

"That said," Director Simmons went on, "it's been a very long while since a diviner made it into a realm portal and came back out again—at least not sane. Even so, that was well before my father's father's time."

TJ crossed his arms. "So what are you saying?"

"I'm saying, I suppose... Mr. Du Bois, Mr. Bolawe, and this... Adeola, you say? They're gone."

"Gone!?" TJ shot up out of his chair, but he sprang back like a rubber band. Simmons's spell still held him tight. "Are you saying no one's even *trying* to get to the other side?"

"Of course not. Even if I did send someone, and that's *if* they could get a realm portal open at all to begin with... we mortals do not last long in the Orisha Planes. As I said, even those who return are not all there when they get back. We are forbidden. Didn't Mr. Du Bois teach you about Ewatomi Adesanya? The woman had only crossed over for a single day and everyone knows how far gone she was until she died—so the elders tell us, at least."

"Oh, yeah," Ayo said. "Adesanya was her name." He turned to the others. "That's who I was talking about in the library."

If no one could get into the Orisha Plane usually, then what were they supposed to do? How could they even get a portal open to begin with? Without his sister's staff, without an Orisha helping them…

The thought hit TJ like an alligator bucking into his chest. Somehow, deep down, he knew it. That first night at the lagoon, he didn't need anyone to see that orb at the bottom of it. He was special, and that's why he was Eshu's target. Without TJ, Eshu would've never been able to call Olosa like they did. That also meant that TJ could do it again. He knew the magic now. They just had to use him as the key.

Mr. Bolawe was alone. If it was true that a diviner didn't stay sane in the Orisha Planes for long, then there wasn't much time before they lost the man forever. The only reason he was at the camp at all was because he felt indebted to TJ by way of Dayo's memory. TJ couldn't let him fight that fight by himself, especially when he knew he could actively support the man.

He had to make things right. He *had* to.

"I can open the realm portal," TJ said confidently. "And I can help Mr. Bolawe. I have… special powers, special Ashe that can help people. Mr. Bolawe showed me how I could use them over the break. He thinks… he thinks I'm a new Orisha. It's why I've done better this session."

Simmons steepled her fingers, her mouth falling agape. Her attention shifted to Manny and Ayo as though to verify with them.

"We couldn't have opened that portal without TJ," Manny confirmed.

Ayo nodded. "Yeah, he's legit."

"'Special powers' or not," Director Simmons began. "I can't allow my campers to be put in danger. My primary responsibility as director is to make sure you are safe. Don't worry, Elder Adeyemi will be here along with the UCMP soon. They'll handle the situation as best they can."

"Then I'll have to ask for your forgiveness then, Mrs. Simmons," TJ said.

The Director's face went tight. "What do you mean by that? What forgiveness?"

TJ closed his eyes and dug deep into his Ashe. Connecting with it was easy now. "Manny, Ayo. The statue."

"On it!" they said simultaneously, and TJ funneled the Ashe from the statue and from the Director into his friends. When he opened his eyes again, the Oshun statue behind Simmons stirred. Its eyes glowed red, and it creaked to life. In an instant, it brought its long arms around the Director's chest.

"What!?" she exclaimed. "What's this? Let go of me!"

TJ shot a look to Manny and Ayo, who were still helping him keep Simmons locked down with their own Ashe. Translucent wisps wafted from their bodies and drifted toward the Director and her statue.

Simmons did her best to fight back and counter, but TJ just sapped her Ashe and used it for his friends, just like Mr. Bolawe told him. Slowly, TJ worked his own Ashe to free himself and his friends from their invisible binds. Now that he knew what he was doing, it was much easier work than when they had broken into the office before. And within seconds, they were each free of their invisible binds.

"Run!" TJ ordered them.

They bolted for the door. TJ glanced over his shoulder to Director Simmons struggling against the statue. Fire shot from the woman's mouth and ice frosted at her fingertips as she tried to break free. But nothing was working.

All TJ could do was sigh and say, "I promise we'll come back. Please, please, forgive us."

43

OLOSA'S MESSENGERS

"WE'RE GONNA BE IN *SO* MUCH TROUBLE," MANNY HUFFED AS they careened through the woods and back toward the lagoon.

Ayo, who was already lagging behind, grunted through labored breaths, "TJ, that was... crazy, yo. But... what are we... going to do... now?"

"He's right." Manny kept perfect pace with TJ, who hadn't yet looked back. "We don't have the staff. What's the plan here? Simmons is gonna break free any minute now."

TJ hated to admit it, and he'd hoped he didn't have to confess it to his friends, but it was Mr. Du Bois's class that gave him the idea he prayed would work right then. More than pride though, TJ knew if he told them what he had in mind, they wouldn't be running by his side. As they approached the lagoon, however, he couldn't hide it anymore. Along the banks and spilling out from the treeline was Ol' Sally and a dozen other alligators at her flank.

TJ halted his run and hid behind a mossy rock. Manny dropped at his side and Ayo found a tree to hide behind before saying, "Holy shit... Ol' Sally has kids too?"

"Remember that first week in Du Bois's class?" TJ asked. "He kept going on and on about Olosa and all her attributes. But he kept droning about her messengers."

"Yeah, yeah..." Ayo sighed heavily. "But you do know that offerings are required for them, right? Chickens. Lambs. Goats. We ain't got none of those."

"Plus, we sort of need to consult Eshu before making an offering to another Orisha," Manny added.

"We don't need any of that," TJ said. "Mr. Bolawe was able to speak to her—to Ol' Sally. He convinced her to help him get into the portal."

Manny shook her head. "TJ, this is mad crazy. You could get killed. Ol' Sally swallowed Joshua's body like a grape."

"You remember that first day at camp," he reminded her. "She didn't kill me then, I don't see why she would now. I think she knows there's something special in me, something she recognizes…"

Ayo looked unconvinced. "I don't know, man…"

"Go back to Simmons's office, then." TJ stood up. "I'm not forcing you to be here. But I'm sure as hell not leaving Mr. Bolawe alone to go insane or get killed by those Keepers." He turned to the alligators and raised his voice. "Ol' Sally! It's me, TJ. I'm Ifedayo's brother. The promised child's brother."

In eerie unison, the alligators hissed and twisted their long snouts to TJ. A sharp panic tore through him and he had to remind himself that animals got nervous around fearful humans. So he straightened his back and held his chin high.

Pretending the alligators were puppies or kittens would have to do.

It was either that or die, like Ayo said.

"I'm here to make it right." TJ held his hands to his side passively, that's how all those guys did it on BBC nature videos, after all. "It's my fault your…" What was the right word? "Your… your Orisha got trapped. I wanted to speak to Ifedayo. I didn't think we were summoning Olosa." The first of the smaller alligators came within feet of him. TJ held his breath to settle his nerves. "Please, if there is any way you can help me help Mr. Bolawe, any way we can get to where Olosa lived—"

Mother, let us eat him, a raspy voice rang out in TJ's head. It took him a moment to realize it was one of the alligators who spoke. A brush of wind hit his wrist, and he noticed that one of the alligators was mere inches from his left hand. It took all the little courage he had not to jump and run. *This mortal is unworthy.*

"Holy shit, they talk?" Ayodeji whispered at TJ's back.

A second alligator nudged its nose against TJ's right arm. *Olugbala and his companion already fooled us once. Mortals are only good for deception.*

Olugbala, TJ thought. *The leader of the Keepers? Were they talking about Mr. Du Bois?*

"It wasn't us who did any deceiving." Manny braved a step forward, coming close to TJ's back in support. "It was Eshu. Ol' Sally saw him too. We want him just as bad as you do."

A third alligator came straight up the middle and jabbed at TJ's belly. *What can children do against the Orishas?*

TJ stared down his nose without a twitch. Those razor-sharp teeth could open his stomach like a knife to butter. "You'll find we're full of surprises."

Manny leaned into his ear. "Real smooth, Skywalker."

Give them passage, children, Ol' Sally hissed. Her voice was just as raspy, though with the weight of age behind it.

The two alligators that were rubbing against his arms retreated almost immediately. The last one nuzzling at his belly was not as receptive to orders. It kept sniffing at TJ's neck and blowing air against his face. Every muscle in TJ's body told him he needed to have been running yesterday, weeks ago, yet his mind held strong, and he forced himself to root in the mud.

Desiree, your mother says give them passage. Ol' Sally skulked up to her daughter.

Desiree the alligator took a very long moment to take her first steps back, though not before snapping at TJ's ear. The violent gesture brought a yelp from Manny; TJ stood tall. Were it not for Manny's jump, the alligator might've not been satisfied. But the whimper seemed to satiate whatever fear she was trying to instill. It just seemed like she didn't like the idea of being stood up to by a teenager.

A blast shook the ground suddenly, followed by a distant roar. A woman's roar.

"It sounds like Director Simmons is free," Ayo said nervously.

All around through the trees, hints of red orbs sprang alight: the crimson irises of the statue guards, the crunching of wood, the toppling of trees into the swamps grew louder as the tree guards approached rapidly.

"And here come her minions," Manny said.

TJ turned to Ol' Sally. His entire face was smaller than her left nostril. "Please," he said. "Help us. Tell us what we have to do."

Ol' Sally gave TJ a long and slow blink, then said in his head, *You will have to drown.*

"I'm sorry." Ayo cleaned out his ear with a finger. "Come again? We'll have to... what?"

If alligators could smile, TJ was sure that's what Ol' Sally would've been doing. Her eyes grew wide with clear mirth. *To pass over into the Aqua Realm, mortals must make a sacrifice. You must take my tail, come to the bottom of the lagoon... and drown.*

"Um, Ol' Sally," Manny said shyly. "I don't know if something is missing in translation here between, ya know, us mortals and you... err... immortals. But what you're saying is we have to die. That's what we're sort of trying to avoid here. We're trying to keep our instructor alive."

One who cannot make the sacrifice, cannot cross.

Just past Ol' Sally's head, tiny red lights that had barely been discernible before expanded to the size of tennis balls. They didn't have time, and they didn't have a choice. But TJ wasn't willing to die to go after Mr. Bolawe. He wasn't willing to—

A new thought struck him then.

"Maybe... maybe it's a test?" he murmured, then turned to his friends. "Like in the movies... a test of faith and all that, right? That first night Manny pulled me out, I saw that orb at the bottom of the lagoon. I almost made it on my own. I almost drowned, but it didn't feel like I was going to die... I think."

"Remember how I said giant alligators were my bar," Ayo whimpered. "I lied. Drowning is definitely crossing the line for me. Yep, that's a line I won't cross. Let's just hope Mr. Bolawe can handle whatever is going on in the Aqua Realm or whatever by himself. He's a big boy."

"I don't know, *maybe* TJ's right..." Manny trailed off. "But how can we be sure? A test of faith sounds all fine, but we could... *die.*"

"You two Americans might not understand this." Ayo pushed his glasses up his nose. "But making deals with giant creatures is generally a bad idea. Stories like this are usually, ya know, cautionary tales. Bedtime stories. Right now we're talking about being those kids who die in the cautionary tale."

"Mr. Bolawe trusted Ol' Sally, though..." TJ offered cautiously.

"Mr. Young! Miss Martinez! Mr. Oyelowo!" the Director's voice boomed. "Stop. Right. Now!"

"Go on," TJ said to the alligator, grabbing her tail. "I'm ready."

Manny groaned. "Wait, I'm going with you." She grabbed onto a piece of tail as well. "For the record though, this is *mad* crazy."

"Eh..." Ayo started to say, still standing on the lagoon bank hesitantly.

With a light jerk, TJ and Manny rocked forward, deeper into the lagoon. The first pair of statues broke the treeline on the far end. They roared with an odd grunt that sounded something between a bear and a sick frog.

The sight must've stirred Ayo, 'cause he came running with a yelp. "Wait! Wait for me!"

At Ol' Sally's rate and with Ayo's awkward breaststroke, he wasn't going to catch up. "I swear I better not drown off your goofy ass, TJ." One of the alligators gave Ayo a push as the boy tried for a lumbering doggy paddle. A few awkward strokes later and Ayo was with them.

Then, almost all at once, the statues and living trees converged onto the banks of the swamp as one. They climbed into the waters, even as the top of their branches nearly submerged under the dark currents. Miss Simmons sat atop Monsieur Francois' top branches with her staff held aloft. She looked deranged.

"Sally..." TJ trailed off. "A little speed, please."

Hold on tight, she said.

TJ flipped his head over his shoulder just in time to see Director Simmons cast a spell. A gust of wind that looked like a giant octopus came straight for the back of Ol' Sally's tail. TJ felt the tiny brush of it tickle the tip of his nose just before his body submerged under freezing cold water.

An uncomfortable amount of water drew into his nose and into his chest. He hadn't been ready for the plunge and convulsed against the water filtering through his lungs and up through his throat. He blew it out and concentrated hard.

Despite the flashing lights above of red-spotted death orbs, the underside of the lagoon quickly grew dark. Only the lagoon's current against TJ's ears gave him a sense of space. A soft touch came to TJ's arm, and he knew it was Manny reassuring him she was still there, that she was with him until the end. TJ could only assume Ayo was hanging on for dear life behind them.

His gaze turned back to the surface, yet there was nothing to see but more black. All that was left was his breath and making sure he held it tight.

In his uncle's pool, his record was a full minute. He wondered how long it would take to get to the bottom, or if there even was a bottom where they were going to begin with. TJ considered keeping count of his breath hold, then decided against it. If he knew he was at a minute, that would only freak him out because after a minute... well, he never got to that point before in his life.

The pressure of deep water pressed into TJ's temples, and the first involuntary heave shook his body. His brain wanted air, demanded it. Not a frivolous want but a dire, desperate need.

Believe, TJ, he thought to himself. *Believe.*

What felt like a brief eternity passed by.

C'mon, TJ. Don't you dare take a breath.

Two more moments.

Hold... on.

Three more moments.

Then, it was too much for TJ.

Breathing in water was a hard thing to describe. Not a slight breath of water, but a full one. It's not like taking in a little water because TJ timed his breath at the wrong moment. A full breath of water, completely involuntary, could only be described as one thing: utter terror. That's all. Sheer terror. Uncontrollable. Savage. Raw. And during that moment of complete and total horror, TJ's body gave one last flail, one last instinctual attempt to make way for air. And then...

Everything faded to black.

Nothingness.

Void.

44

WAY DOWN LOW

SACRIFICE.

That was the last thought TJ had before the shadow swallowed him whole.

That's what heroes did, right? It's what Dayo would've done. But TJ wasn't Dayo, and neither were his friends. They weren't heroes, and this wasn't some movie where good guys always won. Everything required a pay-up—especially when a mortal wanted to enter a realm not designed for them.

He thought it was a test; he *really* thought so. But if it wasn't, had he walked his friends to their deaths? Nothing bad was supposed to happen to them—nothing so permanent, at least.

A sickening pain snaked through his stomach.

If this was the afterlife… Manny and Ayo were going to kill him. Again.

Am I really dead, though? TJ thought to himself.

No, child, Ol' Sally's raspy voice replied. *Not yet.*

Then why do I feel… different?

Open your eyes. And you will see.

TJ's eyelids fluttered open to a haze of white. He squinted and rubbed the sides of his head to ease the strain that the violent light was pressing into his irises. Slowly, very slowly, the space formed first into a light blue, then a deep indigo.

Ol' Sally's voice spoke again. *One must sacrifice the surety of life to reach the tallest mountains' peaks or submerge to the oceans' lowest valleys.*

The ocean? TJ thought as his vision continued to focus. Somehow

hearing the word helped him make sense of the picture before him—
a literal underwater light show: Giant plants that looked like mush-
rooms glowed orange under their heads. Seaweed ebbed with the
water's current as they radiated green. And through them, all swam
eels, sharks, and schools of fish, each of them painted in glowing
marks across their tails, fins, and heads.

The visage felt eerily familiar to TJ. He thought back on his
dream and realized he recognized the landscape—the way everything
seemed to glimmer, how each plant's light blended and intensified the
vivid shimmer of the sea creatures, how the rising rocks framed them
all as the craggy rubble reached up to a glass ceiling above with blue
and green streaks.

Welcome to the Planes of the Orishas: The Aqua Realm, young one.

"Where are my friends?" TJ gasped and was shocked to find that
the water he inhaled through his mouth felt like air. And when he
breathed the water back out, vibrant bubbles shot forth.

Your friends are adjusting, as you are. They will find you shortly.

TJ ran his hand over his neck. No gills. He looked to his hands.
No webbed fingers. All the movies he watched told him breathing
underwater meant turning into a half-fish. But everything about him
—everything physical anyway—seemed normal.

You are both human and non-human in this place, Ol' Sally said
again. Above the "glass ceiling" swam the silhouetted body of the
giant alligator. *In this place, you will find strength you do not know in your
world.*

As TJ continued gasping in water like he was letting in fresh air,
an energy ran through him from the top of his head to the bottom of
his toes. Ol' Sally was right. Ashe came easy in this new place. Where
before he was exhausted, now he felt... whole. But not whole in the
same way he did when waking from a nap or having a good meal. It
was his spirit, his Ashe, that felt full, more complete than it ever did
before.

A shiver raced down his chest. Could this really be happening?
Didn't everyone say the connection between diviners and the Orishas
had been severed? Why was he able to cross over? He didn't have
Joshua—Eshu—to transport him. He didn't have Mr. Du Bois's
magic to hold open portals. He was just a teenager, only *barely*
passing his classes in remedial magic camp.

What made him so special?

What made him deserve this?

"TJ, over here!" Manny shouted. Relief rushed over TJ as he

watched her swim through a pack of catfish. Her mass of hair looked like packed seaweed as it billowed around her head.

Just to her right, near a jagged outcropping housing tiny octopuses, came Ayo. "Yo, Manny, is that you?"

"Swim up to me!" TJ called to them. "Just up here, near the surface. You see? Ol' Sally is just on the other side of this… this…" He gazed back up at the giant alligator. "Why are we separated? Where are you?"

Ol' Sally nuzzled the water below her. Again, it rippled at her touch. *I am still in Olosa's Lagoon. I cannot pass over without her. You will have to go alone, children.*

"So we're technically under the camp then?" Ayo asked as he approached, floating next to TJ. The boy couldn't stop gaping at every glowing shark or eel that passed by.

Correct. You now travel through spiritual ley lines adjacent to your world.

"Ley lines?" Manny questioned, then turned to her friends. "Like the points for travel portals?"

Yes. And the Gatekeeper is using them as well. He and the mortal are going after Olokun in his mid-Atlantic fortress. They mean to free him.

"That doesn't sound so bad." Manny shrugged. "Aren't we trying to free Olosa from Eshu's staff?"

Ol' Sally shook her head. *The Great Monarch put Olokun in his place for a reason. If he is freed, it will unleash his centuries-old anger… and he is no lover of clouded mortals as of late.*

TJ gulped. Mr. Bolawe was going to be in a lot of trouble if they didn't catch up soon. "How do we find Olokun and the other… erm… mortals."

You must follow the path through the graveyard of ships, along the Great Rift, and then into the depths of the Endless Darkness. There you will find Olokun's fortress.

"I don't suppose you can draw us a map, can you?" Ayo asked, his voice joking, though the slight choke in his throat made it clear how nervous he was. "I always get mixed up between the creepy graveyards and the great darknesses whenever I come through here."

The child will be your beacon. Ol' Sally nodded to TJ, and in that moment, he felt something in his chest direct him out along the rocky ridge where the ocean grew dark. *Make haste, young mortals. Your minds do not hold well in this realm. In the past, many of your kind have tried to journey through our home, only to be forever lost. If you are swift, you may yet stop this and return my maiden to her dominion.*

TJ nodded, steeling up courage in his chest. "Thanks, Sally. You can count on us." He tapped Ayo and Manny on their shoulders. "C'mon, Mr. Bolawe's gonna need our help."

And with that, TJ swam off into the blue where he thought he could make out a dark mass in the far distance. Behind him, Ayo cried out, "And who's going to help *us*!*?*"

✝

TJ NEVER THOUGHT HIMSELF A STRONG SWIMMER. WHEN HE TOLD Dad he wanted to be a Navy SEAL, his old man laughed and said TJ swam like an old, injured dog. Swimming through the realm of the Orishas, however, was like being an Olympic athlete. More than that even—right now, he felt more like a straight-up fish, a dolphin through the break. He, Manny, and Ayo glided through coral reefs, sea ferns, and giant clams with such speed, even the sharks that took an interest in them couldn't keep up.

TJ didn't know how he knew where to go, but his gut was as sure as it ever had been. It was like his chest was being pulled on a line, even as they dipped between confusing rock faces and rainbow-colored reefs.

"You know," Ayo said as he ducked between two leaning rock structures, "this would be nearly impossible to get through if everything wasn't glowing like this. We wouldn't be able to see nothin'."

Manny shot through the gap. "Antonia and Andressa won't believe me when I tell them I was here."

"Who?" Ayo asked.

"The twins."

"Wait, the Santos Sisters *actually* have names?" Ayo exclaimed. "Shooooot, you can try and tell them all you want, but the way I see it, we'd be lucky if we make it back in body bags at this point."

"We will," TJ grunted as he dashed ahead of them, narrowly avoiding a clam that tried to make him its snack. "We're going to make it. Bodies and all."

While Manny and Ayo slowed intermittently to stare at gleaming jellyfish, or what Manny swore was a mermaid, or what Ayo swore was a giant sea snake, TJ never decelerated, yelling, "hurry up, you two" whenever they showed signs of slowing.

After a while, though, he wasn't so sure they were swimming in the right direction. The rock structures and reefs receded far, far behind them, expanding out to a vast landscape of nothing but dark sand. Then, a tiny wave rolled around TJ's body, sending a chill down his neck and all the way to his fingers... his *tingling* fingers. And, suddenly, he knew they were headed the right way.

"The ship graveyard should be coming up soon," he said.

"How do you know?" Ayo asked. "Ol' Sally didn't really give us any concrete directions, just vague mumbo jumbo about rifts and graveyards and you being a beacon."

TJ narrowed his eyes. He couldn't see it, but he knew a deep valley was approaching. "I don't know. I can feel it, though. There's something just over that ridge."

"What ridge?" Ayo complained. "I can't see nothin'."

As TJ approached the rocky rim that he couldn't see but still knew was there, his gaze settled along a valley littered with sunken ships: miles and miles of dead sea vessels. Unlike the stretch of ocean they had come from, here it was devoid of light, everything shrouded under the muted grays of colorless and splintering wood.

But the collection of tattered ships was not the largest draw. Instead, everyone's eyes drew to a gigantic humanoid figure swimming between the ships like a vast shadow.

Nearly half the size of one of the fallen ships, the Orisha stirred fear within TJ with the eerie way she drifted through the ocean depths like a dark specter.

Quickly, TJ hid at the valley's edge near a collection of uplifted rocks, beckoning to the others to follow. He hung on to the rock structure so tightly, he thought his hands would bleed. He couldn't believe what he was seeing.

The Orisha dipped in and out of cracked decks and fallen masts with casual grace. Each time she entered one of the great barnacled carcasses, there was an immense, horrible sucking sound followed by an ever greater exhale. As she passed between the few slivers of light cast from stray glowing seaweed pressed tightly between the ships, or a lone glowing whale or squid, TJ could make out her attire: a thin crown that looked like sharp branches from a pink tree or thorn bush. Each branch was tied with wilted flowers. Only the pink and burgundy roses bloomed brightly. The whole thing came down around her eyes. The train of her fuchsia dress ran so long it didn't look like she had any legs as she glided through the graveyard.

"What the hell is that damn sound?" Ayo floated next to TJ, making sure he was fully hidden behind the rocks in fear. "Is someone tryin' to find the bottom of a milkshake down there?"

"Something like that," Manny replied, her skin paling as her voice quivered. "Look."

She pointed a shaky hand to the latest ship the Orisha had just emerged from. This time, TJ could see a corpse in her hand. She drew the body to her mouth and began that horrific sucking. The rotting skin came away like strips of chicken from the bone, flowing straight into the Orisha's mouth.

"Yewa..." TJ murmured, his insides turning. The same Orisha Adeola referred to at the funeral, the same one whose mask Mr. Du Bois had. They must've been on a first-name basis with the deity, and TJ had the suspicion that Adeola and Du Bois got a free pass through the graveyard. A pass he, Manny, and Ayo weren't privileged enough to share.

"Yewa?" Manny asked once she mustered the courage to do so. "The Overseer of Cadavers?"

"What? *That's* her?" Ayo whispered frantically. "Ain't no one at Ifa or Camp Olosa say nothin' about her eating flesh like that."

"Anyone got any virgin fruit to give her as an offering," Manny joked through a trembling voice.

TJ shrugged. "I guess it's like Joshua said, right? We don't know as much as we think we do about the Orishas, diviner kids *or* adults. I mean, the teachers say she watches over corpses until they are transferred to Oya, yeah?" His eyes drifted back in Yewa's direction. "They just don't know what she does with them in the meantime. Eesh, I hope they don't know anyway..."

"So what are we going to do?" Manny asked, swallowing hard.

Ayo sucked his teeth. "I'm sure as hell not going through those ships while Yewa's over there suckin' faces."

"We don't have a choice." TJ tried to shrug and pretend he was braver than he felt. "This valley is too wide. We have no idea how long it'll take to get around. We gotta go straight through." Ayo gave TJ a look of total horror. "We can do it. There are plenty of ships to hide between. As long as we stick tight together, we can watch out for each other." Ayo groaned; TJ rolled his eyes. "Fine, stay here."

TJ pushed himself off the edge of the ridge and torpedoed toward the first set of dilapidated ships, trying his best to ignore his pounding heart.

45

A GRAVEYARD OF SHIPS

THE GRAVEYARD OF SHIPS WENT ON AND ON, AN ENDLESS EXPANSE of rot and ruin. After passing the first hundred vessels, TJ realized most of them had been slave ships. The *São José, Hermosa, Leusden,* and *Henrietta Marie* were a few he recognized by name thanks to one of Tunde's favorite rap songs—TJ remembered it because the artist spent a full minute listing off slave ships. But among the old vessels were newer models as well: slick, fancy yachts and modern military frigates alike.

"Are we swimming through the Atlantic? The Middle Passage?" Manny asked TJ as they passed under the shadow of a warship. "Some of these ship names are—"

"Yeah, I know," TJ finished for her. They shared a knowing look. "This is nuts. But Ol' Sally said this isn't our world, yet it *is* our world. One that looks like ours just flipped around and, well, all glowy and stuff."

He nudged his head to a boat that looked like a whisk basket with sails. "My mom showed me that one in a book about this dude named Mansa Musa. Apparently, his uncle or whatever tried to sail West before even Columbus did. I guess we know what happened to him and his crew now. They all crossed over here because they, well... drowned. Like we drowned."

"Wait, so we *are* dead?"

"No," TJ answered quickly. "Ol' Sally said we're just... different."

Ayo smacked his teeth from behind them. Far behind them. "Can y'all slow down for a dude? This shit's confusing enough already without y'all slipping into places you know damn well I can't fit through."

A screech ripped over them, and a shock wave expanded overhead from the direction they had come from.

Manny shuddered. "What in the hell was that?"

A second howl bellowed.

"Damn." Ayo covered his ears. The third shriek was directed straight at them. "Deadass, that's louder than a mother—"

TJ shot out his hands at Ayo. "Stop, wait! Don't talk. Stop cussin' like that."

"What I said wasn't real cussin'? And I didn't say f—"

"TJ's right," Manny said, catching on. "Yewa... She's a maiden of modesty or whatever, right? She don't like bad language."

TJ nodded, then whispered, "Right. Until we make it out of this graveyard, let's talk like our parents are here with us."

Ayo mumbled something under his breath, and the fourth and loudest bark ripped over them.

"Ayo!" TJ and Manny shouted in unison.

"What!? I didn't think she'd hear me!"

Behind Ayo, a tidal wave of ships lifted with a fierce jolt, lurching up in the water, their masts speared high above them in a crescendo and crashed down like an avalanche.

TJ pushed Manny forward, then grabbed Ayo by the arm. "C'mon, move!"

They rushed behind Manny as ships collapsed around them in slow motion.

"Ah!" Ayo shouted as his silver chain got caught in a rock face. "I'm too young to die!"

"Manny!" TJ shouted ahead. "Head inside that big black submarine over there. We just gotta wait Yewa out, then slip away again."

Manny peeled off to the dark submarine lodged between a cluster of barnacles. Once she dipped into the nearest hatch, TJ kicked his feet hard to spin around to Ayo. With his hand outstretched, summoning his Ashe, a slice of water splintered from his fingers with such force it blew his arm back with shocking recoil. The end of his water line split through Ayo's chain, snapping it.

"That chain was Hermès limited edition!" Ayo cried.

"Thank me later." TJ shook his head and hoped Ayo could keep up. After a dozen strong strokes between falling ships, he passed into the bowels of the submarine.

A large and low *boom* sounded from behind.

"Yo, yo! I'm stuck again!" Ayo shouted from behind.

Is it a designer watch this time? TJ thought bitterly as he turned around to see Ayo struggling against an old rudder that had him pinned against a massive rock. Turning, TJ looked for Manny to help him, but she wasn't there.

"Manny!" he hollered.

Nothing but his own echo came in answer. There wasn't time to go looking for her. Who knew how deep the submarine went or how hard it'd be to hear his voice through the tight corridors?

TJ groaned and flipped back toward Ayo. "Hang on, man."

Thrusting his arms ahead of him, TJ gathered his Ashe into his belly. Just like that first day at camp, he thought of the lesson Mr. Bolawe had taught them about parting duckweed. This was the same, right? Just bigger. A lot bigger. Except at that moment, TJ's pool of Ashe was much larger, just as Ol' Sally said: *In this place, you will find strength you do not know in your world.*

"*Gbè òmi lọ,*" TJ recited with vigor.

Even before the last word was out, a bubble the size of a car swelled and pushed the old rudder away from Ayo. It crashed and crumbled against a cliffside, where little crabs scurried away to avoid the impact.

Ayo, now free, rushed for TJ, saying a quick "thank you" before brushing past him and into the safety of the submarine.

A great screech waved across the graveyard of ships, and a thorn crown crested the horizon of the still crashing vessels. It was the giant bright white holes for eyes that made TJ scream louder than he thought he ever could. Yewa looked massive at a distance. At that moment, however, merely a football field away... she put even Ol' Sally to shame.

"Move your ass, TJ!" Ayo called out ahead of him.

Another screech from Yewa blared, unabated by distance, which sent utter fear through TJ's bones.

TJ spun around and followed Ayo inside. The hatch behind them was as heavy as an elephant, but they pulled with all their might. Just as they got it to swing inward, he saw Yewa push ships aside like they were no more hefty than bags of rice. Just before the door closed, TJ locked eyes with her—if he could call those white, radiating irises eyes—and shuddered as the hatch slammed shut.

A chill sliced through TJ. His muscles tensed as he waited for the submarine walls to cave in from some thrown ship or a giant, raking hand.

But no impact ever came.

They were just left to the dark of the submarine.

That was close, he thought. *Too close.*

Ayo groaned at TJ's side. TJ snapped his fingers to light a fire; then, he saw the boy rubbing at his leg as he leaned against the submarine wall. "Yo, when did you start doing magic like *that*? That was better than anything I've seen, like... *ever*."

"Ol' Sally told me in this realm our Ashe is more powerful," TJ explained. "You can do it too."

"Homie, you didn't think I was trying to get that big a—" TJ gave him a look. "That *big ol'* thing off me? My Ashe didn't get no boost. Nada. Squat." Ayo shook his head. "Where's Manny, anyway?"

TJ peered down the dark corridors. "She probably went down this way. Let's go find her."

They surged through the old submarine, using the grooves and pipes jutting from the sides to pull them along like they were in a space station instead of an underwater boat. It only took a few moments for them to round the corner to the submarine's bridge, where light inflections of sobs and sniffling were echoing down the corridors.

The space was small, buttons and switches stretched across the wall, and seaweed grew between every control panel. A large viewport stretched from wall to wall, showing the graveyard of ships outside. The light from it spilled gently into the room, revealing Manny slumped over the captain's chair, crying into her forearm. Ahead of her loomed a ghostly image of a young woman who looked almost like her—except for a lighter complexion, sharper jaw, and less matted, wavier hair. But the thick eyebrows, the wide mouth, and the long neck were unmistakable. Whoever she was, she was related to Manny.

"You messed up, Manuela," the figure said in the same accent Manny had. "With everything that's happened. Everything your family has done for you, and you can't even take a chance. You want to know why you're so scared? Because you know you'll fail, just like your *papai* failed, just like your *mamãe* failed. That's all your family knows how to do."

Manny cried. "No, that's not true. You're lying."

"If I'm lying, then why did you leave, huh? Why did you leave me?"

"Manny, who is that?" TJ asked, but Manny didn't seem to hear him. The young woman utterly transfixed her. No, not a woman. A teenager. Barely older than they were.

TJ pushed forward, but Ayo pulled him back. "Don't go over there, man. This looks like a curse. The entire room, probably."

"I can't just leave her alone." TJ shoved him off. "I think... I think that might be her cousin."

Ayo's eyebrow flipped up. "Cousin?"

"Long story. Just..." TJ turned to Manny and the young woman. "Just pull me back or something if I get all messed up or whatever."

TJ swam forward, reaching for Manny, but he barely got two strokes into the room before his sister materialized in front of him. His heart stopped, and he whispered, "Dayo? Is that really you this time?"

"Yes, it's me... you worthless little weirdo."

TJ jerked back. He knew this wasn't right. He knew Dayo would never say a thing like that to him. But something unnatural curling through him made him believe the words. Something deep down chewed away at his heart.

"Why are you wasting Mom and Dad's money? You let them sell everything just so you can—"

"I didn't. I told Mom I didn't want to go—"

"Be quiet and listen for a change!" Dayo shouted him down. No, not Dayo. TJ had to remember that this wasn't Dayo. It was some sort of illusion, some trick. It didn't matter, though. It didn't matter what was true or false. The words hurt him all the same.

"You always wanted to be just like me," she rasped. "But how could you? How could you ever measure up to Ifedayo Young? You're nothing. Less than nothing. Just a pathetic little boy with no backbone. Oh? You're going to cry now?" TJ didn't even realize tears were floating from his eyes near his cheeks. "Oh no, don't wipe them away. Let us all see how worthless you really are. You think Manny likes you? She just feels sorry for you. And Ayo? You think he's changed? You should hear the things he says behind your back."

"That's not true, man," Ayo's voice came from behind, though it was barely above a murmur. Far off. Distorted. "I mean... yeah, sometimes I gotta keep up appearances with LaVont and Jimoh—"

"You're nothing, Tomori Jomiloju," Dayo hissed, her teeth baring like fangs. "Nothing!"

TJ realized he was on his knees. How had that happened? When had he slumped over the rusty old control panel?

"Seriously, dude. Don't listen to her," Ayo's voice went on. "Like I said, I was *way* out of pocket about your sister at camp. And yeah, you're different... So what? You should own it."

Own it... TJ thought, and the image of Mr. Bolawe sprang to mind.

"*I don't want you to say it,*" the man had said. "*I want you to own it.*"

But he couldn't. TJ couldn't own it. His sister was right. There was a reason she hadn't come back home for three years. He didn't matter to her anymore. He never mattered.

"That dorky stuff you're into..." Ayo's voice came again. "That stuff you talk about with Manny. I mean, I don't understand it, but that's you, man. That's you stayin' in your lane."

Dayo hissed, "You know nothing about who you are, Tomori."

Ayo's tone tightened. "None of us know who we are, bro. You just gotta... be who you are. That's all you gotta do."

Be who I am... TJ thought. Now the image of Mom came to him.

"*Tomori, be secure in who you are,*" she had told him. "*Envy no one.*"

But his faux sister said the opposite. "Worthless. Foolish. Meaningless. Weak. No backbone."

TJ swallowed hard. He didn't know who to believe.

"Listen, man. It's Yewa messing with you and Manny," Ayo explained. This time his voice came clearer, more resolute. "Don't listen to that illusion. You a real one, dude. Dedicated to who you are. That's what I like about you. And you mean a lot to a lot of people. I can actually be myself around you."

The image of Dayo gave TJ a wicked smile. "Go ahead, just cry and give up. You're good at doing that."

TJ felt his body slump, but something deep within held him firm before the fall.

"No, you're wrong," he told his sister. "I matter. Everybody does. We just need some help sometimes. It's like Mr. Bolawe said. The book hasn't been written for me yet."

He lifted himself upright, felt the pressure of the water pressing against his skin...

That's right! He was in the submarine. He was with his friends. He was going to save Mr. Bolawe.

Slowly, Dayo's wispy form started to dissipate.

"You can't hurt me," TJ went on. "You're not real. And even if you were, you don't know me anymore, Dayo. You don't know what

I've gone through this summer—through all those years you were gone."

Dayo's doppelganger was nearly gone now. Barely a ghostly visage.

"I'm going to help Manny, and then we're all going to save Mr. Bolawe. And I'm going to find out what happened to you, too. Nothing's going to stop that. Not even the power of the Orishas."

And then she was no more.

A brief silence cut through the submarine bridge before Ayo said, "Dang, bruh. I didn't think that was *actually* gonna work."

A pair of sniffles brought their attention back to Manny and her ghostly cousin. TJ rushed over to them, but his nose smashed into an invisible barrier.

"Same thing happened to me." Ayo pointed to his silver-rimmed glasses. The left lens had a crack in it. "It's Yewa's curse. Playing tricks with... with the dead."

"Why didn't you get affected...?"

Ayo ignored the question. "You just gotta talk to her. Talk to Manny. You'll do a better job than me."

TJ nodded, then glanced back to Manny. He couldn't see her face. Her head was still embedded into her forearm like it was glued there. She kept saying, "I'm sorry, Jessie. I'm so sorry."

TJ cupped his hands around his mouth. "Listen to me, Manny. I know what you're going through. Don't listen to Yewa. You're the best person I know. You haven't failed us. You haven't failed anyone. You've been helping me with giant alligators and missing elders all summer. You didn't have to do any of that."

"Yeah," Ayo added. "You could've left him alone like I told you to that day in the library. But you stuck with him. If that's not loyalty, I don't know what is."

Manny's sniffling stopped, and the edge of her eyes peeked from under her forearm. But she didn't seem to know where she was or where TJ's and Ayo's voices were coming from.

"I couldn't have done any of this without you, Manny," TJ continued, his voice low and earnest. "Forget what Jessie is telling you. That's not your cousin. She's not real. I know if you guys were close, then she would know how amazing you are. You're talented, and you're kind, and you're my friend. Your cousin wouldn't say any of that stuff. Yewa is saying all that for her. And Yewa doesn't know shit about you."

"Language..." Ayo murmured, looking around nervously.

"No, I don't care. Do you hear me, Yewa? You don't know anything about Manny. But I do. And I *know* she can fight through this." TJ floated lower and turned his voice to Manny. "Come on. You can do it."

Just as Dayo had disappeared before, so too did Manny's cousin. It was slow, and Jessie kept hissing insults of "failure and two-faced," but eventually, she drifted away into the waters like sand pulled from a beach.

TJ stuck his hand out; the barrier was gone.

He rushed over to Manny and hugged her tight. She wrapped her arms around him too. "Thank you, TJ," she said into his shoulder.

"Don't mention it. You'd do the same for me."

"Guys!" Ayo called from behind. "I'm seriously not trying to ruin the moment, for real, for real. It's a beautiful thing—but there is a giant face looking at y'all right now."

TJ and Manny lifted their heads from each other's shoulders to glance at what Ayo described. And sure enough, a pair of very large eyes—enormous white orbs with no pupils—were staring straight at them from just outside the submarine viewport.

"There are very few mortals who can break my illusions," Yewa said with an ethereal yet husky voice. "Especially ones so young. Is Eshu aiding you as well? Is he there with you?"

TJ bit his lip, that tiny throb of betrayal resurfacing on his lips in a scowl. "No, no, he's not," he gritted. "We're looking for him, though. Ol' Sally—I mean—Olosa's messenger told us he's after Olokun. We're trying to stop him and the mortals who are with him."

"You're trying to *stop* that scheming fool?" Her brow lifted her pink crown up her forehead. "Why didn't you just ask me to pass? I thought you were Eshu and that mortal Olugbala coming through again."

TJ did an internal facepalm. They could just ask? Then he remembered how Yewa was sucking flesh from bones. No one sane would go up to someone doing that and ask for help. Still, slight pangs of embarrassment laced through him, and he avoided his friends' eye contact.

"Olugbala?" Manny questioned. "Who's that?"

"The leader of the Keepers," Ayo explained. "He's the 'Savior of the Diviners.' At least that's what all his followers say."

"You young ones seem ill-prepared," Yewa intoned. "I can transport you back to where you came from. Eshu and Olugbala will be far more a challenge than I was to you—hold on. You, young mortal. I am familiar with your energy." Yewa's gaze focused on TJ.

"Trust me, this is the first time we've met."

"No… no. You are the oddly familiar energy that crossed over not too long ago. The one who connected."

TJ recalled that word "connected." That's what Mr. Bolawe and Elder Adeyemi said to him after he came too at Dayo's funeral. So those shadowy figures were… other Orishas?

"Come with us, Yewa," Manny suggested. "We could stop Olokun from getting free if we squad up."

Yewa shook her huge head, long and slow. "No Orisha has been permitted entrance to Olokun's Domain since he was set there by Olodumare. Eshu can pass because he is the gatekeeper, but I and the others cannot. If you leave now, young ones, you may be able to *convince* them to stop. But to stop them outright—with force—is a fool's gambit."

"But you said that Olodumare set him there," Ayo countered. "He's the most powerful Orisha, right? How can someone break a bond like that?"

"There *are* ways… Though, they'd take time. Five chains bind Olokun to his domain. One for each limb and another for his neck. To break even one chain would take at least three Orishas, and—"

"They have three Orishas," TJ said, fear slicing through him at the thought.

Yewa's eye quirked. "Pardon me?"

"They have Eshu, Olokun… and they have Olosa. It's a long story. Partly my fault. But she's stuck in Eshu's staff."

Yewa fell suddenly very quiet—her face seemingly turning to stone.

"Uh oh…" Ayo trailed off. "You know it's bad when an Orisha is lost for words."

"Young mortals, you must go now," she said darkly. "The Great Rift is merely two leagues east and north of here. But I'm afraid you may already be too late."

46

WRATH IN THE DEEP

TJ, MANNY, AND AYO DARTED THROUGH THE LAST OF THE SHIP graveyard so quickly that TJ hoped there wasn't a police system in the Aqua Realm—because they'd definitely be breaking speed limits.

Yewa made it very clear that Eshu and the Keepers had just enough power to free Olokun. TJ tried to calculate how much time it had been since Eshu dived into the portal and how long it would take for them to catch up. Yewa couldn't give them an exact figure, but TJ reckoned Eshu had to have broken at least half of Olokun's binds by now.

"You know, maybe it's not so bad if Olokun is free," Ayo said as they rushed over an open area of sea kelp fields. "I mean, that's kind of messed up being locked down there that long."

"He deserved to be locked up there," Manny shot back. "He tried to drown humanity with the ocean! He'll just try it again like before."

Ayo did a backstroke and shrugged. "Maybe he's changed his ways. That's what jail is supposed to be for, right? To rethink your wrongs?"

"More like… let your hate fester," TJ replied darkly. "Most dudes who come out of jail don't come out rehabilitated. They just fall back into what they was doin' before. Or worse. I got an uncle like that. You know, the kind of uncle you don't talk about."

"And if Olokun's been alone all this time," Manny added, "he won't be in no good mood."

"All right, all right, forget I said anything, just trying to be an optimist here."

"Ayodeji, an optimist?" TJ cracked his first smile since they got there. "Man, you've been hanging out with us too much."

"Pfft, I'm *always* positive. Look here... we're doing pretty great!" Ayo said sarcastically as they passed into the valley of the deep rift. "Joshua turns out to be Eshu hiding in a kid's body, Director Simmons is pissed at us, we survived a flesh-eating Orisha, and now we're headed for one of the most powerful water deities there is. Why would I want to be anywhere else?"

Manny chuckled, and TJ couldn't help joining her. It was nice, the laughter. It almost helped TJ forget that they were gliding deeper and deeper into a darkness that could've birthed any number of dangers.

"I don't know how we're supposed to leave when we're done here, though," Manny said, her tone turning serious.

"Once we come back with Olosa, Yewa can show us the way back." Or at least TJ hoped.

He pushed along a craggy wall traced with white glowing lines. The markings stretched down the dark basin, almost as a guide to where they needed to go. After a time, however, the radiant carvings look less like guiding arrows and more like scars. Deep ones that pulsated subtly with white light.

"Scorch marks." Ayo ran his hand over one of the deeper craters. "This is big-big spell work."

Manny touched it too. "How can you tell?"

"Manifested Ashe has certain properties. Look here. Only a curse could've created this spiral design."

Swimming ahead, TJ stopped at a fork in the deep valley where the largest wound left on the rocks was revealed. Like the others, the marks throbbed with a bright hue of white. TJ brushed his hands over the great cavity. An atomic bomb must have hit it, it was that large.

As the craggy surface prickled under TJ's touch, a whisper trilled in his ear. And the impressions of a voice followed it. He couldn't discern the words—if he could even call the stream of whistles real speech at all—but he knew it was his sister this time. Not Olosa. Not anyone or any*thing* else. It was the same sensation he had felt at the start of the summer back in Dayo's room. He was sure of it. He couldn't begin to work out why he'd thought the illusion in the submarine was really her, especially now when he was so certain.

"How old do you think these are?" TJ asked, hoping Ayo would say the carvings were no more than a few months old... young enough to line up with his sister's death.

Ayo and Manny swam to TJ's side and stared up at the gaping hole with him. Then Ayo sighed. "I can't be sure, but... these seem extremely old. You can tell because of how dull the scorch marks are. A huge battle went down here, for sure."

Manny gasped. "Oh shoot. You don't think this is where Olokun fought with Olodumare, do you?"

"Makes sense. We're headed for Olokun's fortress. These markings are what was left over, I guess."

Despite dashed hopes, TJ didn't feel down on himself. Answers were coming, and they were coming soon. But he did have one inquiry. "I didn't know spells left marks like this."

"Most don't." Ayo swam up the length of the scar to touch more of it. "Well, none do, really. Only spell work from the Orishas could do something like this. But even then, those would have disappeared. There's only one Orisha I know whose mark could last this long: the Great Monarch himself. There ain't a lot of times in the Orishas' history where he has shown his full power like this. This fight must've been *crazy* savage."

At Ayo's words, a hollowed shriek stretched from the abyss of the valley's great wound. Ice trickled through TJ's legs, his chest, his head. Whatever waited for them at the end of the hole wasn't anything to play with. If Olodumare had this much trouble simply chaining Olokun up, what in the world were *they* going to do to keep him there?

TJ clenched a fist. They would do it because they had him, he decided. Ol' Sally was right. He was more powerful in this place. Yewa and his friends could attest to that. And now Olokun would know it too.

But most of all, TJ was looking forward to making that known to the Keepers and Eshu.

"Let's go," he told the others, gliding forward. "It's time to show the Keepers and these Orishas what we're made of."

☩

THE JOURNEY THROUGH THE TUNNEL WASN'T LONG ENOUGH FOR TJ to steel his nerves, especially with more and more spell wounds etched across the cavern wall. As a clearing opened up before him and the others, he felt extremely small in the face of the splendor ahead:

A fortress that dwarfed the tallest skyscrapers on Earth.

A fortress designed for giants.

It was unlike any structure built by humankind. Instead of sand-stone or concrete walls, giant clams slatted atop one another to create the peaks of several towers. Sea kelp snaked around the edges of the clam-wall, swallowing the structure's foundation in their eerie ebb as they spiraled up each of the towers. And were it not for the amber hue spreading across the fortress from the lava moat surrounding it, the whole space would've been shrouded in black.

"Who needs a lava moat around an underwater fortress?" Manny asked jokingly. "How does that even work?"

"Magic, Manny," Ayo answered. "Magic."

Like the path leading to Olokun's Domain, the fortress itself told a story of battle: Several white-streaked columns upholding its left side had been blown out. The remainder splayed out near the grand moat, suffering beneath their burden.

As per the usual since they had arrived in this strange world, TJ pushed forward, leaving Manny and Ayo to follow. He was glad to hear nothing from them. No complaint from Ayo or furtive gasp from Manny. It meant they were focused on what they were about to do.

Or perhaps they were simply like him, scared into silence and faking it until they made it.

Swimming over the moat, its heat licking at his chest, TJ kept his eyes intent on a gaping hole ahead where the fortress' main entrance must've been once. Above it rested a crumbling raised portcullis, its pointed spikes like teeth ready to sink into his back as he passed through its threshold.

"You know," Ayo said. "When passing an entrance like this, I would normally make a short prayer to Eshu—Master of Thresholds and all that, but... I don't know how I feel about that right now."

The shakiness in his voice was undeniable, no matter how much he tried to cloak it. TJ didn't comment on it, though. Ayo was there with them instead of with Yewa or Ol' Sally. No need to make light of his very understandable jitters.

Streams of gentle blue light spotlighted the grand foyer as they entered the fortress. It was clear the place was meant to house the Orishas themselves. To either side of the room rested lounging couches embedded into clams the size of large boats. A grand stair-case sat at the room's center, leading up so high that TJ had to crane his neck to see where it ended. At the very top, a pair of jellyfish had a figure wrapped between their tentacles—a figure that looked very much like a man wearing a Camp Olosa dashiki.

"Mr. Bolawe!" TJ propelled himself forward like a torpedo.

As he ascended the mountain of a staircase, he noticed more scorch marks of green and red cut between the starfish and shells bedecking the banister. The higher he climbed, the more frequent the damage showed itself along the grand steps. They started as mere marks, no more than a blemish to the Orishas' colossal halls, but quickly the light scoring turned into full-on devastation. Halfway up, an entire section of the stairs had been blown through, its edges still simmering with red.

TJ rushed past it all, doing his best to suppress the worry that threatened to take him. What were those jellyfish doing? And where were the other adults?

When they were only fifty yards away, TJ called out to his friends. "I'm gonna need your help. Ayo, go for the jellyfish on the left. Manny, focus on the one to the—"

TJ halted his forward rush so quickly, Manny nearly tumbled into his back. The man held between the jellyfish wasn't Mr. Bolawe.

It was Mr. Du Bois.

TJ stared at the man in horror. Their instructor's face was one of the most grotesque images TJ had ever witnessed. Mounds of black and blue bruises the size of golf balls peppered his forehead where his brow should've been. His lips had ballooned as well, like he had been trying to blow a trumpet and got stuck puckering. TJ didn't like the man, perhaps even hated him at that point, yet he didn't want to see him disfigured like that. It felt wrong. It made his stomach twist into itself.

"Ò je ẹlẹtàn," Mr. Du Bois murmured once, twice, thrice. "Ò je ẹlẹtàn."

He was speaking in Yoruba. Even if he weren't speaking through sausage lips, TJ probably wouldn't understand him. So, in his own murmur, he asked Ayo, "What's he saying?"

"'Traitor. Traitor.'" Ayo repeated. "'He is a traitor.' No, 'she is a traitor.' I can't tell without more context. He's just repeating the same thing."

"Who's he talking about?" TJ asked but quickly realized Ayo wouldn't know. So he directed his question to Mr. Du Bois. "Who are you talking about? Huh?"

Despite his consistent repeat of the phrase he seemed obsessed with, Mr. Du Bois's puffy eyes were dead. TJ wasn't even sure the man was aware they were there. Some "Savior of Diviners" he was.

Two resounding booms echoed from deeper in the fortress.

"Let's leave him," Manny told them. "It sounds like Mr. Bolawe's still putting up a fight." Her words had added weight as she nodded to Mr. Du Bois.

Ayo hummed under his lips. "Dang, Bolawe put in work on Du Bois's face. I didn't think he had it in him."

It didn't even occur to TJ that it would have been Mr. Bolawe who did all that to Mr. Du Bois. But it made sense. He was sure he had no other choice, especially when two Keepers and an Orisha outnumbered him. Still, even as he swam off down the long and wide corridors, TJ couldn't help taking several glances over his shoulder to Du Bois's face.

Were it not for the sounds of a vicious fight ahead, he might've kept looking.

And so they chased the battle's staccato melody of spell against spell through enormous halls, grandiose libraries, treacherous bridges, and finally the monumental keep. TJ was first through its wide arches, through the throne room's majestic door frame.

Three silhouettes crossed over the backdrop of a cracked wall with lava sloughing over it. The first silhouette was easy to pick out —large, steady, and with flowing hair that went down his back, was Olokun himself: obsidian skin, flowing long hair, shirtless with muscles built on muscles. He looked like some sort of supervillain the way he floated there in the water with crossed arms, and his heels snapped together above his whale skull throne.

A single chain tethered around his neck remained.

The other four had already fallen to the floor.

He was nearly free…

On Olokun's left, Adeola drifted in her long robes, spinning her staff overhead in a series of sparks that pinwheeled toward the last silhouette on the far right: Mr. Bolawe, who had his own staff lifted aloft in defensive posturing.

Their spellcasting was so wild, TJ and the others had to swim up to cover behind the tall pillars just to stay out of harm's way. But even then, their security wasn't a sure thing.

"Where's Eshu?" Manny asked from TJ's side as he ducked under a spell that looked like a shooting star.

A series of mumbles sounded below them from the throne room's cracked floor. They each gazed to the center of the room, where Eshu wiggled in a set of chains. He sat inside a giant clam with a pearl stuck in his mouth, which muted his annoyed outcries. Mr. Bolawe must've trapped him and gagged him for good order. The trickster Orisha got what he deserved, as far as TJ was concerned.

"Not so bad," Ayo said shakily, sucking in his gut so he wouldn't get hit by a streak of lightning that passed by. "One Orisha down. And Olokun is still chained. Well, *barely* chained."

Somehow, TJ only *then* noticed the difference in size between Eshu and Olokun, as though his sense of scale was warped somehow by the magic of the Orisha Plane, or maybe just by the sheer size of the fortress around them. Eshu was only slightly bigger than a normal human, whereas Olokun was the height of a redwood tree.

The battle continued to rage before TJ and his friends. Adeola and Mr. Bolawe dived, zipped, and catapulted left and right around the throne room's pillars as they fought each other with spells and curses TJ never thought one could manifest with Ashe. It was like the elements had come alive in the form of enormous fire snakes and jets of water that looked like giant tidal fists.

Olokun played as their audience—though not a very captive one. His face was unmoving before the play of mortals in front of him. TJ couldn't even tell who he was rooting for.

Fear seized TJ's heart as Mr. Bolawe got tagged by a lightning bolt aimed at his shoulder. He defended against the next attack, but a third was heading for his left flank.

"Mr. Bolawe!" TJ shouted.

He wanted to take his call back the moment he said it.

Mr. Bolawe turned his head to see who was calling out to him, his guard slipping at the worst possible moment. The lightning bolt clipped Bolawe on the side of his face, and the man fell back onto the ground. Hard. His staff flew out of his hand and fell into the darkness with a *clang*.

TJ, Manny, and Ayo jerked back, feeling the pain for the man as though it were their own. Bolawe hadn't been very good at fighting at the funeral either. Though, to be fair, he'd done a ton already if he was able to fight off Mr. Du Bois and Eshu before that point.

At the back of the throne room, Olokun went from crossed arms to an akimbo stance. His face was as impassive as ever. Now that TJ's eyes had adjusted to the dark space, he could just make out that Olokun, like Eshu, had been gagged, though his binding appeared more permanent: a metal slab covering his entire jaw instead of the single pearl that compressed Eshu's tongue.

Mr. Bolawe rubbed his nose clean of the blood that ran free from it. Red-tinted water bubbled up in front of him. Adeola lifted her staff overhead, swam to the throne room's floor, and slammed it down like a jackhammer. The throne room's tiles rose and snapped down around Mr. Bolawe's legs, trapping him on the ground.

"It's about time someone took you down!" she shouted.

Adeola flung a stream of fire directed at Mr. Bolawe's head, but the man held his hands out to capture the line of flame in a ball of water. TJ was glad to see even rudimentary spell work had application in a real fight. But the bubble was small, very small. It only gave him a sliver of protection. The line of fire was barely an inch from toasting Bolawe's face.

The hungry flame inside his bubble fought against his feeble shield, trailing in an unstable line back to its source: the tip of Adeola's staff. She almost looked like an old-school soldier outstretching a spear in a thrust as her lined face told of her utter determination. Except no ordinary soldier would've had a spear spewing a line of flames that looked like snakes trying to bite at Mr. Bolawe's face. Slowly but steadily, she pressed her magical weight forward, right into Mr. Bolawe's nose.

TJ's mentor resisted Adeola's power, her pure and raw Ashe. Shango himself must've been empowering her inferno. Yet the longer she held the connection of the curse, the more snakes seemed to birth from the trail of fire.

Bolawe looked beat up: a cut lip, what looked like a broken nose, and a Camp Olosa dashiki that was ripped to near nothing, revealing Bolawe's quivering muscles underneath. Even if Mr. Bolawe was Adeola's equal, which he seemingly was not, he was at a great disadvantage. Staff magic against staffless magic was almost always an auto-win for the staff wielder.

As the orange line grew and the individual snakes with it, no room was left on the tether, and the fire snakes fell off to slither on their own. Bolawe threw up more, smaller bubbled walls to protect against their strikes. But for each defensive move he made, the central bubble blocking Adeola's main curse shrunk and shrunk again.

He wouldn't be able to take much more.

TJ closed his eyes, inhaled deeply, bringing his Ashe into his chest, then exhaled in Bolawe's direction. As he had seen and done all summer, the wisp of his Ashe shot forth and spiraled around Mr.

Bolawe, enabling the man to hold out longer against Adeola than he had any right to.

TJ dived deeper into his magic and started stripping Adeola of her Ashe, a feat that seemed so much easier and without fatigue in the Orisha Plane, when a voice rang out...

"Ta-dah-aight," Eshu mumbled. "Ta-dah-aight."

Ayo cupped his ear and squinted. "What? Huh?"

A fire snake snapped at Mr. Bolawe's right ear, burning it. TJ refocused and helped Mr. Bolawe empower his next water bubble shield.

"Eshu's calling out Bolawe's weak spots!" TJ gritted. "We gotta help him."

"Just one problem." Manny pointed forward. "We've got about two dozen fire snakes between us and him."

"We have to try." TJ outstretched his hand, and a current of water bubbled from his palm. He flung it outward and caught five fire snakes. The little things flew back in the water and broke up into embers, but they quickly reformed into their solid forms once more.

"Your Ashe isn't fast enough to break that spell before they come back," Ayo stated.

"Ya think?" TJ shot back. "It's hard enough helping Mr. Bolawe keep his shields up and using my own Ashe."

"Oh, you're using your special trick?" Manny asked, then turned to Ayo. "Then we gotta do our part too."

TJ's gaze darted around the throne room. Whenever it was last used, there had been a meeting of some sort. Chairs lined the great hall. Many of them were fallen over or in complete shambles. Next to one of the closer overturned chairs, lying to Mr. Bolawe's head, lay Eshu's staff, whose crystal shined a sickly green.

"Ta-dah-aight," Eshu mumbled again. "Ta-dah-aight."

Then TJ understood what was happening. Eshu was trying to let Adeola know that his staff was "to the right." It was Mr. Bolawe's only play against her, and Eshu wanted to make sure she did him in.

"We gotta get Eshu's staff!" TJ shook his head. "Any ideas on how to get past the fire snakes?"

Manny and Ayo looked at each other, and in unison, said, "The Jester's Gambit."

"Uh, translation for the guy who doesn't know any crossover plays, please?" TJ said, straining against Adeola's Ashe and supporting Mr. Bolawe's magic.

"Spread. Four corners. Delay game. Keep away and run the clock down until we get the best look. Or as I like to call it, the 'on your left' Endgame move." Manny winked at him.

Comic book movies *and* basketball? She was perfect.

TJ smiled. It would be just like the basketball games back home.

Without another question, he sped off, imagining himself on the blacktop down one at the end of the game as he twisted and dove between fire snakes.

Adeola didn't stand a chance.

TJ flipped like an acrobat as he snatched up the staff, fire snakes biting at his ankles all the while. He spun around to make sure that most of the fire snakes gave chase to him, which they did. Good. That's exactly what he needed. TJ imagined Manny was Jordan, and Ayo was Christian from school. And it was always TJ's job to be the distraction.

Before the fire snakes could jump and block him, TJ threw the staff through the water like a thrown spear toward Ayo. The fire snakes that had lagged behind turned their attention from TJ to him, and none of the remaining snakes huddled around Manny anymore. It was just like the YMCA junior basketball leagues. All the kids chased the ball instead of guarding where the ball—or rather, staff in this case—*would* be. TJ's father would have called it low basketball IQ. His mother would have called it a lack of wisdom. TJ was just glad the snakes weren't as smart as Adeola, or it would never have worked.

Just like back at school recess, the play was perfect. Ayo threw the staff to Manny after he caught it. Manny snatched it above her head and stuck it out and ready. TJ settled his concentration on her, leaving Mr. Bolawe to his own power.

Please, work. Please, work.

In that moment, TJ was Manny, the Ashe inside her working through her mind, ignited by the spoken counter curse she uttered. TJ felt the energy roil within her like a star about to go supernova, and he was her fuel. Then, as all the fire snakes sprang around Manny, that bright energy manifested in a huge beam of light that broke the connection between Mr. Bolawe and Adeola.

TJ's ears rang as his connection with Manny severed and his entire vision filled with pure-white. He rubbed his eyes vigorously, and when his vision finally stopped being so spotted around the edges, the scene before him cleared: Manny and Ayo were blown back across the throne room. The force of Manny's untamed counter was too much for them both, it seemed. Neither of them was moving.

Fear sliced through TJ, and he was about to check on Manny when Mr. Bolawe stirred on the ground. But only a few feet from him, Adeola was getting up as well and faster. Her staff was closer too.

Rushing through the ocean current, TJ snagged up Mr. Bolawe's staff and deftly pointed it at Adeola's. With what seemed to be his signature move now, TJ trapped the young woman's staff inside a water bubble. Then, with a flick of his wrist, the staff whipped into his outstretched hand. With one swift breath, TJ swung both staffs in a cross swing straight toward Adeola's chest.

"Wait!" Adeola managed to get out before TJ's air blast caught her full in the chest. She flew back into one of the room's gigantic chairs, which exploded behind her in a shower of seashells and kelp.

TJ hadn't meant to unleash such power. It felt like a tidal wave was rolling through him with the combined focus of his staffs held akimbo.

He couldn't believe it. He actually beat her. They actually did it.

Then he remembered why Manny's spell was so strong, why his own Ashe manifested with such force. Olosa and her power were still trapped in the Eshu staff. If Adeola and the other Keepers had got their hands on something like that, he couldn't imagine the power they could've unleashed.

TJ's gaze drew up to Olokun, who was still at the back of the room with the single chain binding him by the neck to his throne. This time, his empty white eyes actually met TJ's own—that was the impression TJ got, at least—for the first time. The Orisha lifted an inquisitive brow. He probably would have said something were it not for the metal swallowing his jaw.

Mr. Bolawe let out a sigh so deep and great, it could've probably been felt back in the mortal world. "Thank you... Tomori. Your sister... would've been... proud."

TJ gave him a helping hand. Instead of taking it, Mr. Bolawe beckoned for his staff. TJ outstretched his arm to offer it, and Bolawe took it in his hands with a firm but shaking grip. He was putting on a strong face, even though he was clearly at his wit's end. TJ didn't want to think what could've happened if he and the others had shown up any later.

Manny! Ayo! TJ thought, twisting around to search for their slumped bodies again.

"Your friends will be okay," Mr. Bolawe assured him. "Miss Martinez didn't expect to draw on that much power. She'll be passed out for a little while, no more. And young Oyelowo didn't throw up a shield in time, but he's still breathing."

"H-how do you know that—"

"In time, and with proper training, you'll be able to read rooms and the life within them too. But for now." He gestured for Eshu's staff. "Let's finish this thing, shall we, Mr. Young?"

TJ handed it over. "But how come that spell didn't blast me back like everyone else?"

The only other entity in the room who wasn't fazed was Olokun himself, who still watched placidly. TJ wondered if the chains did more than stop his physical movements, but his emotions and Ashe as well.

Mr. Bolawe gave TJ a smile that TJ thought would've looked more friendly had it not been for the blood caking the man's gums. "Because, Mr. Young, the book hasn't been written for you yet. Go on." He lifted his chin. "Check on Miss Martinez and Mr. Oyelowo. They are alive, but they could use their friend."

TJ nodded and floated over to Manny's body first. But as he hurtled through the water, he heard chains breaking behind him. His muscles tensed as he turned around, expecting to see Olokun somehow free of his centuries-long prison. What he saw instead was worse. Much worse.

Mr. Bolawe had freed Eshu from his chains.

47

THE GATEKEEPER'S STAFF

"Thanks, Olugbala." Eshu rubbed his pudgy jaw. "That Du Bois knows his way around a plastering charm, eh? Wouldn't have been so bad if that woman hadn't used that clam trap. I forgot Olodumare put those there. I should've seen it coming, but I gotta respect the deception."

"Come." Mr. Bolawe gestured to Olokun. "We've only got one more chain left."

There had to be an explanation.

Perhaps there was some strange Ashe in the air that was making TJ hallucinate. But he couldn't deny what he saw before him: Mr. Bolawe and Eshu working together. Eshu and Mr. Bolawe sharing in congratulations for one another.

TJ's stomach was a sinkhole. He didn't move, *couldn't* move, even as the man and Orisha glided toward Olokun and spoke some ritualistic words that made the chain around the giant's neck glow. A bright orange line started to cut around the shackle.

None of this made sense. Ol' Sally had let Mr. Bolawe through the portal. Mr. Bolawe had known TJ's sister. He defended her casket at her funeral. He was a friend; he was a mentor. Not this... not a Keeper, not Olugbala—their leader, of all people!

Then it hit TJ all at once.

"Who was the one who allowed me to bring my staff into camp?" he said slowly at first. "Who was the one who replaced a long-time elder who just up and left Camp Olosa because... reasons?" This time he gave his voice more weight in the direction of Mr. Bolawe and Eshu. "Who was the one who convinced me to return to camp?" At this, Mr. Bolawe looked over his shoulder. "And you've been working with an Orisha pretending to be a camper all summer long, right?"

Now that he thought on it... when Mr. Bolawe had come up to Ol' Sally, he had said, "*I'm going to get Olosa back.*" How could he even know Olosa was gone without being there?

He knew everything. It was *him* who set everything up from the start!

"Tomori, you have to understand," Mr. Bolawe started to explain, "this is what your sister would've wanted. This is what we were building to for years—"

"You're a Keeper!" TJ shouted. He felt powerless without a staff, but perhaps his words could do something. "You were pretending that whole time!?"

Eshu's head bounced from TJ to Mr. Bolawe like someone watching an engrossing tennis match.

"TJ." Mr. Bolawe sighed with genuine concern in his eyes. "TJ, there's something you have to know. You're all wrong about the Keepers. You don't really know what we're about."

"Crashing funerals and messing around with my sister's staff?" TJ scoffed. "I know enough, *Mr.* Bolawe. Or do you prefer Olugbala? 'Savior of Diviners', or whatever. There's something special about me like you said; you didn't lie about that. But you were just using me like a key to capture Olosa, and—"

"Ifedayo was a Keeper, Tomori," Mr. Bolawe said flatly. "Your sister was one of us. She was *our* promised child."

TJ was already revving up for his own rebuttal, but his mind caught up to his mouth a second too late. What did Mr. Bolawe just say? That couldn't possibly be true. Dayo would've never; she could never... Bolawe was just trying to trick him like he had done all summer.

This time, TJ wouldn't be fooled.

"You liar!" TJ's Ashe swelled in his belly and shot out from his mouth and fingertips by way of several strong currents of water.

In unison, Mr. Bolawe and Eshu turned around with their staffs and halted TJ's torrent like the blast was hitting a steel wall. That didn't stop TJ, though. He kept pushing his Ashe to its limits, shooting out deluge after deluge and simply hoping he could break the dam that was Bolawe and Eshu's combined strength.

"Tsk, tsk, TJ," Eshu chided after TJ's dozenth attack. "I told you,

you have to be trickier with your spell work. Feint a left or right sometimes, don't just attack the central line. It's not a game of strength or speed; dueling's a gambit of timing and deceit."

After TJ's latest volley of attacks, Eshu and Bolawe swam off behind one of the chairs. TJ turned his power to their hiding place and blasted the furniture to bits. But Eshu and Bolawe weren't there.

"See what I mean, kid?" Eshu's voice chuckled from the side, nowhere near the broken chair where he was supposed to be.

A chain wrapped around TJ's ankle and anchored him magically to the chipped marble floor below like a magnet. Eshu and Bolawe had never moved their position, still freeing Olokun from his chains.

Eshu had just thrown an illusion.

The Gatekeeper beamed a jester's grin. "Pretty good distraction, eh?"

And with those words, the last of Olokun's chains and the mouthpiece around his jaw fell to the throne room floor in a thundering boom that shook deep in TJ's chest and all throughout the fortress with the force of an earthquake. As bad as Eshu being freed was, it was nothing, *nothing* compared to this. As Olokun's final chain fell, TJ fell with it, his legs shallow, his feet devoid of strength.

Olokun drew in a long and slow intake of water, then let it out in a stream of bubbles that enveloped the entire chamber. It was a steady surge of a breath held in for several centuries that was finally free to swell and flow. Gradually, one by one, each bubble dissipated to reveal Olokun rubbing at his neck and cracking it several times.

"I am very, very tired," he said in a surprisingly effeminate voice. "All I ever did was try to protect our diviner children. And this... this is how the Skies repay me: Centuries of imprisonment. In my own home, no less." He rolled his shoulder and flexed his bare chest and muscle-layered torso. "Yes. I am very tired indeed."

Mr. Bolawe prostrated himself before the ancient Orisha—or the closest movement to prostration as one could manage in the water. Mom had always said full prostration was only meant for the highest displays of respect.

"Great Olokun," Bolawe said. "Overseer of the Deep. I am your servant, as ever, forever."

TJ tried to shake free of his chain. He needed to wake up Manny. She'd know what to do. And if he could just get Ayo awake, the boy would tell them about some weakness Olokun had or something. TJ couldn't do this alone. Not while he was chained and plastered to the ground and without his friends to aid him.

"Do you have my daughter Olosa?" Olokun asked evenly.

Eshu lifted his staff aloft for the Lord of the Deep to see. Olokun drifted down to level his head with the staff. He seemed to be sniffing at it. "And she is secure in the crystal? There are no means for her to escape, correct?"

"She will remain there as long as you wish it, *Ọbá*," Mr. Bolawe said, still bent low. "As will the others, when it comes to it."

"Good. My daughter has been particularly rebellious in time's past."

Eshu drew his staff back an inch in question. "'The others'? What's that mean?"

Mr. Bolawe, who still hadn't been told he could rise, said nothing. So Olokun answered for him. "We have a deal, Trickster. An agreement. With my help, Olugbala here will be taking control of the Orishas beyond the Aqua Realm while I maintain the seas and waters, as is my right. I get my vengeance on the other Orishas and the clouded who have enslaved my people, and he gets to keep his people's power."

Now TJ had a few thoughts about why so many slave ships were littered just outside Olokun's Domain.

Eshu turned a look on Mr. Bolawe's back. "Sounds like this deal was made between the two of you *only*." He thumbed between himself and Bolawe. "*This* duo is made up of him and me. Not you, Lord of the Deep. I don't intend on keeping Olosa trapped very long... Just a few years if she apologizes to me. We're just here to teach her a lesson about taking direct offerings without consulting me, not—"

"This is bigger than some foolish squabble, jester." Olokun's words cut deep with condescension. "Olugbala, explain it for your... 'partner.'"

Mr. Bolawe lifted up again and spoke steady and plain. "We diviners are outnumbered in this world, Lord Eshu. If we're to have any chance against the clouded and their new forces, we'll need to entrap the power of even more Orishas."

"That was never in any deal I agreed to." Eshu drew back from them. "Come on. It was simple. Trap Olosa, help free Olokun for some good old-fashioned mayhem, then let Olosa loose again and enjoy the show!" The lines creasing his face seemed unnatural for an Orisha aligned with jolly mischief. His slitted glare redirected to Olokun's passive one. "It's not like everything wouldn't all just go back to the usual boring norm afterward. Gods fight, mortals fight. It all sorts out by the end. But this isn't the same at all! There's a reason the Great Monarch has never given power like that to the mortals. They just don't get the balance right." He turned to Mr. Bolawe. "No offense." Mr. Bolawe didn't react. "This kind of pendulum swing out of left field like this really will wreck the world."

"Ruin does not have to be wrought," Olokun narrowed his eyes, "so long as all parties cooperate."

"Josh—E-Eshu..." TJ croaked. "Look, man." The Orishas and Mr. Bolawe turned slowly toward TJ. "I know our friendship was just a lie for you, but whatever it was for you, for me, it was real. More real than anything you've got going on with this bastard, that's for sure!"

Olokun let out a guttural chuckle, a mocking laughter that cut TJ deep. "Oh, the mortal child is trying to appeal to an Orisha? How... amusing."

TJ scowled but otherwise ignored Olokun. His words were only for Eshu. "Our friendship was real. You can't say the same for Mr. Bo—Olugbala, though. Look what he's doing right now!"

"Tomori, you don't understand—" Bolawe started to say, but Eshu cut him off.

"Kid, I've got this covered. No need to worry yourself over me."

"Oh, you think you can trust them to keep a deal with you?" TJ made fists and jerked against his chains. "I trusted Olugbala, and look where that got me!"

Both Eshu and Bolawe wore frowns. Olokun, however, was ready for a second set of chuckles, his lips quivering on the edge of amusement. If TJ's next words didn't work, he wasn't sure what would. "Okay then... how could *you*," he started, "the Orisha of Mischief, allow yourself to be duped by a mortal and an Orisha like them?"

The silence that filled the throne room then was tangible, like a weight set upon everyone's shoulders. But none heavier than on Eshu's, TJ knew. TJ hoped.

"You know something." Eshu edged his chin up to Olokun and then down to Bolawe. "The kid's got a point."

A flash came at the head of Eshu's staff, and a shockwave blossomed outward. The aftershock of the spell would've blown TJ halfway across the room had he not been tethered by the chain around his ankle. Mr. Bolawe, however, went head over heels into the marble floor, cracking the ground with each of his tumbles.

Olokun, like before, was barely taken aback. With oscillating hands, he tore away the pillars along the wall and magically flung them at Eshu. Eshu, being as small as he was, easily avoided each attack. But the crashing pillars nearly knocked TJ out.

"No!" Mr. Bolawe crowed. "Don't hurt the boy. Leave him!"

Olokun didn't listen, already lifting another pillar to throw. Mr. Bolawe raised his staff and shot something dark and misty at Olokun's wrist.

But it was like Mr. Bolawe's magic was a pebble hitting a skyscraper.

"You dare strike me?" With another flick of his giant fingers, Olokun forced Mr. Bolawe to hang from his ankle upside down. Then, with a swift splay of his hand, Mr. Bolawe went crashing into the far wall.

He didn't move again. Out cold.

Eshu pelted past TJ. "Keep to the nooks and crannies and follow me close, kid."

"What are we going to do?" TJ asked as the weight of the chain around his ankle suddenly dropped free. "And what about my friends?"

"You're no good to them dead. Keep up!"

TJ rushed behind Eshu and kept pace with him through the halls. Behind them, the throne room doors burst into shrapnel and came hurtling at their backs.

"To your right," Eshu shouted as TJ careened just under the zip of an overhead splinter.

TJ righted himself and dived through the gap of an elevated banister leading out onto a courtyard with a statue of Olokun.

"Good work!" Eshu congratulated. "Way to keep to where he can't get you. That's why I always stay small."

"Yeah, great, I get to live another second." TJ barrel rolled away from a follow-up projectile, another broken pillar by the look of its debris against the courtyard's statue. "But I can't keep this up forever. He's gonna tag me, eventually. What's the plan, Mastermind!?"

"First. *You* are going to hold this." Eshu handed TJ his staff. "Then we'll need to go find Yewa to help us put Olokun back in time-out. Oh," he sighed, "did you see Yemoja on the way down here?"

"You mean Yewa?" TJ ducked under another blast.

Eshu pushed TJ aside just before a statue's arm could smack him across the cheek. "Oh yes, I did give her the slip on the way down, didn't I? No, I mean Yemoja. Olokun's wife."

"No. Should I have?"

"Hm, I suppose she wouldn't be down here during the full moon. She'd be nearer to the surface. Once she hears about Olokun, though—"

Another blast impacted near a tower as they passed through another large courtyard.

"Josh—I mean—Eshu! Focus. Giant deity trying to blast us into smithereens here, remember?"

"Right, right. Let's survive first. Recruit help later." He nodded to the staff in TJ's hand. "Just remember to think like me, feel Olosa's flow, and we may have *half* a chance of success."

"Only *half*?"

They zoomed to the underside of a drawbridge and dove deep into a wide cavity where a school of fish that looked more like zombies with big bright eyes drifted gently. An explosion of rocks boomed, and a shadow loomed above—Olokun's massive form, no doubt—slicing through the waters behind them.

Okay, TJ, you got this. Think like Eshu, flow like Olosa. No sweat.

But that was easier said than done. After all, he was still just a teenager barely passing his remedial classes. He hadn't learned the intricacies of Eshu-style illusions or how to harness the power of water and alligators like Olosa.

As TJ followed Eshu through the tight valley at the fortress' base, a rocky surface blasted near TJ's side, scraping him along the knee. Hot pain seared through his body. He expected to see blood in the tear in his jeans, but there was only a glowing white streak across his skin where the wound on his knee should've been.

"Stay still, mortal." Olokun's voice rumbled from above.

"He did *not* just say that." Eshu rolled his eyes and beckoned. "So cliché. Gotta keep moving, TJ." He dipped between crevice after crevice like a guppy avoiding a much, much larger fish. "There's a shortcut through here near his lava moat."

TJ could barely make out Olokun's glowing eyes above them, searching, as he dived deeper into the darkness below. It was too tight down there, and TJ feared they'd get trapped if Olokun decided to just blast the whole valley.

What they needed to do was shoot back up and around Olokun, where there was at least some space to maneuver.

TJ's signature tingle wrapped through his fingers and along his staff's surface. The power was tangible, but he just didn't know what to do with it. He and the other campers never learned illusionary magic. That was supposed to be an advanced use of Ashe and very obscure—according to Mr. Du Bois, anyway. So he focused on Olosa instead. After all, he was surrounded by water.

"Where are you going?" Eshu twisted to TJ. "Shortcut is through here."

"*You* might make it, but I can't keep up. I'll just get trapped."

As he rushed back up through the crags, his mind darted back to that first week of camp and the lesson of the water bubbles. And just as the thought occurred to him, the staff's crystal radiated a solid, pulsing green.

If that wasn't a go sign, he didn't know what was.

"TJ, wait!" Eshu called out.

TJ didn't listen as the valley opened up again ahead of him, the enormous fortress looming large. Just to his side, a collection of pillars sat crumbled and broken. As Olokun shifted his blank gaze to TJ, TJ started catching pillars the size of baobab trees in enormous water bubbles. When he came out the other end, he shot them out toward Olokun. It didn't even feel like the magic was his own, as though Olosa herself was helping him along, and he was just giving her a path to unleash the pillars like arrows going the speed of trains.

But the pillars halted amid the water as though stopped by an invisible wall. "You cannot use my own element against me, child!" Olokun bellowed. "With or without my daughter's help. This is futile. Lay down the staff and give Olosa to me."

The pillars frosted and fell along the rocky ocean floor, shattering into pieces. The move, thankfully, gave TJ an opening to get past Olokun and shoot up out of the trench.

"TJ, over here!" Eshu called from near the drawbridge they had come from, way high up. How did he get up there so fast?

"Gatekeeper, this does not concern you." Olokun lifted a single finger and shot a jet of water in the shape of a spear, but Eshu spun over it like it was nothing. Olokun shot water spear after water spear, and still, he could not land a blow despite some of his attacks grazing Eshu.

A tug came at TJ's hoodie. "We were nearly there, silly mortal!" Eshu gritted.

TJ turned his head to see he was being pulled by Eshu. A *second*

Eshu. "Open waters wouldn't be *my* first choice, but we'll just have to commit now."

He really was a master of illusions.

And just like that, a distinct thunk sounded from behind. TJ twisted his head over his shoulder to see the Eshu copy get run through with a water spear, where it embedded him into the side of the fortress. When Olokun went to examine the second Eshu, it fell away in black and red mist.

"Gatekeeper!"

With TJ and Eshu out in the open as they were, there was no way they could outmaneuver or out-swim Olokun for long. At least two football fields separated them from the cavern scar leading back out the way TJ had come in. They wouldn't get a quarter of that distance. But there was one thing TJ *could* try...

He grabbed Eshu's hand. "Do that trick again!"

Before Eshu could shout a complaint, TJ concentrated, clutched his staff, punched it above his head, and imagined him and Eshu being invisible. He could feel his energy coursing through Eshu, felt as Eshu's own Ashe seemed to catch on and help the spell along. TJ might not have known the function, but at least he could fuel the magic.

Olokun rushed out from the shadow of his fortress just as TJ felt a sensation of coolness come over him. The colossal Orisha squinted, looking everywhere that TJ and Eshu weren't as he passed over his moat, which threw an eerie orange-red light across his face.

Did that really work? TJ thought as he and Eshu did a slow backstroke to their exit.

The quiet that hushed through the water was so silent, TJ could hear his own heartbeat. Olokun noiselessly stalked them, hunted them like a shark in a reef, curling around the tower of his fortress, dipping between open bridge ways, and back out to open water.

TJ just had to hold on, siphon Eshu's energy, implant it in the staff, and back out for Eshu to use again like Mr. Bolawe told him he could. He couldn't let go, couldn't let his focus slip, or he'd be dead.

Then, as though catching a whiff, Olokun stopped and narrowed his eyes on the only place TJ and Eshu could escape. The colossal Orisha lifted his giant finger, and a white light bubbled and pulsated from its tip, shooting out a sleet of water. The water sheet impacted against the ground and kicked up rocks from the ocean floor. Then came another light and another explosion.

Light. Explosion. Light. Explosion.

"Keep doing whatever you're doing," Eshu whispered to TJ. "He's just shooting at random."

But the shots and blasts kept coming, and with each one, more rocks flew up to float back down slow, very slow. Some came so close that TJ and Eshu had to adjust their awkward backward swim to work around them.

TJ peeked ahead. *Only one football field left to go. We're almost home free.*

"Hang on, TJ," Eshu murmured. "We're going to make it."

At the behest of his staff, TJ was moved bodily out of another white streak's path that came straight for him. But even that wasn't enough. The beam sliced along TJ's back, and he screamed in pain, letting go of Eshu's wrist. The impact sent him soaring far, far back as pain seared up his back with every convulsion of his muscles.

It was like being hit by a paintball, only much, much worse.

Was this what it felt like to get shot, TJ wondered? There was a burning, aggravating sensation along his spine, growing outward from where he was hit. He'd had that described to him once before. It was the same sensation his cousin said she'd felt when she got hit with a stray bullet back home. TJ never thought he'd actually get shot, least of all in the Orisha Plane.

He kept tumbling through the water, rolling until his back crumbled against what felt like an old and dying reef. His whole body screamed of sores.

"Stop fighting the pain," Olokun called out from far away, somewhere near his fortress. "Show yourself."

Show himself? There was no way he held onto that illusion while taking that tumble. Then he realized he was hidden, half-submerged in the debris of the rocks and reef.

"Gatekeeper!" Olokun's voice boomed again. "You could have been an ally, and now you need to learn to stay out of my affairs. This does not concern you."

"Stay quiet," Eshu said in TJ's ear somewhere from his side. "He'll find you, but don't freak out when he does. Trust me. Just remember, think like me, flow like Olosa."

"Ah, there you are." Olokun's baritone rumbled through the rocks —and through TJ's chest. TJ felt pressure along his legs and arms, lifting him against the rocks. He was being trapped by a water bubble of Olokun's own as the rocks cleared away.

"You have potential, young mortal." He said, confidence dripping from his very being. As if he knew his win was inevitable. "But you are no equal to me. Nowhere close."

TJ rose level with Olokun's eye line. Fear should've cut through him, but the chill of calm serenity wafted through instead.

It clicked for TJ.

"You're right," he told Olokun. "I am no match. But I don't have to be."

It was so obvious to TJ now. He wasn't supposed to think of Eshu and Olosa's magic separately but as one. He needed to think like Eshu *while* flowing like Olosa. TJ caught the image of Eshu wiggling out of the rocks and circling behind Olokun in the water.

"There's something you don't know about me," TJ grunted.

Olokun gave him a lazy expression as he continued wrapping TJ in a water ball, which slowly turned to ice. "Oh, yes? What might that be, child?"

"I'm a lucky charm."

TJ flung out his Ashe, empowering Eshu. A mound of rocks came crashing down from the great cavern's ceiling, headed straight for Olokun's head. But, somehow, with impossible speed, the Orisha dodged aside in time. His smile was a wicked one. "You think I didn't expect something from the Trickster, really?"

TJ returned the smirk, pointing up with his free hand. "That was thinking like Eshu." Then he jabbed his chin just behind Olokun. "And that is flowing like Olosa."

Eshu sprang behind Olokun with his hands uplifted, and with them came a tidal wave of molten rock. Like a conductor, Eshu flung out his arms, and a chorus of angry lava flowed over his head and snapped around Olokun's legs, bringing him down to the ocean floor. The Orisha fought against the magma but sunk deep into the molten mess at his feet.

Eshu zipped forward, freeing TJ from his ice cage with a single tap of a finger. "Not bad, kid."

"You said to flow like Olosa... what flows better than lava?"

"Water. But still, points for creativity."

A large, guttural scream came from within the lava sloughing over Olokun.

"That's only going to slow him down." Eshu pointed down. "You know this, right?"

"Swim away, then?"

"Yes, swim away!"

They both dashed away as fast as they could go, Eshu several paces ahead of TJ. Not believing how well that had worked, nervous energy surged through TJ as he pushed toward their exit. They were so close now, they could actually make it through this!

A cacophony of shrieks, wails, and hollers sounded from behind them, making the surrounding water vibrate violently.

Eshu took a quick peek behind. "Oh dear. Do me a favor and don't look back."

"What? Why?" TJ totally looked back. What he saw made his jaw fall slack.

Olokun was barreling for them with a violent speed that made the water behind him a sonic storm. Swarming around the rippling waves was a horde of possibly every type of sea creature: Fish, sharks, octopuses, eels, turtles, and stingrays, all glowing. Every scary thing TJ had seen on his journey through the Aqua Realm was in hot pursuit. TJ could even make out the impressions of *actual* merpeople, which to him looked more fish than human.

A blast shot from Olokun's hand, hitting against the top of the cavern's split wound—TJ and Eshu's exit. Rocks exploded, and an underwater avalanche collapsed and blocked their path, just a quarter football field away from them getting away.

No, it couldn't be! They were *right there*. They'd done everything right. TJ had thought like Eshu and flowed like Olosa. This wasn't how this was supposed to go.

"Well," Eshu shrugged, "we gave it our best shot, TJ. You did great. Now. Repeat after me."

"Huh?" TJ questioned.

"*Mò pé àpèjọ kàn,*" Eshu said in Yoruba.

"*Mò pé…* what?"

Eshu spoke slowly and clearly with Olokun just mere yards away. "*Mò. Pé. Àpè. Jọ. Kàn.*"

"*Mò. Pé. Àpè. Jọ. Kàn.*"

"Close enough. Now turn around and say that with me in three. Two. One."

TJ whipped around, thinking they were going to be committing some last-ditch kick-butt spell that would turn Olokun into little butterflies or something.

"*Mò pé àpèjọ kàn!*" they both shouted in unison.

And, in almost an instant, everything froze. The mob of sea creatures. Olokun himself. And TJ's heart...

"What kind of spell was *that*?" TJ asked in shock.

"Uh… it wasn't," Eshu replied.

TJ didn't get it. Everything was very clearly stuck in place. But then he saw it. Olokun's nose was flaring, pulsating ever so slightly. His brow caved, and he balled his fists before gritting through his teeth. "Skies, Gatekeeper. If you were going to just parley, why not call it from the start and save us wasting all our time with this pointless chase through my fortress!?"

48

PANTHEON'S PARLEY

THE PICTURE AHEAD OF TJ WAS LIKE A SCREENSHOT FROM ONE OF his favorite video game cutscenes: A huge deity in front of him, flanked by his crew of killer sharks, eels, and merpeople, all back-dropped by an enormous fortress in some underwater world. No one —not even a diviner—would believe him if he ever got out of this to tell the story.

TJ whispered to Eshu, "What did we just say to him?"

"Uh…" Eshu leaned in to murmur back. "In English? 'Pantheon's Parley.' Essentially, we Orishas can call a council meeting at any time, and the other party must hear the other out honestly before continuing. Don't worry. I'll work it out and get us out of this thing. *No wahala.*"

Olokun huffed out of his nose, brushing loose rock from his shoulder. "State your terms, Gatekeeper."

"How about this?" Eshu clapped his hands together. "We give you the staff, and you let us go free. We have no qualms with you, Great Olokun."

"We can't give him the staff!" TJ blurted.

If Olokun was this powerful after a very long sentence, one could only imagine the type of devastation he could cause with the power of even more Orishas at his fingertips.

"If you two can't agree, then perhaps this parley is broken." Olokun raised his hand, and with it, his horde of sea creatures stood at attention, a thousand different eyes glaring down in unison.

TJ lifted his hands in a rush. "No, no, nothing broken. But how about this... What if... What if..." He thought back to Mr. Du Bois's class and the quiz he had totally failed. What did Olokun want again... oh yeah! "What if we make the clouded do what you wanted? We can fix the stuff that you're angry about."

"So, you make the promise to remind those of the coast to honor my name as they once did in time's past?"

"Y-yeah." TJ shrugged. "S-sure, we can... spread the word."

Was that really it? Was that all Olokun wanted in the end? Some appreciation, some *respect*?

"And," Olokun went on, "you shall do away with Eko Atlantic?"

"If that means letting me and my friends go, yes. We can do that, no problem." TJ had no idea what Eko Atlantic was. But the only other option was getting eaten by a thousand sea creatures, so yeah, he could definitely commit to whatever it was he was promising.

"And you, Gatekeeper, you bear witness to this?"

Eshu floated in an exaggerated bow. "Of course. The kid regains your praise and then does away with Eko Atlantic, and we get to go."

"Good. You will have until February's new moon."

Half a year? TJ thought. *That shouldn't be so bad. This was almost too easy.*

If he could blast away ships in this place and contend with Yewa and Olokun... doing away with whatever Eko Atlantic was couldn't have been so bad.

"Deal," he said.

Olokun lifted a finger and turned his gaze on Eshu. "One issue remains. How will the mortal boy be bound? A mortal cannot make a deity's contract."

"This mortal boy is... different."

Olokun canted his head. "How so."

"You don't sense it? I mean, he gave *you* a little trouble back there, didn't he?"

A thoughtful silence sat between them as Olokun stared at TJ, assessing him more intently than he ever had until now. The look was familiar. One TJ likened to the slitted gaze leveled on him by Ol' Sally at the start of summer.

"Very well." Olokun uncrossed his arms. "I agree to your terms. And if you do not do as you say, I will drown the coast as I have done before... Gatekeeper, will you do the honors?"

"Of course." Eshu put his hand out, then nudged his head for TJ to do the same.

TJ canted his head. "I just... touch your hand?"

"That's right."

With a bit of hesitation, TJ outstretched his hand and placed it on Eshu's own. Then Olokun lifted a single finger—which was five times bigger than their whole hands. The moment they all touched, a bright energy surged through TJ, and a ballooning of pure white light gleamed around them. TJ held still for a moment, wondering if anything else would happen. He tried his best not to stare at the group of merpeople who held tridents aimed directly at his head. But as the surrounding light gave way to the dim shadow of Olokun's fortress, their weapons lowered. Even the sharks and the eels started to turn around and swim back off toward the palace to circle their towers, slither through the lava moat, and float among the wide-open spaces surrounding the great structure.

"So..." TJ trailed off nervously. "We're, uh, all good, then?"

Eshu nodded. "Until February's new moon, at least. Olokun will not take any action against Eko Atlantic. But if you renege on the agreement, he will have full capacity to do as he wishes. In return, he will allow us to leave freely along with those you call friends. You are both bound by the Orisha's ancient binding ritual."

"And the staff will remain with the Gatekeeper, as he is our impartial party," Olokun said. "Again, if you go back on your word, mortal, the staff with Olosa inside is my claim."

A slight whisper brushed over TJ's finger, where he made contact with Eshu and Olokun. And he noticed at the tip of his finger what looked like a faint little tattoo glowing a soft white: a curious forked line on what looked like a cross.

"Great," TJ said nervously. He still felt like this was all one big trick. "So, you'll let us out now?"

"Of course." Olokun dropped his head slowly, his long hair falling over his dark shoulders. TJ couldn't get over how reasonable he was since they had called out that phrase—a far cry from the murderous gaze he had held just a moment ago.

But TJ was alive and whole, so he couldn't complain.

"Would you like me to bring the other mortals you call friends to you as well?"

TJ gave Eshu a sidelong glance, then looked back to Olokun in bewilderment. "Um... yes... please."

"A moment, then. I shall return shortly."

TJ watched as Olokun drifted back to his ever-looming palace, back over his lava moat, and into the gaping hole TJ, Manny, and Ayo had entered before.

TJ let out a sigh so large, his head went light and dizzy. "*How* in the *hell* did that work?"

"We Orishas are not savages." Eshu smiled. "Sure, we have some scuffles here and there, but if you ask to talk, we'll talk."

TJ clutched his staff tightly. "Why didn't we do that from jump?"

"Because you don't want to get yourself into bad deals. I didn't know you could do away with Eko Atlantic in half a year. But you were so confident that I—"

"About that..." TJ swallowed hard, his previously sharp tone tapering into a half murmur. "What is that? Something here in the Aqua Realm? I figured with your help I could just—"

"Oh, kid..." Eshu threw his hand onto his forehead. "Eko Atlantic is on your plane, your world. It's a district near Lagos. You never heard of it?"

"No." TJ wasn't feeling so good about the deal anymore. "Is it a... *small*... city?"

"Oh, it's only one of the largest land reclamation projects you mortals have ever done. When Olokun got word about it, his anger only grew. And Olosa allowed it despite him wanting her to ravage the coast with tidal waves. That used to be his coast, you know."

"Oh, great..."

"Don't look so fretful. We'll figure something out." He winked. "I have a few friends, you know."

TJ spent the next several moments quietly freaking *all the way* out until Olokun brought his friends back. Manny and Ayo floated at his flanks, still unconscious. Manny's bushy hair had fallen over her gentle face, and Ayo's glasses clung just to the tip of his nose, one of the lenses cracked.

"Are they... okay?" TJ asked. "Can we wake them up?"

"It would be best to keep them in this state until you cross back over," Olokun explained.

Eshu nodded and added. "Their mortal bodies do a great job of protecting themselves when unconscious... uh... sort of like a small coma. It's a surprise they've managed as well as they have so far, actually. But I expect that has something to do with you..."

"*Their* mortal bodies?" TJ questioned, thinking back to what Mr. Bolawe said about him at the cafe. "What about *my* body?"

Eshu and Olokun traded looks between them, as though vying for which of the two would explain. Eshu spoke first. "Your body is... different, somehow. I couldn't figure it all out over the summer, but it is."

TJ gazed down at his sister's staff. No, Eshu's staff. He had one idea of how he was different. "At my sister's funeral. When I touched her... I saw a place with all these figures and this new energy. Is that normal?"

Both the Orishas shook their heads, and it was Olokun who spoke next. "You are a rarity even among this realm, mortal."

TJ frowned but wasn't sure how he should feel exactly. Then something hit him. "Oh!" he turned to Eshu. "My sister's staff! At the lagoon, you said—"

"Oh, right!" Eshu beamed, snapping his fingers. "The original shall be returned to you. It is currently being kept at New Ile-Ife. Just speak to Elder Bamidele."

"Can't you just manifest it right now or something?"

"Not across the realms, no. Besides, that staff is bonded to your late sister. It will not heed me willingly. That's why we had to do the whole charade to begin with this summer."

"About that," TJ said. "I'm still mad about what you did."

"Ah, yes. Most are when I put them through their journeys. Give it a few years. You'll be thanking me for all that's happened before too long."

Olokun cleared his throat. "Thank you again, young mortal. I look forward to your fulfillment of our deal."

"Wait, what about Mr. Bolawe and Adeola? And Mr. Du Bois?"

"You asked only for the ones you call friends." He gestured to Manny and Ayo, who still floated in their little stupors. "I did not sense a bond with the others, not as strong as these two, though the woman and Olugbala were interesting..."

TJ thought about it for a moment. Had this been the beginning of summer, he would've wanted Adeola and Mr. Bolawe, but he wasn't sure what to think of them. He wanted to talk to the others at least, ask Mr. Bolawe what he meant about his sister being a Keeper, and question Adeola about what she was doing all summer too. Mr. Du Bois was never exactly a friend to TJ, so that was a big fat no. Though now... he wouldn't call him a bad guy either. All said, somehow, TJ knew that if he lied, it would be detected in whatever mystical deal he brokered with Olokun.

"The mortals will remain with me, then," Olokun said, understanding what TJ's silence meant.

"But they'll go crazy, won't they?"

"Not if I tend to them, no." Olokun floated ominously, but TJ knew his words were true. He had no reason to lie. "I've a few questions for them before I release them. Farewell, young mortal."

And then the big guy swam off again.

☩

DESPITE TJ NOT BEING SURE WHETHER ADEOLA OR MR. BOLAWE could still be called people he cared for or admired, as he and Eshu swam back out the Great Rift, through the Graveyard of Ships, and back up to where Ol' Sally had left them, he knew for sure he owed Mr. Du Bois the biggest apology ever. If this had been an hour ago, he wouldn't have believed Olokun's word about releasing the others eventually, but then TJ wondered if they would be released the same... and whole.

He wasn't entirely sure what was what or who was aligned with who, but he suspected that Mr. Du Bois and Adeola had been working together *against* Mr. Bolawe. If Olokun returned them like he said he would, TJ hoped to get his answers when Adeola woke up. He had a bad feeling he wouldn't get any coherent response from Mr. Du Bois, though; he had already seemed pretty crazy when they found him.

At the very least, he'd have Manny and Ayo to talk it all out with. They still floated at their sides in their sleep-states. Eshu showed TJ how to pull them along with a sustainable water charm. Unlike in the Mortal Realm, TJ got it down pat with little explanation and no exhaustion.

He was going to miss that about this place. How everything came so easy to him there. Then he thought back to what the Orishas told him. How he was different, even among them. What did that even mean? Why couldn't anyone explain what was going on with him?

Despite the clarity of magic he felt in the Orisha Plane, TJ still couldn't say it was his favorite place, though, between ship graveyards and ancient fortresses that tried to kill him. He was most definitely, positively, and absolutely over it all.

"Well, this is where I leave you," Eshu said as he tapped at the ocean's "glass ceiling" to call Ol' Sally. A great silhouette started to grow larger from above. He held out his hand for his staff, "I'd like to have that back, please."

"You're not releasing Olosa?"

"Not until the deal is done come February's new moon. As witness, I must take no part and safeguard the staff and Olosa."

"But that stuff about the promised child. It was *you* in that mask in the library, wasn't it? You lied, didn't you?"

"Oh, yes," Eshu said, remembering. "Sorry about all that. I didn't completely make up the story, just the stuff about the path leading to the lagoon. But the business about '*a promised child will rise with the light of a dying, falling star, and the Lost Monarch will return once more*' was true. It's just that none of us knows the true ending of the Great Oracle's words. Hard to know when these days Orunmila spends most of his time in the stars." Eshu snapped his fingers. "Now, please, kid... the staff."

"Wait... you're not coming with us?" TJ asked, holding close to the staff in his hands. He knew now it wasn't really Dayo's, but he was still attached.

"I'm afraid I can't. Not in the same way you knew me before, at any rate. Just as a whisper whenever you walk through a doorway or face hardship in life. Why do you think I needed my Joshua persona?"

"But how will we figure out this whole deal with Olokun?"

"Prayer and a lot of hope." Eshu chuckled. "But I'll do as much as I can on my side. Olokun must have some means to return to your world, and I gotta figure out what he's got cooking up long term. But if you need Eshu, just remember... I lay between the thresholds. Find one and call to me. I'll speak to you then."

He beckoned for his staff once more.

"But," TJ handed the staff over, "everyone says they can't commune with Orishas."

"TJ, you should be catching on by this point... You're not everyone." Eshu touched him on the forehead, sending a mystical chill through TJ. "See you around, Tomori Jomiloju Young."

And in a blink, everything was dark once more.

☦

TJ WANTED TO TAKE BACK WHAT HE SAID ABOUT HAVING ENOUGH of the Orisha Plane the moment they returned. He forgot how much his muscles ached in the mortal world, how much strain it took to breathe through his normal lungs, and how sweaty a swamp climate could be.

The morning sun peeked over the heads of cypress trees. TJ felt moist mud at his back, water lapping at his feet as he fought to keep his eyes open—he'd almost forgotten what mortal exhaustion felt like. All his fatigue seemed to come on at once. Even as a huddle of figures rushed to his side, even as one of them grabbed at his wrist, touched his throat. Were they checking for a pulse? Men and women wearing robes from different parts of the world converged on him: some with pointed caps, others with monk-like shawls, most with the aṣọ òké robes of Nigeria.

One of the latter was speaking to him, a woman, he thought. But her voice came so low he couldn't be sure. Did he recognize her? Her face was long, and her outfit shimmered... shimmered like the stars in a galaxy. Yeah, he knew who that was. But the effort it took to call out Elder Adeyemi's name was the straw that broke TJ's back. The energy it took to form the words on his lips was just too much.

His body called for sleep, and he gave into it.

49

A SUMMER FOR THE AGES

THE FIRST TIME TJ OPENED HIS EYES, THERE WAS ONLY WHITE before him. Just like when he had fainted at his sister's funeral, he only heard voices.

"*Director, look. He's opening his eyes.*"

"*Mr. Young, hold on, your parents are coming.*"

TJ tried moving his lips to ask about someone named Manny and Ayo, to warn the voices about two other names he didn't quite understand: Olokun and Bolawe. But the only thing that came out was an indistinct mumble. Even as the voices responded to him, they, too, sounded like they were at the end of an endless tunnel. TJ strained against his body. He needed to make it move.

Where was he?

I'm Tomori Jomiloju Young. I'm fourteen years old—fifteen in October. I got a mother, father, brother, and sis—

TJ felt himself thrashing on sheets, but it was like he was in a dream moving slower than he should've been. His sister. His sister was gone. His sister was a hero. No, his sister was a Keeper. Wait, what?

"*What's wrong with him?*" a voice asked. Did it belong to someone named... Simmons?

The *click-clack* of heels echoing around the large tunnel that was TJ's distorted hearing rang out louder and louder. Then a hand touched his wrist gently. "*Rest, Mr. Young. Hold your memories as best you can.*"

And he was back to sleep again.

☦

WHEN TJ OPENED HIS EYES AGAIN, HIS VISION WAS BACK TO normal, if perhaps a little blurred. A great brown blob was staring down at him, but little dark lines cut between them, and he knew it was a wooden ceiling. Then cricket squeaking and frog croaking attacked his ears, a gentle breeze caressed his cheek, and that unique salt air of a marsh filled his nose.

He was in a cabin, a cabin near a swamp.

Camp Olosa!

TJ's tongue was like sandpaper as he moved it around his desert of a mouth. He needed some water...

"He's awake! He's awake!" shouted a voice at his side.

TJ tilted his head sluggishly to see his brother hopping up and down, his dreadlocks jumping with him. TJ couldn't remember the last time Tunde was so happy to see him.

"Tomori!" Mom exclaimed as she rushed TJ in a hug.

Dad ran a hand through TJ's nappy hair, then gave him a cup of water. "We was worried 'bout you, son. But I told your mother we Youngs are fighters."

Mom kept pecking TJ's cheek, leaving it a wet mess. For once, TJ didn't mind it. "Are you okay? Is your memory fine?"

"Memory?" TJ asked. "Yeah, why?"

A storm of footsteps thundered across the cabin floor. Manny and Ayo came bursting into TJ's room. Each of them had pale skin with IV poles in their hands rolling along with their run. TJ peered down to his own arm to see his own IV stuck in his hand. But the liquid in it was green, bubbling, and sloshing instead of clear.

"I told you two to stay in your beds!" came the voice of Miss Gravés from the other room.

TJ's friends ignored the woman and shouted at the same time: "What happened in the Orisha Plane?"

TJ almost didn't hear what they had asked, too filled with joy to see their beaming faces. Outside of a few healing wounds and bruises, they looked all right. Then he realized what they had asked him. "What... you were with me. You don't remember?"

"I remember some things..." Manny said. "Mostly feelings, really. Whenever I sleep, I dream about this submarine and my cousin being there..."

"And your memories will return, eventually. If. You. Get. Some. Rest." Miss Gravés, stocky as ever, stood akimbo behind Manny and

Ayo's shoulders. "Mr. Young, good to see you awake. Shall I expect you back on my field soon?" TJ really hoped she was joking.

"What's going on?" he sat up a little in his bed, returning the water cup to Dad. "Why don't Manny and Ayo remember anything?"

"Like Director Simmons told you all," Miss Graves grabbed Manny and Ayo's arms to pull them back, "Mortals who go to the Orisha Plane have difficulty remembering what they did when they cross back over. If you kids were in there much longer, you might've lost your minds entirely. Which I've told Mr. Oyelowo and Miss Martinez several times, but they keep gettin' out of bed at any sound that you've woken up."

Manny and Ayo traded a pair of embarrassed looks, and TJ couldn't help but smile.

"So…" TJ trailed off. "Why do I have my memories?" He knew the answer, though. It was like Mr. Bolawe said and how the Orishas had treated him. He was different.

"You really do?" Mom asked. "You remember everything?"

"Yes, all of it."

A hush spread across the room as everyone exchanged glances among each other, Mom and Miss Graves in particular.

Dad was mostly confused, as usual.

"I'll go inform Elder Adeyemi." Miss Graves turned on her heel and walked out of the room. "Mr. Oyelowo. Miss Martinez. You come with me too!"

"Well, I guess we gotta go then." Ayo stuck out a fist. TJ gave him dap. "This spirit goo is pretty strong. We should lie down."

"You'll tell us everything we missed when we get out, right?" Manny asked, her dimples deep and eyes bright.

TJ gave them both a look of the obvious. "Of course, guys. Rest up."

Manny gave him a warm hug, and TJ whispered in her ear. "There really were merpeople down there. Try to remember, okay?"

"I'll work on it," she replied, smiling.

Ayo lifted his chin in subtle acknowledgment—his form of a hug. Then they too left the small room, leaving TJ with his family once more.

"So Elder Adeyemi is here?" TJ asked. "For real?"

"Oh yes," Mom said. "Her and the rest of the UCMP. Whatever you and your friends did caused a whole bunch of hoopla."

TJ couldn't believe they didn't remember any of it. How would anyone ever believe everything he had to say without them to back him up? How would he break it to Mom and Dad that Ifedayo might've been a Keeper... or that Adeola was one?

"What about Adeola? We were with her and Mr. Du Bois and—"

Mom put a hand to TJ's cheek. "Both are okay—"

"If you call crazy okay," Tunde cut in.

"Babatunde!" Dad chided.

"My bad, my bad!"

TJ gave Mom a confused look, and she explained, "They were found on the banks of Lagos. Mr. Du Bois keeps repeating the same phrase, but they were able to keep him alive. He got transported to Babalu-Aye Medical just this morning. Adeola, too. Her memory is just as foggy as your friends'. Manuela told us she and Mr. Du Bois crossed over before you did. So it'll be some time before they're back to normal. But since you remember everything..."

Did that mean Mr. Bolawe forgot everything as well? Was he still in the Orisha Plane with Olokun? Or did he leave, too?

"What about Mr. Bolawe?"

Mom shook her head. "Your friends mentioned him going in, but not much else. He hasn't been seen. But don't worry, I'm sure—"

"He's a Keeper. He's *the* Olugbala."

The color in Mom's face flushed for a moment. "What... how can you be sure?"

"He told us... he said—" TJ bit back the truth about Dayo, and an awkward silence sat among them.

Thankfully, Tunde broke it. "They sayin' that a bunch of other Orishas are showing themselves to diviners. There's news all over Evo about it."

"I told you not to use that thing," Mom said, narrowing her eyes at Tunde. "It'll rot your brain with all those tin-foil theories."

The boy shrugged nonchalantly. "It's got the quickest news."

This was all too much. Orishas coming back. TJ being the only one with his memories. Elder Adeyemi and the UCMP wanting to speak with him?

"Can I get some air?" he finally asked.

"Of course you can, son." Dad helped get TJ out of bed. TJ's legs were like noodles, but he eventually found his balance. "There's a back door right out there—a nice little porch with a view of the swamp. Take a few minutes. We'll hold off those elders as long as we can."

☩

For once during that summer, TJ appreciated the beauty of the swamp and Camp Olosa. He'd been so busy trying not to fail classes and chasing voices on the water that he realized he never got to just sit and... be.

Sure it smelled like rotten eggs sometimes, the air was moist, and the moss hanging from low-hanging trees was creepy as hell, but still, it had a certain charm to it.

Okay... it was still just a swamp.

But it felt like *his* swamp, his home. Whatever was going to happen once he went back in to talk to all the elders, he knew he'd miss his time at Olosa's little plot of land. He'd miss the whispering wood, where he and Manny really got to know each other, the late-night sneak outs, where he realized Ayo wasn't all that bad, and the mess hall, where, TJ realized then, Eshu loved to stuff his face because he never usually got to eat mortal food. He couldn't think how anything could ever top his summer.

A giant tail flopped out of the lagoon and back under the black waters.

TJ waved back. "Mornin' Ol' Sally."

Morning, young one. She lifted her round green eyes over the waters. *You did well. I knew you were truly divine.*

"So I really am an Orisha or something? Mr. Bolawe told us both lies, but I don't know how I could go through the Orisha Plane without being dead or crazy if he was wrong about me."

An Orisha? Ol' Sally blinked long and slow. *Not exactly. You are something else... something new.*

TJ was hoping the old alligator could give him a different answer. He sighed. "Yeah, new. Mr. Bolawe said there are new Orishas every few gener—"

TJ stopped short at the sensation stirring at his side. A moment before Elder Adeyemi spoke, he felt her somehow, felt her Ashe stirring near the porch as she stepped from the lagoon in yet another dazzling set of robes that seemed to reflect the swamp itself.

"Good morning, Mr. Young," she said. "You know, I had a wager with my sister how long you'd be out. I'm sad to say I owe her two tickets to Nigeria vs Ghana next month. You weren't supposed to wake up for a few more days yet."

TJ turned back to Ol' Sally, but she was already swimming down to the far end of the swamp. "I forgot to ask my parents how long I was out."

"Not long. Two days, twenty-three hours, and..." Adeyemi

peered at her dainty little watch, "Twenty-three minutes. Give or take."

"Well," TJ sighed, "At least I got five minutes to myself. I guess my parents did everything they could to stop you."

"Oh, no, they don't know I'm speaking with you now." She leaned against the porch's wooden railing and dipped her head close to TJ. "Between you and me, your mother scares me. And I didn't want to face her wrath for disturbing you."

TJ smirked. "She scares me too sometimes. But that's probably a good thing. It's okay, though. Manny and Ayo already did that, though without the wrath part."

"Ah yes... they are quite fond of you. Both in the top five of the camp, I believe."

TJ gave her a nod, almost forgetting about the camp's rankings. Before they did their little moonlight ritual, Joshua was at the top, followed by Ayo, Manny, Lorenzo, and then Andressa.

"You know why I am here, yes?" Adeyemi asked.

"The Orisha Plane?"

"The Orisha Plane." The elder nodded. "I'm sorry, I would let you rest more and have your time, but diviners who have crossed over usually lose their memories, and I must make sure to speak with you while you're still fresh. That being said, if you wish to dismiss me, I will go back to join the others. I've told them I needed to use the ladies' room."

"Nah, it's fine. But under one condition."

Adeyemi quirked an eyebrow. "Oh?"

"Did you see Adeola? I heard she's doing better, but... you know."

"Ah, there is good news there where she is concerned. She's still not able to communicate normally, but I am quite accomplished at speaking directly to her ori."

"Speaking to her ori?"

"Telepathy, essentially. Like um... the way Darth Vader spoke to Luke at the end of *Empire Strikes Back*." TJ's eyes shot wide. "Miss Martinez told me you are quite fond of the classics."

"So... what did you hear from her? Adeola, I mean."

"Well, apparently, she and Mr. Du Bois were partners this summer. They were attempting to serve as your guardians. I don't know the full extent of it, but from what I could discern from her thoughts, they were looking into a possible infiltration of the camp."

"Yeah, there was this kid named Joshua who was actually Eshu.

But I don't understand. Mr. Du Bois was hiding this mask that looked like a Keeper mask. And he took my staff and didn't tell anyone about it."

"He wasn't sure who to trust, from my understanding. In fact, that day you and Adeola crossed paths in the library, the both of them had a little talk. That's when he realized she was a Keeper, but she revealed she had a change of heart when your sister passed."

A brief silence cut between them, peppered only by the croaking of frogs. TJ never got a solid confirmation about what happened to Dayo. And that was one of his key goals all summer. He had his suspicions, of course. And they all brought a stab to his heart.

"Do you know how she was killed?" he asked quietly.

Elder Adeyemi took a few steps toward TJ, then leaned along the porch banister. "Adeola didn't let me in that far. She suppressed that memory."

TJ frowned, rubbing at the cool IV pole he had wheeled out with him. "So, Adeola *was* actually a Keeper?"

"For a few years now, yes." TJ almost thought Adeyemi was going to ask if his sister was a Keeper too, but instead, she asked, "And... is it true that Olufemi Bolawe also goes by the name of Olugbala, or the Savior of Diviners, the leader of the Keepers?"

TJ dropped his head down at that. "Yeah. Yeah, it's true. I thought he was... I don't know. My friend or something."

"Me too." Adeyemi sighed and peered out into the swamp. The morning sun poked through the trees in rays, reflecting off her emerald dress and sparkling in her brown eyes. "I had hoped you would say I was mistaken. Sometimes my readings can be wrong. But it seems my interpretation of Adeola's thoughts was correct. However, I am having trouble with one detail. And it is very important that you remember if you can. Olokun. Is he still bound to his fortress? Did Olugbala free him? Adeola's memories get particularly foggy at this point. From what I could discern, Olokun was still chained."

TJ's throat swelled with shame. "He... he got out. I tried getting him with Eshu's staff, but me and Eshu—he ended up helping me by the way—we said this phrase." TJ tried to recall what it was. "I think it was... *Mo pe apejọ kan.*"

"Pantheon's parley," Adeyemi whispered almost to herself. "If that's the case, it's a wonder Olokun has not revealed himself to any diviners like some of the others these past few days."

"So it's true? Not just some Evo conspiracy theory?"

"Ah, so you know of that search engine, do you? Yes, some Orishas have been manifesting themselves, but only for a few moments. I've only confirmed a handful myself."

TJ gave his IV pole a little punch. "I could've done better. I could've trapped him again."

"I'm curious," the elder said. "This parley. It was between Eshu and Olokun, yes?"

"Uh... not exactly," TJ said as Adeyemi tilted her head in question. TJ lifted his finger to show her the crossed mark on his finger. "It was between Olokun and me. He promised not to drown the coast of Nigeria so long as I got the people to appreciate him again."

"That seems a fair trade."

TJ groaned. "That's not all." Heat rushed through his ears. "I also promised to get rid of Eko Atlantic without knowing it's a city. And I have until February to do it, by the way. How big is it? The city, I mean."

Adeyemi blew through her mouth and stared up into the trees. "Oh, only the biggest land reclamation project in all of West Africa to date."

TJ groaned again. "Yeah, Eshu said something like that. I didn't have a choice though! Olokun was going to feed me to merpeople!"

There hadn't been enough time to dwell on his not-so-quick-witted decision-making. But he had the feeling over the next half a year he'd regret it gravely.

"It's quite all right. We'll figure all that out. It's amazing you survived a bout with an Orisha at all." TJ looked away from Adeyemi at that. "I heard what you were saying to Ol' Sally. Your friends had some stories about that as well."

"I don't know what to believe at this point," TJ admitted. "But... Mr. Bolawe told me that sometimes there are new Orisha every few generations."

"Hmmm, that would be one explanation for why your memories are intact. And how you fared so well."

"Maybe. Sally said I had more power in the Orisha Realm. Plus, if it wasn't for the staff and Eshu helping me, I probably wouldn't be here."

"Very interesting. I'll have to converse with Elder Akande about that."

"Elder Akande? She's okay?"

"Oh, yes. She and Elder Whittaker were found in the Forests of Canada wandering aimlessly and feasting on fish heads and berries."

So Mr. Bolawe didn't kill them. Now that TJ thought of it, Mr. Bolawe didn't want to hurt TJ either.

"Now, I can only wonder what Olufemi is up to with Olokun. You are familiar with Olokun's story, yes?"

TJ nodded. "Mr. Du Bois drilled it into us this summer. Something about him being angry with humans and wanting to flood the lands."

"Yes. And I'm sure a few centuries of being chained hasn't altered his plans. I expect the other Orisha only showing up momentarily and at sacred sites has something to do with why he's not returned yet. But regardless, we have the UCMP watching the most populated coastlines — Lagos in particular."

TJ shook his head. This whole time, he thought Dayo was inside him. Ever since the funeral. He didn't think he'd be... whatever it is he was. There were times that summer when he really thought he heard her voice, but it was just Olosa all that time.

"What are you thinking about, Mr. Young?"

"You can't read my mind and find out?" TJ asked incredulously.

She smirked. "It doesn't quite work like that. You'll learn that when you continue your magical education."

"Let me guess," TJ said. "You're going to let me off with a slap on my wrist even though I brought in a staff, set a statue on your sister, and went into the Orisha Plane without adult supervision, all because Ifedayo Young is my sister?" TJ's thoughts were back on Mr. Bolawe that day after he fought with Ayo.

To TJ's surprise, Elder Adeyemi snickered. "Oh, no. In fact, once you and your friends are back to full health, I and some of the other elders are to escort you off the premises. From this day onwards, you are banned from Camp Olosa. My sister is quite... what do you kids say these days... heated?"

"Oh..." TJ trailed off in surprise.

"But on the subject of your magical education. I do have one more question, if you don't mind. Then I'll pretend I've come back from the bathroom, and you can walk back in to see me for the 'first time.'"

TJ nodded, wondering what was coming next. A lifelong ban from all the magical schools across the world?

"Tomori Jomiloju Young, the priests have agreed. You are invited to attend Ifa Academy of Tomorrow's Diviners. Do you accept?"

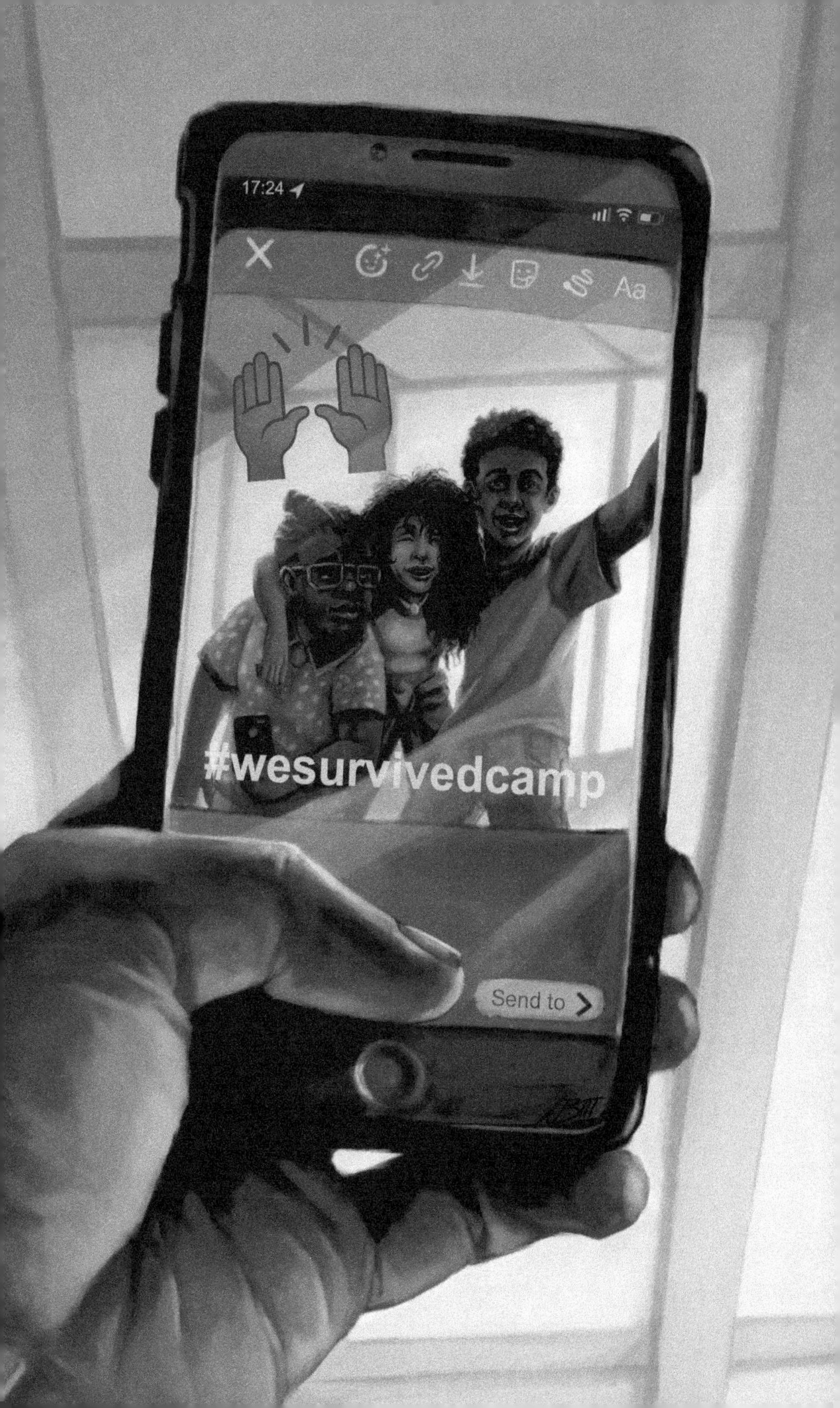
17:24
Aa
#wesurvivedcamp
Send to

What happens when a deity needs
to reconnect with humanity?

They go to New York City, of course.

The story doesn't stop here. You can read
When the Wind Speaks, a short story epilogue following
the Orisha of Storm, Oya.

visit this link and read the story:
antoinebandele.com/when-the-wind-speaks

Never make a deal with a deity.
Promises with one are impossible to keep.

14 going on 15-year-old TJ Young spent last summer fighting to unlock the secrets behind his sister's mysterious death but found himself battling the magic of the ancient Orishas instead. And some of the answers he sought came with a promise he might not be able to keep: to do away with new human intervention on the coastline of Lagos, Nigeria by the start of spring.

But how does a teenager do away with years' worth of infrastructure in only half a year?

He'll need to enlist the help of new allies, mortal and immortal alike. And thankfully, after surviving the grueling magical curriculum of Camp Olosa the year before, he's now headed to the most prestigious magic school in West Africa: Ifa Academy for Tomorrow's Diviners.

But will that be enough as he prepares for what can only end in an all-out war between mortals and gods?

Find out in this young adult fantasy based on the mythology of the West African Orishas, where TJ will encounter lost tales, the uncompromising corporate world, and the ancient secrets of the Orishas.

visit this link:
antoinebandele.com/stay-in-touch

ALSO BY ANTOINE BANDELE

TJ YOUNG & THE ORISHAS
The Gatekeeper's Staff

The Windweaver's Storm

ORISHAS AMONG MORTALS
Will of the Mischief Maker

When The Wind Speaks

TALES FROM ESOWON
The Kishi

THE SKY PIRATE CHRONICLES
By Sea & Sky

Of Ruin & Silk

For Code & Honor

LOST TALES FROM ESOWON
Demons, Monks, and Lovers

Gods' Glass

CHRONICLES OF UNDERREALM
The Legend of Cabrus

ABOUT THE AUTHOR

Antoine lives in Los Angeles, CA with his girlfriend and cat.
He is a YouTuber, producing work for his own channel and others.
He is also an audiobook engineer.

Whenever he has the time, he's writing books inspired by African
folklore, mythology, and history.

antoinebandele.com

✞

To my beta readers:

Autumn Amara, Sherry Burch, Jordan Fortuin,
Lukas Gibson, Negus Lamont, Brian Letang, Cair-Paravel Emyth Brenn De
Luney, Francesca McMahon, Andrea S.U., Mel Tong, Chu Xue Ying

Thank you for your time and dedication to this project.
The story wouldn't be what it is without you delightful diviners.

GLOSSARY

- **Àgbádà:** a Yoruba tunic.
- **Ashe:** a Yoruba philosophical concept through which the power to make things happen or produce change is conceived. Within the diviner community, it is known as the source of magic.
- **Aṣọ òké:** a narrow strip-weaving technique and variety of Yoruban fabric often incorporated into formal wear.
- **Bàbálàwò:** a priest of Ifa, also known as the Shepard of Mysteries.
- **Bruxa:** the Portuguese word for "witch."
- **Bùbá:** a Yoruba blouse or top.
- **Cara:** the Portuguese word for "guy."
- **Clouded:** a term used to described those of non-magical lineage within the diviner community.
- **Ìlèkẹ:** spiritual beads often worn at the neck by devotees of Ifa.
- **Ẹmi:** the Yoruba word for "spirit," also the class title for spiritual guidance at Camp Olosa.
- **Ere Idaraya:** the Yoruba word for "exercise," also the class title for physical training at Camp Olosa.
- **Eshu:** the messenger for all Orishas. The Orisha of trickery, crossroads, misfortune, chaos, and death.
- **Ètùtù:** Yoruba ritual in light of propitiatory performances for the Orishas.
- **Evo:** short for "Evocation." An unlisted search engine

used by underground diviners for news not savory enough for most publications.

- **Fìlà:** a Yoruba cap.
- **Futebol:** the Portuguese word for "soccer."
- **Gèlé:** a Yoruba head tie.
- **Ìde̩:** spiritual beads often worn at the wrist by devotees of Ifa.
- **Ifa:** the name for the system of divination practiced by diviners and devotees.
- **Ile-Ife:** the original city, the homeland of diviners, which in modern times has been moved to New Ile-Ife.
- **Irenku:** in Yoruba funeral tradition, this is the final day of observance, often coupled with a small parade for the dead.
- **Ìrènókú:** in Yoruba funeral tradition, this is a day set for games.
- **Ìró:** a Yoruba wrap-around skirt.
- **Ìtàóku:** in Yoruba funeral tradition, this is the day relegated to feasting and celebration of life.
- **Itis:** African American slang meaning the drowsy sleeping feeling one gets after a significant meal, often after Thanksgiving.
- **Ìyá:** the Yoruba word for "mother."
- **Ìyá Àgbá:** the Yoruba word for "grandmother."
- **Jovem:** the Portuguese word for "young person."
- **Mamãe:** the Portuguese word for "mother."
- **Naira:** the currency used in Nigeria.
- **No Wahala:** the Yoruba phrase for "no problem."
- **Oba:** the Yoruba word for "king."
- **Obatala:** the Architect Orisha, the Healer, or the Shepard of the Imperfect, characterized by his gentle personality and eternal patience.
- **Ode Buruku:** the Yoruba word for "bloody fool."
- **Oduduwa:** the Doted Orisha, the Divine King, characterized by his clear and focused mind.
- **Ogbon:** the Yoruba word for "wisdom," also the class title for Ifa studies at Camp Olosa.
- **Ogiyan:** the Crushed Cassava Orisha, characterized for his ultra specialization of the cassava harvest.
- **Ojo Isinku:** in Yoruba funeral tradition, this is the time relegated to prayer and donation.

- **Oko:** the Agriculture Orishas, the Keeper of the Farm, characterized by his protection of plains, once a hunter turned farmer.
- **Olodumare:** the Almighty Orisha, the Father, or the omnipotent, characterized by his great power and all-knowing pools of knowledge. He is all things.
- **Olokun:** the Orishas of the Deep Blue, the Ruler of the Seas. Husband to Yemoja, and parent to most other water Orishas.
- **Olosa:** the Lagoon Orisha, characterized for her abundance, prosperity, and fertility.
- **Òlòṣí:** the Yoruba word for "bastard" or "foolish person."
- **Ọpọn Ìfà:** a divining board of the Ifa divination system, often made of wood and circular in shape.
- **Ori:** sometimes referred to as an Orisha, oftentimes refer to a state of mind relating to spiritual intuition and destiny as it relates to human consciousness.
- **Orunmila:** the Divination Orisha, the Miracle Worker, characterized by his separation from other Orisha. Whereas most Orisha do have some interaction with the world, Orunmila spends most of his time in the stars.
- **Osain:** the Orisha of the Wood, characterized by his healing nature and distinguished by his Cyclops-looking appearance.
- **Oshun:** the Orisha of Rivers, characterized by her sensuality, love, and purity. One of the wives of Shango.
- **Oya:** the Orisha of Storms, characterized by her tenacity and compassion. One of the wives of Shango.
- **Papai:** the Portuguese word for "father."
- **Patakí:** a scared story, song, or myth in the Ifa faith system.
- **Pẹlẹ̀:** a Yoruba shawl.
- **Qi:** the circulating life force whose existence and properties are the basis of much Chinese philosophy and medicine.
- **Shango:** the Thunder Orisha, the Lionhearted, or The Overseer of Masculinity and Masculine Beauty, characterized by his loud personality and substantial presence.
- **Ṣòkòtò:** Yoruba trousers.

- **Sūrú, ẹrọ, and ètùtù:** in order, patience, gentleness, and coolness needed in Ifa ritual.
- **Tchau:** The Portuguese word for "bye."
- **Velho:** the Portuguese word for "old person."
- **Yemoja:** the mother of all Orishas. The Orishas of creation, water, motherhood, and moonlight.
- **Yewa:** formerly the Orisha of lagoons, now the Orisha of graveyards.
- **Zobo:** a Nigerian hibiscus drink of deep red made from Roselle plant flowers.